She k

God help her, Madison knew.

She could feel what her mother was feeling, and her mother, Lainie, was afraid. She was being threatened, and she was trying to argue in return. She was pleading desperately, in a placating voice. She was trying to…

Madison went dead still, shaking, drenched in an icy sweat. Because she wasn't just feeling what Lainie felt.

She was *seeing!* Seeing what Lainie saw.

And Lainie saw a knife raised high above her.

**What reviewers are saying about
Heather Graham Pozzessere:**

"**Award-winning Pozzessere combines
mystery with sizzling romance.**"
—*Publishers Weekly*

"**As always, Heather Graham Pozzessere
creates (a) spectacular and dazzling work of
romantic suspense…**"
—*Affaire de Coeur*

Also available from MIRA Books and
HEATHER GRAHAM POZZESSERE

SLOW BURN
EYES OF FIRE
FOREVER MY LOVE
NIGHT MOVES
BRIDE OF THE TIGER
DARK STRANGER
ANGEL OF MERCY
STRANGERS IN PARADISE

Coming in October 1997

A PERILOUS EDEN

HEATHER GRAHAM POZZESSERE

IF LOOKS COULD KILL

MIRA BOOKS

If you purchased this book without a cover you should be aware that this book is stolen property. It was reported as "unsold and destroyed" to the publisher, and neither the author nor the publisher has received any payment for this "stripped book."

ISBN 1-55166-285-X

IF LOOKS COULD KILL

Copyright © 1997 by Heather Graham Pozzessere.

All rights reserved. Except for use in any review, the reproduction or utilization of this work in whole or in part in any form by any electronic, mechanical or other means, now known or hereafter invented, including xerography, photocopying and recording, or in any information storage or retrieval system, is forbidden without the written permission of the publisher, MIRA Books, 225 Duncan Mill Road, Don Mills, Ontario, Canada M3B 3K9.

All characters in this book have no existence outside the imagination of the author and have no relation whatsoever to anyone bearing the same name or names. They are not even distantly inspired by any individual known or unknown to the author, and all incidents are pure invention.

MIRA and the star colophon are trademarks of MIRA Books.

Printed in U.S.A.

This one has to be for family and friends:

Dedicated with love to Victoria Graham Davant, my sister and my best friend, because I couldn't imagine life without her.

To Lisa Charge Alvarez, for being the stuff of which heroines are made.

To Katey and Same DeVeuno, for not only being family, but also for being the nicest, warmest, most giving people in the world.

To Mary Pozzessere Durso, Auntie May, for her unwavering support, and so I can make absolutely sure she gets a copy of this one.

To Ginger Crosbie, for doing such a great job of getting us all together.

And to Keith Pozzessere, for being so proud of the name, and for always making sure that he's part of our family.

Prologue

Madison could hear the voices coming from the bedroom, and she was afraid.

She was twelve, nearly thirteen, so it wasn't a matter of being easily frightened, or even a matter of not knowing what went on in the world—she did. Her beautiful, volatile mother had married the equally volatile and temperamental artist Roger Montgomery, and ever since then, voices and sounds had often come from the master bedroom.

But tonight...

Something was different. It wasn't just the usual passionate argument that was going on. They weren't hurting accusations of infidelity at one another. There was a different voice in the room, a hushed voice....

A menacing, sexless voice that sent shivers racing along Madison's spine. The voice was evil. Madison *knew* it. She told herself that she was being fanciful—that it might even be her mother's voice, since Lainie Adair was such a highly acclaimed actress, known for her uncanny ability with accents.

But it wasn't her mother. Madison was certain.

She knew that her mother wasn't playing games

or acting out some sex fantasy. Someone, something…evil…was in the room.

She wondered if Roger was there, as well. She
didn't know. She could hear her mother's voice, rising, falling, a note of hysteria, of pleading, in it.
Then she heard the whispered, sexless voice again.
The different voice.

The evil voice.

The voice that made her skin crawl.

Without thinking, she'd come out of her own
room, and now she stood in the hallway, a trembling
wraith in her oversize cotton T-shirt. She moved
along the hall, anxious to reach her mother, but at
the same time afraid. She'd never been afraid this
way. She could watch the most gruesome horror
movie without flinching; she was always willing to
accept a reckless dare. She had defied the very real
possibility of monsters in the closet or under her bed
as a young child, telling herself that she simply
wouldn't be afraid. The darkness didn't frighten her;
she wouldn't allow it to.

But tonight…

Oh, God, she was terrified. It was the voice. That
voice, with its undercurrent of sibilant, menacing
evil. The hallway seemed to be a million miles long,
though it couldn't have been more than forty feet
from her doorway to her mother's. The harder she
tried to make herself move, the more weighed down
she seemed to be. Fear constricted her throat, so she
couldn't cry out, and yet she knew that she shouldn't
cry out, that she couldn't let the voice know she was
coming.

She had to move, to see the person connected to
the voice.

She wanted to run, but she couldn't, because something terrible might happen if she did.

Except that something terrible was *already* happening, and she absolutely *had* to be brave. She had to stop the evil.

The evil was in the air around her, pressing down on her. It made the air thick and heavy, so that it was a struggle just to walk down the hallway. It seemed to make the door to her mother's room swell and bulge against the doorframe, while the light within seemed to radiate out in strange shades of bloodred evil.

She tried to be rational.

Surely her mother and Roger were just fighting.

She needed to be calm, rational. To pound on the door and remind her mother that she needed a few hours of uninterrupted sleep. Of course, if Lainie was fighting with Roger, it was quite possible that they would make up before Madison even reached the door, and then, if she went storming in, well…

She wished she would interrupt Lainie and Roger at some wickedly sexual enterprise, but she knew she wouldn't.

She *knew*. God help her, she *knew*.

She could feel what her mother was feeling, and Lainie was afraid. She was being threatened, and she was trying to argue in return. She was speaking desperately, in a placating voice. She was trying to…

Madison went dead still, shaking, drenched in an icy sweat. Because she wasn't just feeling what Lainie felt.

She was *seeing!* Seeing what Lainie saw.

And Lainie saw a knife.

Big, glinting silver, wickedly sharp. A butcher's

knife. Madison had seen it before, in the kitchen. It belonged there, in the block of chef's knives that sat on the counter. It was raised high in the muted light of the bedroom, high above Lainie.

Lainie watched...and through her eyes, Madison saw.

The knife slashed downward with brutal, merciless strength.

Lainie screamed, but Madison didn't hear her mother's cry, because she was screaming herself, doubling over. Feeling. Feeling what her mother felt.

The knife.

Tearing into her. Through flesh and muscle. Ripping into her, just below the ribs.

Madison staggered and began to fall. She leaned against the wall, feeling the agony of torn flesh, the chill, the fear. She gripped her middle and looked down, and she saw blood on her hands....

She was cold. Blackness was surrounding her. Her hand on the wall, she struggled for support. She tried to talk, to scream again, to cry for help, but the blackness overwhelmed her, and she sank to the floor.

"Madison. Madison!"

She woke to the urgent sound of her name. She opened her eyes. She was lying on the living room couch, and Kyle was there, Roger's son. Eighteen now, five years and a few months older than she was, a dozen years older in his superior attitude. Black-haired, green-eyed, Mr. Jock, quarterback of his football team. She hated him half the time, especially when he called her ''squirt,'' ''airhead'' or ''bimbette.'' But when his friends weren't around and he wasn't busy impressing the cheerleaders, he wasn't a bad kid. Solid. Down-to-earth. When she was convinced she was a product of the most dysfunctional family of all time, he told her to stop whining, that lots of people had step- and half brothers and sisters. In fact, if he hadn't been her stepbrother, she might even have had a crush on him. But since he was, she wouldn't even let herself think about that.

Okay, so maybe she had a few more than most. And okay, so Lainie was an unusually cool mom; in fact, she was *hot*. It wasn't so bad to have Lainie for a mother, or Roger for a stepfather. Her real dad, Jordan Adair, was a world-renowned writer. And who actually cared how many stepmothers she'd had, huh?

Sometimes Madison hated Kyle, but other times, when she had reached the pits, he could make her laugh. And sometimes, *sometimes*, he even made her feel warm. As if she belonged somewhere.

But now he was staring at her, green eyes shining with tears. "Madison?"

"Madison...are you all right, Madison?"

She turned slightly. Roger was there, as well. Roger, who was openly crying.

"Roger, move aside."

It was her father who was speaking. *The* Jordan Adair, a handsome man in his forties with a headful of long silver hair, a silver beard, dark, penetrating eyes. Leave it to her mother. Lainie would only marry men who were different: a rock star first, a writer, an artist. Jordan liked women in the arts, as well, but he didn't seem to be quite as picky. He'd been through an opera singer, a stripper, a ballet

dancer and Lainie, and had now broken the pattern
to marry a sex therapist. He'd always loved Lainie,
though. Always. And Madison knew that he loved
her, too.

Like Roger and Kyle, Jordan had tears in his eyes.

She became aware of the sirens then. And the fact
that the foyer was filling with cops. Roger moved
away. She saw more of her family, her sister and
her step- and half-siblings, standing awkwardly in
the living room.

The girls, Jassy and Kaila. Jassy, her father's
daughter from his first marriage, was pretty and delicate, a dark-eyed blonde. Kaila was her only full
sister. She and Kaila were both just like Lainie, redheads with blue eyes.

Her other brothers were there, as well. Trent, her
father's son from his second marriage, had sandy
hair and Jordan's piercing dark eyes. Rafe, Roger's
son from his first marriage, twenty now, was completely different from Roger and Kyle in coloring;
his eyes were a misty silver, and his hair was a shining Nordic blonde. Like the others, he was pale now,
scared-looking, quiet, his cheeks streaked with tears.

Kaila, just a year younger than Madison and
nearly her twin in looks, suddenly began to sob.
Loudly. Her knees buckled, but Rafe slipped an arm
around her before she could fall.

Suddenly Madison remembered.

She began to scream and scream, shaking. There
were paramedics at the scene, and even as she
screamed and thrashed and tried in her hysteria to
explain, someone came with a needle, pressing it
into her arm. She could hear someone saying she
couldn't possibly talk to the police yet, and even if

she could, what good could it do? Then the tran-quilizer slipped into her, and everything went black once again.

This time she woke back at her father's house, Kyle sitting by the side of her bed. She heard soft sobs coming from another room. One of her sisters.

"My mother is dead," she whispered.

Startled, Kyle looked up. He stared at her com-passionately and nodded.

"Someone killed her, Madison. I'm so sorry. Your dad is with Kaila, but I can get him for you if—"

"I saw it, Kyle."

His eyes narrowed sharply.

"I *saw* it."

"What do you mean, you saw it? You were in the hallway. Did the murderer run past you? Did you see who did it?"

She shook her head, looking for the words to de-scribe what had happened. Tears welled up in her eyes. "She was terrified, absolutely terrified. She saw the knife. I saw it, too. I felt it."

"Madison, you were forty feet from her room when we found you. Had you been in there?"

She shook her head.

"Then you couldn't have seen anything."

"I saw the knife."

"Who killed her, then?"

"I don't know. I didn't see a face. Just the knife. Just the knife, coming down at her. And I felt it. I felt it ripping into her." She started to shake and sob again. Her mother had been killed, and it hurt as if a million tiny knives were digging into her heart. Lainie had been wild, headstrong and reckless, but

Lainie had also been her mother, the one who held her, cherished her, laughed with her, shook her head over her, took the time to make red pipe-cleaner hearts with her class last February. Her mother was dead, and she didn't think she could bear it.

Kyle didn't try to say anything else. He sat beside her on the bed, taking her awkwardly into his arms while she cried and cried. Eventually her father came to the room and took her from Kyle, and she kept crying. She tried to tell her father that she had seen the knife, had felt Lainie die.

Her father was gentle and tender, and he pretended to believe her, but she knew he didn't.

In the days and weeks that followed, the police investigated the murder with energy and zeal. They questioned Lainie's various husbands extensively, certain that either Roger or Jordan had murdered her in a crime of raw passion. The tabloids picked up on the murder, as did the major magazines.

The cops talked to Madison. Lots of them. City of Miami cops, Metro-Dade cops. She told them that she had seen the knife, had felt her mother die. They didn't believe her, either. But there was one cop who was at least nicer than the others. Jimmy Gates. He was fairly new to homicide, young, with warm brown eyes and sandy hair and a gentleness about him that soothed her. He wanted to know just what she had seen; he made her think back. When he questioned her, she saw the hand holding the knife. And she knew then that the killer had worn thin, flesh-colored gloves, like a doctor's gloves.

She was amazed to realize what she could see, and also disturbed.

Roger was nearly arrested for the murder; her father was nearly arrested, as well. But there was no evidence that either man had killed Lainie. Kyle, Kaila and Madison had all been in the house at the time of Lainie's death; Roger had arrived soon after. Kyle had immediately called Jordan Adair. In their questioning, the police said that Roger might well have killed Lainie, left by a window, disposed of the weapon and returned to pretend to find his wife. And Jordan's home was well within walking distance, so he could easily have committed the murder, disposed of the weapon and reached his own house within a matter of minutes. Oddly enough, neither Roger nor Jordan accused the other. And with no evidence to go on, the police finally had to leave both men alone.

Time, Newsweek and *People* ran articles with headlines like Can Money Buy Innocence?—American Justice.

Jimmy Gates continued to talk with Madison. He listened gravely each time she went over and over what she had seen and felt. He tried to get her to see more, but try as she might, she couldn't see beyond the gloved hand. Her father told Jimmy that he couldn't torment her anymore, but she told her father she wanted to see Jimmy.

Two months after her mother's murder, a suspect was arrested.

He was a crazy old derelict by the name of Harry Nore. Madison had seen him walking the streets of Coconut Grove most of her life. He begged at the corner of Bird and U.S. 1. Sometimes he shouted about Jesus and the Second Coming; sometimes he stood on the corner in the night and cried that Satan was coming and would devour them all with a sea of flame. He was first arrested for breaking into the house of a neighbor. He had stolen food, which the neighbor would have forgiven, but he had also filled his pockets with the family's jewelry. The police found him in the kitchen, cutting bread.

With a butcher knife.

Harry Nore was also wearing a gold Saint Christopher medal that belonged to Roger Montgomery, which was what first made the police begin to wonder if the man was more than a thief. In examining the butcher knife Nore had been using to cut the bread, the forensic crews found minute traces of blood.

Lainie's blood.

Nore's fingerprints matched some of those lifted from Lainie's bedroom. And he had a record. He'd already served time for killing his wife with a similar knife.

However, Harry Nore—the bug-eyed, lice-infested derelict—never went to trial for the murder of Lainie Adair Montgomery; he was judged incompetent to stand trial. When confronted with the murder, he began to rave. God had dropped the knife into his hat. God told him who was good and who was evil. He confessed to killing Lainie. In his confession, he stated that it was the devil who had come for her, because she had been one of his own brood. Lainie had been beautiful and evil, so beautiful that she led men to distraction and acts of perversion and violence. She was the devil's spawn, and the devil had come for her. Looks could kill.

Harry Nore was evaluated and then incarcerated in a north Florida institution for the dangerously insane. He had a frightening, nearly toothless grin that was spread across the nation on the covers of the major magazines. He looked the part of a homicidal maniac, and the police and the investigators and the folks from the D.A.'s office were pleased, telling Madison and her family that at least they would not have to live with the agony of an unsolved murder. Nore had been found with the murder weapon, and he had confessed to the crime. Madison couldn't understand why she didn't feel as satisfied as she should that justice was being done. She wondered if it was just because locking Harry Nore away wouldn't bring Lainie back. Or was it the presence of fingerprints, when she knew the killer had been wearing gloves?

The police were happy, and even Harry Nore was happy. He didn't have to beg out on U.S. 1 anymore. He was fed three times a day.

Life went on. Madison had never thought that it could; but it did. She never stopped hurting for her mother. But though the ache remained, the raw, jagged edge of pain was dulled by acceptance. Even the sensationalism at last died down, and only now and then would a cable channel run a program about Lainie and her wild life and tragic death.

She and Kaila went to live with their father. Kyle, Jassy and Trent went away to different universities. Rafe finished at Florida International University and went to New York to work on Wall Street. Madison went to school, dances and parties, tried out makeup, shaved her legs, pierced her ears and temporarily dyed her hair a brilliant blue for Halloween. Seasons passed; she fell in and out of love. Her father married twice in three years. Both women were gone so quickly she barely remembered their names.

She began to forget that she had actually *seen* the knife coming down as it killed her mother.

Began to forget...

She was young, and life went on. She would always love Lainie, always remember her. But each day the little things began to matter more. Her sisters and brothers. Jassy, who looked after her. Kaila, who needed her. Rafe and Trent, who were gentle with her. Kyle, who was kind for a while, then infuriating, then strong, or gentle, when she needed help the most. Life had to be lived.

Pain and fear gradually faded.

But she was the spitting image of her mother.

And the terror was destined to follow her.

1

Madison felt the dream wash over her, and instinctively, even in her sleep, she fought it. She tried to
awaken. No good—she was entangled in it.

She heard herself laughing, except that it wasn't
really her. She was the other woman, the woman in
the dream. Pretty, auburn-haired, charming. Out for
the night with a charismatic man. She was so excited. The feel of anticipation was exhilarating. They
were going to make love. She wanted to. She wanted
to be swept away, seduced, and when the weekend
was over, she would finally share him, his name,
with her friends. She would laugh and tell them what
a wonderful lover he had been; at work, she would
share intimate little secrets about how incredibly romantic he was, how erotic their affair could be, and
she would be so happy, a woman in love with her
handsome lover, a man who loved her, as well....

Madison knew that something was wrong. She
screamed inside the dream, but to no avail. She was
the pretty woman, and she was swept away by the
excitement, the longing, the human desire to be

touched and adored.... Oh, God, there was something so pathetic about being so needy.

The landscape swept by the car. Madison did and didn't recognize it. She wanted to wake up, to stop what was happening, but she couldn't.

The couple laughed and teased. She couldn't see the man's face, but she saw the woman's beautiful dark red hair whipping in the wind as they drove.

Darkness descended. Time elapsed....

They were in a bedroom. A shadowy hotel room. She was laughing again, so delighted. They kissed, murmuring. He undid the buttons of her blouse... one by one...touched her, stroked her....

Madison wanted to look away; she felt like a voyeur, watching such intimacy. The redhead was willing to do anything. Anything to please her lover. Naked, they entwined on the bed. She let him turn her over, onto her belly. His fingers threaded into her hair, drawing her head back. She only twisted her head slightly, looking back at her lover, and it was then that she saw...

The knife...oh, God, the knife, descending...

Madison woke up, desperately choking back a scream. Carrie Anne was watching a video in her room; she couldn't alarm her daughter. Oh, God, she was still shaking. She hadn't had such a horrible, realistic dream in a very long time.

She looked at her watch. It was nearly five in the afternoon; she'd promised to sing tonight. She hadn't intended to fall asleep, hadn't meant to nap. And she certainly hadn't meant to dream. And, oh, God, such a dream, so horribly, painfully vivid and terrifying...

She got up and paced her room for a moment, then dialed Jimmy Gates at the office. He was still at work.

"Madison?" he asked when she started talking, explaining.

"Jimmy, this dream..."

He listened as she talked.

"Jimmy, has anything happened? Do you know anything about what I'm telling you?"

He hesitated, and she winced. Yes, something had happened.

"I don't know.... I mean, I'm not sure if the scenario's like you're describing or not, but... Listen, I'm on an investigation. I was going to call you anyway, after the weekend. I need your help. You're spending the weekend down at your dad's, right?"

"Yes."

"I'll pick you up at your place Monday morning. We can get going from there, huh? Try to have a good weekend. Give Carrie Anne a kiss for me, will you? Maybe I'll even get down there. And don't worry—there's not a thing you can do for anyone now except yourself, okay?"

She nodded and hung up, then sighed, glad because the terrifying vividness of the dream was already fading. She hated it when she had such dreams.

She drew a brush through her hair. Well, she'd called Jimmy. She would do what she could, as she had a few times in the past. Thankfully, it was rare that the dreams came to her. When she could help, she did. Yet she knew that she couldn't cure all the evils in the world. She couldn't even cure all the problems in her own family.

The dreams had started with her mother's death.

She lay down on her bed again, staring up at the ceiling, wishing she didn't feel so overcome by memories. She hadn't had any strange visions for five years after her mother's death.

Then she'd had the first of the dreams.

In her dream she was walking away from an unknown house. Quietly. Tiptoeing. She realized that she held a gun. She heard noises and saw a car. She was angry, somehow aware that it was her car, and that someone was trying to steal it.

She crept out and raised the gun....

There was a violent pain in her arm, and she cried out, then woke up, rubbing her arm and shaking.

She was in her bedroom at her father's house, the room she shared with her sister Kaila. Kaila was across the room in her own bed, just waking up, rubbing her eyes. "Madison? Madison, what's wrong?" She jumped out of bed and came hurrying over to Madison's bed, sitting beside her.

They often fought, as most sisters, especially those so close in age, fought. But there was also a warmth between them. They were very unalike in personality, yet so similar in appearance that they might have been identical twins.

"It was nothing, just a dream," Madison assured Kaila quickly.

"Did you hurt your arm?"

"What? No?" But she was still rubbing her arm, even though there was nothing wrong with it. She shook her head sheepishly. "No, no, I'm fine. I had a nightmare, but it's all right now. Sorry I woke you."

"What was it about?"

"It was stupid. I was somebody else, in a different house. Someone was trying to steal my car, and I had a gun and was going to stop what was happening—then someone hit my arm, and I woke up. Dumb, huh?"

Kaila shrugged. "Well, different. You sure you're okay now?"

Tomorrow they would be fighting over makeup or who had taken whose new jeans. But for now... Madison nodded, and Kaila gave her a quick, fierce hug and went back to bed.

A few days later, when Madison still felt the dream nagging at her, she called Jimmy Gates. He wasn't in, and, feeling foolish, she left no message except her first name.

That afternoon, when Madison was driven home by Darryl Hart, the Hart-Throb of the school, she was startled to see a car in her father's expansive driveway, with a familiar man leaning against it. Detective Jimmy Gates. He was a little bit older now, showing premature signs of silver at his temples. He looked distinguished, befitting a man who'd gotten a number of promotions and citations during the five years since Lainie's murder.

She stared at him, feeling increasingly uneasy. She shouldn't have called him. She'd just had a dream, that was all.

Darryl behaved like the perfect high school stud he was, setting protective hands on her shoulders. "Who is he? What's wrong?"

"Nothing's wrong, Darryl. He's an old friend of the family. I think we probably need to talk alone. Call me later tonight?"

"Sure. Except maybe I shouldn't leave you alone

with him. So much strange stuff happens these days.''

"It's all right, Darryl. He's a cop.''

Darryl drove away unhappily, watching her in the rearview mirror as he backed out of the drive. Jimmy smiled at her. "Hi.''

"Hi, Jimmy. You still playing 'Miami Vice'?'' she asked him.

He shrugged. "You know there's no such thing,'' he said.

"Homicide,'' she said flatly.

"Yeah, I'm still homicide. And I need to know why you called.''

She hesitated, then told him about the dream, apologizing for calling him while trying to sound matter-of-fact and not like a fool.

Jimmy looked off into the distance, hesitating, then stared at her. "Have you heard about the Peterson case?''

She nodded and tried to pretend that a strange, cold sensation wasn't sweeping over her. She'd heard. Everyone in the city had heard. Earl Peterson had gotten his legally licensed handgun out of the cabinet where he kept it carefully under lock and key, to go outside when he heard noises by his car. He had tussled with someone outside and been killed with his own gun. He'd been found by his wife at six o'clock the following morning.

"I think maybe you can help me,'' Jimmy said.

"You do?'' She shouldn't have called him. She felt ill. It wasn't that she didn't want to help him— she just wished she didn't have the knowledge to do so.

"You have something, Madison. Something special. Will you help me?"

She hesitated. Her father wouldn't like it, but she was almost eighteen. She had seen Mrs. Peterson sobbing softly on television, and if she could do anything to ease the woman's suffering, she would.

She walked toward the car, and Jimmy opened the passenger door for her. She slid into the seat.

They drove to the crime scene.

A BMW sat in a tree-lined drive. Madison walked over to it, so alarmed by the cold, dark sensation sweeping over her that she nearly backed away. Only the memory of Mrs. Peterson's tearful appeals kept her moving.

Then she stood still.

She closed her eyes. She had a vision of night; of a feeling of anger. She could hear breathing, controlled, growing heavier. Mr. Peterson. She saw his hand, saw the weapon he held as he carefully, angrily moved around the BMW toward the large, shadowy figure trying to break into the car. She started violently as a second figure—unnoticed until then—suddenly stepped from the shadow of a large palm tree to slam his arm down on Mr. Peterson's. Mr. Peterson dropped the gun with a gasp. Madison cried out, feeling the pain in her arm—the same pain she had experienced in her dream. She hunched down, hugging her arm to her body. Seeing.

The man picked up the gun. Mr. Peterson looked up at him. "Now, wait—" Peterson began.

The gunman, a tall, thin white man with a blond crew cut, looked down at Peterson and calmly pulled the trigger twice.

Madison felt the force of the bullets ripping into

her chest. She didn't cry out, but she clutched her breast, feeling the impact.

And the cold. The awful cold assailing Peterson as his lifeblood began to drain away...

And still she saw. Saw the killer turn with his shadowy companion and race across the street into a heavily overgrown vacant lot.

The killer paused and started to run back, but his companion stopped him, urging him forward again. Madison saw them run again, saw until the icy fingers of death eroding Peterson's vision turned the picture to black.

Jimmy was at her side, helping her up, trembling himself. "I shouldn't have done this. Jesus, look at you. You're soaking-wet, shaking..."

She shook her head vehemently. "I'm all right. I'm all right. Honestly." She hesitated. "I can give you a description of the killer."

Jimmy ran his fingers through his hair. "I'm not sure I believe this myself. How am I going to get anyone else to believe that you can...see things?"

"Cops do make use of...of..." she began, but broke off, wincing.

"Psychics," Jimmy supplied.

She shook her head. "I'm not psychic. This has only happened to me twice. But I can give an artist a good description of the killer."

Madison did give the police a description, and an artist created a damned good sketch of the man.

Through the sketch, they found the man and brought him in for routine questioning. Thinking that the police had more on him than they did, he broke down and confessed to the killing of Earl Peterson.

After that, Jimmy made Madison promise to call him anytime she had strange dreams.

But the next time she had such a dream, it was far more personal. And it changed her life.

Madison graduated from high school with honors. She intended to go to school in Washington, D.C., and major in criminology—just like Kyle, who had recently acquired his master's degree and gone to work for the FBI.

Kyle came to her graduation. They hadn't seen much of each other in recent years; he had been away, and Lainie's death had more or less split up the "family." But he came to her graduation, along with all her other assorted siblings.

He brought his brand-new wife. Her name was Fallon, and she was perfect for Kyle, being perfectly beautiful. He was so tall, dark, well-muscled and good-looking; she was petite, blond, amber-eyed, slim and hourglass-shaped. Madison was surprised to find she wanted the woman to turn out to be a bimbette; however, she wasn't. She, too, had just gotten her degree and had taken a job with the Smithsonian. She was sweet and charming, and Madison had to admit to liking her very much. She told herself that she would have been incredibly critical of any woman clinging to Kyle's arm, because he was her... No. Because he was Kyle. And though she told herself that she didn't have a crush on him, she did. She was jealous.

That night she slept with Darryl Hart for the first time. Darryl was madly in love with her and intended to follow her to the same university. She was the envy of all her friends.

He did everything right. And though it was

slightly painful, it wasn't horrible. It just wasn't what she had read about, though Darryl assured her that it got better for women.

She certainly hoped so, though she tried very hard not to let him know just how disappointed she was. Darryl was a good guy.

She dated him for her first three years of college. Then...she had another dream.

She had known that Fallon was expecting a baby. She and Kyle lived relatively near one another—she in Georgetown, he in a suburb in Maryland, just outside downtown D.C.—but she avoided him. She and Darryl and Kyle and Fallon had met for dinner a few times, and everyone had had a great time—except her. So she made excuses not to see them. She told herself that she was a bitch, a horrible person. She should be happy for Kyle and Fallon. Kyle was her friend. He had helped her through the worst period of her life, so it was natural for her to feel a strange kind of dependency on him. It wasn't a crush. She needed to appreciate Darryl. He was even-tempered. He adored her and was unfailingly considerate. He was handsome, built like a young Adonis. She *did* appreciate him.

Together, they were perfect.

She was with Darryl when she had the dream about Kyle and Fallon.

It was terribly uncomfortable. It was almost as if she were with them. In their bedroom.

Fallon was on her side of the bed, tossing and turning. She was hugely pregnant, round as a tomato, yet still beautiful, her blond hair a tangled fan around her delicate, pinched features. She was racked with pain.

Kyle, at her side, was up, trying to help her, support her. "It must be the baby. We've got to get to the hospital."

"It's too soon, almost two months too soon!" Fallon cried.

"But you've been sick. We've got to get you there now." He stood, naked. Muscled, tanned. In her dream, Madison tried to look away, but she couldn't. It was as if she were there.

He dressed hurriedly, eschewing socks and underwear, slipping into his jeans and a T-shirt, and sliding his feet into his loafers while he dialed the phone. Fallon was distressed that he'd called for an ambulance, but he told her, "Babe, you're burning up. We need some help, fast."

Madison felt Fallon's heat. She was burning, burning, burning...like a fire. But there wasn't pain, there was just heat. And Kyle was there, holding her hand. Fallon was happy to feel his hand in hers, it was just that the heat was so terrible, and then she was shivering, hot and cold, hot and cold....

"Madison, Madison!"

She started, her eyes flying open. Darryl was shaking her awake, looking concerned.

"Madison, honey, you're having a nightmare. You have to wake up. Madison, what is it? What's wrong?"

She was soaked. She'd kicked the covers away. Darryl had his arms around her, and instinctively she clung to him in return.

"Want to tell me about it?" he asked her.

"No, no, it was nothing. I'm okay. I, uh, thanks. Thanks, Darryl. You're great." She kissed him. But when he wanted to take it further, in his efforts to soothe her, she curled away from him, a nagging sensation of worry refusing to leave her.

Three days later, a message from one of Kyle's buddies at the FBI on their answering machine told her that her dream had been real. Fallon had died as the result of complications from a virus, along with her premature, stillborn daughter. The funeral was Friday, in Manassas, Virginia.

Madison's entire family attended the funeral. Her own father had always gotten along exceptionally well with Kyle and Rafe, and Jordan Adair and Roger Montgomery still remained friends. Darryl, naturally, attended with Madison.

Kyle looked like hell. He wasn't quite twenty-six, but he'd already acquired a few silver strands of hair at his temple. His grief was terrible. Madison felt numb.

In church, she remained on her knees, head bowed, through most of the ceremony. She wondered if she might not be a terrible human being, if her jealousy might not have killed Fallon. The logical side of her brain tried to assure her that it couldn't be so, but she still felt somehow responsible, and it was an incredibly bad feeling. She wanted to run away.

She had only a few moments alone with Kyle. He came to her while she was kneeling by the coffin during the family's last viewing.

He knelt at her side, and she tried very hard not to cry while he adjusted the prayer book in his dead wife's hands. "At the end, she told me that you knew," he said suddenly. He stared at her in a way that gave her chills. "She said you were with us, that she was glad you were there. She told me I should look out after you."

He wasn't staring at her, though, as if he wanted to look after her. He was, in fact, staring at her as if she were a demon straight out of hell, as if he wished she would get as far away as possible from the beloved body of his wife.

Madison stared at him in return. "I have no idea what she meant," she lied. "I'm sorry, Kyle. I'm so, so sorry."

"You have no idea?" he repeated. And his voice was deep, rumbling with a strange anger. "What kind of a witch are you, Madison?" she thought she heard him whisper. And she saw his hands, folded prayer-fashion over the coffin now, tighten. Tighten with power and anger. Then he stretched his fingers out, as if aware of his terrible tension. He stared at them, handsome face taut with grief, blue eyes glittering. His hands slowly began to clench again, as if he would like to wind them around her neck, as if he, too, wondered if she couldn't somehow be responsible....

"No!" Madison whispered beneath her breath, then hurried from his side. She forced herself to go through the funeral and over to Kyle's house, where friends and family gathered after the service. When she said goodbye to Kyle and Roger, who stood at his side, she said it with a new sense of finality.

Madison immediately changed her major from criminology to communications. She'd always avoided acting, because of her mother, and writing because of her father, but she discovered she had a flair for photography, and though she had avoided modeling because of Lainie, she found herself giving in to friends in the school of photography who needed help putting together portfolios for job interviews.

On a spring break trip to Las Vegas, she married Darryl. Nine months later to the day, she gave birth to Carrie Anne Hart.

Darryl went to work for an engineering firm in Fort Lauderdale. Madison did runway modeling and an occasional photographic shoot while being a mom and working on her own photography.

Two and a half years after their marriage, Darryl came home to find Madison in tears. He wanted to know what was wrong. There was nothing wrong, she said. *She* was wrong. Their marriage was wrong. He was wonderful, but she didn't love him the way that she should.

Well, he wasn't so wonderful, he told her. Then he admitted to having an affair with one of his file clerks.

Madison wasn't sure why she was so furious, when she was appalled at herself for never having really loved Darryl. He wanted to patch things back together. He was so contrite that it was terrible.

In the end, oddly enough, they managed to part as friends. Good friends.

But Darryl accepted a job offer in the D.C. area. He needed to start over; she understood.

When all three of them could manage it conveniently, Madison saw to it that Carrie Anne went to stay with her father for a few days to a week. On those occasions, Madison began to accept more and more modeling jobs. While she was off on location in the Keys on one of them, she and some of the other models got a little giddy on a drink the bartenders were calling a Storm Front. She was surprised to find herself singing on stage with the hotel's poolside band, and even more surprised to discover that she was good.

She was alarmed when one of the photographers showed her a few of the pictures he had taken while she was performing.

She looked exactly as Lainie had looked before her death. Long, thick auburn hair, large, bright blue eyes. She was taller, about five-foot-eight, but her face was Lainie's classic oval, her nose, her mouth...just like Lainie's. She had loved her mother, even though she hadn't wanted to grow up to be her, wild, headstrong, going through husbands like toilet paper, heedless of the feelings of others....

Joey King, leader of the hotel band, wanted her to take a job with them. He was young, excited.

"We're on the brink of something really good happening. I've sold some of my songs, we've had the big music people down to see us—"

Madison finished her drink and stood. "Joey, I don't want to be a performer. I have a daughter. I have a career that's going better than I actually wanted it to."

"Because you look like your mother," he said.

She stared at him, and he shrugged.

"Sorry, but she was famous. I've seen lots and lots of pictures of her, and you do look just like her. Is that why you don't want to perform?"

"Joey, honestly, I just don't want to go out on the road—"

"All right, all right, no going on the road, I promise."

"Groups can make it or break it on the road," she reminded him.

"I have a wife and two kids myself," he told her. "Lots of groups have survived nicely just by doing local gigs and being studio musicians, and we have some great studios here. My sizzling desire for fame and fortune has been somewhat dampened by the reality of life," he added dryly. "So, would you do a few demos with us? Would you sing live with us now and then, when we've got some of the suits in the audience?"

His flames might have been dampened, but he was still a determined dreamer. And she liked him. He was blunt and honest, not to mention she'd had fun singing with the band.

She shrugged. "Sure," she told him. "Sure..."

Madison closed her eyes for a moment, then swung her legs over the side of the bed. Time to stop thinking about the past. Time to get moving.

Life had settled into a pattern for her, and she was happy, she told herself firmly

Well, okay, maybe not completely happy—she was too restless to be happy. She was a young divorced mom living in the same city as most of her family, so she had people who loved her around her—yet she was independent.

There were still the dreams, and when they came, she called Jimmy. But the dreams weren't all that frequent, and she was resigned to having them. Sometimes she would go with Jimmy to a crime scene, and sometimes she was able to get a feel for something, or have a flash of insight. She was seldom tormented by the visions.

As she had been today.

She straightened her hair and skirt, and caught sight of herself in the mirror again. "Don't whine, Madison! If you're not happy as a little lark, at least you're basically content in life!"

But her reflection remained grave. She felt restless. Uneasy.

As if, suddenly, things were going to come full circle.

As if the past itself were going to come back and haunt her life....

She gave herself a serious shake. She was working tonight. And come Monday, she would help Jimmy. She'd helped him before. Tonight it was time to have some dinner with Carrie Anne and her dad, if he was around, and get going.

Yet as she started for her daughter's room, she still couldn't quite shake an uncomfortable feeling. Not just the fear and pain the dream had evoked for a stranger.

An unease that curled around her heart...

Much, much closer to home.

2

Kyle knew that he fit in fine. He might be a "suit" from Washington now, but he was a Florida boy from way back, and he knew how to sit in a Key West bar and blend in with the scenery.

He was wearing cutoff jeans, scuffed Top-Siders and a worn short-sleeved cotton shirt, open at the throat and halfway down his chest. He wore dark sunglasses and a baseball cap pulled low over his forehead, and he sat at a table located in the rear, where shadows fell, leaning back in his chair, legs sprawled on the chair before him as he nursed his beer. He could pass for a tourist—or a local. He guessed that he was actually somewhere in between. Jordan Adair owned this particular place, and it was popular. Folks coming down to Key West liked to have a drink at Sloppy Joe's, famous as an Ernest Hemingway hangout, but they were equally anxious to fit in with the modern so-called "literary" crowd, which could include just about anyone. Jordan Adair wrote gritty suspense; his friends included mystery writers, true-crime writers, sci-fi and romance writers, those who dealt in history, in general fiction, in nonfiction—and those who were just so famous they could write books that would sell just because they were who they were. Along with the literary crowd, the place offered music—and the music was as varied as the clientele.

Jordan was not only cozy with the attorneys, cops and pathologists he consulted for his work, he was also friends with the film crowd, since a number of his books had been adapted for the screen. Tourists loved to flock here just to see who they could see, with the assurance that—should the crowd be quiet—the music would be good. At the moment, it was late afternoon, and a technician was just finishing fussing with the wires to one of the microphones.

Today, some of those who wanted to be seen were out. A young starlet with an entourage of bodybuilders was at the bar, drawing her share of attention from the tourists, as was Niall Hathaway, author of the latest publishing phenomenon, a hardcover about a priest brought back from a coma through the prayers of his congregation—and dreams about a life with the woman he had once loved and would love again. The book had been on the hardcover bestseller lists for over a year now; the movie rights had gone for well over a million dollars. Didn't matter. The old guy just wanted to take his newfound wealth and go fishing. Key West was a good place to get on a boat with a rod and a few knowledgeable fishermen.

Kyle wanted to get out on a boat, as well. He wanted to get into the water, fish, dive. Lie back, crisp himself in the sun, drink beer in the breezy heat that usually fell over the water here. And he would. He didn't have his own boat anymore, but Jordan had told him that the *Ibis* was his for the length of his stay, however long it might be. He hadn't had much of a chance to talk to Roger yet; he hadn't had much of a chance to do anything. He'd just arrived via a commuter flight through Miami International from Washington National, and it felt good just to sit in Jordan's tavern. Key West wasn't exactly home, but it was certainly home away from home. It was a good break before starting out in Miami with the local boys from Metro-Dade and Miami. He'd already done some preliminaries, but the Miami authorities had just turned to the FBI, so they were in the early stages of an investigation into what appeared to be a serial crime spree.

Odd, how life moved along—and it *did* move along. His memories of Fallon still hurt, but the pain was like that of an old knee injury; the flesh had healed over, but the joint would never be quite the same. Still, enough time had passed that he could smile now and then, thinking about her, and recollections of good times, of her smile, mingled with the pain, and sometimes it was okay. Still, it hadn't been the tragedy of Fallon's passing that influenced his life most strongly.

Lainie's death had charted the path his life would take. In coming to terms with what had happened then, he had come to believe that only justice could make things better, could ease the pain her horrible death had brought to her family. Not to mention the fact that his father had been suspected of murder, just as Jordan Adair had been. Following the cops and the lawyers around, he'd been horrified to discover just how hard it could be to catch a killer. Crimes of violence fell into two categories: crimes of passion against loved ones, friends or acquaintances; and then the crimes that were growing alarmingly more frequent as time went along—crimes of random violence. As he tagged along behind Jimmy in his search for clues to Lainie's killer, he had come to know that the victims of a crime were often those who were left behind to come to terms with a new life and the injustice of their loss. Nothing could bring back a loved one, but closure, knowing what had happened, helped put people on the healing road to sanity.

Crimes of passion against loved ones, Jimmy had taught him, were often the easiest to solve. Science had come a long way; DNA samples could be used in a courtroom, along with fingerprints, hairs, fibers and more. A rapist could be convicted on a semen sample.

Random crimes, on the other hand were hard to solve. Even if the cops could lift a dozen fingerprints, it wouldn't help if those fingerprints weren't on record somewhere. Random crimes kept the cops looking for needles in haystacks.

Which was why he'd wound up going into the psychological business of profiling killers. It narrowed down that haystack for the cops.

Closure. It was so damned important. Arresting and imprisoning a killer allowed those left behind a sense of justice—at least the killer had been stopped, and others wouldn't have to feel their pain.

His work was important. He was glad that it still broke his heart to study the victims of the killers he sought; pain for others let him know he was still living. Because though, it might have been his stepmother's death that had influenced his life's work, it was his wife's death that continued to haunt his own life. He was grateful that she hadn't been brutally killed, but she had suffered even so, and he couldn't help but be bitter that someone so young, with everything to live for, had died. There was no justice in her death, no rhyme, no reason. No sense. Fallon had not just been young, beautiful and full of life. She'd been kind, caring and warm. She couldn't pass a bum in the street without giving him a dollar; she couldn't let a stray dog run by without setting out a bowl of food. Kids had loved her. She would have been a great mother to the daughter who never managed to draw breath. There was an emptiness inside him as well, a pain that remained for the child he would never hold.

Kyle had been told that time could heal what reason could not. He'd been told that God would give him strength at a time when he couldn't find it in his heart to believe in God. One thing he could say was that time did go on. He was a survivor, so he lived. He breathed, ate—and drank. Heavily, at first. moderately now. He slept with other women. Sometimes there was something of a relationship there, and sometimes he just hoped for good sex. Life went on, and he did his best with his work and with other people. True justice wasn't coming in this lifetime, and he knew it; still, it somehow mattered more than ever now that he make his very best effort toward achieving whatever justice he could help achieve.

''Hello out there!'' a husky masculine voice suddenly boomed over the sound system. A lanky, good-looking young man of perhaps twenty-eight or thirty had come to the microphone at the center of the stage, which was to the left of the bar. ''Welcome, to our locals, our old friends…and to you out there enjoying a spell in our fantasyland. We're the Storm Fronts, and we're going to keep you entertained this afternoon while you kick back, eat, drink and catch some rays. My name is Joey King, and with me are David Hamel on bass, Sheila Ormsby on keyboards, Randy Fraser on drums and, I'm happy to say, Ms. Madison Adair herself is with us this afternoon on vocals. Ladies and gentlemen... enjoy.''

Kyle was suddenly glad that he was in the shadows, because he certainly wasn't prepared for Madison. Especially Madison as he saw her this afternoon.

The band members filed casually out onto the rustic stage as their names were announced, Madison arriving last. It didn't seem that it had been so long since he saw her last, but it had, of course. It had been a lifetime.

She was the same; she was different. There had still been a little bit of tall, gawky teenager left in her the last time he saw her.

And now...

Now there was not.

She walked with an easy, confident sway. Her smile was as breezy and sensual as a hot summer's day. She was tall and slender, without being too slim; there were definite curves to Madison. She managed to be elegantly slim and voluptuous, all at the same time. Her hair remained red—like a sunset, deep and dark in the underlayers, sun-tinted with searingly gold highlights. She wore it long down her back, thick and wavy. Her face had matured; her features were fine against the lean oval of her bone structure. Her eyes were large, and a brilliant, crystalline blue. She hadn't dressed in a way meant to allure; she didn't need to. She wore a midthigh-length denim shirt with a simple soft-knit short-sleeve pullover in baby blue. Her long, tanned legs were bare, and she wore sandals with inch-high heels.

She was electrifying. The minute she breezed onto the stage, she drew all eyes. It was more than her intense, vibrant, dramatic coloring, more than the stunning beauty with which she'd been genetically blessed. It was her walk, her ease, her confidence, her smile. Her every casual movement seemed to be as naturally, sensually lithe and arrogant as that of a cat.

Yes, she was startling, certainly. Attractive, beyond a doubt.

But, God, oh, God, it was more than that.

She looked like her mother. Exactly like her mother.

Longer hair; shorter skirt, but she might have been Lainie.

Back in the shadows, he felt a grim smile slip onto his face. Funny. She'd always been a little cat. Cute, and more. And he'd always been drawn to her. Yet, curiously, at the same time...

He'd always wanted to keep his distance. There were too many things that Madison could see. And he didn't want to be seen.

Kyle had been doing no more than sipping his beer. Watching Madison, he suddenly downed the rest, then nodded as a bronzed blond waitress in short-shorts came by to silently query him about a refill.

Madison had been his stepsister. She'd often made him smile with her tart comments on her world, observations that were far too wise for her years. Yet he wondered suddenly if it wasn't the fact that she was such a dead ringer for Lainie that had really kept him at arm's length all these years. Was she like Lainie? Lainie's death had been terrible and tragic, true, but Lainie had also been capable of being one hell of a bitch, heedless of whose life she played with—or destroyed.

Madison was speaking now. "Welcome, folks, to A Tavern. It's my dad's place, for those of you who don't know, and I'm always happy to be here. There's something special about Key West. Everybody's kind of free to be themselves down here, and we take pride in taking the time to smell the flowers—and the sea air and dead fish, of course." Her patter was casual, as the band members tuned up their instruments. She flashed a quick smile at the young man, Joey King, who had introduced the group, and he smiled back. "Anyway," she added, adjusting her mike on its stand, "we're about to get started with one of Joey's ballads, just fit for the island. It's called, "Love's on the Rocks, So I Just Swim in My Beer." Chime on in with the refrain anytime you so desire."

She flashed another of her brilliant smiles. The musicians were suddenly all tuned up, and Madison was swaying with the beat.

She had a great voice. Fluid, solid, husky. The song had a Jimmy Buffett quality to it, which seemed natural, considering the time and place. The tavern grew crowded as the music wafted out to the street; the crowd laughed with the lyrics, clapped appropriately and sang along as invited. By the time the music ended, the place was so full that Kyle wouldn't have been able to see the musicians if they hadn't been standing on a raised stage. The waiters and waitresses, proving themselves to be contortionists, nimbly slid and slithered through the crowd, delivering pitchers of beer, margaritas, and soda, along with food and various outlandish concoctions in souvenir glasses.

The band did another number, a Top 40 rock hit. Then they played another original, this one a softer ballad called "Getting On with You Gone." Another Top 40 hit, another original, this one about a no-good son of a gun. A few more songs, and then Madison announced the last number before their break. Again it was slow. People were dancing in the limited floor space between the tables and the stage. Toward the end of that final song, Madison looked his way at last.

She might be nerve-rackingly psychic, but he could tell that she hadn't known that he was there. She stared at him, and she suddenly fell silent. Madison could be one tough, sophisticated cookie, but she was staring at him then like a deer caught in headlights. Well, he must have been quite a surprise. They hadn't seen each other in one hell of a long time. He'd stayed away, and in his healing process, he'd realized somewhere along the line that just because she'd somehow known what was going on in his life, he'd maybe tried to blame her for it. And even now, he'd come here for work, not exactly to make peace. Still, he was ready to admit to the ill manners he'd demonstrated in his grief. Yeah, he was ready. But maybe, he thought with an inner shrug, life didn't work that way. The way Madison was looking at him, he felt as if he'd been hanging on to a rope—that she'd just cut clean through. Well, what the hell. They both had their own lives. Maybe there was no reason to make amends.

He lifted his beer glass to her. "Sing," he mouthed.

Her fellow band members were staring at her, nimbly covering, playing the same beat and chords over and over. Madison seemed to give herself a mental shake, and her eyes left his.

She flashed the audience that pure-charm smile of hers and picked up again, singing her heart out.

Then the music ended, to a burst of applause, and Madison promising that the group would be back.

Kyle thought she might just ignore the fact that he was there. He was somewhat surprised that no one had told her he was coming.

Maybe everyone had just assumed that she'd *know* he was coming down to Miami to work. Hell, Jimmy should have told her. Her father should have told her. But maybe Jordan Adair had thought it wouldn't mean anything to her, one way or the other.

And maybe it didn't, though the look she'd given him suggested otherwise.

But she didn't ignore him. She threaded her way through the crowd, acknowledging those who stopped her to speak or compliment her and the band, until she reached his table. By that point he'd moved his legs from the chair where he'd been resting them, but he was still wearing his dark glasses and baseball cap, so she couldn't have seen much of his features in the darkening shadows of the coming night.

She stood in front of the table, looking down at him with her perfect features composed in a cold and aloof expression. "What the hell are you doing here?" she demanded.

"Hello, Madison. It's great to see you, too."

"Right. What are you doing here?"

He shrugged, smiling. Lifted his hands. "Drinking beer. Listening to music."

"What are you doing *here,* in Key West? In my father's place?"

"I'm in the Keys on business. I'm here because your father invited me."

He heard a whistling sound as she sucked in her breath with involuntary surprise.

He used his foot to push out the chair opposite from him. "Have a seat, Madison."

She sat. Not because she wanted to be with him, he thought, but because she was so shaken.

"Want a drink?" he asked.

She shook her head, blue eyes intently on him. "I'm still working. So…when did this all come about?"

He shrugged. "I was told last week I was coming down to give some assistance on a local investigation. Your father invited me here for the weekend."

"You're staying at my father's house?"

He nodded, wondering why her blunt hostility was so disturbing to him. He ignored that question and instead said, "Your band is good."

"Yeah," she said, still just staring at him.

"I heard about your divorce. I'm sorry about that. I thought you kids were good together."

"It's all been over quite a while now. You needn't be concerned."

"Look, Madison, I'm really sorry if you have a problem with this. Your dad invited me down. I didn't know you'd be here, and it wouldn't have occurred to me that it would upset you even if I *had* known you were here."

"I'm not upset," she snapped quickly.

"Angry," he said.

"Surprised, is all."

"I can't imagine why your father didn't mention it to you."

Her lashes lowered. Maybe *she* knew why, he thought. Maybe she and Jordan weren't getting along. They were both temperamental, and sometimes argued passionately, though they loved one another dearly.

"Have you talked to your dad this week?"

Madison didn't answer. The waitress was hovering near, watching her. "Did you want a soda, Madison? Some mineral water?"

Madison kept staring at Kyle. "No, I'll have a draft."

"I'm sorry, what?"

"A draft, please," Madison repeated.

"But—" the waitress began. Madison looked at her, and the other woman shrugged and walked away.

Kyle grinned. "I was trying to buy you a drink. Let me put it on my tab."

"This is my father's place. I don't need to put my drinks on your tab."

Kyle straightened in his seat, then leaned forward. "Look, Madison, I'm at fault here. I was pretty rude the last time we met, but—"

"You weren't rude, you were hateful."

He shook his head painfully. "Madison, my wife had just died."

"And I was very sorry," she said quietly. "And you treated me as if were the Wicked Witch of the West, straight out of Oz, as if I'd somehow caused it to happen."

"Look—"

"No, *you* look, Kyle. I don't understand my sense of second sight. God knows, I don't want it. But I can't make things happen, and I'm not—" She broke off, a look of pain flashing across her beautiful features.

"You're not what?"

She shook her head.

The waitress returned, setting her beer in front of her. Madison thanked the woman as Kyle leaned forward.

"I'm not different from anyone else," she said through gritted teeth. She picked up the beer and drank it down. She didn't chug, he noticed. Or, if she did, it didn't look like chugging. Madison was too elegant for that.

"Madison, I'm trying to say I'm sorry. We were family once, close family—"

Her mug landed back on the table. "You're not my family, Kyle. You were my stepbrother, but my mother died. You're not my family. We're not related—"

"We *were* family, a totally dysfunctional family. Remember? That's what you always called us. But you're right, I'm not your brother. Still, death doesn't change relationships, and I'd like to make peace—"

"You were the one firing off the ammo," she reminded him politely.

"And I'm asking for your forgiveness."

"What? Won't Dad let you use his boat if I don't think it's just great that you're back?"

He smiled, shaking his head. "Madison, you're acting like a brat. First, my job pays decently—I could rent a boat if I needed one. Secondly, you're overestimating your power over your parent. He has his own mind."

"Oh, really?" She started to sip her beer, then realized her glass was empty. She looked around, as if she wanted another. Quickly.

Kyle leaned closer, somewhat amused. "I don't think you should be drinking yourself silly—over me. Don't you have another set to do?"

"I'd never drink myself silly over you, Kyle Montgomery. I'm just so damned mad—"

"Ah! So you *are* hostile."

"Hostile? That's an understatement."

"I hurt you, Madison. And I'm sorry."

"Since we're talking about overestimating things, I think you're overestimating *your* power, Kyle. You don't have the power to hurt me."

He shrugged, looking around. He saw the waitress and motioned to her. "I'll take another beer, please—honey."

He'd added the last on purpose. The waitress didn't notice, but Madison winced.

"Madison…?" the girl asked.

"Ms. Adair is still working," Kyle said pleasantly.

"I'll have another draft, Katie, thanks," Madison said.

Katie walked away to fill their order. He couldn't help smiling as he stared at Madison, except that, as he looked at her, he felt a sudden tremor streak through him, hot as fire, constricting something vital in him. She was angry, nasty, could be bitchy as hell.

God, he wanted her.

He exhaled a long breath, staring at her, glad of his roomy denim cutoffs and the table hiding his arousal from her.

She'd been cute and clever at thirteen. Beautiful in college. He'd felt affection for her when she was a kid, pride when she was older, and, always, a strange pull. Now she was pure, sensual elegance. It was startling to realize the strength of what he was feeling for her at that moment.

She'd been his stepsister, for God's sake, he reminded himself. But they weren't biologically related, for which he was grateful, considering the purely physical reaction she was causing in him now.

Except that he cared about her, too. Even though part of him wanted to be a million miles away from her. Even if he was...

Unnerved.

That was it. Completely unnerved by her.

He cleared his throat. "Did you drive here, Madison?" he asked her.

"Yes, why?"

"Because you shouldn't drive home. I'll wait for you."

The beers were set before them. Madison stared at him, her eyes hard. "You're not my big brother. You don't need to wait for me."

"You're drinking too much."

"Oh, *I'm* drinking too much. So I should ride home with a beach bum who's been sitting here drinking for hours?"

Kyle grinned slowly. "I'll go to coffee next."

"Don't bother on my account."

"Are you staying at your dad's place?"

She hesitated. "Yes."

"Then I'll wait."

"Maybe I have a date."

He looked past her, studying the band members, who were again readying their equipment.

Kyle lifted his beer. "Are you sleeping with one of them? Joey King, maybe? He looks like your type."

"He's married, with kids."

"Glad to hear that would stop you."

"Damn you, Kyle—"

"Sorry, sorry, I just haven't seen you in a long time."

"Who I sleep with is none of your business."

"Maybe it's the natural concern of an older brother."

"I thought we'd established that you're not my brother."

He shrugged. "Have it your way. Old habits die hard. I'm just trying to ascertain who you'll be seeing after your gig."

"Maybe I sleep with the whole band. At the same time."

He smiled, lowering his head slightly. "Madison, you have the tolerance level of a baby when it comes to alcohol."

"Really? You haven't seen me in more than six years! You think I'm drunk already? You think you know my tolerance levels? Then maybe you don't want to stick around. I'm Lainie Adair's child, remember? If I'm so loaded, you should watch out. I might resort to some kind of wild strip show up there.''

He grinned, tugging on the brim of his baseball cap. ''Well, cool. You did just remind me that there's no blood relation between us. Our kids wouldn't have two heads, or anything like that. I'll be watching and waiting.''

''Our kids? Oh, Kyle, never, not even if the survival of the species depended on it.''

''I think they're waiting for you, Madison.''

She stood up with sudden anger, then bent down, whispering vehemently, ''Don't wait for me.''

''I'm not having any traffic fatalities on my conscience. I'll be here when you're done.''

''Kyle—''

''I'll be waiting, Madison.''

She straightened. Turned. Wavered.

She really didn't have any tolerance for alcohol. None whatsoever.

She banged into a table on her way back to the stage.

But she sang just fine. Her voice was great. She moved sensually to the music.

And when she finished, he was waiting.

3

Madison could have kicked herself. She prided herself on looking at life with level, matter-of-fact vision, and here she was, behaving like a two-year-old.

Because Kyle Montgomery had suddenly stepped back into her life.

To make it worse, she reflected, he was behaving well. Apologizing. Putting the past in the past, trying to establish a friendship.

She could be mature, too. She *could*. He had just taken her by surprise, that was all. And, of course, he did know her. She had no tolerance for alcohol whatsoever—which seemed absurd, considering what her father could put away without the slightest slur in his voice. But that didn't matter; she had a handle on that now. During the second break, she had laced herself with strong black coffee. By the time the group finished for the night, she was clear-headed. Tired, but clearheaded. So much so that she was able to insist with quiet, mature dignity that she could drive her own car home.

Still, when she drove through the gates to her father's Key West "bungalow," Kyle was right behind her. It would have appeared rude to rush in ahead of him and slam the front door in his face, so she stepped from the driver's seat of her Cherokee, closed the car door and waited. She wasn't going to appear rude. And she wasn't going to fight with him like a child. She wasn't going to embrace him with enthusiasm, however; she was going to be cool, aloof and unerringly polite. Courteous. Naturally, he was welcome in her father's house. At one time, as he had said, they had been a family, however dysfunctional.

"So, how is being back home in the land of sun and fun?" she inquired as he stepped from his rented Honda and started along the path toward her. He looked good. As if he spent lots of hours in the gym. There were the larger touches of silver in his dark hair than the last time she'd seen him, as if life had beaten him up a bit. It had; she knew that. His face was more striking now, with a few sun lines working their way around his mouth and eyes. He was tanned. He might use good sense and sunblock now and then, she thought, but vanity would never keep him from the outdoors, which he loved. It was, in fact, strange to think of him spending so much time in the Washington area without coming home. She knew that his house was actually in northern Virginia, near Quantico and the office where he worked most frequently, with a lot of beautiful scenery nearby, as well as museums, theaters and sporting events. But he loved the sun and the things to be done in the sun, swimming, boating, diving, fishing. Maybe staying away had been some self-imposed punishment after Fallon died.

Nearing her, he arched a dark brow, apparently surprised by—and perhaps wary of—her conversational tone of voice.

"It's good to come home," he said, staring up at the "bungalow." Jordan Adair's "Key West shack"—as he referred to it on talk shows—had eight bedrooms and baths, and sat on a patch of man-enhanced private beach. "Not that I would presume to call your father's house *my* home," he said, a small smile curling his lips.

Madison shrugged. "Well, we were definitely the strangest family in the world. My father and your father used to play at being rivals, now they're each other's best friends." She hesitated, determined to keep a grudging tone from her voice. "I'm sure my father considers this place home for you."

"That was quite magnanimous of you."

She shrugged. "Well, I'm exhausted. And five-year-olds wake up early."

"Your daughter is here?"

"You didn't know that?"

He shook his head. "I drove in, dumped my gear in an empty guest room, saw your father briefly— he had one of his Enter at Your Own Risk, Madman Working signs on his door. He said I should go on over and have a few beers, he'd probably show up."

"He didn't mention that the group would be there tonight?"

"No."

"Sounds like Dad—he also didn't think to mention to me that you were coming in."

Madison turned, walking along the gravel drive that led to the tile path to the house. A few steps brought her to the rustic front door—the place was a mansion with every conceivable luxury on the inside, but the weathered wood exterior made it look like something of a crab house. Kyle followed her inside.

The foyer led straight through to a massive living room that opened out onto the patio and pool. On either side, the house sprawled out, kitchen and four bedrooms to the right, Jordan's office and another four bedrooms to the left. Beyond the pool was a separate building that housed a Ping-Pong table, a billiard table and a multitude of games and coin operated machines. Next to it was a storage facility for scuba and fishing equipment. The patio was always lit, so even though the house was darkened, there was plenty of light for the two of them to see one another.

"Well, as I said, welcome back."

"And as I said, I'm sorry."

She shrugged. "Apology accepted." She hesitated. "How long are you down for?"

"I don't know yet. I have to be in Miami on Monday. From there, it depends on how things go."

Miami on Monday.

Madison felt an instant chill, but she didn't intend to say anything to Kyle. She didn't want him asking her what kind of a witch she was again.

"What's going on that you've been called down?" she asked casually.

He shrugged. "You don't know?"

She shook her head. "No, I don't know." That was the truth. "I don't see everything, and I don't control what I see, and I wish to hell that you'd stop treating me like some kind of freak!"

"What?" He seemed startled.

"I'm not a freak."

He frowned. "I never said you were."

"Well, you've acted like it."

He shook his head again. "No...I... No. Madison—it was just a bad time. Hell, I've said I'm sorry."

"Yeah, well, welcome home. I guess I'll see you around."

"Good-night."

He didn't move, continuing to look at her.

She hesitated, wishing she knew more. "You still didn't tell me exactly why you're down here."

"No, I didn't. It's a long story. Want to go out on the boat with me tomorrow?"

"No."

He shrugged. "Well, a boat is a good place to tell a long story."

"Maybe I'm not that curious. And maybe I could just ask Jimmy—or Jassy—what's going on in Miami."

"Maybe you could. Suit yourself."

"I can't just take off with you in the boat. I have a five-year-old. And we always spend Saturdays together, unless she's with her dad."

Madison thought that a streak of pain flashed through his eyes, but it was gone so quickly that she decided she might have imagined it. But then, he should have had a little girl, too.

But he was smiling at her then, so guilelessly that she was sure she had imagined the darkness in his eyes and soul.

"Your five-year-old is Jordan Adair's granddaughter. I'll bet she just loves a day out on the boat."

She hesitated.

"Hey, sis, come on. I'm just trying to make peace. Honest to God, once upon a time, we were friends."

"Maybe. We'll see. It depends on when you're leaving."

"Early. By eight."

"You're out of your mind."

He smiled again with a casual shrug, tugging on his baseball cap. "Maybe. We'll see."

He turned then, walking toward the left wing of the house. She was glad that her bedroom was to the right.

Get a grip, Madison, she warned herself, hurrying through the shadowed house. Her fingers were trembling. Great. All those years. She'd married, then divorced. She'd found a life; she was happy. Or at least, she got on just fine. And here he was, back for a matter of hours, and she was shaking.

Fuck him.

She winced and tiptoed toward Carrie Anne's room, cracking the door and looking in on her sleeping daughter. She walked into the room, stood by the bed and smoothed back her daughter's hair. Carrie Anne was beautiful. She was blond, like her dad. Her features were fine, like Madison's own. She had wide, generous lips, and the best smile in the world.

She'd made a lot of mistakes, Madison thought, for a lot of reasons. But even if her marriage had been a pathetically bad mistake and her own fault, it had surely stood a purpose, and she knew that her ex-husband thought so, too. Carrie Anne was worth whatever heartache they had caused one another. And oddly enough, they were doing a fine job of keeping Carrie Anne's best interests at heart.

She planted a kiss on Carrie Anne's forehead, then

walked through the expansive bath that connected
their two rooms. She entered her own room, allow-
ing the night-light from the bathroom and the patio
lights from beyond to serve as illumination. She
flung herself back on the bed and stared up at the
ceiling. She loved her dad's "shack." Her room was
large, her bed was plush, and she—like her other
siblings—had a complete entertainment center, as
well as a working fireplace for those few nights each
year when the temperature dipped as far down as the
low forties. Her father had spared no expense on his
children's part-time rooms. Carrie Anne's decor was
handsomely Disney, with a little Dr. Seuss thrown
in. Madison herself had opted for a white-marble
floor with ebony throw rugs and a red-black-and-
blue motif that was vivid and passionate. Roger
Montgomery, a frequent visitor, had applauded her
taste, telling her that she was far more artistic than
she was willing to admit.

"Just like my—" he'd begun.

"Your what?" she'd asked with a smile.

"Son," he said quietly, looking away. "Kyle. He
can draw like a son of a gun."

"I didn't know that," she'd murmured, straining
to maintain her smile.

"My point exactly. Kyle doesn't like to let people
know he can draw. That might make him too much
like his old man."

"I'm sure he loves you very much."

"Well, I guess you can love someone and not
want to be like them."

"Maybe. What about Rafe?"

Roger had shrugged. "Rafe's a great kid, but he

can't manage a stick figure. He's a mathematician, like his mother.''

"Ah. Well..."

And then she'd managed to change the subject.

She sat up now and slid off the bed. She stepped out of her shoes, slipped off her skirt, blouse and bra, and dug under her pillow for her nightgown, a tailored cotton confection from Victoria's Secret. As she did up the buttons, she caught sight of herself in the mirror over her dresser.

For a moment she felt a terrible chill and stood dead still.

Oh, God, she did look like her mother! So much so that it was really frightening.

She turned away from the mirror and curled into bed. She put her head down and reminded herself that her life was good. She adored her daughter; she had a good job and good times, and everything was great.

Everything was great, and yet...

All right, there was a lot that sucked, too. Somehow, she hadn't noticed that. Not until Kyle came striding back into her life tonight.

She prayed for sleep. Kyle was here. He would help solve whatever crime he was here to investigate—or the killer he was after would move on and remain a mystery to everyone. One way or the other, Kyle would leave. Maybe he would keep coming home for holidays, now that he'd been here, but he wasn't really a part of her life again.

She tossed and turned.

Kyle was here. After her dream. Reporting to work on Monday. And Jimmy was going to pick her up on Monday. She wished she knew what was going on.

She wanted to sleep; she didn't want to sleep. She was afraid she would dream. She shivered. One way or the other, she had to sleep.

Eventually she did.

And no dreams invaded her slumber.

She loved weekends. Adored them. Not that her schedule was such a brutal one—she knew many women who worked much harder!—but she did have a child in kindergarten, and she did wake up at six-thirty most mornings to get Carrie Anne to school on time. That made Saturdays and Sundays great days, when the alarm didn't buzz rudely in her ear and she could sleep as late as she wanted.

Not that morning.

It was as if her eyelids had been fixed with robotic alarms themselves. They just suddenly sprang open, and she was wide-wake, staring around her room, where light was just beginning to filter in.

She closed her eyes and wiggled down into the covers. She told herself how deliciously comfortable her bed was. How she could sleep for hours if she wished.

No good.

After a minute, she sat up. She glanced at her watch and swore softly at herself in disgust. It wasn't even six yet. She wondered bitterly if there wasn't some silly system inside of her that wanted to go out on the boat with Kyle.

Too bad. She wasn't going. Carrie Anne was still sleeping, after all.

Thank God for Carrie Anne. Her daughter would

keep her from foolishly seeking out the company of Kyle Montgomery.

She had barely started the water running before she heard a little voice.

"Mommy, can I come in with you?"

She froze, then pulled the curtain back as the water beat down around her. "Hi, sweetie. What are you doing awake? Did I wake you up? I'm sorry."

Carrie Anne, large blue eyes wide, solemnly shook her head. She lifted her hands and grimaced. "I woke up. Just like that." She frowned. "There isn't school, is there? We wouldn't have come down to Grandpa's place if there was school, right?"

"No, there isn't school. Put your shower cap on and come on in."

Carrie Anne squiggled out of her Barbie nightgown and undies and piled her blond hair into a cap. Madison helped tuck her daughter's curls beneath the elastic rim before bringing Carrie Anne in with her. They both sudsed up and rinsed off, Madison making sure Carrie Anne did her toes and ears, before Carrie Anne asked her, "What are we doing today, Mommy?"

Madison hesitated. She turned off the shower, reached for towels and swung Carrie Anne from the shower to the plush rug at its side.

She took all that time, but then it seemed that she talked before she really thought. "Want to go out on the boat?"

"With Grandpa?" Carrie Anne asked.

Madison shook her head, wrapping a towel around her daughter's. "I don't think Grandpa's coming. He's really into one of his books right now. But an old friend is down... He used to be my stepbrother."

"How can somebody used to be your brother?" Carrie Anne asked, truly mystified.

Madison opened her mouth to answer, then shrugged. "Well, once his dad and my mom were married. So we were what people call stepbrother and stepsister. But you know that my mommy died—"

"And went to heaven," Carrie Anne supplied.

"And went to heaven," Madison agreed softly. "And then my stepbrother and I didn't really see too much of one another anymore. Anyway, his name is Kyle. And you know Kyle's daddy, Roger. You know his brother, Rafe."

"He's Uncle Rafe's brother?" Carrie Anne asked, pleased. Rafe was always great with the kids. Madison often wondered why Kyle's older brother had never married and had his own kids. Of course, he, like the rest of them, had watched such a multitude of marriages go wrong. Rafe had spent a few years in New York, on Wall Street, and in that little bit of time, he'd made a fortune. Now he was based in Miami, where he played at the stock market and being an entrepreneur.

"Actually, he's Uncle Rafe's half brother," she said. "But we usually just say brother or sister, because except for Auntie Kaila and me, we were all half sisters and brothers or stepsisters and brothers." She was confusing her daughter, and she smiled. "Honey, Kyle is related to Uncle Rafe. But he's not really like Uncle Rafe."

"He's not nice?" Carrie Anne said with a frown.

"No, no, he's just different. You know, the way Aunt Kaila and I are different."

Carrie Anne shook her head. "You and Auntie Kaila look just alike, Mommy."

"Right—but we're different."

"You act different."

"Yeah."

"You act happy. Most the time. Auntie Kaila doesn't."

Madison frowned, looking at her daughter. She acted happy? Life was a thrill a minute. But it was true that Kaila hadn't seemed particularly happy lately. Madison wondered what was so wrong, that a five-year-old could intuitively sense a problem.

"Don't be silly," she told Carrie Anne. "Auntie Kaila has a beautiful home, a supernice husband and three great, cute little kids just like you. She's happy."

"I don't think so," Carrie Anne said, then let it drop. "Let's go on the boat!" she enthused suddenly.

"Okay…then go get your bathing suit on, the new one with the matching cover-up—"

"I will, I will, I know, the sun can be murder," Carrie Anne said, smiling.

Madison nodded. "I'll get dressed myself and see you in a few minutes."

"You should wear your new bathing suit, too, Mommy," Carrie Anne advised. "The one with the matching cover-up." At five, Carrie Anne already loved clothes. She took good care of her own and liked to advise Madison on hers.

"Okay," Madison agreed. "Let's get to it, then."

Fifteen minutes later, she was dressed in her new turquoise-and-gold two-piece from Bianca, along with a sleeveless thigh-length cover-up, and ready with a bag filled with snorkels and masks, suntan lotion, and clothing to change into for both her and Carrie Anne when the sun and salt became too brutal to bear anymore. The boat was complete with a shower in the head, so she wouldn't have to suffer the salt. She packed several books, her own CD player and headphones and Carrie Anne's tape recorder and tapes.

Just in case they all ran out of conversation.

Then, hand in hand, she and Carrie Anne walked down the hallway to the outside patio.

She saw her father first. He was definitely a unique man, with something of a Hemingwayesque quality. His thick silver hair fell to his shoulders. He wore a straggly beard and his customary clothing—cutoffs, no shoes, no shirt. He loved the image of being an island bum. She knew that women still found him attractive, that his dark eyes were described in interviews and reviews as "brooding" and "charismatic." Kyle—in cutoffs, as well—was in the chair next to her father. He was wearing dark glasses, but no baseball cap today. He wore his dark hair cut to a medium length, not too long, but long enough to curl slightly at his nape and leave enough to brush back over his forehead now and then.

He was in very good shape. It was easy to see that now, with his chest bare. Lots of dark hair grew across that broad expanse. His shoulders, too, were broad and bronzed.

Jassy was with them. Madison hadn't known that her older sister was coming. Tiny and blond, but with her father's dark eyes, Jassy was a dynamo. Despite her fragile appearance, she had gone into pathology and now worked for the Dade County medical examiner's office. Jimmy had told Madison about the cops who initially didn't want to take Jassy seriously; one look from her dark eyes and one sure swipe of her scalpel assured them that she was all business.

Madison wouldn't have minded observing the threesome for another few minutes, but it wasn't to be. Carrie Anne slipped her little hand from Madison's and went rushing out to Jordan Adair. "Morning, Grampa!" She sat right on his lap, took his whiskered face between her hands, wrinkled her nose and kissed him on the forehead.

"Hey there, munchkin!" Jordan said, giving her a fierce bear hug in return. "What are you doing up and about so early?"

"I'm going out on the boat," she said happily, smiling and squinting at her aunt Jassy. "With Rafe's brother, who mommy says is very different, but nice, too. Are you coming, Aunt Jassy?"

"Where's your mother?" Jordan asked Carrie Anne.

"Here, Dad," Madison said, stepping out onto the patio. A coffeepot and cups sat on the counter by the breeze-through to the kitchen. Madison helped herself to coffee and took the fourth chair at the patio table. Carrie Anne was still on her grandfather's lap, but the three adults were staring expectantly at Madison.

She sipped her coffee. Black. "Good morning."

"You're coming on the boat?" Kyle said politely. If he was surprised, he didn't show it. If he was pleased, he didn't show that, either.

"You asked us."

"Yeah, I did." She couldn't see even a hint of his eyes behind the glasses.

"You can't come, Dad?" she asked her father.

He shook his head. "I'm in the middle of some research."

"I told you I'd help you later, Dad," Jassy said sweetly, winking at Madison.

"When I need help from you, you little whelp, I'll let you know," Jordan grumbled.

Jassy shrugged. "Suit yourself."

"Are you Kyle?" Carrie Anne asked, looking straight at him and inspecting him curiously, the way only children can.

"Carrie Anne..." Madison murmured.

"We did forget to introduce them," Jassy reminded her.

"Yes, I'm Kyle. And you must be Carrie Anne. I've heard very nice things about you. Nice to meet you." He offered her his hand. She shook it, smiling.

"It's nice to meet you. Mom said that Uncle Rafe was nicer, though."

"Carrie Anne, I said no such thing—" Madison began, startled and appalled.

"Did she say that? Well, she's wrong," Kyle told Carrie Anne, grinning. "I'm a lot nicer." He sat back, and though Madison couldn't see his eyes, she could feel them.

"I said no such thing," she protested lamely. She looked quickly to her sister. "Are you coming out on the water, Jass?"

"I don't know. Dad's decided to plan a party to-night—"

"What?" Madison said, interrupting her.

"Yeah, I thought a big get-together would be

nice," Jordan said, shrugging. "It's not too often that so many of our family and friends are around. Rafe and Roger can come on down, Jass is already here, Kaila should make it with the kids in a couple of hours, and her husband is supposed to make it back by about seven." He hesitated for a minute, looking at Madison. "Darryl's been down for a few weeks now, but we haven't had a chance to see him, and—"

"You invited my daddy?" Carrie Anne said, delighted.

"You don't mind?" Jordan said brusquely to Madison.

She didn't mind in the least; she and Darryl got along fine. Probably because deep passion—involving love, spite or jealousy—had never gotten in the way of their divorce, as it did with so many people.

But she felt Kyle watching her, and she flushed. Angry at her own reaction, she said coolly, "It will be fine."

"Jimmy Gates will come down," Jordan continued, "and a bunch of locals. Your band, Madison, and Trent and Rafe can both make it. And Roger Montgomery, of course. It will be like a big family reunion."

Right.

Their big, dysfunctional family.

Minus Lainie.

And the other mothers, too, Madison admitted silently to herself. She knew almost nothing about Rafe's mother, except that she had been sick a long time before she died. Kyle had been just a few years old when his mother was killed in a car accident. Jassy's mom, at least, was alive and well, in Portland, Oregon, studying the effects of carcinogens on sharks. Jassy had definitely inherited her medical inclinations from her mother.

As to Madison's half brother Trent's mother, she'd been a very gentle scientist working to cure the world of the common cold. Her dedication and nobility had apparently appealed to Jordan as a young man, but marriage—and a life in the remote regions of Montana, where she worked—hadn't been for Jordan. Trent's mother had passed away quietly of a heart attack just a few years ago. Madison thought that Trent was the lucky one of her father's offspring. He had his mother's slow, easy nature. He was hard to rile, and not as passionate, pigheaded or angry as she could be herself.

As Lainie had so often been.

Trent loved literature and had spent most of his formative years with his father. He and Jordan had remained close. He, Jassy, Kaila and Madison met for lunch at least once a month, usually with Rafe. It was a firm date.

Kyle was the only member of their strange "sibling" group who was consistently missing.

And now he was here.

The prodigal son returning. And her father was planning a great feast.

Curious. Well, Jimmy would be here. Maybe she could learn a little bit about what was going on.

Jordan turned to his oldest daughter. "There's no reason for you not to go out on the boat, Jassy. You'll be back in plenty of time." He threw up his hands suddenly, shaking his head and turning to Kyle. "Can't get this one married off. But she makes a great hostess for the old man," he added affectionately.

Jassy plucked a grape from a bowl of fruit on the table and made a face at her father. "To some of us, the concept of marriage means monogamy—and those vows, you know? 'Till death do us part'? Some of us take those things seriously."

"Every good woman needs a man, Jassy," her father told her sadly.

"Maybe, Dad, she's holding out for a good one," Madison said sweetly.

Jordan sniffed.

"Then again," Madison added, sipping her coffee thoughtfully, "maybe she's found her good man but has the good sense to keep him away from us!"

Jordan wagged a finger at Jassy. "There'll be no running off without my knowledge, young lady," he told her.

"God forbid!" Jassy said dryly. "I'm *only* thirty-one."

"That's not young, Auntie Jassy," Carrie Anne said gravely.

Madison groaned, but Jassy only laughed. Jordan snickered, and not even Kyle could hide a smile.

"Carrie Anne, that was a terrible thing to say to your aunt," Madison chided.

Her daughter looked at her with wide blue eyes. "Why? Being old is great. You can drive and eat all the candy you want and stay up late and everything."

"Yes, but—" Madison began.

"Maybe we should make our exit now," Kyle said, rising. "Jass, you coming?"

Jassy hesitated, looking at the jeans and shirt she was wearing. "I don't have my suit on—"

"There's plenty of stuff on the boat," Madison said. She wanted her older sister around. "Come with us."

"Yeah, why not?" Jassy gave her father a kiss on the cheek. "Bye, Dad."

Carrie Anne gave Jordan a fierce hug, and Madison brushed the top of his head with a kiss. He told them all to enjoy their day and watched as they started down the dock.

Kyle's gear was on board, already; Madison threw her bag on board, then handed Carrie Anne off to her sister.

For a moment Madison paused on the deck, startled by the sudden sensation of unease that spilled through her. Despite the penetrating heat of the rising sun, she shivered.

It's Kyle. After all these years, it's Kyle. I should be staying away from him.

She gave herself a shake, and the feeling was gone, as if it had never been.

Kyle released the dock ties and revved the motor, and they eased out onto the open water.

4

Once past the buoys, Kyle released the throttle, and they motored at a high speed east-northeast. Jassy changed, which Madison checked out the contents of the galley; then she and her sister and daughter took juice in plastic bottles out onto the front deck and stretched out in the sun. They lay in quiet for a while as the boat slashed through the water. The motor drummed, and the sound of the waves against the hull was lulling.

Jassy rolled halfway over. "It's good to have him home, huh?"

"Sure," Madison murmured, flopping over to tan her back. She heard Kyle cut the motor.

"I like him," Carrie Anne volunteered. She sat up restlessly. There was only so much simple sunbathing a five-year-old was going to enjoy. "Mommy, can we *do* something?"

"We *are* doing something," Madison teased. "We're out on the boat."

"No, can we do something on the boat?"

Madison didn't have to answer. She'd brought a bagful of things to do for Carrie Anne; she just needed to gather the energy to roll over and find a few of them.

"Want to help me fish?" Kyle asked. He'd

dropped the anchor and leaped from the small wheelhouse to the deck. Madison was glad of her own dark glasses then. She couldn't resist an assessment. Kyle looked good. Fit in every way. Broad-shouldered, deeply tanned, sleek, well muscled. She reminded herself that she lived in the Sunshine State—it was filled with hard bodies, scantily clad and spread out on a multitude of beaches. She modeled for part of her living, sharing her time with some of the best male bodies known to man.

His was better.

Real.

Mature.

Stop, Madison, she warned herself.

Despite herself, she imagined him completely naked. She blushed, and was glad of sun and her glasses once again. Carrie Anne, all innocence, was able to look up at Kyle with pure childish pleasure.

"I can help you fish? Really?"

"Really. If you'd like."

"Sure!" Carrie Anne said excitedly, her eyes alight. "Can I, Mommy?"

"Maybe Mommy will fish, too," Kyle suggested.

"Mommy is going to dive over the side in a bit. You two fish," Madison said.

"Jassy?" Kyle asked invitingly.

Jassy stretched and yawned. "Maybe. In a few minutes."

Kyle took Carrie Anne aft. Madison could vaguely hear the deep drone of his voice and her daughter's happy laughter in return.

"Five. It's a great age," Madison murmured.

"Umm. It's before a woman finds out about men," Jassy replied dryly.

Surprised, Madison leaned up and looked at her sister. She smiled. "So what *is* up with you?"

Jassy shrugged. "Nothing new."

"You seeing someone?"

"Yeah. Maybe."

"Tell me!"

"Umm...give me a little time, huh? I want to make sure it's not like a..."

"One-night stand?"

"Well, 'three-date deal' would be more like it."

"Are you sleeping with him?"

"Madison!"

"Fair question."

"None of your business."

"If you can't tell a sister, who can you tell?"

"It's private."

"Have you or haven't you?"

"Okay. Once. Just once."

"Whoa! So it's serious."

"I still need to be careful. I have...reasons. God, he's charming, though!"

"But who is he?"

"Not yet! And don't you dare say a word to anyone, promise?"

"What can I say? You haven't told me anything."

"Please, I don't want anyone even knowing there's a man in my life."

"All right, all right! But now I'm going to be eaten alive with curiosity."

"Eaten alive with curiosity! Now that will lead to an interesting autopsy!" Jassy said.

"Ugh."

"It's a fascinating science," Jassy said seriously. "There's so very much you can learn from the dead when they can't speak for themselves anymore."

"I'll grant you that." Madison leaped to her feet. "But look around you. The sun, the sea—it's a great day. Take a break from the dead, huh? I'm going in. You coming?"

"Yeah," Jassy agreed. "I'll be along in a few minutes."

Madison dived in.

Kyle had brought them to anchor just off a sandbar. They were near a few of the smaller reefs, but even having been away for a while, Kyle would have been careful to anchor far from a coral shelf—anchors damaged the precious living coral. They had remained far to the southwest, avoiding John Pennecamp State Park, an underwater park that protected the reefs and the sea creatures living there. There was no fishing out of Pennecamp, though it was a beautiful place to dive.

Madison swam down, estimating that they were in about twenty-five to thirty feet of water. The water was perfect, warm near the surface, cool and pleasant beneath. She shot down deep, touched and stirred up the sand, then kicked to the surface again. She looked to the boat, ready to shout to Jassy to come join her.

But Jassy had moved aft. Madison heard her laughter, Kyle's deep voice, Carrie Anne's shrill giggle of delight over something.

Her invitation to her sister died on her lips.

"How's it going, guys?" she called instead, keeping her distance. The fishing lines would run with the current, and she definitely wasn't in the mood to catch a hook.

"Mommy!" Carrie Anne cried happily, running to the portside rail to stare down at her. "I just caught a red snapping!"

"Snapper," Madison corrected automatically. "Great!"

Kyle joined Carrie Anne at the hull, bronze chest glazed in a sheen of sweat, eyes shaded by his glasses. "I was just thinking, Madison, you might want to come up. Jassy was telling me they had a shark attack out here last week."

She frowned, looking at him. "Kyle, you know that a shark attack is about as common as being struck by lightning. That diver was spearfishing and holding on to the fish he caught by sticking them in his swimsuit. In case you haven't noticed, I'm not carrying any dead fish."

"But we're fishing, and Carrie Anne's snapper is a pretty big guy. He did some heavy-duty wiggling. Lots of distress signals going out in the water."

"I just want to swim over the reefs for a minute. You can see me. I'll come back in just a few minutes."

Kyle shrugged, but didn't look happy. He wanted her out of the water, but he knew that his argument wasn't all that strong. Any offsping—or pseudo-offspring—of Jordan Adair had grown up in the water.

As Madison swam from the boat she could feel his eyes on her. She dived beneath the surface, heading toward the reef.

Water was wonderful. It was the one great escape still known to man. Under the surface, there were as yet no cellular phones. It was beautiful; it was freeing; it was a different world.

She surfaced for air, judging that the coral tips were not more than ten feet beneath her trailing toes. She dived again, swimming carefully around the coral, not touching it. A tiny, brilliant yellow tang darted by her; sea fans waved before her. She very carefully skirted a few dusky red-orange stands of fire coral and came upon a monstrous grouper. The fish looked like a plump, outraged British butler.

She surfaced, then dived again, enjoying herself and oblivious now to the fact that Kyle was watching her from the boat.

A shy moray eel moved away from her with such speed that it looked as if he'd been sucked back into the coral. She swam on to the outskirts of the reef and noted something lying in the sand.

Too bad she hadn't taken the time to put on a mask and snorkel. She couldn't see the object clearly, and she was running out of air.

She surfaced, then dived again, going straight for the object in the sand.

As she neared it, she felt the all-too-familiar cold settling over her again.

She was somewhere else. Laughing, then not laughing. Laughter turning to fear.

She was in a hotel room. As a very pretty young redhead.

Black phone on the side table, Holy Bible beneath the phone. TV remote by the Bible. She'd come because she wanted to come. She'd been so happy, then...

The flash of steel.

Madison blinked, desperate to free herself from

the vision. She had slipped back into her dream, there under the water. She had to surface.

But she had thrown herself to the ground. And as she returned to the present, she could see the object.

It was an arm. Weighed down with a red building brick.

A human arm, from the elbows to the fingers, with the tips missing. Gnawed. She could see bone at the elbow, raw, puffed, bloated flesh.

She started to scream, inhaling as she did so, and then began to choke.

Her vision was clouding again, this time with blackness.

She couldn't think....

Kick...

Suddenly, someone was with her. Kyle. They were shooting toward the surface. They broke it.

She gasped for breath. Choked. Her lungs and abdomen were killing her. She breathed deeply. And looked at Kyle.

In the water, at least, his glasses were gone. His green eyes were impatient and angry.

"Madison, damn it, I told you to come out, not scare us all to death by disappearing that way. Jesus Christ! Your daughter is in tears up there! What the hell is the matter—"

"Arm!" she managed to croak.

"What?"

"Kyle, there's an arm in the water. A human arm. A woman's arm. Elbow to hand. The fingertips are gone."

"Madison, maybe it was an eel. Things beneath the water are distorted—"

"Damn it, Kyle, do you think I'm an idiot, or that

I'm so nearsighted I can't tell the difference between an arm and a fish? There's an arm down there!''

"All right, Madison. Get out, throw me a mask and snorkel. And get me some diving gloves and a few of those large freezer bags from the galley.''

She nodded, still so unnerved that it seemed to make sense just to obey him.

She climbed up the ladder at the aft of the *Ibis*. Jassy was there, her pallor showing that she knew something was very wrong. But Carrie Anne was standing by Jassy, and Madison had to be careful.

"Carrie Anne, go into the cabin and get one of Grandpa's masks and snorkels, and a pair of gloves, will you, sweetheart? And hurry for me.''

Carrie Anne was a child, but not a fool. She stared at her mother and nodded grimly, then ran off to do as she had been told.

"What is it?'' Jassy asked.

"There's an arm down there.''

"What?''

Madison sighed with exasperation. "There's an arm down there!''

"Human?''

"Yes, human, what the hell do you think I mean?''

"I'm going down—''

"You don't need to. The FBI is on the case.''

"Yes, but he's the FBI. I'm a pathologist, for God's sake!''

"He'll bring it to you.''

That wasn't good enough for Jassy. Carrie Anne retrieved the mask, snorkel and gloves, and Madison tossed them on down to Kyle, who disappeared.

A moment later, Jassy dived over the side of the boat.

"What's going on, Mommy?" Carrie Anne asked.

She hesitated. "Somebody had an accident. We're going to have to go back to shore, honey."

Carrie Anne slipped her arms around Madison's waist as they stared at the water. "I'm sorry, Mommy."

She glanced at her daughter, surprised. "Hey, sweetie, I'm the one who's sorry."

"It's okay," Carrie Anne said, and hugged her tighter.

Watching the surface of the water, Madison wondered uneasily if the man in her sister's life could be Kyle. They'd both looked so comfortable that morning, sitting at the table with her father.

Kyle had just arrived in south Florida, she reminded herself. But then, Jassy had said that her affair was just beginning. And most of their pseudo-family had visited Kyle through the years, including Jassy.

Madison fought back a wave of sick jealousy, trying to tell herself again that Kyle was no longer a part of her life.

Still...

Jassy had talked about keeping things quiet. About having "reasons." Madison felt a knot in her stomach.

A few minutes later, the two broke the surface.

"Got it!" Jassy called cheerfully. "Radio in, Madison. We've got to get the law out here."

Jassy. Cute as a button. Smart as they came. Perfect for Kyle? There wasn't a squeamish bone in her body. Where Madison had nearly panicked at the sight of the severed arm, Jassy found the discovery intriguing.

Madison radioed in, then took Carrie Anne with her to the galley to make coffee.

A Coast Guard cutter arrived. Madison got her first chance to see Mr. FBI in action when a loud-mouthed lieutenant started in on Jassy and Kyle for having picked up the arm. In a cool, polite tone, Kyle informed the man of who he was and why he was in Florida. Then he introduced Jassy and informed the man of her position. All very politely. But by the time he was done, he was receiving ingratiating apologies, and he and Jassy were being invited for a dive down to see if any more body parts might be found.

They both declined. Jassy, however, was upset to realize that the arm wasn't actually hers to investigate. She was Dade County, and this was Monroe. However, the lieutenant assured her consolingly that since the facilities in Dade were so excellent, the Monroe authorities would likely be glad to allow Dade a look at the specimen. Especially considering the recent occurrences in Dade.

Madison didn't have anything to say on the way back in, and when they reached her father's house, she immediately took Carrie Anne in for a shower. Once her daughter had, surprisingly and obligingly, slipped into bed for a nap, Madison closed the door softly on her room and hurried down the corridors of the house.

Her father's office door was locked. When he was busy and no one was to interrupt him unless death

threatened or the sky was falling, he taped a picture
of a growling bear on the door.

The picture was in place.

Madison glanced outside and saw that Kyle was
stretched out on one of the pool lounges, facedown.
His bathing suit was wet, so he'd been in the pool.
She slipped out the glass doors and went to his side,
taking a seat on the lounge beside his.

He turned over immediately.

Shades in place.

He sat up, as she was doing, looking at her. "Carrie Anne okay?"

"Of course."

"Does she have any idea what we found?"

"I'm sure she does, but she hasn't really said anything. I told her that there had probably been an
accident of some kind."

Kyle looked down, nodding. "Yeah, an accident,
all right."

"Kyle, what are you doing down here? In the last
year or so, Miami has had its share of bizarre killings. There was the guy who went after the prostitutes on Eighth Street, and the man who murdered
the poor homeless people and set them on fire.
And—"

"And the cops worked those killings," he told
her. "But they were heavily patterned, easier to profile, and the cops had a better handle on the type of
killer they were after." He hesitated. "Plus, it's sad
but true. Who worries about the homeless except for
the rest of the homeless—and some guys who actually work the streets and remember that they're
people, just like the rest of us. And prostitutes..."
He lifted his hands. "People have a tendency to

think that pimps and prostitutes get what they deserve.''

"No one deserves to be murdered,'' Madison said indignantly.

He arched a brow. "Even by the law?''

"I don't know what you're saying.''

He shook his head with sudden disgust. "I guess I'm just at that stage of life where I'm not sure what's right and wrong all the time. The last time I was called out, it was up to Massachusetts. This particular perpetrator had already been convicted of child molestation and murder, but because of the laws, he was given two simultaneous fifteen-year sentences. His behavior in prison was outstanding. He chiseled away at his time, was put into special programs.... He was let out of prison on a weekend pass. In two days, he killed two boys and a little girl. How could such a man ever be let out of jail?''

"So you're saying there should have been a death penalty and it wouldn't have happened again?''

He shook his head, looking out at the setting sun for a minute. "What happens when one innocent man or woman is executed? You can't dig them back up and say you're sorry. Then again, take a Ted Bundy. Who's going to say that a man like that doesn't deserve to die? The parents of his victims must have thought that electrocution wasn't nearly cruel enough.''

"You're not answering me,'' Madison reminded him softly. "What are you doing down here?''

"Oh...''

She spoke slowly. "Those other killings were solved. And I haven't heard anything about another suspected serial killer in the news.''

He shrugged. "Because no one quite knows what's going on yet, except that certain evidence is pointing toward a serial killer."

"What evidence?"

"Madison, you don't really want—"

"Kyle!" she said, then hesitated, still not willing to tell him about her latest dream. "I can't get as excited about a severed arm as Jassy, but I'd like to know what's going on," she said firmly. "I live alone with a five-year-old and a housekeeper. I'd like to keep my child as safe as possible."

"Well, this man isn't after children."

"You're certain it's a man?"

He nodded. "I am."

"Others aren't, but you are?"

He smiled. A crooked smile. "I'm a profiler. It's what I do. And I know it's a man."

Madison found herself smiling, as well, shaking her head. "I thought you weren't even starting until Monday?"

"I got all the paperwork right before coming down. And I think I have a good picture of what we're looking for." He hesitated, looking at her through his dark lenses, then shrugged. "First month, right around the fifteenth, a young woman is reported missing. Beautiful young woman, a Debra Miller. She'd talked to her co-workers about a special date she was going on, no name given. She goes home. Goes out. No one knows where. The neighbors remember seeing her jump into her car and wave goodbye."

"And...her body was later found?"

He nodded. "In the Everglades. Badly decomposed."

"God, I remember that. That was in the newspapers."

"Next month, a similar situation. This time it's a young Latino mother of two, recently divorced."

"And her body—"

"She remains missing."

"Well, then, perhaps—"

"Perhaps she's just missing. True. Third month. A third victim, twenty-five-year-old Julie Sabor, who'd very excitedly told her co-workers there was a new mystery man in her life, disappears. There's a possibility she's a Jane Doe in the Dade County morgue right now."

Any of them could have been the woman in her dream, she thought unhappily.

"But, still…"

"All on or around the fifteenth of the month, all young and beautiful, all with plenty of loving, caring family." He studied her for a moment. "You didn't know anything?"

She shook her head. "I remember there was a story in the *Herald* when Debra Miller's body was found. And I might have seen an article about a disappearance, but there haven't been any sensational news stories, and you know how things are down here. The local stations thrive on sensationalism."

"Well, the cops haven't let too much out yet. They're afraid they'll lose what few fragile bits of information they share with the killer."

Madison felt him watching her through his dark glasses. The sun was nearly down. He didn't really need them anymore. The light now was part of what made the Keys so spectacular. Pink light, gentle light. Soft streaks in pastel colors.

"I wish you weren't divorced," he muttered.

"What?"

He shrugged, lifting his hands, studying his palms. "What I see so far is a killer every bit as clever and charming as Bundy. He's smart. His psychological problems are incredibly deep-seated, and well hidden. He's growing increasingly violent, and more obsessed with mutilation with each murder. He has an association with the middle of the month—not the full moon, but the middle of the month, doesn't matter what the moon is doing. He's attractive and accepted. He could walk into the best restaurant in the state and look exactly as if he belonged there. I think that he's looking for something from his victims...and doesn't get it. Or hasn't gotten it yet. Then he grows angry. And then..."

His voice trailed away, and he looked at her, his mouth grim. "I just wish you were still married, because I don't think this guy goes for married women. He's looking to charm someone, and he wants something in return."

She exhaled a long breath, looking out across the pool. "The fact that serial killers exist in the modern world is not a good reason to stay married, Mr. Montgomery." She stared at him suddenly. "Would you give Jassy this warning?"

He frowned. "Jassy is just so... She's so full of common sense."

Madison arched a brow. "And I'm not? Kyle, how on earth could you pretend to know that now? To judge me now?"

He ran his fingers through his dark hair impatiently. "I guess I just can't say the right thing to you, Madison. I care about all of you—Jassy, you,

Kaila. I don't want anything to happen to any of you. Jassy always has her nose in a book. Kaila is married. You're out in the world. I worry more about you.''

Madison stood. ''Don't try to profile all of us, Kyle,'' she told him quietly.

''For God's sake, Madison, I'm not trying to be offensive. You're a model. Out with photographers, other models, men. You're more susceptible.''

''Right. Any handsome, charming man comes my way and I'll just say, 'Why the hell not?' and drive away with him.''

''There you go again, acting defensive. You're divorced! You're in a dating mode!''

''Excuse me, then. I'm just going to go get dressed and put on some makeup. After all, my dad's having a party. I need to show up in a dating mode,'' she told him tartly, then smiled sweetly and spun around.

''Madison!'' he called after her.

She didn't stop.

''Madison!''

She turned. ''What?''

He walked to her, setting his hands firmly on her shoulders. ''For the love of God, Madison, I don't want anything to happen to you. And...''

''And?''

He hesitated, still studying her. ''And I'm glad that Jimmy Gates has left you alone, and that you're not part of this case.'' He paused, frowning. ''He has left you alone—right?''

''You're mistaken if you think that Jimmy forces me into helping him.''

"So he still calls on you for your hocus-pocus," he said bitterly.

Madison stared at him, feeling the resentment building in her heart once again. "He doesn't always call on me."

"You call him?" he demanded incredulously.

"When I feel I need to, yes, I do! I didn't ask for whatever it is that I have. I hate it. I really, truly hate it. It's terrible to have to hurt for other people. But it's worse to feel that you can do something and not do it. It's worse to think that you could help ease someone's suffering and ignore it."

He winced. "Madison, listen, I just have a bad feeling on this one. My turn to have a bad feeling, a really bad feeling. You need to keep your distance."

He hesitated for a minute. She was painfully aware of the heat emanating from his fingers as he clenched her shoulders. She liked Kyle's hands. They were big. He had long fingers. He had his father's hands. Artist's hands. Capable of a light touch, and yet very powerful.

The warmth of his touch reminded her of the chill she had felt today.

Was he right on this? She'd never felt so unnerved as she had since last evening. Of course, she'd had that feeling, and then he'd arrived.

She had the dream, and then...

She looked down suddenly and remembered the unease she had felt when they were about to set out on the boat. Seeing again the flashes of a life she had seen in her dream, when she was diving toward the arm.

The hotel room. Being in someone's else skin. The euphoria, and then...

Then the flash of the steel.

"Madison!"

He lifted her chin, putting her at a disadvantage again, studying her eyes while his remained hidden behind dark lenses. "Madison, I'm certain that the arm we found today belongs to a victim of this killer. He's ranging from Miami to the Keys. Your territory, Madison. I don't want you hurt. I don't want you involved."

She had to be involved. She had no choice. She opened her mouth, ready to tell him about her flash of insight.

But she didn't want to tell him what she had been seeing. Jimmy was the one who had believed in her from the beginning, and she knew that she was only given a great deal of credence now by most of the homicide guys thanks to Jimmy.

Not Kyle. She couldn't tell Kyle. He was still staring at her through his glasses, his touch, his tone, passionate and intense.

"Madison, what you see is dangerous, don't you understand? You don't dare be dangerous to this killer. I mean, I know how I felt when I thought you were invading the privacy of my life. Imagine a killer..."

She pulled away from him, staring at him furiously. "Invading your life?" she repeated softly.

"Madison, that's what it felt like. Like I said before, I was in pain at the time, in agony, and I'm sorry about the way that I acted. But if this killer became aware that you could enter into his very thoughts...if he somehow came in contact with you, if he happened to be someone you met in a social situation…''

"I'll be very careful regarding who I sleep with in the near future, Kyle," Madison informed him blithely. "Thanks so much for your concern."

Then she turned on her heels and forced herself to walk slowly back to the house.

5

By eight o'clock Jordan Adair's party was in full swing. A trio was playing by the pool, and family and friends had arrived.

Kyle's father had been among the first to arrive, and they had greeted one another with a long hug and a lot of emotion. Then Rafe had arrived, and they had greeted one another warmly, as well.

Jimmy Gates showed up, having become a close family friend. He'd cared deeply; they'd all known that.

Kyle and Jimmy greeted one another with a careful, professional assessment. They would be getting down to business come Monday.

Then Kaila had shown up with her three little ones—hassled, harassed and busy. Kyle, Rafe and their father had helped her deal with her brood while she explained that her husband, Dan, was running late. Kaila looked badly flustered. But Jassy, cute and sleek in a sleeveless, clinging black cocktail dress, came to take the baby. A minute later Madison—barely acknowledging Kyle, though she was friendly and warm with his father and brother—took the two older children. Older! The baby, Anthony, wasn't quite two; Shelley, was three and half, and the oldest, Justin, was five. Kaila seemed deeply relieved to have the respite and was delighted when Rafe made her a piña colada and she had a few minutes to sit in peace.

Kaila, like Madison, had a wealth of long, deep red hair, huge blue eyes and finely chiseled features. Kyle thought she was very pretty and might have been mistaken for her sister, except that their personalities were so different, they moved differently. Kaila was always anxious; her movements were abrupt. Madison... Madison was subtle. Graceful. Agile. More...

Sensual, he thought dryly.

And furious with him once again.

Tonight she was wearing emerald green. Redheads weren't supposed to be able to wear green, but she pulled it off spectacularly. She was wearing an emerald green halter-topped dress. Her hair was swept up, and her back was bare.

It was a sin to have a back so perfect, he thought. He was tempted, every time she was near him, to run a finger up and down its bare length.

So tempted, he thought dryly, just as any other man would be.

Once Madison had the kids settled and playing in Carrie Anne's room, she moved among her father's guests with incredible ease.

Kyle noticed that she didn't come near him. Well, she was angry with him again. Naturally. He didn't seem to be able to express himself very well with her. He was concerned, that was all. And she didn't seem to understand that whatever else her strange power might be, it was also very dangerous. Watching her talk, listen and laugh, he felt a strange knifing within himself. He tried to forget the way she had looked that afternoon, the passion in her eyes when she tried to explain how she couldn't see the suffering of others without helping if she could....

If only her damned power would go away. He'd hoped it might have done so. Apparently not.

It wasn't easy seeing Madison again.

He thought of the women with whom he'd slept on a casual basis. No involvement, no great emotion.

Easy to sleep with a woman when he didn't care.

This time, he did care, but even if her temper ever waned enough that she was willing, it couldn't happen. He cared too much.

Now, though he tried to be covert, he couldn't keep his eyes off her as she sipped champagne.

In moderation, he noticed. She kept the same glass with her all night.

Darryl Hart arrived among the later guests. Kyle was irritated to feel an instant hostility toward the man—especially since Darryl greeted him with a firm handshake and a sincere welcome, and seemed genuinely interested in his life.

Madison greeted her ex-husband with a warm hug and a kiss on the cheek. Studying her, Kyle wondered curiously what could have come between the two of them. They seemed to be good friends. Still close. They seemed like a perfect couple. Darryl was a good-looking man, big, built—hell, he'd been a football hero through high school and college. Madison was vibrantly stunning. They'd been Ken and Barbie, homecoming king and queen. She was still quick to smile at whatever Darryl said to her. They both took the greatest pleasure in their daughter. He had a feeling that Darryl was still in love with his ex-wife. What were Madison's feelings?

What the hell had broken them up?

Though he maintained his distance from Madison, he milled close enough to her to hear some of the things being said to her.

"Madison, you need to let me paint you in that dress."

His own father.

"Madison! Just for a weekend. Fly in, fly out, you on the white-sand beach of Cozumel!"

A renowned, gay advertising executive.

"Honey, I know you don't like exploiting your name and family in any way, but if you'd pose for the poster for the art fest, I just know that it would do incredible things for business—and all the proceeds go to children's charities!"

An attractive silver-haired matron, obviously a patron of the arts.

"Kyle!"

He turned.

His half brother, Rafe, handsome as a beach boy with his blond hair, silver eyes and perfect tan, was approaching him, a little brunette on his arm. "Kyle, meet Sheila Ormsby. Sheila is with—"

"The Storm Fronts," Kyle said, shaking the girl's offered hand. She was cute, with dimples and a wide smile. She was probably in her late twenties, he thought. He'd seen her playing the keyboard last night, while Madison was singing.

"I didn't get a chance to meet you last night," Sheila said, smiling broadly.

The dimples were great. Deep and charming.

"I hadn't seen Madison in a very long time."

"So I understand. Rafe tells me that you're kind of like the prodigal son returned."

Kyle arched a brow at his half brother. Rafe hunched his shoulders.

Oddly enough, his family—and extended family—members, had been trying to introduce him to women all night. Being a widower seemed to bring out such conduct in others.

"Well, Sheila, it's a pleasure to get to meet you, and I'm sorry we didn't get a chance to say hello last night. How long have you playing?"

"All my life," Sheila said.

Rafe grinned and walked off, leaving him to discuss music with Sheila. As they talked, his father returned, bringing the elegant silver-haired patron of the arts along with him—along with her daughter, a voluptuous girl with a headful of sleek, shiny black hair inherited from her Colombian father.

Then Trent came up to him, beaming proudly, as if he'd created the pretty sandy-haired entertainment reporter on his arm specifically for Kyle.

As they talked, Kyle noted Kaila checking her watch nervously, then excusing herself and heading for the house.

Madison, apparently watching Kaila, as well, excused herself.

Jassy did likewise.

Curious, Kyle excused himself and walked to the self-service patio bar, then looked through the partially open glass doors into the living room. Kaila was on the phone, talking too quietly to be overheard. The other two hovering worriedly nearby.

He slowly set ice in his glass, concerned. He wasn't sure why. He'd been gone a long time, but it didn't really change things. Once upon a time, before Lainie's murder—or perhaps before Fallon's death—they'd all been close. He cared deeply about them. All of them. Yet...

Why the hell was he eavesdropping?

He didn't know.

Yes, he did.

He was worried. Worried about Madison. He wanted to keep his distance from her. She was trouble; she could slip right beneath his skin. She could slip into his damned mind, for Christ's sake. He would be better off hundreds and hundreds of miles away from her....

Not only was she trouble, but, damn, if she just didn't seem to be Lainie reincarnated!

All true.

And all immaterial.

He wanted her. Naked. Panting. Hot. He wanted to—

Whoa. Not so graphic, he warned himself.

The pictures in his mind were graphic as all hell.

He started, dropping an ice cube heavily into his glass as Kaila hung up the phone with such angry force that the slam could be heard on the patio.

As she hung up, the other two looked away uncomfortably. Madison cleared her throat, staring at Jassy in perplexity, then looking back to Kaila.

"Kaila," she said quietly, "you can't get so angry every time Dan can't make something. He's an attorney—"

"Yeah, and attorneys don't have lives?" Kaila asked acidly.

"Kaila," Madison said patiently, "Dan's a good guy. He worked his butt off to get through school, and he works diligently now. He knows that you come from money, and he wants to provide for you.

He's very honorable about never wanting to borrow money from Dad, or touch your trust fund, or—''

"Oh, he's just a fucking saint!'' Kaila lashed back.

Madison tried again. ''Kaila—''

"Hey, come on, now, watch the language!'' Jassy said, trying a teasing approach.

"Kaila, seriously, come on now—'' Madison tried.

"Oh, yeah, right! Marriage is so sacred! This from the woman who divorced Mr. All-American!''

"Yes, and divorce isn't pleasant! But you and Dan love one another—''

"Oh, shut up, Madison! You don't know anything. Madison, Madison! Everything is Madison! Madison would look so lovely in a poster for the art fest, Madison, can't you please fly to Cozumel just for a day, darling? Madison, you look so much like your mother! Well, damn it! Madison, I look just like you, and still I'm just Kaila, with three little kids, PTA meetings, McDonald's lunches, a regular baby factory. Naturally I nursed my children. A rich kid like me with nothing to do but raise my beautiful children and be Dan's wife. While you—you're the goddamned, all-glorious Madison!''

Kyle couldn't help watching Madison's reaction. Part of her must have wanted to tell her younger sister to go straight to hell. But he watched her gain control before she spoke; it was obvious she loved Kaila, and she seemed to realize that her sister was only lashing out in pain.

"Kaila, what the hell is wrong?'' Madison asked her softly.

"Nothing. Nothing!" Kaila snapped. But her huge blue eyes were becoming liquid with tears.

"Kaila—"

Kaila went dashing off down the hall toward her bedroom. Madison started after her.

"Leave her for a few minutes," Jassy said.

"Jassy, something is really wrong, for Kaila to be acting like that!"

"And you should talk to her. Just give her a few minutes first."

"All right."

Madison turned around, heading out to the patio. Kyle sheepishly realized that he had been a miserably intrusive eavesdropper, and he moved away from the bar.

Luckily the art patron's daughter with the great head of black hair was nearby. He quickly engaged her in conversation. Madison walked by, to all outward appearances composed, except that she didn't even seem to notice him.

Maybe she didn't.

He wondered if he should go talk to Kaila himself. He couldn't. His stomach was clenching. He couldn't help watching Madison. He wondered, if he could just fuck her once, would the feeling of obsession go away?

Madison couldn't wait too long; she was too anxious. She slipped back into the house and hurried down the hallway. She paused at the door to Carrie Anne's room and heard Martique, her father's amazingly patient Haitian housekeeper, reading to the kids in her beautiful singsong voice.

She hurried on to Kaila's door. She knocked

softly, but didn't wait to be bidden to enter. She went on in, treading softly.

"Kaila?"

Her sister was stretched out on her bed, staring at the ceiling. She stopped crying, but her cheeks were damp with tears. "Oh, Kaila!" Madison said softly, and hurried across the room. Kaila half rose, ready to meet Madison's hug.

"Oh, Madison, I'm so sorry! It's just that he never shows up, and I never really know where he is, and I just keep thinking that there's more going on! I know he's sleeping with someone else. God! If I just had the balls to have an affair myself!"

"Kaila! That wouldn't help anything."

"Yeah, it might. It might make me feel wanted. Special."

"Kaila, I know that Dan loves you."

"You just want that to be the truth! And you don't understand! Everyone loves you. Everyone! You're beautiful. You're perfect. People fawn over you all the time."

"Kaila!"

"It's true."

Madison shook her head, a crooked half smile on her lips. "You picked the wrong girl to blow up at, if you're talking about relationships. Don't you dare tell a soul, but the closest thing I've had to a sexual relationship lately is a really hot, steamy romance novel one of Dad's friends gave me a while back."

Kaila straightened. "You're kidding!"

Madison shook her head.

Kaila was still stunned. "You meet so many people. Guys are always after you—"

"Joey's one of the best guys I know, but I'm

crazy about his wife and kids. I'd never consider fooling around with him, and he's never made a play for me. Of the men who *have* seemed interested..." She paused. "Well, there are just so many diseases out there. Marriage does have its benefits, you know. In my whole life, Darryl was my one big romantic relationship."

"Oh, my God! How do you survive?" Kaila whispered in horror.

Madison laughed. "People *do*. Sex isn't everything."

"It's a hell of a lot. I mean, I may not like it all the time, the way... I mean, with... I don't know what I mean."

Madison smiled again, hugging her sister. "I know what you mean. I still remember my marriage, you know. Sometimes you're in the mood, and sometimes you're not, and sometimes you oblige because you know your partner will just be pissy all day if you don't!"

Kaila laughed. "Yeah, kind of..." She frowned. "And then I feel badly sometimes because..."

"Because?"

Kaila shrugged. "There's nothing really wrong with Dan. I mean, he's..."

"Good in bed, functions like a pro, all parts in working order!" came a cheerful voice from the doorway, and Jassy stepped into the room.

"Jassy, you can be incredibly clinical!" Madison told her, grinning to take the sting out of her words.

"Clinical?" Jassy protested.

"And the both of you are just woefully nosy and personal!" Kaila told them accusingly.

"That's what sisters are for," Jassy assured her,

and glanced over at Madison. "No sex life—at all?" she inquired incredulously.

Madison groaned. "We can't all be having secret affairs."

"Who's having a secret affair?" Kaila demanded.

"Jassy," Madison informed her.

"You weren't supposed to say anything!" Jassy gasped.

"Oh, God, I'm sorry," Madison said guiltily.

"It's all right, because you've told Kaila. But Kaila, if I told you who the guy is, it wouldn't be a great secret affair anymore."

"Did she tell *you?*" Kaila demanded of Madison.

Madison shook her head, then frowned, looking past Jassy to the door to Kaila's room.

Jassy hadn't closed it all the way. Now Madison thought she saw it move, thought she heard the faint sound of footsteps behind Jassy in the hallway.

"What's the matter?" Kaila asked.

Madison shook her head, wondering why she was suddenly certain that someone had been listening to their conversation.

Furtively.

"Nothing," Madison said, but she was still frowning. She rose and walked to the door, swinging it open.

The hallway was empty. She had to be imagining things.

"Madison?" Jassy said worriedly.

Madison shook her head. "It's nothing, honest."

But it *was* something. A strange feeling she couldn't quite shake.

"Let's go back to the party," Kaila said, smoothing her hair. "I've got a great sitter in my dad's own house, and here I am, sitting in this room and feeling sorry for myself when I have a chance to talk and party with adults and flirt a bit."

"That's the spirit, kid," Jassy assured her.

"Yep. Let's go on back out," Madison said.

In seconds they were headed back to the party.

"Madison!" Sheila said cheerfully, calling to her and waving her highball glass in the air. Scotch. Straight Dewar's. Sheila had once told her that Dewar's was the drink of choice—never mix it with soda, soda was what caused hangovers. Sheila could drink Dewar's all night and not look a tad the worse for wear. Madison envied her that ability.

Sheila weaved her way through the crowd until she reached Madison. "Great party—it was really nice of your dad to think of inviting all us Storm Fronts."

"Dad's a pretty good guy most of the time," Madison assured her.

"You know, your brothers are all cute, but this newest one...wow."

"Kyle Montgomery?"

"Is he really your brother?"

"His father was married to my mother."

"Oh, my God, that's right, I forgot all the scandal when she died— Oh, there's my foot in my mouth again. Sorry, Madison."

"It's all right. I just come from one of those families that's prone to scandal," Madison said dryly.

Sheila smiled, her dimples deep, her eyes bright. "Makes life interesting. I wouldn't mind being surrounded by gorgeous males all the time. You do have the life. Your ex looks like Mr. Universe, Trent is incredibly handsome—''

"Trent is my biological half brother, my dad's own son," Madison reminded her.

"Okay, so avoid incest at all costs. But Rafe— what a cutie. So studious and handsome—just like Clark Kent. And now this new one...umm. Actually, I guess it's a good thing he's not your biological brother. The way he looks at you. And the way you look at him."

"I don't look at him! In fact, we had something of an argument several years ago."

"Umm. So it would be okay if..."

"If what?"

"If I made a play for him."

"I— Of course," Madison said quickly. What the hell difference did it make who made a play for him? He'd been surrounded by every female in the place all night.

"You don't sound sure," Sheila observed, smiling. Madison sighed. Sheila wasn't exactly a wild woman. They'd been in the band together for a long time, and they'd certainly become good friends. They were complete opposites, Sheila so petite, Madison so tall. Sheila was, if anything, a connoisseur of men. She didn't want to go through the dinner-and-flowers routine of casual dating; she studied her possible partners, and it was instantly all or nothing. She was careful and discreet and, Madison was certain, responsible and careful. But if she wanted a man...

"Sheila, don't be absurd. Make a play for whoever you want. Do I look like I'd ever want to get involved with...with...my own...my own..."

"Stepbrother?" Sheila suggested.

"Umm..."

Sheila studied her for a long moment, and her smile deepened. "Honey, you're right. You don't look like you want to get involved with Kyle."

"Right."

"You just look like you want to fuck him. But that's okay. I'll take what you're saying at face value. But then again...anytime you want to stop me, just say so."

Smiling sweetly, she walked over to the group surrounding Kyle.

Madison wanted to smack her.

In a mature, dignified manner.

The party was winding down.

And Dan wasn't coming.

Okay, so he was an attorney. That didn't mean a man had to work every Saturday. He was always gone. And she was always home. He was always dressed up in a suit and tie. And she was always in jeans or shorts and T-shirts stained with the latest foods—baby applesauce, chocolate fudge, grape drink—or spit-up or diarrhea. She loved her kids. God forgive her, she really loved her kids.

But she was just so...

Restless.

Hurt. Worried.

She was twenty-five years old, and most of the time it seemed that her life was over. That she would never be young again. It was different for Dan. He went out; he worked. His job was important. She was supposed to understand. Anytime she was on the phone, he was free to interrupt her with a crying baby.

Anytime he was on the phone, she was supposed to make sure that you could hear a pin drop throughout the house.

Yet tonight...

He was here.

And at last he approached her, as she had known he would. Casually. But so nicely.

"You okay?"

She felt a strange sense of excitement just at the husky warmth of his words. "Fine."

He hunched down next to her where she sat, dangling her bare feet in the pool. Her heeled sandals and piña colada were at her side.

"You look gorgeous."

"Thanks." She looked at him. "You're not bad yourself."

He smiled back. "God, Kaila...Dan has everything I want. Everything in the world, and he doesn't even know it. Great kids. And a beautiful wife. If you were mine, I wouldn't leave you alone for a minute."

"That's sweet of you to say."

"You should give me a chance."

"What?"

"Trial run."

She stared at him, feeling a flush spread through her. She was tempted. God, he was good-looking.

"I'd give up ten years of life just to see you naked," he whispered.

She thought he was teasing at first, trying to make her feel better. But then she looked at him. And he wasn't teasing.

"I'd die just to touch you...to..." He moved his lips closer to her ear and whispered a few graphic words describing with explicit simplicity what he wanted to do to her.

"It would be wrong!" she whispered.

"Why?"

She shook her head.

She should have been horrified; she should have stood up, slapped him and walked away.

Except that she was tempted. And his words were both soothing to her wounded ego and...exciting.

Exciting as...fantasy? she asked herself. Or reality?

She wasn't sure.

"I...I...can't..." she whispered.

"You're not ready. And you don't believe that I love you. And that I need—no I crave—to be loved by you in return. You don't take me seriously. You can't imagine how much I'll love your children, how good I'll be—how I can share being the caregiver."

"I..."

"You need time. I'll be waiting."

He rose and moved away.

He was great. So charming. So handsome. So many women were quick to crowd around him....

And she might not have this chance forever!

But still...

Kaila hugged her knees close to herself. She'd been married a long time. She didn't really know any other man, and she was afraid. Surely, as mad as she was at him, she loved Dan.

Didn't she?

Or was he just a habit in her life?

She leaned her head down, feeling dizzy. Too

many piña coladas. She should be happy. On paper, her life looked perfect. They were financially secure, and they did have three happy, healthy, beautiful children. What kind of a horrible human being was she to be so miserable?

She didn't know.

She just didn't know....

Jassy stepped from the house onto the patio. The guests were beginning to leave. The night was growing quiet.

She walked around the pool and toward the dock, staring out at the water. The night was beautiful. She felt wonderful.

Arms suddenly slipped around her. She would have cried out from surprise, except that a hand quickly covered her mouth and a husky voice whispered, "Shh..."

Her heart pounded furiously.

The hand slipped from her mouth; the arms holding her eased.

She spun within his now gentle embrace and kissed her new lover. The kiss deepened. His hands wandered, cupping her breasts. Tongues met and mingled. At length, Jassy drew back, groaning softly.

"Not here, not now!" she whispered breathlessly.

Her lover sighed. "I don't know why we can't just—"

"It's too soon. I want to be taken seriously."

He smoothed his fingers along a straying strand of her hair. "We need to go somewhere," he said, kissing her again.

She barely broke her lips from his.

"Can't."

"Have to," he whispered against her mouth.

"Can't," she repeated, her mouth against his again.

"We need to be together."

She broke the kiss at last with a sigh. "I can't leave here tonight. You know that. Not without a lot of explanations."

"You're a doctor—have an emergency."

"I'm a pathologist. Dead people don't have emergencies."

"Ah, come on. Sure they do...."

"Other people are on duty."

He caught her hand and drew it down the length of his chest, then lower, pressing her fingers against the bulge beneath the button fly of his jeans. "See what you're missing?"

"A waste," she agreed sadly.

He smiled and kissed her cheek. "Fine. Miss you. Love you. Monday will be an eternity."

"Monday," she agreed softly.

They exchanged one more hot, sloppy kiss, and he slipped away in the shadows. Jassy watched as he greeted someone on the porch. She felt good. Great. God, being in love was wonderful!

He was in agony, absolute agony.

It was dark. Late. Very late. His room was dark and oddly misted. He was bone-weary, but he couldn't sleep. Because of her.

The whole thing was ridiculous. How could you see someone after so many years and want them so badly that it was a physical thing, an ache that couldn't be controlled?

Then there was the way she looked at him.

Angrily. As if she wanted to kill him.

Then...

With something else. With a strange blue glitter in the wide depths of her amazing eyes.

He stood up, restlessly pacing the room, like a tiger on the prowl. All he had to do was walk down the hall. She was there. Just walk down the hall. Wake her up. Wrench her out of bed for a showdown. Look, we both want this, let's do it, get it over with, get on with our lives....

He was moving. Quietly opening and closing his door, entering the hallway. He was wearing a white terry robe, nothing more. Didn't matter. The house was quiet. It was deep night; he knew in his heart that nothing, no one, was going to stop him.

He threw open the door to her room.

A soft night-light threw its yellow-red luminescence over her. She was lying back on her pillows in a black silk gown, her hair a cloak of fire. She saw him, and she didn't say a word. She just slipped gracefully from the bed, staring at him all the while. She walked toward him, nearly reached him. She slid the black silk gown from her shoulders and stood in naked glory before him, breasts full and firm, pubic triangle the same deep flame red as her hair.

She reached out. He let the terry robe fall. Her fingers scraped down his chest. Down...so close...

Her whisper was right against his lips. The soft fall of her hair teased his flesh.

"Look, we both want this. Let's do it, get it over with, and get on with our lives...."

"Yes..."

He lifted her by the waist, walked her back to the bed, set her down, caught her legs, spread them, dragged her back to him. No time for play. Oh, God. He...

Woke up.

Shaking, sweating bullets, Kyle jerked himself from the dream. For a moment it was hard to convince himself that he'd imagined his every step.

But he had.

He was sitting in the guest room. Drenched. Worse.

He groaned aloud, gritted his teeth and threaded his fingers through his hair, pressing tightly against his temples. Damn.

This wasn't working.

Kyle slept late.

He went to the ten-o'clock mass, having heard that Madison and the girls had gone to the eight o'clock. They hadn't returned.

He grabbed coffee at a doughnut stand and walked the streets of Key West, watching as the early "Conch Train," full of tourists, explored the city's attractions.

Finally, around noon, he wandered back to the house.

Madison had already started back for Miami with Carrie Anne. Jassy and Kaila had started back with her, so that Madison and Jassy could stop with Kaila for a few rest breaks along the way and help out with the kids.

Kyle spent the afternoon fishing with Jordan, his father, Rafe and Trent. It was a good-ol'-guys kind of afternoon. They caught plenty of snapper, kingfish and brightly colored dolphinfish, and polished off several six-packs of beer. They fried the fish back at the house, and Kyle slept for several hours.

Then he, too, headed for Miami.

Monday morning was coming.

And along with it...

Body parts.

6

"I'm not sure I'm going to be very helpful," Madison told Jimmy Gates. As planned, he'd picked her up on Monday morning. However, she hadn't known that they were going to the morgue. She'd never gone with him to the morgue; he'd always taken her to crime scenes.

Of course, it wasn't that she never came to the medical examiner's office. And that wasn't because she had taken to visiting the dead, but because Jassy worked here.

Still, Madison didn't often walk down these corridors. She met her sister in her office when they were going to go to lunch.

Jimmy glanced at Madison, and she gazed back at him. He had just celebrated his thirty-seventh birthday, and he still looked like a kid, with his continually tousled reddish hair, freckles and warm brown eyes. But those looks were deceptive. He could be relentless, ruthless, tough as nails, when it came to hunting down a killer. Luckily, his looks had kept him out of a trouble a few times when he sidestepped the law to get the information he wanted.

"Bear with me, Madison, huh? I just have a hunch on this one."

"Okay."

A morgue, despite the best efforts of the cleaning crews, smelled like a morgue. Looking at tile, stainless steel and glass, Madison felt a chilling sensation.

Creepy, Carrie Anne would have called it.

Jimmy pushed open a door and they were in a fairly large room. An autopsy room, Madison thought. There were stainless-steel gurneys set beneath microphones. In a far corner, a group of four, covered in hospital greens, were working over the naked body of a man. To the side, their backs to her, a couple of suits—plainclothes cops?—were watching and listening as a man's voice droned into the microphone with the details of death.

Death. So damned impersonal. Stripping the last vestiges of dignity from the human soul.

"Madison." Jimmy tapped her on the shoulder. He was speaking in a soft whisper. "Here. Right here."

He led her through a doorway into a side room, turning her around. There was a lump on one of the antiseptic stainless-steel tables, covered with a green sheet. A mousy-looking female pathology assistant, apparently impatient with her work, stood by the lump. Jimmy stared at Madison.

She looked from him to the lump, feeling a chilling, trembling sensation sweep over her.

Jimmy's hunch had been right. She could already feel something. Something she didn't want to feel…but she was going to be able to see something.

Oh, God.

But perhaps she could help.

But she didn't like this. She didn't like this at all.

"Uh...uh, brace yourself," he warned Madison, and nodded to the pathology assistant.

The woman pulled the sheet back. Madison's first instinct was to be sick. Violently sick. The lump was a head. Set up at an angle, but obviously gnawed at the neck. The eyes had been eaten away. The flesh was so pasty that it might not have been real; it should have come out of some special-effects studio.

A sound escaped Madison; she gripped her stomach and closed her eyes, afraid that she going to pass out. Her knees were buckling; she was going to fall....

She suddenly felt rough arms around her, holding her up. To her astonishment, she heard Kyle Montgomery's voice.

"Jimmy, what the hell's the matter with you, bringing her in here to see something like that?" He was furious.

"Oh, come on, Kyle! She might be able to help."

"Jimmy, Jesus Christ!" Kyle was still holding her, supporting her.

"Kyle, damn it, this is Madison, not some squeamish little kid. Her sister is one of the leading forensic scientists here. She knows what blood looks like. It's not like I'm going to shock her or anything."

"Damn you, Jimmy, that head shocked me, and I promise you, I've seen some of the worst."

Madison didn't want them fighting, and she didn't want to stare at the head.

But she stood, stiffening her spine to steel, determined to be strong enough to stand without Kyle's help—despite the fact that she had to stare at the heart-wrenching sight before her.

She couldn't help herself, because a chilling sensation had settled over her, and though she was staring, the sight of the head was fading; she wasn't seeing what was in front of her. She was seeing a pretty, vivacious redhead. She wasn't sure if it was the same woman she had seen before, but if not, she was similar in height and build, and she had the same beautiful, streaming hair. She was laughing as she opened a car door and slipped into the driver's seat. Someone was with her. They were driving…on the highway. Then they were on another road. There was an occasional huge bird's nest up on a telephone pole on one side of the road. There was water on both sides, as well.…

They passed a sign. Lake Surprise. She knew the exact spot they were driving by; it was on U.S. 1, on the way to Key Largo.

"The Keys," she said suddenly.

"What?" Kyle said.

"The Keys," she repeated, still staring at the head.

"Will you please cover that up?" Kyle demanded of the mousy little pathologist.

The woman started to oblige.

"Wait a minute," Jimmy protested. "Madison is getting something, she's seeing things."

The sheet came back up.

"She isn't seeing anything else!" Kyle snapped. Which was true, but how he could possibly know, Madison had no idea.

"I'm all right!" Madison lied. She was going to be strong. She was determined.

Like Jassy. Madison wasn't going to fall apart like

a fragile female so she had to be held up by the strong male. Kyle.

"I'm all right," she repeated, and it sounded much better.

It didn't matter.

Kyle led her out of the room and back into the corridor. Jimmy followed irritably behind, but Kyle didn't stop until they had left the corridor of death and come to an employees' lounge. It was empty except for a tattered sofa, which Kyle forced her down on.

He ran his fingers through his dark hair. "Madison, you're as white as a sheet. Are you sure you're all right?"

She nodded.

"Of course she's all right," Jimmy said impatiently. "Right, Madison?"

She wasn't, of course. She was shaky, damned shaky. But she didn't want Kyle to know that fact.

"I'm fine. Perfectly fine," she said, staring at Kyle. "I don't need a big brother looking out for me." She lowered her head quickly. She was doing it again. Lashing out. Acting like a two-year-old, when what she wanted to be was aloof and remote and dignified.

"Madison," Kyle said impatiently, "even the pathologists cringe at some sights. Cops who think they've seen everything see something else and get weak knees and throw up all over. You don't have to be the damned Rock of Gibraltar."

She shook her head slightly. "I really am all right."

"What did you see, Madison?" Jimmy demanded impatiently.

Again, she hesitated. She could have killed Jimmy. This wasn't playing fair. He'd asked for her help. He hadn't told her that Kyle might be involved. She didn't want Kyle here. She didn't want him seeing her in action and thinking, as he had thought when his wife died, that she was some kind of a...

Freak.

"Madison? Please, Madison, for the love of God, this is a bad one, a real bad one. We think it's part of the case we asked for Kyle's help on."

Her head jerked up, and she stared at Kyle.

"I didn't want her involved in this, Jimmy," Kyle said.

"It isn't your call," Madison informed him, but she could tell by the way he was looking at Jimmy that it wasn't going to end there. Maybe it *was* Kyle's call. He was FBI, and Jimmy was a local cop. She frowned, watching him. "I—I didn't even see you when we first came in."

"I was watching the autopsy in process."

He'd been one of the suits. Of course.

"Madison..." Jimmy said, pressuring her.

"Jimmy, she shouldn't be involved."

"Kyle, I *am* involved." She looked at Jimmy. "I can see the woman right before she died. She got into a car with someone."

"Whose car?" Jimmy asked.

"Her own—I think. She was driving. Someone was in the passenger seat. She was smiling and laughing, ready for a longish drive. She was excited, as if she was getting ready to go away for the weekend with someone she was comfortable with, with..."

"A friend?" Kyle suggested.

She shook her head, looking at him, wondering why she felt such a flush creeping to her cheeks.

"A lover. A new lover. She was excited, breathless, happy. Maybe she thought she was heading out for her first real time with this man."

"Can you see the man?" Jimmy asked.

"Is it definitely a man?" Kyle inquired.

Madison shook her head, then stared at Kyle for a moment. "I thought you knew it was a man?"

"My mind is always open."

Like hell, she thought. She turned back to Jimmy. "I'm really sorry, Jimmy. I assume it was a man. But I really can't say. All I saw was her...." She paused, then drew a deep, shaky breath. "She was very pretty, so vivacious, full of life. She smiled, she got in with someone, and she started to drive. To the Keys. I'm certain."

"Why are you so certain?"

"I saw a few cormorant nests up high in the telephone poles. And then I saw the sign for Lake Surprise."

Kyle and Jimmy glanced at one another.

"Where from there?"

Madison shook her head.

"Okay, where did she wind up?" Jimmy asked.

"In the sea," Kyle said wearily. "I'm willing to bet that head goes with the severed arm."

Jimmy shot Kyle a quick glance, frowning. "Monroe hasn't gotten us the arm yet. But that isn't what I meant. Where did they go when they got to the Keys?"

"I don't know, Jimmy."

"Do you feel that you know for sure that the man

in the car with her was the one who murdered her?'' Kyle asked, his green eyes sharp on her.

"No, I...I don't know," Madison said, feeling somewhat confused herself.

"Madison, come on, can you give me anything else?"

Once again she paused and looked at Kyle. "You think that the arm and the head are from the same person? Why do you think that?"

"No real reason. A hunch." He shrugged. "Okay, so it's Miami. We still don't usually come up with too many body parts that aren't somehow related."

He was watching her intently as she spoke. Thinking what a witch she was?

She looked back to Jimmy. "When I was in the water, off Dad's boat, diving down toward the arm...I had a flash of something. Something very similar. A girl. A very pretty young redhead. Lots of energy—and faith in her fellow man and woman. Open, trusting. She knew the person she was with. She was excited. She expected to be having a lot of fun. I saw a room, a typical hotel room. Not grungy, not luxurious. Bed, Bible, black phone, TV remote changer. Same pretty red hair, same smile, same emotion. It could easily be the same girl. I saw her happy as a lark, and then...then the flash of a knife. She was killed in that room."

"Does it coincide with your other dream?" Jimmy asked Madison.

"What dream?" Kyle demanded harshly.

"Friday—Madison had one of her strange dreams and called me. I didn't involve her in this because I like to make her miserable, Kyle," Jimmy said.

Kyle looked at Madison. "Anything else you haven't told me?"

"I had a dream," she murmured. "You don't like to hear about my dreams."

"Well, I'd damned well better hear about them now!" he snapped.

Jimmy cleared his throat. "You are helpful, Madison. Thanks. Thanks a lot."

"Has there been an identification on the head yet?" Madison asked.

"Not yet. It's only Monday morning. Preliminary investigations suggest that she was killed sometime Friday—" He broke off, flushing as both Madison and Kyle realized that she had probably been killed at a time corresponding to Madison's dream. "But," Jimmy continued uncomfortably, "the head was thrown in the water. Two kids fishing in a canal found it. We're waiting on a match-up with a missing-persons report."

Madison nodded.

"We're also waiting to get the arm in. The Monroe authorities said they'd be glad to turn it over—other counties like it best when we keep the grisly murders here in Dade," he said with a wince.

"But if she was killed in a hotel room in the Keys—"

"The head came from Dade."

"The woman had lots of other body parts," Kyle murmured.

"We'll have to see where they turn up," Jimmy responded. He shook his head, looking at Kyle. "Jeez, we've got to catch this guy."

"Is Jassy here? Has she been assigned to this case?" Madison asked.

"Jassy's in the lab right now. I'm sure the head man will give her a crack at it. I mean, I'm sure the chief medical examiner will let her have a look and... Oh, jeez..."

A lab tech stuck his head into the lounge area. "Lieutenant Gates? Dr. Sibley has a report for you on the drifter who came in last week. Says he knows you're here on other business, but if you've got a few minutes...?"

"Sure, sure," Jimmy said absently. "Madison, can you give me a few minutes? I hate to keep you at the morgue—"

"I'll get her home," Kyle said.

"Hey, guys, I can just grab a cab," Madison said. "Kyle, you might want to hear whatever Dr. Sibley—"

"No, that's all right, he doesn't need to be here for this," Jimmy said. "This one's totally unrelated. This guy had no ID, he's almost as old as Moses, and I think he got bumped over the head for the ten bucks he had just panhandled. Kyle can get you home, no problem."

"Thanks," Madison murmured.

Kyle escorted her out.

It was a spectacular day. Brilliant sunlight, incredibly blue sky.

"How about some lunch?" Kyle asked, once he had her seated in his rental car and was jockeying out of his parking space.

"I thought you were mad at me?"

"I am. Lunch?"

She wrinkled her nose. "Lunch?"

He shrugged, a half smile curving his lip. "All right. How about a drink?"

"Can you drink on duty?"

"I could probably manage a beer."

"Sure you want to take a chance giving a drink to someone as susceptible to the intoxicating properties of alcohol as me?"

His smile deepened. "Yeah, I'm willing."

She looked forward, at the traffic ahead. "Sorry, it's too early for me."

"Be daring."

"I have to pick up my daughter."

"I'll pick her up."

"It's your first day on assignment."

"What time does Carrie Anne get out of kindergarten?"

"Two o'clock."

"I'll be back on the job by two-thirty. I started this morning at six, and I'm my own boss on this one."

Madison still hesitated. He thought of her as an intrusive witch—when he wasn't trying to pretend that she was a complete quack. Being near him was pure torture.

When she was near him…

She simply wanted him. Sex. Only sex, of course.

But there was a possibility that he was carrying on an affair with her sister.

She shrugged. They would talk, have a drink. She could surely manage to be courteous for that long. "One drink."

"And by then, you may be hungry."

She thought about the head.

"I may never be hungry."

He drove out the causeway to Key Biscayne, stopping at a place that sat directly on the water. They had their drinks, two microbrews, outside at a wrought-iron table and watched as pelicans swooped hopefully around the pleasure craft out on the bay.

Madison was looking out over the water when she felt the intensity of his eyes.

Behind dark glasses.

He was a "suit" today, wearing a stereotypical pinstripe shirt, rep tie and a deep navy suit cut handsomely to the proportions of his body. It was very sunny; she was wearing shades, too. Still, it felt as if he were staring right through her.

"Damn Jimmy," he said softly, shaking his head. "And damn you. If he doesn't involve you, you involve yourself. But he shouldn't allow it."

She looked away from him, swallowing her beer. "Kyle, you've been away a long time. Jimmy's been a friend for years. He's never abused the relationship."

"And I thought you were busy playing singer-slash-model."

"I do model. And I love jamming with the band."

"It's just jamming?"

"That and some demo material. Touring doesn't work well with the concept of family."

"The modeling takes you out of town."

"When I've got the time."

"Amazing. You could probably have two flourishing careers and you rein back on both of them."

"I have a daughter."

"And you don't want to be famous. Like your mother."

She stared at him. "I hear you draw exceptionally well."

He stared at her for a very long moment, a slow,

rueful smile curving his lip at last. He lifted his microbrew to the sun. "Touché—maybe. I'm not even sure myself."

"Have you used your drawing in your work?"

"On occasion. Computers have really changed everything, you know."

"Computers still have to be programmed."

"True." He was staring at her again, shaking his head. "I didn't want Jimmy calling you on this one."

"I think you already told him that."

"I don't think either of you listened."

"Look, Kyle, there's no real difference between this case and any other."

"There *is* a difference."

"What?"

"I don't know."

"Feelings of hocus-pocus?" she asked, taunting him.

Then she sighed. "Look, Kyle, I can't begin to understand all that you've learned about the psychology of killers, but this man mutilates people and chops them up, so he's probably as psychotic as they come—"

"Or smart," Kyle suggested.

"Sick."

"Sick—and smart." He sighed, folding his hands together. "The two can go hand in hand. And if you look at the law, no matter how sick something may be, the person doing it may be judged sane and responsible for his actions, depending on his understanding of them at the time. Bundy was sick—and judged sane to stand trial. Cutting up a body and disposing of it with weighted bricks or in the muck of the Everglades is bizarre, but think of the Everglades. Things can disappear there forever. Between what we've found and what witnesses have told us about the victims, we know we're talking about someone who chooses his victims carefully and is charming enough to get them exactly where he wants them.'' He shrugged, lifting his hands. ''Look, Miami recently had Conde—who killed prostitutes. But to the best of my knowledge, you haven't been turning tricks on Eighth Street, so it's quite unlikely you could have been a victim of his. But this guy...''

''Kyle! There are more than three million people in this area! Why would *I* be in particular danger?''

He shook his head. ''I don't know. I just don't like it.''

He smiled at her suddenly, swirling his beer. ''What a world! Some murders are just as sad and terrible as others—but easier to solve. I remember one down here years ago, when a young cop comes down the street and sees a naked guy walking around with a severed head. He tries to throw the head at the cop. Lucky for the cop, he misses. It was his girlfriend, but he said she was the devil. He'd stabbed her over a hundred times before severing her head. There's a crime of passion for you. Heartbreaking for the poor girl's family, but you've got your killer quick. People can shake their heads and sympathize, but they can sleep at night, as well. This guy is dangerous because he doesn't go walking around naked, he doesn't carry a head, he doesn't suggest that his victims are the devil. Whatever his fantasies are, he keeps them hidden. He leads a normal life. He's smart. He probably lives alone. He has his own transportation easily available. He might have started off pulling the wings off of flies as a kid, throwing rocks at dogs, burning kittens. Whatever he started with, he escalated to murder. And he's enjoying the hell out of himself right now, knowing that he's left very few clues and that the cops are going to be scrambling all over themselves trying to find him." He hesitated, then winced. "Well, I guess I haven't done a lot to make you hungry enough for lunch."

She smiled. "We can order."

They went inside. Kyle ordered snapper; she opted for the grilled mahimahi.

"So Darryl's down," Kyle murmured, taking a swallow of coffee. "How does that work out?"

"What do you mean?" she asked warily.

But there didn't seem to be any underlying insinuation to the question; his glasses were off, and he seemed to be asking out of concern and curiosity. "Carrie Anne. She's a very sweet, charming and outgoing child—and she seems to have a wonderful relationship with you both."

Madison smiled. "Thanks. We're lucky. Really lucky. Neither one of us played any games with Carrie Anne or tried to use her to hurt the other. Darryl adores her, and he's a great father. Until kindergarten, he had her one week out of four. I'd fly up with her and leave her with him, then he'd fly back with her and leave her with me. Now that she's starting 'big kids' school,' as she calls it, we've worked around her schedule. When there's a holiday or they have teacher-conference days, she goes up to see him. I didn't have that much of a chance to talk to him the other night, but it seems he's going to be working down here for several weeks, at least.

Which is great. Carrie Anne will get to spend a lot of time with him.''

"And do you spend time with them, as well?"

Madison arched a brow, sipping her iced tea. "Sometimes," she informed him.

"Why the divorce?"

"None of your business." She took another sip of tea. "How about you?" she suddenly demanded.

"Me, what?"

"No steady woman in your life?"

His smile faded, and he shrugged, attacking his salad with sudden interest. "No."

"You've become celibate?"

He looked at her. "No."

"A host of one-night stands?" she inquired.

"It's none of your business."

It hurt. Funny, it hadn't felt hurtful when she said it to him.

She pushed back the salad she'd been toying with and folded her fingers together on the table. "No one will ever be Fallon, but sex is a natural instinct, so when the urge occurs, you follow?"

He looked back up at her. "Is that how you view intimacy?"

The way he was staring at her, she wanted to slap him. But her heart was suddenly thumping in double time; her palms were clammy, and a hot streak was saturating her bloodstream.

Instinct, yes. They could manage a few civil exchanges, but then they were at one another's throats. And yet he **was right**, that was exactly how she was viewing things.

Pity they had to talk at all.

If only she could just...touch him. She wanted to

feel his flesh, his lips against her skin. It had been a very long time....

She felt her cheeks growing warm and red, and remembered what Sheila had said to her at her father's house the other night about her wanting to sleep with Kyle.

How awful.

But it was true.

Get a grip, Madison! she warned herself. And she leaned back. "Kyle, you son of—"

Thankfully, the waitress made a timely arrival with their check. She was a chatty young woman, and she pointed out the weather—clouds brewing in the east. "Spring—it's just that time of year!" she said cheerfully. "The mornings can be absolutely gorgeous, and by afternoon, wham! Pitch-black skies, lightning to rip up the sky and buckets full of rain. Of course, the great thing about south Florida is that after the rain, the sky is all blue and beautiful again!"

"Yes, it's a great place," Kyle said.

"I mean, bad things do happen, but they can happen anywhere, right?" the girl said, her smile still in place.

"Definitely," Madison agreed.

"It *is* going to storm soon," Kyle commented.

"Storms are great to watch from here," the waitress said cheerfully.

She left the table, hips swaying slightly. A nice girl, friendly, vivacious.

Like their killer's victims, Madison thought suddenly.

She looked from the remains of her fish to Kyle

and realized, as his eyes touched hers, that he was thinking the same thing.

"Think you ought to warn her?" Madison asked.

Kyle didn't seem surprised, or unnerved, that she had read his thoughts.

"Yeah, probably. When we leave, I'll suggest that she not go anywhere with anyone without telling someone close exactly what she's doing." He looked at Madison. "You need to live the same way. Don't go anywhere with anyone without someone else knowing exactly what you're doing."

"Kyle, I'm not a fool!"

"Damn it, Madison, don't be so defensive. We're not at war."

"But I'm all right. I've been living my life—"

He exhaled on a long, explosive note. "Please! Madison, I'm worried about you."

"Well, you know, Kyle," she said quietly, "I was really worried about you at one time, but you were a grown man and there was nothing I could do except to accept the fact that you didn't want me around. I'm grown up, now, too, Kyle. You don't need to be worried about me."

He stood up so suddenly that his chair nearly toppled over. He caught it, sliding it with a vengeance beneath the table.

He caught the waitress near the hostess stand and paid the check. Madison watched as he spoke with the girl, being both charming and earnest.

She seemed charmed in response, but she was an open, friendly girl, and she turned back to Madison, smiling sweetly and waving.

Obviously she thought that they were a couple.

They left the restaurant and drove to Carrie

Anne's school in silence, except for a few brief directions.

Kyle drove on to her house. Madison was quiet as Carrie Anne chatted excitedly about her school program, coming at the end of the year.

Kyle was good with her. He knew how to listen to kids. He seemed as interested in her kindergarten program as he would be in some crime-lab technique.

He dropped them at Madison's house, and though he surveyed the outside of her Old Spanish golf-course home, he refused to come in when she politely offered him coffee, even though Carrie Anne excitedly urged him to do so.

"I have to get back to work," he told Carrie Anne sadly, scrunching up his nose. "First day on the job down here. I have to be good."

"You can't come in just for a minute?" Carrie Anne asked wistfully.

He shook his head, his eyes strangely clouded, as he reached out the window and tousled her hair. "There's nothing I'd rather do than spend the afternoon with such a lovely young lady, but I really have to go to work."

Carrie Anne accepted that. Madison felt a strange tremor snake along her spine as she watched Kyle.

He had meant that. Of course. He had to be wondering if his own daughter would have been like Carrie Anne if she ever had a chance to draw breath.

Then his eyes were on hers. And she wasn't thinking about children, or the killer on the loose. She was looking back at him, and the tremors that raked her were suddenly as hot as flaming coals.

Sex.

Just sex.

If they were alone…

If he was naked…

Oh, God.

She waved, took Carrie Anne's hand, and headed quickly into the house.

7

His phone rang at five.

Kyle reached over and answered it, staring at the clock as he did so. His alarm had been set for six.

It was Jimmy on the phone. "We've got a torso."

Kyle rubbed his chin. "Where are you?"

"Out on the Trail. Right off Krome."

"I'll be there as soon as I can."

"We might have something. A clue."

"Yeah?"

"A tattoo just below the navel. A rose, with thorns. The medical examiner on the job out here says it looks new."

"A rose...with thorns?"

"There were fresh roses in Maria Garcia's house, the still-missing second victim. And our Jane Doe in the morgue—"

"Rose tattoo, upper left buttock," Kyle said, quoting from the forensics report he had read while still in Washington. "I'll be with you as soon as possible."

He hung up and jumped out of bed.

Their killer had revealed something of himself, leaving his calling cards.

Roses...

With thorns.

* * *

Kaila Adair Aubrey wound her fingers into the sheets at her sides and gritted on her teeth, staring up at the ceiling.

"Talk to me, baby, talk to me."

Talk.

Men wanted women to *talk.*

She just didn't have a damned thing left to say right now. It wasn't that Dan wasn't a decent lover; he was. Or he could be. But sex seemed like everything else in their lives to her right then—all *him.* And this just wasn't doing a damned thing for her. She wasn't in the mood for a big fight or a showdown; she didn't know how to articulate all that she had to say as yet. And if she couldn't get her thoughts out right, he would dismiss her completely—as males were so wont to do—by assuring himself that she was just being a bitch with PMS and he was the poor, misunderstood, hardworking provider. "Kaila..." He groaned her name.

At least he still had that right.

She'd been growing afraid over the past few months, with his everlasting work hours, his constant business dinners, that he was sleeping with someone else. She still thought he might be, and the thought hurt, but it was the same as everything else. When she even hinted at such a fear, he got hurt and furious and impatient. Of course, she was in a better position than lots of young wives with small children who were worried about their husbands; she could run home to a rich daddy. No, it wasn't the money that kept her quietly in her home and with her husband. It was the insecurity, the confusion, the not knowing. Was there something—someone?—else out there for her? Or did she love her husband? Was he really what she wanted? Was she just tired, feeling old, feeling used up, feeling that she'd never be decently thin again after so many children so quickly? God forgive her, she was grateful that the kids were fine and healthy, but...

But she was a mess.

And would she go crazy if she let Dan go and he did fall in love with someone else, forgetting all about her? She did love him, she did, she was just so...

Wound up.

And not in the mood.

But she'd been obliging rather than argumentative, though right now she simply wasn't involved at all, despite the fact that he was all slick and sweaty and grinding into her.

At last he climaxed. Fell on her. Heavy. Rolled to the side.

He tousled her hair.

They lay in silence.

A few minutes later he started touching her. She gritted her teeth again, but then, to her surprise, she began to feel aroused. She pressed into him. They kissed. His hands ran up and down her. She eased against him, rubbing her body against his. Nuzzled the thick mat of hair around his navel.

"Come on, do me, baby, do me," he groaned.

It was as if she had been doused with cold water.

Kaila held still for a minute, her head lowered against his belly, her lower lip caught between her teeth. She knew what he wanted, of course. And she could have slid on down the length of his body and taken him in her mouth, just like he wanted. Except, she just didn't feel like it.

She didn't feel like talking him into an erection, or working hard at arousing him, either. She wanted to be seduced, swept off her feet.

She stood up suddenly. Her husband opened his eyes, staring at her in surprise.

"I can't *do* anything but oatmeal," she said irritably, walking toward the bathroom. "The kids will be waking up."

She heard him brushing his teeth while she was in the shower. When she stepped out, he stepped in. He didn't look at her.

He showered. She brushed her teeth and moisturized her face.

He came out, toweled himself. She looked at him in the mirror. Dan had dark-blond hair, neatly cut— good legal hair. He kept himself in shape. He had light blue-green eyes and managed to keep a good tan, as well. Having kids didn't do things to men at all. He was tall and well built and good-looking. She wanted him; she didn't want him. She loved him; she hated him.

She wondered if she was suffering from some strange disease.

He wrapped his towel around himself. "If you don't want to do something, Kaila, just tell me."

"I did—"

"No. The first time. It was like making love to a dead tree."

That one hurt.

"I'm sorry."

"All you had to do was say something."

"I was trying to be a good wife."

"Yeah. Sure. There's nothing like making a man

feel totally inadequate to make him feel he's got the best damned wife in the world.''

"Go fuck yourself," Kaila told him softly.

"I'd definitely have more fun," he assured her.

Stung, she stood perfectly still.

She had known that she was unhappy.

It hadn't occurred to her that *he* was miserable, too. And now she wondered more than ever if he was having an affair.

He walked out to the bedroom and started dressing. Shaking, she slipped into a robe and hurried out of the bedroom, closing the door behind her.

She went mechanically through the functions of the morning, waking Justin and Shelley, starting breakfast.

Shelley was quickly howling and in tears because she couldn't find one of her sneakers, and she had to wear her sneakers, because they were getting new playground equipment that day.

Anthony—who was mostly weaned, but not completely—threw his kiddie cup on the floor and screamed for her.

Justin decided to help, with his own cornflakes, and spilled the milk all over the table and on the floor. Naturally, that was when Dan walked in.

"Jesus, Kaila," he said. "Looks like I'll be a little late," he muttered.

"You might have thought of that earlier," she bit out cattily.

"I should have thought of that earlier."

He started mopping up Justin and the table and the milk. Kaila knew she was about to burst into tears. "I've got it, just go. Just get out. You can be late for everything else in the world, but don't be late for that precious job of yours.''

''Well, you know what, Kaila? At least, at work, people like me. Amazing how that can make you feel happy to be somewhere!''

He threw down the towel with which he'd been soaking up the milk and stormed out of the house.

The rest of the morning seemed to take forever. She got Justin and Shelley off to their various schools and finally had Anthony happy and in a good mood. Her housekeeper, Anna, arrived. Anna was a wonderful Latin woman with a flair for handling children. She whisked through the kitchen in a matter of minutes, got the laundry going and came into Shelley's room, where Kaila was looking through piles of toys to find the still-missing sneaker. ''You have tennis this morning, no?''

''I was going to take a lesson, but...''

''You go. You get out of the house. Have a good time.''

''Things are kind of in a shambles this morning.''

''Kaila, I work for you, yes? I'll pick up the shambles. That's my job. I'm good at it. You pay me well, and you have cute, good little children. Go, go, shoo!''

Kaila went to her lesson. The weather was already hotter than Hades. She saw a few friends on the courts, and they asked her to lunch.

She called Anna, who had no problem picking Shelley up at one and Justin at two.

She went to lunch at the country club. She had two piña coladas. Her head was spinning.

She said goodbye to her friends, then headed back to the locker room to change. Her sneakers seemed to slap against the cement as she entered the changing building, walking down the hallway between the men's and ladies' lockers, rest rooms and showers.

It was oddly quiet.

She was startled and nearly screamed when she felt a hand on her shoulder.

"Kaila!"

She spun around.

He was there. Looking so handsome. He'd been playing tennis. He was in white. His skin was so bronze. He flashed his teeth in a perfect, tender smile.

"You look scrumptious!" he told her.

She smiled. She felt somewhat silly; two drinks laced strongly with rum in the middle of the day were a bit much.

"Thanks."

"You ready to have an affair with me yet?" he asked. His tone was light, but his eyes were serious. He backed her gently against the wall, his fingers moving over her face.

"I...can't."

"You know you will."

She smiled, looking at him, shaking her head. "We just really couldn't... I mean...it wouldn't be right. I mean, not at all."

She giggled. Damn the piña coladas.

He pressed against her. His lips were suddenly on hers. Molding, passionate. She felt a stirring. The piña coladas, she told herself. She was kissing him back. Just a kiss. More than a kiss. Tongues meshing. Wet. Stifling. She needed more air. Strange. She was both excited...

And repelled.

A slight sense of panic pervaded her. His hands were on her, molding her breast, sliding up her thigh. She felt his touch against naked flesh, dangerously close to intimate.

"Sleep with me, love me..." he whispered fervently against her lips.

She suddenly wanted to push him away. But he broke away from her. "I love you. I can wait until you're ready. The time is coming. I can taste it when we kiss..." he whispered. "There's so much more I want to taste, to lick. To kiss. I want to make it so good. Lick you here...here..."

He moved his fingers to show her. She inhaled sharply, shocked. She'd only been toying with this idea so far. This was more than play. More than fantasy.

It was too real.

"But I can wait. I *will* wait. Because it will be so much better when I wait.... You'll want me. When I finish with you, I promise, you'll want me."

"I..."

She couldn't speak.

He brushed her cheek tenderly, deep understanding in his eyes.

He walked away from her whistling.

An acquaintance passed him by on the way to the men's lockers. They spoke, jovial, laughing.

Kaila leaned against the wall, her knees buckling. She was shaking.

Once again, she didn't know what she wanted.

Fantasy had been so much fun. Imagining a lover. Handsome, charming, devoted entirely to making her feel wonderful. Adoring her, a lover who knew just where and when and how she wanted to be touched…

But she suddenly felt…dirty.

She was getting exactly what she had wanted, except that she didn't really want it.

She wanted to cry again.

She finally managed to push herself away from the wall and head into the locker room. She had to get her relationship with him back on a friendly keel. Unless, of course, Dan *was* having an affair. Then she would be so mad that she'd sleep with the first person available.

Him.

She paused before her locker, smiling. The feeling of repulsion for her almost-out-of-the-question would-be lover faded. He was a sweetie. A charming man who knew how to make her feel better. Like an attractive, desirable woman again—even if she did occasionally wear oatmeal and spit-up.

He'd left her roses. Beautiful red roses. A dozen of them. They were lying on the bench directly in front of her locker.

She picked them up, smiling, then muttered, "Ouch!" and sucked on her finger where she had acquired a tiny drop of blood.

These roses had thorns.

Still, the very idea of roses was so romantic and sexy and sweet.…

Kaila took a long shower at the club, trying to clear her head before going home.

The world looked a little better when she returned. Anna had the house in wonderful shape. Anthony was napping; Shelley was playing with her Barbie dolls and Justin with his trucks while they watched a Disney video.

She walked into the kitchen to find Anna cutting up vegetables for the stew she planned that night.

Yet, looking through the kitchen to the dining room, Kaila started suddenly.

There was a huge vase of roses on the dining room table.

"Anna?" she said.

"They arrived an hour ago."

"From?"

"I don't know. The card is addressed to you."

Kaila walked into the dining room. There were at least two dozen roses beautifully arranged in a pink glass vase. She found the card and opened it.

It was very simple.

"Kaila, I love you. Dan."

They sometimes went for days, weeks, even months, without a significant break in a case.

And, of course, there were those horrible instances when a killer was never discovered. The good thing about most serial killers was that deep in their psyches, they wanted to be caught. They knew their behavior was abhorrent, and they wanted to be stopped. And so they left their calling cards; they taunted the police, leaving clues each time. And every year, with more and more scientific techniques available, it became possible to irrefutably link more murderers to their victims. Fingerprinting, fibers, teeth marks, DNA, all contributed heavily to locking away—or executing—numerous criminals.

Once they were caught.

That was where profiling came in.

Kyle spent the morning with Jimmy at the site out on Krome, where the torso had been found buried in the embankment. He watched back at the coroner's office as the pathologists did the initial investigating and determined that the head, arm and torso all belonged to the same woman. He asked for numerous shots of the tattoos on Jane Doe's buttocks and their newest victim's torso. By the afternoon, he had scanned the shots into the computer and checks were being made across the country for any similar "signatures" on the bodies of victims in other states.

From Broward south through Dade and Monroe Counties, the police began investigating tattoo parlors.

Kyle worked late in his Coconut Grove hotel room, playing with random information and the computer. At seven he was deeply involved, and ordered up room service. By nine he was frustrated and restless. He turned off the computer, turned on the television.

His telephone rang.

"Kyle."

"Hey, Dad," he told his father. "What's up?"

"Nothing. It's just a luxury to have you in the city again. Thought I'd check in."

"Things are going well. We have a few interesting breaks in the case."

"Yeah?"

"Something that may be significant. Two of the victims seem to have had tattoos done recently."

"The papers have mentioned body parts," Roger said dryly.

"So much gets released to the public, there's not

much we can do. And unfortunately, the papers seem to thrive on anything gruesome.''

''That's true. Well, you think you'll get some free time this weekend?''

''I'm sure I can manage some.''

''Good. Remember the opening I was telling you about the other day?''

Kyle went blank, then felt guilty as hell. Yes, his father and a friend and fellow artist were opening a gallery to highlight local artists. Their own work, along with that of a number of other area artists, would be on display. It was to be a black-tie affair Sunday evening.

''Hey, Dad, if there's a way, I'll be there.''

''Good. Rafe will appreciate your presence.''

''Oh, yeah?'' Kyle inquired, amused.

''Your brother says that maybe the press will leave him alone if you're there. They're always after him, wanting to know why he never went into art. Says telling them he has no talent never works. Maybe they'll be after you on Sunday instead of him.''

Kyle laughed. ''Leave it to Rafe to tell them straight-faced that he can't draw a stick figure. Fine. If you see him before I do, you can tell him I feel guilty for living out of state and leaving him to take all the whatever-happened-to-your-artistic-genes heat.''

''He'll be glad to hear it. See you there, son, if not before.''

''Yeah, Dad. Hey, wait, Dad, is the rest of the family coming?''

''The rest of the family?''

Kyle winced slightly. "Yeah. You know. Jordan and his brood. And Trent."

"Yeah, sure, of course. I imagine they'll be there. They're all invited, anyway. We've never failed to be supportive of one another, and they know this place means a lot to me. Is there a problem?"

"No, of course not."

They said goodbye and hung up. Kyle rose and stretched, tired but restless.

The phone rang again. Kaila, just calling to say hi. His second line rang, and it was Trent. A third call came from Jassy, who involved him in a lengthy conversation regarding forensic findings before telling him it was really just a social call and it was nice to have him home.

The phone rang again. He told himself he wasn't hoping it was Madison.

It wasn't. It was Rafe. He'd just taken a date to the movies at Cocowalk. She lived in the Grove and he'd just dropped her off, so maybe he and Kyle could meet for a drink.

It sounded good to Kyle.

Coconut Grove, even just after ten o'clock on a weeknight, was alive and bustling with tourists from all over, along with the local crowd.

Kyle wandered through the bookstore—open until eleven on weeknights—and picked up a few newspapers, then wandered back over to Cocowalk, where he was meeting Rafe at Fat Tuesday's. Rafe was already sitting at the bar with a beer, watching the hockey play-offs.

Kyle sat down beside him and ordered the same. "Didn't stay with the date, huh?" he inquired.

Rafe smiled slowly and shrugged. He wasn't quite

two years older than Kyle—Roger had gone through wives quickly when he was young—but though they were close in age and size and shared a love for the sun, they weren't alike in much else. Rafe had been a great student, he was serious and dedicated and, though not artistic in the least, he was a financial genius. He'd spent several years working as a stock trader, then started investing his savings. He'd been able to quit his job and now made a good living off his investments. His time in the sun had turned his blond hair platinum, and despite his serious nature, his eyes were a silver that could quickly come alight with rueful amusement, as they did now. "Staying with the date was on my mind, but I wasn't invited. Well, I'm working on it for next time. She's an R.N.—has to be at the hospital at six. Nice girl. We'll see how it goes."

"It's about time you got serious about a woman."

"I'm serious about all women," Rafe assured him. "Now, how about you? How's it going here in the wild, wicked city?"

"Not too badly. I've only been here a few days, and we've had a couple of breaks." He told his brother about the torso and the tattoos, and the roses delivered to Maria Garcia's house, warning him that they weren't letting that information out to the public. Then he shrugged unhappily. "Jimmy had Madison in, as well."

"So?" Rafe said. "She's worked with him before. It makes sense that he'd want her help on something like this."

"I don't like it."

"Why? What is Madison seeing? How close is she getting?"

Kyle shook his head in disgust. "All she's seen so far is the victim."

"She mostly sees the victims. She never saw her mother's killer, remember?"

"She's seen more on occasion. Sometimes she sees what the victim sees. But you're right. She seems to have a blind spot for the killer on this. All that's happened so far is that she feels pain for the woman who was killed. I just don't like her being involved."

"What can you do?" Rafe asked him with a sympathetic shrug. "Jimmy is going to use her, and Madison is over twenty-one."

"I just don't have a good feeling about it."

Rafe toyed with the label on his beer bottle, hesitating. "I think you just came home and got nervous because Madison looks so much like Lainie did...when Lainie was killed."

Kyle shook his head, wondering why his brother's words were suddenly making him feel as if he had missed something. "It's not that. Besides, Harry Nore was certifiably insane, and he was caught."

Rafe shrugged. "I don't think Madison ever believed that Harry Nore killed her mother."

"She accepted it. The cops had him, along with the murder weapon—with traces of Lainie's blood still on it."

"She accepted it because she was a kid and she was told that was what happened. She had no choice."

"The evidence against Nore was damning, and that's my point. Madison has gone through enough."

"Oh, she's stronger than you think. Besides, little bro, you can't just come waltzing back into town when you've been gone for years and think you're going to boss the family around."

"I don't think that," Kyle said with a scowl. "I just don't like...I don't like her being involved. It makes me nervous as all hell."

"Then get her uninvolved."

"How?"

Rafe laughed. "How the hell do I know? You're the damned FBI agent!" He sobered suddenly. "Okay, so this is a nerve-racking case. More and more about what's going on is making its way into the newspapers, and lots of people are getting nervous. Maybe this is a bad one. Maybe you're right and Madison shouldn't be involved. Find a way to keep her busy elsewhere. Have her kidnapped to a desert island for the time being."

"Right. Then the FBI will be after *me*."

Rafe laughed easily. "I'm sure you can think of something. Do your best to keep her out of it."

Kyle stood suddenly.

"Where are you going?" Rafe asked.

"I'm going to call her. I've heard from everyone else—hell, Trent even gave me a call. I just want to make sure she's okay."

"She's a big girl now," Rafe reminded him.

Kyle nodded and headed toward the phones. He had a cellular, but he hated the damned thing, and he'd left it in the hotel room.

He dialed Madison's number. Her machine picked up. "Madison, it's Kyle. Pick up. Madison, I'm going to wait. I'm going to keep talking. It's Kyle. Pick up."

She didn't do so. He tried ringing her number once again. Once again he got the machine.

He hung up and walked back to Rafe, glancing at his watch. "Eleven o'clock on a weeknight. Where the hell is she?"

"Out on a date?" Rafe suggested.

"She has a kid."

"Yeah, well, women with kids go out on dates."

He cast his brother a glare. "Then the baby-sitter would pick up."

"Right. But you're forgetting that Darryl is in town. Maybe Carrie Anne's with him. Maybe she is, too."

"Madison and Darryl are divorced—"

"Yeah, well, they're still close. Real close. Friends. Who knows, maybe once they've both sown a few wild oats they'll get back together again. Kyle, she's all right. Wake up and smell the coffee. She's probably sleeping at Darryl's house. You can't come home and start chasing her around."

"I'm not trying to chase her around. I'm worried about her."

"Kyle, she's all grown up. You're not even really related to her, plus you left her life years ago. I'm telling you, you can't be her guardian angel now."

"Maybe not."

They talked about stocks, Rafe telling Kyle where he should invest.

"You're going to have to make good investments, there just aren't that many really rich FBI agents," Rafe reminded him.

It was late when Kyle finally left his brother.

Late when he went to bed after two beers.

He should have slept quickly, and well.

He didn't.

At first he lay awake wondering what it was that

he should be seeing and just wasn't realizing. Something in the pictures of the victims, in the forensic reports.

He crawled out of bed and started going through the reports once again. What was it?

Then it hit him, and he realized it had taken him so long because the picture he had of Julie Sabor was in black and white.

Redheads.

They were all redheads.

Maria Garcia had been very dark, but still, there were traces of red in her hair. And the corpse today...

He felt ill. More worried than ever about Madison. He tried her house again.

She didn't answer.

He hung up. Rafe had all but told him that she still slept with her ex. He could check with Darryl, except that he didn't have any idea where Darryl was staying.

It was really late, but he called Jassy. She came on the line sounding really sleepy. "Madison could be at Darryl's, but she's probably home. She turns the ringer down on her phone after ten all the time because Carrie Anne is such a light sleeper. Call her in the morning, Kyle. I'm sure she's fine."

He thought about driving out to her house then and there, and banging on the door until she acknowledged him. She would be really ready to kill him, though, and more prone than ever to ignore his warnings. He had to be calm, had to tell himself that it was a good thing she was probably sleeping safely with her ex-husband, that he should get a grip and wait until morning.

He lay awake.

Finally he dozed.

And he dreamed.

He dreamed once again that he and Madison were in the same house. And he was moving down a darkened hallway, trying to get to her. He was wearing a towel. He'd showered, and he was intent on one thing—Madison. It was simply time. It didn't matter that they always argued when they talked. It was time. She knew it just as well as he did. It didn't have anything to do with the kind of emotion that had tied him to Fallon. It had nothing to do with the past or the future, and she knew that, too.

So he walked down the hall. And in his dream the hallway was dark and misty. Long.

Like the hallway in the house Lainie Adair had shared with Roger Montgomery, all those years ago.

Madison was at the end of the hallway, in her room. There was a soft yellow light emanating from her room, sweeping around her. She was wearing a towel, as well. Her hair was dry, burning red in the strange light, creating a cape around her naked shoulders as he walked down the hallway. Her chin was up, her eyes were bright, her lips were poised to speak. She was going to tell him what he should be doing with himself, except it didn't matter. What she said didn't matter. She was waiting, because they both knew that there had to be an outlet for what they were feeling.

His groin tightened.

He met her eyes. Felt the electric fury that burned within her because she wanted him and he knew it. She didn't want to want him, and she definitely didn't want him to know that she wanted him....

He just smiled. And walked closer.

That was when it happened....

When the darkness suddenly deepened. When she suddenly seemed so far away from him. When the air itself changed. When he felt...

A presence.

Someone between them.

Someone lurking in the shadows that were suddenly becoming deeper and deeper. Someone waiting. Someone evil, threatening Madison...

Out of the pitch-darkness he suddenly saw the silver glitter of a knife. Big, long, a butcher's knife, wickedly sharp. It hung in the air, as if suspended in the darkness of a haunted castle in an amusement park, the strings hidden by the eerie lack of light.

The silver streaked through the air.

The shadows shifted and moved.

Madison screamed....

Kyle awoke, drenched in sweat.

For several long seconds he sat there, realizing he'd been dreaming, that he was in his bed in his hotel room, that morning's light was just beginning to filter into his room.

Six-thirty.

The alarm went off.

He nearly jumped off the bed.

Get a grip! he warned himself in silent self-disgust. He crawled out of bed and into the shower, jumping when the water hit him, cold as ice at first.

The water warmed, and he lifted his head, letting it stream over him. Maybe he shouldn't have accepted this assignment. There were criminals all across the country. He should never have come home.

The phone was already ringing when he left the shower. He picked up the receiver. His assistant, Ricky Haines, was calling from Virginia. They hadn't found any matchups with the rose tattoos so far, but he would keep looking.

Kyle thanked him, hung up and glanced at the clock. Nearly eight. He called Jimmy, who was usually in by seven-thirty, if not earlier.

Jimmy was in, and he had information.

There had finally been an identification on their Jane Doe. She was in fact Julie Sabor; dental records brought in from Cincinnati had clinched the ID.

"We think we've got a name on our weekend victim, as well," Jimmy told him. "Holly Tyler, twenty-eight, worked as a receptionist at a med-tech lab. Only child, parents deceased, friendly, well liked at work. She was incredibly excited and secretive Friday afternoon. She was getting off early for a 'wild weekend'—and she told the girls at work that she wouldn't whisper a word until she saw them again come Monday."

"She never showed up on Monday?"

"Her friends in the office even hesitated about calling in this morning—they thought she might be planning to call in sick or something. But then one of them noticed an article in the paper this morning about the torso we found yesterday and decided to call in. I'm expecting Larraine Harrison and Betty Kilbride, two of the girls she worked with, to come down and identify the body—well, the head—in about an hour."

"I'll be there," Kyle said, and hung up.

He dressed quickly, then tried Madison's number. He still got the answering machine.

He swore, then decided to drive by her house.

Her beige Cherokee was in the drive, but she didn't answer the bell. He knocked on the door, then walked around the house, pounding on the windows.

"Damn you, Madison!" he muttered out loud.

Finally he used his cellular phone and called Jimmy. "Have you got Madison with you down at the morgue again?" he demanded angrily.

"No, I don't have Madison at the morgue," Jimmy informed him irritably. "What the hell's eating *you?*"

"She didn't answer her phone last night, and she's not here now."

"Well, you know, Kyle, she *is* over twenty-one."

"I'm going in, Jimmy."

"Kyle, I'm sure that—"

"Doesn't matter. I'm going in."

"Fine. I'll be there in five minutes. Five—"

Kyle had already hung up.

8

"Gorgeous, absolutely gorgeous. Now, no smiles for this. Be sultry. Seduce the camera, Madison. We're not being playful here, we're smoldering, my darling. You are pure sensuality.... Give me movement, subtle movement, just a tiny bit of movement, face, eyes... Part your lips, just a hair. That's it, perfect, perfect...."

Jaime Marquesa's camera clicked away as he gave her his instructions. It was an outdoor shoot, on a small private spit of beach at Key West, and as Jaime moved around with his camera, his two assistants hovered in silence behind, ready to move any obstruction or raise aluminum sheets against the sun if the shot demanded it.

Madison liked Jaime, and she liked working with Michelle Michaux, a local woman who had come from Miami's inner-city area to excel in fashion design. Of Haitian descent, Michelle had a beautiful, soft accent. Her swimwear was becoming so popular that the onetime dollar-an-hour seamstress was frequently quoted in *Forbes*. But she also had a deep-seated belief in giving back to her community. Today, she, Jaime and Madison were all donating their time and talents for a poster campaign to support the local arts and students interested in pursuing careers in fashion and the fine arts. The concept was Michelle's. The theme was To Soar Where We Can Dream. To Madison, with Darryl working in Miami and anxious to spend time with Carrie Anne, the opportunity to take the few days necessary to work on the project had seemed incredibly fortuitous. She'd also been anxious to get away.

She'd been curious to discover if she had the willpower to force herself to leave Miami and slip away, knowing that Kyle was there. But if he and Jassy were getting together, she needed to keep herself out of the way. And if she had been misreading the signs...

"Sand!" Jaime exclaimed suddenly—and unhappily. He took up an admonishing stance and stared at one of his young assistants, a handsome New Yorker of Nicaraguan descent named Hector. "Sand!" he repeated.

Hector shrugged and came running forward with his little brush, carefully removing every spec of the offending sand from Madison's buttocks.

"Thanks," she murmured.

He winked at her with a casual shrug. "Bugger of a job, Madison, but someone's got to do it."

She smiled back. He wasn't being offensive. He was Jaime's lover.

"And I get to hold the sun shields!" George Nathan, Jaime's other assistant, said with a sigh as he checked a light meter. George was sandy-haired, lanky, a recent graduate of the University of Miami. He'd already won a number of prizes for his own photography, but he was working with Jaime to learn from the best.

"Sun shields are important," Hector assured him.

"But sand is more fun."

"Boys, we're working here!" Jaime commented with an exaggerated sigh. "Once again, same look, Madison, sultry, dreamy... Okay, she needs the scarves now. Okay, with the scarves, Madison, you play. Just play. Have fun. Run with them, keep them flying in the breeze. We are showing that dreams are spun like fine silk, that they float in the air, that they are what we make them, yes, you understand? Go with it, run with it...."

She did. Jaime was good, the best. She was certain he could have talked a five-hundred-pound bearded lady into feeling that she could be dressed up and dusted off to look just like Cinderella on her way to the ball. Playing with the silk scarves, running up and down the sand, was fun. Hard work, because—despite the fact that it was growing late in the afternoon—the sun remained intense and Jaime seemed to be taking thousands of pictures. They'd been at it all day. The stylist and makeup woman had left after the last break, and Jaime kept promising that they would be done any minute. His concept of a minute was apparently a bit different from the norm, but he brought out the very best in her, and she knew it.

At a brief pause in the shooting—with Hector once again dusting her flesh free from sand—she was stunned to look up and see Kyle Montgomery standing in the back, beside Jaime and Michelle. He was talking with them but watching Madison. He was dressed for the beach in nothing but a pair of pale blue cutoff jeans. His head was bare; he wore sandals on his feet and, in the sun, his inevitable sunglasses. He looked a lot more like part of the shoot than a dedicated FBI agent. Dark hair fell casually over his forehead; his flesh was incredibly bronzed and covered with a sheen of sweat. He might have been a lifeguard.

At times, she mused, he had been. He had worked as a lifeguard during his last two summers before college.

That was a long time ago. He was no longer a local boy.

So what was he doing here? He was supposed to be working.

Despite herself, she felt her blood begin to race. Her heart pounded; breathing became difficult. She wished Kyle had stayed in Washington.

She commanded her knees to quit feeling so weak. She chided herself in silence for letting him affect her in any way. She wondered whether, if she closed her eyes, he would disappear.

She tried it. He didn't.

Jaime indicated with a smile that Kyle was welcome to go talk with Madison. Kyle nodded, then started walking toward her. The casual beach-boy look of his clothing was immediately belied as she felt his damning stare, despite the darkness of his glasses. He stopped dead in front of her, and she was certain that he was using all his willpower not to reach for her and shake her.

''What are you doing here?'' she asked him, annoyed to realize that she didn't sound at all casual. Her voice was irritatingly shrill. She couldn't quite seem to control it around him.

''Trying not to slap you silly,'' he responded irritably.

''Why? What the hell is the matter with you?''

she asked. She was genuinely puzzled, and her tone was curious.

"You," he said simply, snatching his glasses from his face as he stared at her, eyes as sharp as green gems. "You!" he repeated, and he appeared restless and angry, running his fingers through his hair in an aggravated manner. "Damn you, Madison, what the hell are you doing here?"

Startled by the depth of his anger, she replied, "Excuse me, this is my job. I belong here. Actually, at the moment, I'm being exceptionally good. I'm working gratis for the community. You got angry when I was involved in your work. Well, I've taken myself far away from it, and far from you, so just what the hell is your problem?" She was proud of herself. She had spoken in a very even tone.

"It didn't occur to you to tell anyone where you were going?" he demanded furiously.

"Darryl knows where I am—he has Carrie Anne."

"Darryl! That's it?"

"Wait, now, let me think. Should I have told the father of my child—who would be taking care of that child!—where I was going, or should I have thought, no, no, let me tell the stepbrother I haven't seen in more than five years? The one who isn't satisfied with a single thing I do?"

He did grab her then. He reached for her arm with a sudden movement that was violent in its sheer speed, drawing her closer to him, as if he needed to make sure that she could hear his every word. "No, Madison, not me. Maybe your sister, your father, someone else."

She tried to pull free, but he wouldn't let her go. She opted against the indignity of struggling.

"I left quite suddenly. I intended to call Dad when the shoot was done today, to let him know I'd be at his place, since he's back up in Miami getting ready for your father's show. But then, my father isn't down here acting like Henry the Eighth."

"Irresponsible little bitch!" he muttered.

Madison was completely stunned by the depth of the anger in his voice. She stiffened and forced herself to remain cool and collected. "Really? I'm so sorry you don't approve. But I need to be responsible to Carrie Anne, not to you. And I would have called my family—"

"I thought I'd made you aware that there's a serial killer on the loose!"

Madison held her breath, feeling as if icy waves of fury were cascading over her and giving her new strength. "There's always a serial killer on the loose somewhere, isn't there? I mean, isn't that why you have your job?"

"This is different and you damned well know it."

"So how did you find me?"

"I called everyone—including Darryl."

Madison bit into her lower lip and sighed. "Look, you didn't want me involved. I'm staying away."

"Madison, damn it, they're all redheads. Every last one of the victims—"

"They're redheads, and they're women, and they're young. And I have the intelligence to be careful, Kyle."

He frowned. "You knew they were all redheads?"

"You just told me so."

"But you knew before I told you."

"The girl in the vision I had was a redhead. That's all I knew. Kyle, I can't stop living because I'm a young woman with red hair!"

"Damn you, Madison—" he began, but he broke off, wincing, because Jaime was calling out to them.

"Agent Montgomery?" Jaime came hurrying over. He was obviously concerned. "I know how important your work is, Lieutenant, but if your conversation could wait just a few minutes more... We're ready for the next shots, and we're losing our light."

"I think the agent is done," Madison said.

"No, he isn't done," Kyle said, staring at her hard, his dark lenses back in place. "But I can wait," he added politely.

"Don't you need to get back to Miami? Follow up on some clues?"

"I'm with you, Madison. Talking with the psychic. I am working."

"Madison?" Jaime said anxiously.

"I'm ready," she said, staring at Kyle.

He walked back to join the others. Madison was painfully aware of him, standing with his arms crossed over his bare chest, watching as the shoot continued.

He made her feel awkward. Like a little kid again, trying to play dress-up, trying to be beautiful, mature, impressive.

Jaime started sighing.

Hector went into a fury of sand-dusting, which seemed to make everything worse.

"Come on, Madison, we're losing the light. Remember, this is for the hopes and dreams of lots of people!" Michelle said, wrinkling her nose. "I had help, Madison. My mama was on welfare. I'm not. We're working to make people believe they can create a better tomorrow.''

"*Sí, sí,*" Jaime said. "Good speech, but, Madison, I don't want a militant look here. We're not burning bras. Right now, we're going for soft. Sexy.''

"All she has to do to look sexy is be awake," Michelle said, complimenting her chosen model.

"She'd be sexy as all hell eyes closed, sound asleep," George added in a husky tone.

"Play with the camera, play with it!" Jaime reminded her. "Make love to it, yes…?"

She wanted to kill Kyle. This was an important shoot. She had to forget that he was there. She had to be completely professional. She didn't know why Kyle made her feel as if she were a little girl, pretending she knew what she was doing. Somehow, she had to forget him!

Sure.

And so she began to use the fact that he was there. She would never be able to laugh and play and flirt with Kyle. She might as well be seductive through the camera.

She hoped she could make him suffer.

She played with the camera. She laughed, smiled, pouted, posed. She felt the luxury of the silk in her hands, felt the sun, the sand, the sheer sensuality of the day shimmering around her. The sun, sinking against the horizon. Touching, feeling. She was damned well going to be sexy. She was going to show him what he'd chosen to throw away all his life.

At last the light was gone. By that time, though,

Jaime was as happy as a clam. Michelle, too, was delighted, Hector was assuring her that she'd just made him bisexual, and George was sweating.

Kyle was completely impassive.

Hector slipped a robe over her shoulders as she took a bottled water from an ice chest as they wrapped up. She knew that Kyle was behind her.

"I don't know why you hung around. It's boring for onlookers. Sorry, I guess there was something you wanted. Or did you come all the way back down here to yell at me for not letting more people know I'd be gone a couple of days?"

She swallowed a long drink of her water and looked at him.

His arms were still crossed over his chest; there was no sun left, but he still had those damn glasses on.

"We can talk later. Your friends and admirers want to celebrate a successful shoot and get something to eat."

"Are you referring to my professional associates?" she inquired politely.

"Yeah, the gay guys, the woman and the tech with his tongue hanging in the sand. Them. Your professional associates."

"Is George's tongue really in the sand? How sweet," Madison murmured pleasantly.

"You just might wind up with the wrong man drooling after you, Madison," Kyle warned.

"And then again, there are those men who are completely unaffected," she murmured. "Excuse me, I'd like to change."

She brushed past him, hurrying up to the small

house on the beach that belonged to a friend of Michelle's.

Michelle came in to collect the bathing suits used in the shoot and help her change. Michelle, dressed in a casual, brilliantly colored sarong, was shaking her head in amusement. "My, my."

"My, my, what?"

"That boy, he'd have been fine on the poster, as well. He's a sexy man."

"He's an FBI agent. They aren't allowed to be sexy."

Michelle arched a brow. "He must be mighty fond of you, *chérie*."

"He's mighty mad at me, is what. I'm twenty-six, but apparently I didn't ask the proper permission to leave town."

Michelle made a *tsk*ing sound, shaking her head, smiling in an annoyingly knowing manner. "People only worry when they care. There are only angry when they care deeply."

"Well, of course, I suppose…he cares about me. In his way. We were stepsiblings at one time."

"Stepbrothers do not naturally care about stepsisters. Especially when… Well, your mama died and the relationship ended, yes?"

"My mother was murdered, and I look like my mother, and no one was able to help her. I think he has a strange sense of feeling responsible that nothing bad should happen to me."

"You do look just like you mother, *chérie*. Just like."

"Exactly. It's all psychological. He has this idea set in his head that something might happen to me, too."

"Looks *can* kill, sweetie. You be glad that big strong boy is looking after you. Now, if it were me..."

Madison tied the cotton halter dress she was wearing and looked at Michelle. "If it were you?"

Michelle winked. "I'd sleep with him."

"I should sleep with a man just because he's concerned about me?"

"No, no, you should sleep with him because he has good arms, a nice chest...and a good butt, too, I think. Nice skin, rugged, masculine, very good face. Take that from an artist."

Madison couldn't help laughing. "The goods measure up?"

"You're a young woman. You want to sleep with a wrinkly old man?"

"No, I don't want to sleep with a wrinkly old man—until I'm a wrinkly old woman. Honestly, Michelle, women aren't supposed to sleep with men just because they have good bodies. There's supposed to be a magic, a desire...." Michelle was staring at her with arched brows. Madison let out a long sigh. "I just never thought of making love with a guy simply because I'd inspected him and he had the proper body!" She was only lying a little.

"Then you are the only woman alive who has not looked at a hot body and wondered at the fantasy of a stranger. Ah, but you want love. Foolish girl. You want to fall in love. Well, let me warn you. Women, *mais oui*, we want to fall in love. We want romance. Men want to have sex. Good sex. Women emote, and men are moved by primal instinct." She waved her dark, elegant fingers in the air expressively. "Men—they think with their anatomy. They look at what a woman's body has to offer. Love is good. But if you want to fall in love…well, love is hard. Sex is easy. Maybe too easy for some people, but right now, for you?'' She quirked a brow, smiling. ''Be daring, *chérie*. You may look like a Barbie doll, *oui?* But you are real, and must live and breathe and make love, eh?'' Again, she smiled. ''This may be the age of electronics, but there is nothing like a flesh-and-blood man. Especially for a Barbie doll.''

''What does *that* mean?''

''Good things. That you are reserved. You spend your time with family, with little Carrie Anne. I'm trying to tell you to take a chance. Be daring.''

''Sometimes,'' Madison said slowly, ''chances aren't good. Other people can get hurt.''

''And *you* can get hurt. It's part of the way it goes. Pain can be the greatest teacher. It can be good. That way, we know when there is pleasure and happiness, as well. *Non, ma chérie?*'' Smiling like the Cheshire cat, Michelle waited for her reply.

''Michelle, he's the wrong hunk for me. He thinks I'm a witch.''

''Witches can be good. Earthy. Nurturing. And very sexy.''

''Michelle, you're hopeless. And you don't un-derstand. Kyle and I have…a past.''

''No, *chérie,* you don't understand. The past is gone, the future lies ahead, and the present is to be lived.''

Smiling, Michelle left, closing the door behind her.

Madison walked to the window and looked out. Michelle was talking to Kyle, her laughter melodic.

"Flirt!" Madison murmured, shaking her head as she watched her friend.

It was nearly eight o'clock, and the brilliant array of colors—oranges, crimsons, mauves, pinks, blues and golds—that streaked the sky with sunset was fading to gray.

Kyle, she saw, was watching the sky, as well. Listening to Michelle, but watching the sky. Sometimes, when she was young, they had sat together in silence in the late afternoons, watching as the sun went down. She knew that he loved the colors of sunset as much as she did. How had he stayed away from home so long?

She shook her head and swept up her purse, impatient with her moment of nostalgia. "Why can't they make that man go to work from nine to five? Who the hell gave him permission to come down here in the middle of a case?" she muttered irritably to herself.

Madison walked out of the house, telling herself that she was cool, collected and ready to meet the others.

"I think we're almost ready. George is getting the last of our equipment," Hector told her cheerfully. She stood with him while they waited, watching as Kyle talked to Michelle, a few steps away, until he excused himself to take a call on his cellular phone.

George finished packing the equipment, and he, Michelle and Jaime joined Madison and Hector. George told a joke, but Madison discovered that she wasn't listening. She felt an uneasy sensation slipping over her, as if she were being watched.

She looked around. Beach behind her, the house before her, foliage, now rustling in the night sea breeze, scattered across the area between homes in the exclusive private neighborhood. She could see no one, nothing suspicious, and she couldn't even get a feel for an area from which someone might be watching her.

There were gates and a security guard outside the small compound of private homes. It was so unlikely that anyone could be watching them.

And still, goose bumps covered her arms.

Kyle finished his call, clicked his phone shut and returned to them.

"Well, then, where shall we go?" Jaime asked.

Everyone chimed in with a suggestion. Except for Madison.

She didn't care where they went, as long as they left. Except that even once they started driving, she still had that uncomfortable feeling of being watched.

Kaila was tired, bone-weary, in body, in spirit. Dan's flowers had been great—but a poor substitute for him. She'd gotten the flowers...

And then a phone call. He had to be out of town for a few days. He was so sorry. He would make it up to her. He loved her.

Yeah, yeah, yeah.

Anna had stayed home sick; it had been hour after hour of the kids squabbling, spilling, spitting up. She'd reminded herself all day that kids did those things, that she loved her kids, that she'd wanted kids.

She just hadn't planned on raising them alone.

But at eight, they were all in bed at last. She walked into her bedroom, stripping as she went. She was usually careful. Kyle had warned her sternly to be careful, and she loved Kyle, knew that he loved her and was concerned about her safety. But she was tired. And so she forgot to draw the drapes and blinds throughout the house.

She left her jeans, T-shirt underwear and bra in a pool on her bedroom floor—she just hadn't been able to bear the scent of spit-up on herself one minute longer. She drew the water for her shower, then wrapped her hair on top of her head and covered it with a shower cap while she waited for the water to grow warm. She stepped beneath the spray, felt the tension-relieving jets of the water, then turned the tap to make her shower even warmer. God, it felt good. If she wasn't afraid of falling asleep and drowning, she would have taken a bubble bath. As it was, just standing under the hot water was great, feeling it beat down all around her.

But then...

She thought she heard something. Like the glass doors that connected the master bedroom to the pool and patio sliding open.

Despite the heat of the water, she froze.

And waited, listening...

It had been a very long day for Jassy, dramatic in many ways, exciting, frightening.

She was sometimes amazed herself at her ability to sympathize with the victims of violent crime, yet still turn to the sleuthing of pathology with such energy and passion. An interviewer had once asked her if she felt guilty, cutting into the bodies of those who had met with violent ends. She had assured the young reporter that although she often felt sorry that she had to cut into a victim, she didn't feel guilty in the least. The dead could no longer speak; they couldn't seek justice for the violence done against them. With her work, she could seek the justice that the dead could not.

With the discovery of the torso, they were now able to analyze the stomach contents of the deceased. Now, with some good investigative footwork, the police could find out where Holly Tyler had eaten her last meal. From there, they could begin to comb the area hotels and motels, and through luck or some heavenly intervention maybe find the place where Holly had been killed, find witnesses to her arrival there, witnesses who had seen the killer.

She was on a satisfied high when she finally got home that night.

She glanced at her watch, delighted to realize that any minute, the new man in her life would be arriving. She felt a giddy excitement, a feeling unlike anything she had felt since high school, for God's sake! This was so wonderful, so exciting, such a sheer high.

And he loved her, too.

Fifteen minutes.

She slammed her door shut, already crawling out of the clothing she'd been wearing at the morgue all day. Fifteen minutes wasn't a lot of time.

She dropped her shoes and lab coat in the living room, then struggled out of her skirt and panty hose as she moved down the hallway. By the time she reached her bedroom, she was nearly ripping off the buttons on her white tailored blouse and feeling for the back catch on her bra. Her trail of clothing behind her, she jumped into the shower before turning on the water, then squealed with surprise as an icy spray met her face. Muttering, she warmed the water.

Well, the cold had certainly given her a jolt of energy!

She reached for her solid off-the-shelf deodorant soap, then remembered the scented stuff she'd gotten for Christmas. Dripping, she jumped out of the shower, dug under the sink and found her perfumed gel. It was great. She lathered heavily with it—twice in all the intimate places.

Now...what to wear when she got out?

Nothing, she decided. Nothing except her gold dangle earrings, her sapphire pendant and her anklet. That would do it.

But even as she decided on not choosing a wardrobe, she shivered, certain that she had heard a distant clicking sound. She pondered over it briefly.

Oh, shit! Had she locked the front door?

Killer watched the woman he loved.

Of course, his name wasn't really Killer, and he loved all women. Still, she was special.

He called himself Killer because he liked it. Because it was a hardy, swaggering, masculine name.

And, of course, because he was a killer. Talented, clever. And they were all such fools.

He watched her...fascinated.

Watched her move with quick, lithe grace. Watched the clothing fall from her perfect form. She had beautiful breasts, high, firm, perfect. Her hair shimmered over her naked shoulders. She turned around, and he trembled, thinking about touching her. She had a great ass. And she was different. He already knew she was different. For one thing, she knew him. Knew him well, not casually. This wasn't a well-orchestrated but casual pickup, like the others. This time, it could work. She could love him, too. Really love him. She might be the rich scent and sweet softness without...the thorns.

And he might not have to...

Kill her.

She moved again. Soon she would be out of his sight. This was so good, watching her, seeing her, without her knowing that he saw, watched. That he dreamed of tasting her. She didn't know how good a lover he was going to be. Maybe, sometime, he would have to hurt her. Just so that she understood that she wasn't to try to hurt him. And so that she could know just how great her pleasure could be after pain.

He would take it slow with her. So slow...

He started suddenly, unhappily aware of an uneasy feeling—as if he were being watched himself. He looked around quickly, frowning. No one, no one, no one, could see him, except maybe...

The other one. The one he *really* wanted. One day, oh, God, yes, one day! He suddenly felt giddy. She looked and looked and looked, but she couldn't see! he thought exultantly.

He'd seen her!

While she...she couldn't see the forest for the trees. They were all so blind. He felt like laughing as an old biblical saying came to mind.

There are none so blind as those that will not see! Still...

She could prove to be dangerous. And if she came too close, if she threatened him...

It would be slow with her. Because it would be the same as it had been so very long ago. He would adore her, even as he despised her. She was the threat. And he would let her see every single little thing he would do to her, with her.

For the moment, he looked out from the shadows and waited patiently for the clouds to cover the moon before he made another move.

Jassy Adair was certain that they would catch the killer soon. Kyle knew his business, and his profile was undoubtedly an accurate picture of their killer: a handsome, articulate man who could easily charm his way into the trust of women. A man who spent the majority of his time living a seemingly normal life, accepted by his family and peers.

Thanks to her sister, they knew what kind of room to be looking for, and when they homed in closer, she was sure, Madison would be of even greater help. Science and spirituality—or whatever it was that Madison had—could work hand in hand. Science could prove the truth of Madison's visions.

The killer would be caught....

Then she heard a noise, and she wondered again if she had locked the door. Suddenly she was praying that *she* would live to see the killer caught.

She leaped out of the shower, grabbing her towel. Sopping-wet, she tore down the hallway, even though logic was telling her it was the wrong thing to do. She needed to darken the house and somehow make her way to the back door.

Too late.

He was already there.

Dead still, soaking in her towel, she stared at him.

"Doors should be kept locked," he said, very softly. "You should know, doors should be kept locked. You, of all people..." He sighed. "You'll learn."

She opened her mouth to speak.

Words wouldn't come. Because he was already stepping forward. "You're so beautiful. So perfect and beautiful. And the way you talk about body parts..."

Kaila wrapped a towel around herself, letting the water continue to run. She stepped very carefully to the bathroom door and looked cautiously around it, doing her best to keep herself hidden.

Someone was in her house.

Her instinct was to slam the door and lock herself in. She thought of her cell phone, tucked away in her purse by her bed.

She couldn't slam the door; her children were in the house. She had to protect them.

She stared out the bathroom door for what seemed like an eternity. Silently she slid around it. She couldn't see anyone in her bedroom.

But the glass door was partially open. A breeze was lifting the half-closed curtain.

Tentatively, her heart in her throat, she walked toward it.

"Kaila?"

At the sound of her name, she screamed, spinning around, dropping her towel.

Dan stood in the doorway. He had an ice bucket with a bottle of champagne in one hand, two stemmed glasses balanced in the other.

"God, honey, I'm sorry. I called to you when I

got home. The trip's off. I guess you didn't hear me over the water.''

"You nearly scared me to death."

"Honey, I am *so* sorry!" He walked past her, set down the ice bucket, champagne and glasses and closed and latched the glass door, then turned back to her. She hadn't retrieved her towel. He smiled, looking handsome, ruffled, worn, and glad to be home. When she did start to reach for the towel, he approached her quickly. "Honey, don't. You look like a million bucks. I'm sorry about working so much, honest to God. I just can't seem to get out of it...but I do love you, Kaila. You and the kids mean more to me than anything in the world. I swear it." He drew her against him, wrapping her in his arms. She was wet and chilly in the air-conditioned room, and he was very warm. He felt good and secure, and she was suddenly glad of him, wanting him. He could touch her, kiss her, lick her anywhere, and it would feel natural and delicious. It was just that she'd been married so long....

"I love you," she told him.

"I'm off all day tomorrow. I'll take care of the kids from morning till night."

"Oh, God, Dan, that's the most romantic thing I've ever heard!" she told him gratefully.

He started to kiss her, first her lips, then the length of her naked body. His tongue snaked over her flesh, between her thighs...

Stepping up into Jaime's van, Madison suddenly shivered fiercely. She sat in the front passenger seat, buckling her seat belt, fighting the vision that was clouding her mind.

She saw shadows, but within the shadows, two lovers, intimately entwined with one another.

She couldn't really see the people, and she had the awful feeling of intruding on something that was not just intimate but warm and special. She could see that...

The woman was a redhead.

She wasn't watching them through her own eyes, she realized.

Strange words ran through her mind.

Killer is watching, Killer is watching....

The vision faded suddenly.

All that remained was the memory that the woman was a redhead.

And the words...

Killer is watching, Killer is watching...

They kept repeating, a refrain that haunted her mind. And she knew that no matter what argument they might be having, she was going to have to tell Kyle what she had seen with her strange mind's eye.

9

Madison smoothed her hair, collecting herself and ignoring the others as they argued over where they should go for dinner.

The voice and its haunting refrain faded completely, and Madison began feeling rather silly. She was frightened, yet not in a tangible way. She was surrounded by people; she was safe.

Hell, she even had her own personal FBI agent following right behind the van in his rental car.

She realized that Jaime was staring at her, frowning with concern. He had left the decision of where to go to Hector and George, who had agreed on a rustic crab house near Sloppy Joe's.

"You all right?" Jaime asked her as he helped her out of the van. "You look like you've seen a ghost."

"I'm fine, honest."

He suddenly reached forward, pinching her cheeks. It hurt. "Jaime!" she protested.

"That's better! You don't want the government asking the same question, do you?" he queried, arching a brow devilishly.

She started to protest again, then shrugged. "Do I look better?"

"Ah, Madison, you look stunning! If looks could kill, you'd be lethal! Come on now."

He linked an arm with hers. And though the place was crowded, he had the right pull. They were quickly seated.

She had expected that Kyle might feel awkward at dinner, being a stranger to everyone but Madison, but he actually seemed more comfortable than she did. Everyone knew about his father's upcoming gallery opening, and their enthusiasm for Roger Montgomery's work and commitment, were contagious. Madison, relaxing, forgot the strange sensation of being watched that had seized her earlier. The restaurant was boisterous, but not too loud. The company was very pleasant, laid-back.

Kyle was even being merciful and not hounding her about the fact that she had left town without telling anyone. In fact, he assured her early on during dinner that her father knew she was going to be at his house; Jordan Adair had talked with Darryl that afternoon. Then Michelle diverted his attention, but Madison didn't care. She was finally beginning to unwind. The company and drinks were numbing her mind. Even memories of her vision were fading. Then, as they talked, she was startled to hear a pleased squeal from across the room. With an alarming feel of dismay, she watched as a petite dynamo hurried across the room to them. Sheila.

"Madison! What a lovely coincidence! And Kyle Montgomery. What a pleasure."

"Sheila, what a surprise!" Madison said helplessly. Kyle pulled out a chair for Sheila, and Madison introduced her to the others. "Sheila plays keyboards with the Storm Fronts."

"Yes, of course, your delightful musical group!" Jaime said with pleasure. "I've seen you play with Madison, but we have never been formally introduced." He kissed Sheila's hand in greeting.

Sheila was delighted. "Naturally, I know your work, as well! It's spectacular!"

"You're too kind," Jaime protested. "Well, now and then, we all have a stroke of genius, *sí?*"

"Sheila, we'd love to have you stay with us," Madison said. God, she was lying through her teeth! And Sheila was a friend! "Of course, we'll understand if you're here with friends."

"What luck! I was here celebrating my sister's birthday, but she and her husband—and even Mom and Dad—have just left."

"What luck," Madison agreed.

Sheila joined them, advising them on the local beers. Madison hadn't planned on having anything with alcohol, but now she changed her mind. The fresh catch was dolphin, which they ordered for the table, along with a shrimp-wrapped-in-bacon appetizer and conch chowder.

The conversation turned first to music, then to art. Madison, at her end of the table, far from Kyle and Sheila, listened as Kyle avidly joined in the discussion. She watched him, thinking about how he so seldom let others see his own talent. But beyond that, it seemed that he really did love art and had a greater appreciation for his father's interests than she had ever imagined.

He caught her watching him once. And it was a strange moment, because she knew that he was reading *her* thoughts, but somehow that made him strangely vulnerable to her.

A nice switch, she thought.

Conversation was easy. They all laughed. Madison felt comfortable, relaxed, secure.

It was inevitable, though, that someone would ask Kyle about his work.

"I read about some of your work once in *Time*," George said. "Can you tell us what you're doing down here? Is it that serial killer the papers have been writing about?"

"Well, we definitely believe we have a serial killer on the loose in the area," Kyle said solemnly. "Most of the recent developments will be making the late news tonight. Like my breaking into Madison's house," he added dryly.

"What?" she asked, startled.

He shrugged, looking around at the others again. "Over the last four months, there have been four gruesome murders, all occurring around the fifteenth of the month, and each growing more and more violent. The victims were all young, beautiful, vivacious women. When you're working with something so heinous, you have a tendency to worry about the people around you."

"Dear Lord," Sheila murmured, leaning an elbow on the table and propping her head on her hand as she looked at him. She shuddered fiercely.

"And...you broke into Madison's house in pursuit of this killer?" Michelle demanded, confused.

Kyle shook his head, smiling ruefully. "As I said, this killer is preying on young, beautiful women. I couldn't get in touch with Madison last night, and then...when I couldn't reach her this morning, either..." He lifted his hands helplessly, then took a long swig of his beer, staring at Madison again.

"Her lock was easy to pick, but she has a good alarm system. I'd told Jimmy Gates down in homicide that I was going in, but...well, I almost got myself arrested anyway, and I'm wondering right now just how ridiculous I'm going to look on the news."

"I didn't answer my phone, so you broke into my house?" Madison said incredulously.

"Madison, you shouldn't be so snippy!" Sheila advised her.

"Sheila, I'm not! I'm just surprised."

"Thank God you've got a stepbrother who cares so much! If someone in my family couldn't reach me, they probably wouldn't worry for a week!"

Kyle arched a brow to Madison, obviously enjoying the fact that her friends thought she was the one in the wrong.

"Sheila, you're always going off for days at a time," Madison reminded her.

"Well, you still shouldn't be angry!" Sheila said.

"Are you angry?" Hector demanded, grinning at Madison. He looked amused, out to cause trouble.

Everyone was staring at her. She stared at Kyle, gritting her teeth. "Of course not. I told you—I'm not angry, I'm surprised."

"Surprised! *I'm* scared. A serial killer, preying on young women!" Sheila said, and shivered.

"A little fear can be healthy, I'm certain," Jaime said.

"Do you agree, Kyle?" Michelle asked in her soft singsong. "Is it smart for women to be afraid?"

"A little fear can be very healthy. The police weren't exactly trying to keep the killings quiet, at first, but they didn't want to cause a panic, either.

But as of this afternoon, it's been officially decided that it's time to cause a bit of a panic. From comments made to friends by the victims, we're certain that the killer is a charming young man who is seducing his victims into believing they're in for the love affair of a lifetime. He's most probably very good-looking, blends in with a crowd, appears entirely respectable. Not in the least the image of a crazed killer. So, Sheila, you should be concerned. It would be wise for you to be very careful.''

"You know," Hector murmured, "if you're curious about the news... Well, it's gotten late. Maybe they'll have the eleven-o'clock news on at the bar.''

They stared at one another briefly, then rose in one body, moving to the bar. Kyle remained slightly in the background. As the news moved from the latest terrorism in the Mideast to local-interest stories, a police spokeswoman giving a press release appeared on the screen. She said that the police believed that they were investigating four murders that were the work of a single killer, and that young women needed to be seriously on the alert, especially women, and women living alone.

Listening, Madison found herself worrying about Jassy. She told herself that her sister was smart. Besides, she still thought Kyle might be the man her sister was seeing, and if so...

She was going to call Jassy. She had to make sure her sister knew what she was doing.

She blinked. The news was still centered on the killer. There was an interview with Jimmy Gates, who gave out the information that friends of the victims had told police that before each disappearance, the murdered young women had been looking forward to time away with a new romantic interest.

Then there was suddenly a shot of Kyle. He was in his suit, in front of Madison's house. There were police cars everywhere. Kyle looked worn and very aggravated—but still handsome and appealing. He was shown talking with Jimmy as Jimmy arrived at the scene, then he spoke briefly with the press, recommending that women in the area be advised to use extreme caution in accepting any invitations. "Don't go out with strangers. Period. Even if you think you know someone, double-date. Don't go anywhere without a friend knowing your exact destination and who you're with. Leave work in groups, shop with a girlfriend."

"Should women be armed?" a pretty reporter asked anxiously.

"If a woman is going to be armed, she needs to know what she's doing with a weapon, period. A gun is never a guarantee of safety. Bear in mind how many children have been killed with a family gun. To me, the best way to stay safe is to stay smart and cautious."

"What about women living alone?" the same reporter queried.

Kyle had been solemn; now he suddenly smiled. One of those rare smiles of pure charm that sent hearts racing. "Well, if possible, move back home for a while," he suggested.

"Good idea!" someone called.

"And if that's not possible, the main thing here

is to be smart, be careful and don't make yourself vulnerable.''

There were more questions, coming faster and faster, like bullets themselves.

Kyle answered tersely, especially when he was asked why he was at the home of Madison Adair, daughter of the slain movie star, Lainie Adair, his onetime stepsister.

''In fact, sir, didn't you just break into her house?''

''Were you arrested and handcuffed?''

Kyle fielded the questions well, ignoring what he chose to ignore and replying that—naturally—any man was concerned about the young women in his family under these circumstances. Yes, he admitted, he had been worried about his stepsister, but he had since been advised that Madison Adair was fine and away working on a fashion shoot.

Madison noticed that he didn't say where.

When he excused himself and walked away from the interview, the camera focused on the pretty newswoman who had hit him with the most questions. She had done her homework well. She rehashed Lainie's murder and ''scandalous'' life, then brought up Madison's work, her resemblance to her mother and her occasional involvement with the police. By the time the newscast was finished, Madison wanted to sink into the floor.

At the same time, she felt like an absolute ingrate, certain that the news hadn't managed to capture the entire event. Kyle had nearly been arrested for breaking into her house, all because he had been worried.

About *her*.

She looked back at Kyle, who shrugged irritably. "At least they missed the fact that I was nearly shot as an intruder before I had a chance to flash my ID."

"Thanks for worrying," she murmured. "And I'm sorry. I guess, under the circumstances, I should have called Jassy or Dad before taking off, as well as Darryl." She sighed with weary exasperation. "That damned newswoman! She didn't miss any of my life. We got to go through my mother's death all over again."

"Ah, child!" Michelle commiserated.

"They showed your house—right on television. Can't you sue them for that or something?" Sheila asked.

"I don't think so," Madison murmured. "I don't think it matters, anyway. Where I live has never been a big secret."

Kyle was staring at her. He wasn't pleased. From his look, she knew he was thinking that it probably hadn't mattered before if her address was publicly known.

But it did now.

"Well," Michelle said, "this killer will have to think twice now. With such a warning out, surely young women will be very careful."

Kyle shook his head very slowly. "If only that were true. If only they all understood the point. This man is extremely clever—and charming. Most rational people feel that such violent murders must be the work of a madman. They're sure they would recognize such a man, that he must look like a monster, when his real power lies in his ability to appear to be not just respectable, but secure. A protector of the innocent. Hopefully we'll have alerted at least some of his possible victims, and maybe we'll slow him down long enough to catch him.''

Michelle shook her head and made the sign of the cross over her chest. Hector followed suit. Madison was tempted to do likewise as she stared at Kyle.

''Oh dear,'' Sheila murmured, ''what a depressing end to such a wonderful evening.'' She stood very close to Kyle, smiling up at him. ''I admit I'm afraid to go home alone now.''

''Kyle has a car, he'll see you home,'' Madison said, even though she hated the thought of Kyle driving Sheila home.

Was she protecting Jassy? she thought, mocking herself.

She felt a little sick inside. Jassy was newly in love. If it wasn't Kyle, could it be…?

Oh, God, she had to talk to her sister.

''That would be wonderful,'' Sheila said, staring at Kyle. She appeared so petite, charming and wide-eyed with trusting adoration that Madison wanted to shake her.

''Sure,'' Kyle said, staring at Madison. ''We'll take Sheila home before going to your father's place.''

Sheila looked disgruntled; it wasn't quite what she'd had in mind. But she acquiesced, and it seemed that she really was somewhat nervous. She livened up, however, on the drive to her house, chatting away with Kyle in the front seat. She talked about being alone and how much she usually loved her independence. ''Of course, now…but I refuse to allow an animal like that to ruin my life! I don't ever want to talk about him anymore. Madison, I hear your father is attending a gallery opening sponsored by Kyle's father. How intriguing that they remained such good friends.''

"The opening is Sunday," Kyle told her. "We'd love to have you."

"Why, I'd love to come with you. Thank you so very much."

Kyle frowned. "Sheila, I didn't—"

"Oh, there's the house, right there. I'll just run in quickly. I've got my key—of course, I'm all thumbs right now. I hate to be such a nervous Nellie, but would you please come with me and just take a quick look around...?"

Madison kept quiet, all but seething in the back seat. Sheila knew damned well that Kyle hadn't asked her to the gallery opening on a date; it had been a general invitation. But Sheila had stated plainly that she was going to make a play for him, and that was what she was doing.

Kyle parked the car in front of Sheila's. But he didn't follow Sheila along the walk. He got out and looked into the back seat, at Madison. "Come on."

"I'll just stay here and wait for you. I think she wants a kiss good-night."

He shook his head, a slight smile on his lips. "Madison, surely you've seen enough slasher movies. The guy leaves one girl alone in the car, and, well, you know where it goes from there. I'm not leaving you alone. Come with me."

"I'm not in any danger."

"How do you know?"

"I'd sense it."

He shook his head and was suddenly grave. "I think that's my main paranoia in all this. I'm really afraid that you won't sense it if you do become endangered yourself. Besides…''

"What?"

"You might not be in danger, but I am."

"From…?"

"Sheila," he said bluntly. "Get out. Come with me."

"Sheila is just as cute as a button."

"Yes, she is. Now come on, Madison, get out!" He hesitated. "Please?"

With a deep sigh, she obliged. They walked Sheila to the house, where Kyle managed to explain rather charmingly that he couldn't actually bring Sheila as his date, since he was obliged to be his father's gofer for the evening. Sheila promised that she would be there even so, and said that if she could help in any way, any way at all, well, she would be delighted to do so.

They left Sheila's place and drove out to Jordan Adair's waterfront estate. Martique was there, sleepily greeting them in the foyer, despite the quiet with which they approached the house. She quickly went back to bed, and they were alone, facing one another, once again.

Madison was going to tease Kyle about Sheila and the way he'd managed to wriggle out of an actual date, but he turned on her like a Doberman.

"Madison, I'm being dead serious, and you're going to listen to me and pay attention. The news is out. And people will panic. Half the women in Miami will be buying handguns by tomorrow. I just pray that there won't be any accidental deaths caused by someone who's frightened and trigger-happy. But I'm telling you, Madison, and I mean it—don't go off without letting me know again. *Me.* You made a fool out of me today, and you might have put yourself into grave danger.''

"Kyle! Damn it, I'm grateful, but I didn't do anything. You made a fool out of yourself. I appreciate the fact that you were worried, but you're not responsible for me.''

"No? Well, you're not fit to be responsible for yourself, so someone has to be." He dragged his fingers impatiently through his hair. "Madison, give me a break here.''

"All right, Kyle, I won't make a move without your permission!" she muttered sarcastically.

He ignored the sarcasm. "Good," he told her flatly.

"Fine," she agreed.

"Good night.''

"Good night.''

She turned around and started down the hallway to her bedroom.

"Madison!" he said, calling her back.

"What?" she asked, turning to him. She felt strangely on fire. They were here, together. Martique was here, too, but she had retired to her own little room out back, beyond the pool. Madison had been living so many fantasies regarding him. She was breathless, frightened, burning....

"Madison, have you noticed something?''

"What?''

He hesitated. "Well, I've been gone a long time, but...?''

"Yes?''

"Well, Jimmy usually calls on you not so much because you can feel and see from the victim's point of view, but because..." He hesitated as she frowned at him. "Sometimes you can see the killer, as well. This time you can't seem to get so much as a glimpse of the killer. What do you think that means?"

She shook her head, swallowing tightly, because he was right.

"I don't know," she told him. "Do you?"

He shook his head. "No, I don't. But it's curious. And frightening," he added softly.

"I'm all right," she said firmly.

He nodded. "You will be. Good night, Madison."

That time, he turned and walked away from her, down his hallway. She heard the door to his bedroom open...

And close.

She gnawed lightly on her lower lip, then turned and walked the distance to her own room. It seemed like a very long walk.

Filled with shadows.

Kyle stayed up late. He plugged in his computer and modem and, despite the hour, contacted Ricky Haines in Virginia. Ricky didn't care. His wife was a chemist with the bureau, and they were both dedicated to their work.

Ricky sounded a little sleepy, but he assured Kyle that he had been running information through the computer all day, investigating the records of tattoo parlors and trying to come up with some connection in the lives of the four women killed. "Nothing yet, but don't worry, we're on the case. How about you?"

"Yeah, I'm on the case. I'm in Key West right now—"

"Key West?"

"My stepsister is the psychic, remember? I followed her down here on a hunch."

"Yeah, sure. You know your stuff, Kyle."

Did he? It hadn't been necessary for him to leave Miami. He'd just been so disturbed, what with the vivid scene in his nightmare and the fact that Madison didn't answer her phone, that he had to see her. It didn't actually fall under business. And if the case began to break while he wasn't even in Miami...

The case wasn't going to break that easily. Unfortunately.

"Ricky, there is one thing."

"What's that, Kyle?"

"They're all redheads."

"Are they? From the one picture—"

"I know, you can't tell. It just appears that she had dark hair. But trust me, every one of the victims was a redhead." He thought of his stepmother. "Work that angle for a while, okay?"

"Sure."

He instructed Ricky to modem the most recent information on the lives of the victims into his PC, then said good-night. He sat for a while, studying the records of all four victims. Debra Miller, Julie Sabor and Holly Tyler had all been single, never married. Maria Garcia had been a divorcée. She'd left behind two small children. Her picture flashed on the screen, and Kyle got a sick feeling, deep in his gut. Sometimes he could be analytical. But sometimes it was impossible not to be human, not to feel the pain.

From what he had, he couldn't connect the women—except for the red hair. They lived and worked in different parts of town. Their jobs were completely different. Debra had been a Miami native, Julie from New York; Maria had been a Cuban immigrant, and Holly Tyler had been born in Minnesota. All that seemed to link them was the fact that they were all redheaded, young, vivacious and attractive. Maybe that *was* all, and maybe that was enough.

Kyle rubbed his forehead, thinking about the methods and motives of serial killers from the past. There was usually something about a woman that sparked something in a killer's mind. What was it? Just the hair, the vivacity? Where was the killer stalking his victims? Bundy had looked to college campuses, assured that he would find plenty of young, beautiful women there. But these women were slightly older, in their late twenties.

He was getting nowhere. And he wasn't nearly as tired as he wanted to be. He just didn't want to shower, then lie awake tossing and turning all night.

Worse. He didn't want to sleep and dream about trying to reach Madison, just down the hallway, and discover the killer lurking between them, his knife glinting in the moonlight.

Still, he turned off the computer and rubbed his eyes. He rose restlessly, then showered. When he'd soaped and scrubbed, he turned the tap all the way to cold. He stayed under the water for a long while, letting his flesh turn icy.

Finally he emerged from the shower and turned out the lights except for the one in the bathroom, which was just inside and to the left of the door to his room. Years of training had taught him to sleep in darkness and shadows while illuminating any possible entrance.

He closed his eyes, but he couldn't sleep. He opened them and stared up at the ceiling.

He could just get up, and walk down the hallway. No pretense. Just ask her if she wanted to sleep with him.

Too obvious. Oh yeah. Definitely too obvious.

He could just walk down the hallway and tell her that he'd gone for a drink of water, then taken a wrong turn while heading back to his bed.

She was probably sound asleep.

He'd seen the damned vision in his head so many times. He would step into her room, and there she would be. Maybe in a towel, maybe in silk. It wouldn't matter. Coverings would drift to the floor. We both want this, let's stop the arguing, let's do it, get on with our lives, get it out of our systems, maybe...

He couldn't do it; just couldn't. He thought that he knew Madison, thought that sometimes, just sometimes, the way she looked at him, the way she smiled when he caught her off guard...damn, the electricity was just there. If they didn't get to it soon...

He heard footsteps suddenly. Soft, furtive, moving quickly, just outside his doorway.

He tensed, throwing his legs over the side of the bed and reaching quickly into the nightstand for his .38 special.

His door opened slowly....

She was caught in the gentle light pooling from the bathroom through the partially closed doorway.

She stood for a moment, blinded, while he sat in the darkness.

She wore silk.

A long emerald silk robe that clung to her body. Curved with it. Her hair spilled over it like a riot of fire in the night.

She had come to him.

10

"Say it again, say it again," Jimmy Gates teased, planting kisses against Jassy's ankle.

She hesitated, laughing. "Morphometric."

"Umm...more," he begged, moving up her calf.

"Periosteum deposits."

"When you talk medical, I just go mad!"

She burst out laughing, pushing at his shoulder, leaping out of bed.

"Hey!"

"I'm thirsty."

"Oh, great. I'm making passionate love and you're after a Pepsi!"

"You're not making passionate love, you're teasing me, and you're making me laugh so hard my ribs hurt! Can I get you anything?"

He patted the bed. "Just you." He paused a moment and shrugged. "And maybe a Michelob."

"A Michelob, coming right up."

Jassy scampered quickly in and out of the kitchen, naked. The light from the bedroom was enough for her to find the refrigerator. She grabbed a Pepsi and a beer, then a bag of chips for good measure, and ran back to the bedroom.

"What a woman!" Jimmy said, his eyes rolling

dramatically. "Body parts, beer and chips—all in bed. How did I live so long without you?"

"Frankly, I don't know," Jassy assured him, plumping up her pillow so that she could lean back and rip open the chips. "Want a chip?"

"Sounds like heaven."

He sat up beside her, munching a chip and reaching for the remote control. He flicked on the television, where a local station was showing a repeat of the eleven-o'clock news. He watched the events of the morning, shaking his head. "We've got to catch this guy." He glanced at Jassy unhappily. "You know, I've never failed to appreciate your sister, or to look out for her interests, when I've asked her to help me, but Kyle has me spooked on this."

"Why?"

"Well, mainly because he keeps mentioning the fact that all the girls were redheads."

"From what I understand, there's usually something that triggers this kind of killer. There was a case in California where a madman went only for brunettes. This man must like redheads. But I... Oh, I see. Madison is a redhead." She was quiet for a minute. "But I can't see why Kyle would be especially worried about Madison. Kaila's a redhead, too."

"Well, I'm sure he's going to worry about Kaila, too, except that she's married, and she's not likely to take off for the weekend with any new man."

"Kyle went down to be with Madison?"

Jimmy nodded, swallowing a long drink of beer.

"Well, that's a relief."

Jimmy frowned. "It sounds as if you're worried about her, too."

"Everyone in the city is going to be spooked by tomorrow. Not that we don't have our share of homicides to begin with! But a serial killer... Yeah, I'm glad he's with my sister. He'll look out for her." Jassy stared at him. "Why do you still look so unhappy?"

"Your stepbrother has *me* spooked, as well. And you know what?"

"No, what?"

"I've been thinking again."

"About what?"

"Lainie Adair."

"Lainie?" Jassy said.

He nodded. "She was definitely a redhead."

Jassy exhaled. "A redhead with a fiery temper, all right."

"You didn't get along with her?"

"Oh, I did! But that's because I always had my head in a book and I was no threat to her whatsoever. And after she and my father divorced... honestly, I was living with Dad, and I didn't see her that often. She just infuriated me sometimes, because..."

"Yeah, why?" Jimmy said, leaning back and studying her with interest.

"You want the truth?"

"Sure."

"She was such a bitch. My father wasn't enough for her. Roger wasn't enough for her. They were both desperately in love with her. She had something, a special quality. Naturally, she was very sexy. And she was a star. The problem with her was that everything became a drama, or a game. She liked pitting my father and Roger against each other.

She wanted every man in her life to think that she was the one woman he could ever really love. My dad never got over her. When she was mad at Roger, she would come running back to Dad. I don't know if they slept together once she married Roger, but if they didn't, it wasn't because she wasn't willing. Oh, Lainie could be charming. She adored her daughters, and I have to admit that she was always great to both Trent and me. But the way that she manipulated men was just awful!''

"Not that either Roger Montgomery or your father could be considered chaste, monogamous men,'' Jimmy reminded her lightly.

"I guess not. Dad once told me—when she was still alive, of course—that he thought Lainie was God's punishment on him for all the mean things he'd done to other people. Who knows, if she hadn't died, she might have had my father and Roger shooting one another!''

"And instead, they're the best of friends."

"Shared misery and anguish,'' Jassy told him. "They drank together all night after Lainie's funeral.''

"It's interesting now to catch either of them when they're watching Madison.''

"Because she's the living image of Lainie."

"Yes.''

"Strange, Kaila looks just like Lainie, too, but there's something different. I think it's because Madison has Lainie's presence. It's in her walk...the way she moves.'' She glanced at Jimmy and added quickly, "Except, of course,'' she added hastily, "that Madison is very different, too.''

"What do you mean?''

"I mean that Madison isn't a bitch at all. She cares too much about everyone around her. Isn't that odd? She's like Lainie in so many ways, and not like her at all. Lainie was beautiful, spoiled and incredibly selfish. Madison, on the other hand, will go out of her way to be understanding. Actually, lately, Kaila has been the one acting more like Lainie."

"Well, no one ever has to defend Madison to me. I think she's great. The best."

Jassy punched him lightly in the shoulder. "You don't have to sound that enthusiastic!"

Jimmy smiled. "Behave. I care very much about your sister, and you know it. But in an entirely different way. She doesn't know how to talk medical blood and guts at all."

Jassy laughed softly, running her fingers through his hair. "Thank God for my hidden talents."

Jimmy smiled, but his smile faded. "She's a good kid, a great kid. But she *is* a copy of Lainie, and this has just got me thinking.... I don't know, these women, these victims, do resemble Lainie Adair."

"Lainie has been dead a long time now."

"I know, I know. I guess there can't be a connection. But still..."

"Still, what?"

He rose, reaching for his pants. "Jassy, there's something I've got to check on. Lock yourself in. You've got a gun, right?"

"You betcha—and I know how to use it."

"Good girl. You can talk bullets to me later," he said, winking, and left her.

Baffled, Jassy lay awake long after he had gone.

* * *

Madison...

She wasn't an image, a mirage. A dream.

A wet dream.

She was really there.

In silk.

"Madison..." Kyle murmured after a moment. "You should have knocked. I could have shot you."

Her eyes focused on him in the shadows. He saw them widen. He'd been sleeping naked. He almost made an instinctive grab for the covers, but he didn't. He remained exactly as he was, seated, setting his gun on the nightstand. Her eyes moved over him, then met his.

"No. You wouldn't have shot me. Not you. You're far too good at your job," she assured him.

He didn't reply. He thought her cheeks were exceptionally flushed. She didn't say anything for a long moment. Her lashes fluttered over her cheeks. Probably because she'd noticed his growing erection.

He stood, heedless of his state of arousal. After all, *she'd* walked into *his* bedroom.

"Well? What are you doing here?" he asked her, wishing his voice didn't sound so harsh. But his heart was thundering, his breathing was already labored, and his muscles, and more, were twitching with tension.

"I..." she began, then tossed back her hair, swallowed and started anew. "I couldn't sleep. And I felt...maybe you were still awake and wanted to talk."

"To talk?"

She was silent for a moment, staring at him. Then she shrugged.

"All right, never mind. I suppose I didn't really think that you wanted to talk. But really, I couldn't sleep. Oh, hell, Kyle! Let's…let's do this, get it over with, get on with our lives."

He started, staring at her, frowning deeply. "What?" he demanded with husky anger.

"I said—"

"Have you been in my mind, Madison?"

"What?" she queried crossly.

"I said—"

"No, I haven't been in your mind! I'm not a mind reader, damn it. There you go, treating me as if I'm an alien being or strange—"

"You have something, Madison. An ability, ESP, something. And people *do* like their thoughts to be private!"

"This was a mistake. Oh, God, what a mistake."

She was trembling, shaking. It had taken her a lot to come here, no matter what her bravado, he realized.

She started to turn around, hair swirling in a wave of deep fire. She had come, fulfilling his fantasies, and he was about to lose her. Because the words she used had been the very words his own imagination had come up with so often.

He moved quickly, determined to stop her. Because if he let her go, she would never come back.

"Madison!" He caught her arm, drawing her back. She stared at him again, flushing deeply. Her eyes met his.

"We both want this," he said to her. "Let's get on with it…. Hell, yes, let's get on with it."

He pulled the single tie on the emerald silk robe. He'd known she wasn't wearing anything beneath it. He lifted it from her shoulders, then watched, fascinated, as the silk drifted down her form and fell to her feet.

He met her eyes for one minute, arching a brow. "We are talking about the same 'it,' right?"

Her color deepened.

He smiled. And feasted.

He'd seen her before. Seen her in casual clothing, elegant clothing, bathing suits. But he'd never seen anything like Madison naked. Her breasts were high and full, her nipples large, dark and provocative. The hair between her thighs was as fiery a red as that on her head, while everything between was curved and smooth and so damned tempting he was afraid he would climax just looking at her.

Great beginning…

But he couldn't stand there staring for another minute. He would start twitching and spontaneously explode. A strangled grunt left his throat, a sound far more primal and animalistic than was politically correct, but at that moment, he couldn't quite give a damn. He all but wrenched her into his arms, lifting her against him. Her naked flesh rubbed erotically against his. He could feel the pounding of her heart, the rise and fall of her breasts as she gasped for air, her vibrance, her warmth…. He could breathe in the scent of her….

"Wait, Kyle!" she murmured suddenly.

"Wait?"

He paused, holding her tight against him, staring down into her eyes. They were wide, a liquid blue, staring back at him. "Kyle, you haven't…"

"I haven't?"

"You aren't…?"

He swore, ready to die.

"You're not—sleeping with my sister, are you?"

"Your sister? Which sister?"

"Jassy." Her eyes widened farther. "Either of them!"

He smiled, shaking his head. "No. I'm not sleeping with either of your sisters. What the hell ever made you think that?"

"Jassy's seeing someone."

"Not me. Can we get on with it?"

She nodded, still staring at him. Then her eyes closed as his lips molded over hers and he kissed her with a ravaging hunger, plunging his tongue into her mouth, invading, consuming with a sure promise of raw energy, passion and need. He continued to seek her mouth, her tongue, as he held her in his arms, sweeping her off the floor with him as he blindly sought the bed.

He fell with her upon it, his mouth still glued to hers, seeking, tasting, caressing, sharing hot, wet, sloppy kisses. He needed her, all of her. His lips moved from hers to her throat. His hands closed over her breasts, his fingers molding her nipples. His mouth followed, bathing her breasts, suckling the hardening peaks, drawing startled little sobbing sounds from her, his name, from her lips....

Madison...

God, he wanted her. It was painful; it was anguish. He couldn't touch or taste his fill. He had always known that her hair was silk, that her naked flesh would be like satin, stroking him. But she was vibrant, as well, twisting, arching, biting lightly into his shoulders, as he touched her with an ever-greater intimacy, rubbing her belly lower and lower with the brush of his knuckles, sliding his fingers into her...,

Their mouths met again in a long, wet, ravaging kiss. His fingers were still inside her. He felt her touching him. Hands on his erection, closing around him, stroking.

He broke away and looked at her, and her blue eyes looked back into his, glazed, yet ready....

He moved against the length of her with a renewed impetus of passion. He wet her breasts with his tongue, drew moist patterns down her torso, laving her navel. He parted her thigh with a quick thrust of his hands and fell between them, making love to her with the intimate caress of his tongue.

She cried out, fingers knitting in his hair, tugging. He endured the pull. In seconds she climaxed. Blood thundered and pulsed painfully in his aroused penis, and he rose above her, sliding into her with the force of his passion. Searingly hot, wet, she gloved him....

He moved with a fevered, urgent rhythm, losing all sense of thought and reason with the sheer force of his need. He gritted his teeth together hard, trying to remember that he wanted her with him, drowning in the tantalizing scent of their sex, in the erotic feel of her flesh, being within her. Her hips pulsed with his to a frenetic, desperate beat. Then his climax exploded violently from him, and he wrapped his arms tightly around her, drawing her harder and harder against him until he heard a cry of release spill from her lips once again....

He rolled her over and held her against him, content in the feel of intimacy that still pervaded him. She was naked, sleek with sweat, her back curved to his chest, her skin against his own. He touched her again, lightly, drawing a line from her shoulder down her spine, over her hip and the curve of her buttocks.

"Now I know why I've stayed away from you so long," he murmured softly.

"Why?" she murmured.

"You're pure temptation, Madison."

She shifted, turning in his arms, smiling slightly. "So are you."

"Well, thanks, but somehow... Never mind."

"Why did you accuse me of reading your mind?" she asked him softly. "Do you still think I'm a witch?"

He pulled her slightly closer. "Yes, you're definitely a witch. You cast spells. Men fall in love with you, just seeing you on the page of a magazine. They'd die to have you."

"They?"

"And I've been thinking about walking down the hallway and bursting into your room with almost the exact same words."

"Oh."

"'Let's get on with it!'" he murmured. "I think something awful would have happened if we hadn't come to this. I would have exploded."

"Surely not!"

"Little pieces of me would have landed all over south Florida," he told her gravely.

She smiled, but then her smile faded. "Like that poor woman!" she said softly.

He shook his head, realizing what he had said. "Worse," he assured her, and she had to smile, resting her head against his chest. "Well, we did get to it." She was quiet for a few minutes. He absently smoothed her hair, engrossed in the feel of it against his flesh.

"I should go back to my own room now."

"Don't even contemplate the idea."

"But—"

He lifted her chin so that he could look into her eyes. "That was the best sex I've had in my entire life. And if you think that I'm just going to let you walk out of here now—when you're wet and ready and in my bed already, when we don't have to go to dinner, have drinks, figure out how to get one another's clothes off or anything—you're nuts."

She stared back at him. "Funny, isn't it? I thought that I was curious. That I just needed..."

"One good shot?" he inquired dryly.

Madison stared at him steadily. "I thought we'd be at the get-on-with-the-rest-of-our-lives bit by now."

"Are you there? Done with me?" he demanded.

"I wish I was!" she said honestly.

"But?"

"I suppose I shouldn't have come here. Except that I was going crazy, I had to know—"

"Are you done sleeping with me?" he asked, interrupting impatiently. "Have you had all you want?" She hesitated, staring at him, irritated by the bluntness of his demand. "Well?"

"That's an incredibly rude question."

"It isn't rude. I'm dying here. Well?"

"Blunt, crude."

"It's an honest question. Answer it."

"No," she admitted angrily.

"Good." He found her lips and kissed her, in greater control than he'd been when she first came naked into his arms, licking, nipping, teasing, playing, until a rise of passion seemed to stir them both once again.

Then he was inside her again.

And it was true.

It was the best sex he'd had in his whole life.

It didn't matter in the least to Trent Adair how late it was getting. He could keep at it all night. He stared down at the page he was working on, deeply pleased.

Chief Inspector Jésus Hernandez hunched down by the corpse, shaking his head in dismay as he fought the nausea that bubbled in his stomach. With each murder, the killer was mutilating the body with a greater fervor.

She had been a beauty—once.

Young, with hopes and dreams in the crystal blue eyes that now stared sightlessly toward heaven. Perhaps, in her dying moments, she had traveled the path of her soul skyward. Hernandez could only pray that it was so.

For what lay on the ground, the remains of her mortal person, was a tragedy, a crude jest against the hopes and dreams of the young. She had been neatly dissected, her organs removed and displayed about the body, her head nearly severed, the line of blood around her neck so thick that she might have been wearing a gaily colored ribbon...

He sat back staring at his words.   He smiled, pleased.

Damn, he was getting good, and he was going to get published before any of them even knew that he was trying to write a book. He'd kept it a secret, not wanting anyone to think that he meant to get help from Jordan, or use Jordan's influence in any way to help him. He could do it on his own.

The scene was downright gruesome.

Good, but gruesome.

And very different from what Jordan Adair wrote. This was far more graphic.

Real.

Morning came.

Light filtered through the shades into the bedroom.

Kyle awoke slowly, then wondered at first, a frown furrowing his brow, if his dreams hadn't grown frighteningly tangible and far too graphically erotic.

But no...Madison was there. Lying beside him.

Naked.

Still sleeping deeply.

Which was nice. Talking to each other this morning was going to be awkward; he was glad she was asleep, because he just wanted to watch her for a while. She was stretched out on her stomach, her hair a wild red tangle around her shoulders and over her back. She'd casually kicked the sheet aside, so she was barely covered at all, and he had a nice long look at her. Naked—and relaxed. There was only so much he had seen in the sheer heat of passion. It was good to look at her at his leisure now.

She did have the world's most incredible back, long and sleek, caped now with the fall of her dark auburn hair. Her legs were very long and shapely. Madison didn't have the anorectic look that characterized so many fashion models; she was in superb condition, slender, but sleekly muscled. Really nice, tight, rounded buttocks.

He wouldn't allow himself to touch. She might awaken.

But he frowned suddenly, leaning over and pushing aside a corner of the sheet that created a shadow on the right side of her hip.

There…just below where a bikini line might fall, was a tattoo. Tiny, discreet, very pretty.

Yet it made his blood run cold.

A rose.

A bloodred rose.

11

Kyle moved so abruptly that he startled her awake. She rolled over, nearly jumping into a sitting position. He found himself watching as her emotions swept clearly through her eyes: realization of where she was, and dismay that she was still there.

They'd been wild during the night.

But now, with sunlight filtering into the room, she reached instinctively for the sheet, drawing it up to her breasts as she turned a nervous gaze on him. "I...meant to be out of here. Martique must be awake. She'll—"

He cut in sharply. "Where did you get that tattoo?"

"What?"

"Your tattoo. Where and when did you get it?"

"I really don't see that it's any of your business!" she replied irritably.

Kyle took a deep breath, realizing that he was tense and acting like a drill sergeant. "It's important, Madison."

She stared at him for a moment, then started to turn away, as if anxious to find her robe and get out. He caught her arm. "Madison, get back here."

"Let me go, Kyle."

"Madison, two of the murder victims had rose tattoos."

"Lots of women have tattoos."

"Not just tattoos, rose tattoos."

"I hadn't heard—"

"And you won't hear. The police are keeping the information quiet. When murders like these occur, they get dozens of cranks calling in, confessing to them. Information like this helps them weed out the phonies. Trust me, Madison, or hell! If you don't trust me, call your sister. Two of the victims had rose tattoos. Another of the victims had just received a huge vase of roses. Now please, where and when did you get your tattoo?"

She paused, looking at his hand, where it rested on her arm. The look meant that he should let go. He didn't.

"Kyle, I've had that tattoo since my first year of college. I was out with a bunch of my girlfriends. We went to a club, had a few drinks and all decided to get tattoos. Luckily, we weren't too loaded, or it might have been a lot bigger."

Kyle frowned, shaking his head. "What ever made you think about getting tattoos?"

She shrugged, her beautiful mane of auburn hair waving down her back, a small, rueful smile curling her lips. "We were college kids. On break, with too much time and too much money. We were being wild, decadent—adult, or so we thought. I think the tattoo parlor was somewhere in Virginia. Near Manassas, I'm pretty sure. I don't remember. It was a long time ago. It was one of those things kids do— I had blue hair once, too." She sighed, shaking her head. "And as to the rose, well…"

"Yes?"

Her eyes rested on his. "I guess I felt guilty."

"Guilty? How?"

"I spent so much time not wanting to be like my mother. I still worry about it, now and again, I think because I'm the spitting image of her, and I—I don't want to have a life like hers, though it does seem I'm on the path, doesn't it?" She didn't want an answer; she was already talking again. "I did love Lainie. She was a horrible wife, and she was selfish, but in her way, she was a wonderful mother. She was in costume and all made up for a play once, and the director yelled at her that my sitting on her lap was going to mess up her dress. She hugged me tighter and told him that her children were more important that any dress, and for that matter, they were more important than any play. She did love us. Anyway...Lainie had this rose."

Kyle exhaled a long breath of relief. "Your mother had a rose tattoo?"

Madison nodded gravely, then smiled again. "Do you remember how your father used to call her his rose? He'd say that Lainie was just like the most glorious rose, so beautiful and sweet-smelling—and so full of thorns. She had her tattoo done because of your father. She said that she got it complete with thorns because she didn't want him to forget that she had her own defenses. She said she needed her thorns. You wouldn't have seen it, because my mother was hardly going to run around naked in front of you, whereas she felt perfectly natural dressing in front of her daughters. The night I had mine done, I'd had a few glasses of champagne, and you know my tolerance for alcohol. I was probably a little weepy, thinking about my mother, even though she'd been dead a long time by then. My friend Cathy Tarlington had a sailfish done, because her boyfriend was an avid sports fisherman. Jill Anderson got a beautiful heron—she's still working to save the Everglades. And I had...a rose.''

Kyle stared at her, nodding after a moment.

''There's nothing remotely dangerous about my tattoo.''

''I guess not. It's just so curious. An incredible coincidence.''

''You might never have seen it.''

He met her eyes. ''I think you're wrong. I would have seen it eventually. Last night was long overdue, and you know it.''

''It couldn't have been too long overdue. You haven't been down here that long.''

''Well, *I've* been fantasizing since the night I got here. How about you?''

''I hadn't fantasized at all,'' she assured him regally.

''No?''

''No.''

''You're a liar.''

''I'm not.''

''You told me you were so curious you couldn't stand it. Not another minute.''

''I never said that.''

''You said something damned close.''

''Well, I wasn't fantasizing—''

''I see. But your friends have been pointing out the fact that I might be a good lay?''

She arched one brow with elegant disdain. ''What a way with words.''

"How do you want to put it?"

"I don't."

She started to rise, drawing the sheet along with her. He pulled it back. She let it go, spinning around to face him.

"Hey, I'm being honest," he told her huskily. "You're the best I've ever had."

"The best what?"

"You just told me I'm too graphic."

"I didn't say that. Not exactly. The best what?"

He stared at her for a long moment, resting on an elbow. "You're the best partner I've ever had in bed. You're beautiful, erotic and giving. And there's no way in hell I'll ever be sorry."

She paused, watching him. "I didn't say *I* was sorry, either," she told him. Then, moving with pure grace and elegance, she reached down for her green silk robe, but she didn't put it on.

She meant to leave him, he knew. She would be back, he told himself. Oh, God, yes, she would have to come back! Because he was more obsessed than he'd ever been. Still, he luxuriated in gazing at her as she veiled her nudity. She was so beautifully built, and her skin had the perfection of porcelain. He had the sheet now, covering him. But once again, he was discovering that watching her was all he needed for an erection.

It might cause some problem in the days ahead, he reflected.

"Why are you in such a hurry?" he asked.

"It's morning. Martique—"

"Would never dream of saying a word to anyone."

"I have to take a shower and get ready. We're doing some more shooting for the poster today."

"Madison, it's not over six-thirty. And do you really have to do more photos? Jaime must have taken hundreds of shots yesterday. I've got to go back to Miami—"

"And I have to work here."

Kyle stepped out of bed. Meeting her eyes, he took the emerald green robe from her hands. He didn't want to argue with her. Not now.

"I can be really quick, I promise," he vowed solemnly.

"Kyle..."

"Really quick."

He tugged at the robe more forcefully. "Once you get away," he told her, taking the green silk garment from her and letting it fall back to the floor, "I don't know when I'll get you back again. Don't leave me like this." He pulled her into his arms and molded his hands over her buttocks, forcing her against his pelvis.

A smile twitched at her lips. It was good enough for him. He swept her up and laid her down.

And once he had her there...

It was impossible to let her up.

He was nowhere near as quick as he had promised.

Okay, she *had* walked into his room, Madison reminded herself. And it wasn't that she wasn't glad to have done so. Darryl had been a good lover, giving, exciting....

It was just that nothing in life was like being with Kyle. His passion was so explosive, each touch bringing new sensation. When she thought she was tired, he could reawaken her. When she thought she would die from reaching such peaks, he lifted her over another one. It was wonderful. And he was so vocal, telling her that she was the best lover he'd ever had. In defense of her soul, she didn't dare return the compliment.

But sex seemed to make men possessive. Maybe it made women possessive, as well, she thought as she showered, because she knew she would knock Sheila right in the head if she started making a play for Kyle again. And yet, Sheila certainly still had the right to do so. She and Kyle had come together with no expectations, no commitments. Chemistry had been brewing between them from the first, and they'd both recognized it, then acted on it. And it had been good. But that was all. They were supposed to have gotten the obsession out of the way, so that they could get on with their lives.

There was absolutely no way Madison was ever going to admit that she'd been in love with Kyle most of her life, that she was still in love with him and would always love him. He had called her a witch once. And now he thought she was great in bed. Well, what had she expected? Kyle didn't give of his heart or his soul easily. They'd had great sex. Such words did not speak of involvement or commitment, and she was going to keep her own head level on her shoulders.

Except that he was making it so hard.

"I don't like you staying here," he said, shaking his head.

"I'm committed to another day's shooting, but I'm safe with these guys, you know."

Dressed, dark and deadly handsome in a business suit, he nodded gravely as he sipped his coffee, surveying her, his eyes very green against his bronzed skin.

"The frightening thing is that this killer is someone everybody trusts. Someone leading a dual life, walking around every day looking as normal as can be."

"I'll be fine. Jaime is picking me up, and I'll have him bring me home, too. Martique will be here all day, and—" she paused, with just a sparkle of amusement in her eyes "—my dad's alarm system is even better than my own."

"Umm," he murmured.

"Besides, I'm supposed to be the psychic one. The witch," Madison reminded him. "I don't feel any sense of danger here."

He raised a brow, then shrugged. "I can't explain it, but I feel really uncomfortable about this entire case."

"Maybe," she suggested softly, "you've just been at it too long."

"Yeah," he said lightly after a moment, "maybe I need a vacation. Anyway, I'll leave once Jaime gets here, but I'll be back tonight, and I'll drive home with you tomorrow."

"That isn't necessary."

"I think it is."

Madison gave up arguing. A few seconds later, she heard Jaime beeping outside. "I've got to go."

He didn't kiss her cheek, didn't touch her. He just nodded gravely, followed her to the door and watched as Hector stepped from the van to help her into the front passenger seat. Hector waved to Kyle, then crawled into the back, slamming the side door.

"*Mucho macho*, that man," Hector said, shaking his head.

"Indeed!" agreed Michelle from the rear seat.

"He'd make a good model," Jaime said. "Good face."

"Great body," Michelle added.

"He'd be good on the poster," Hector mused. "What do you think, stepsister of *mucho-macho* man? Would he pose?"

"Well, we'll all be together again at his father's gallery opening," Madison commented lightly. "You can always ask him."

"*You* can always ask," Jaime agreed, glancing from the road to Madison with a half smile on his lips.

"Well, that's Sunday," Madison said.

"Right, we have our work today," Michelle said. "Can't think too far ahead. But, Madison, look at you! You're just glowing today. Don't you think so, Hector?"

"She's pure neon," Hector agreed.

"You had a good night, eh? Thank God!" Michelle laughed.

"What?" Madison gasped.

Hector and Jaime laughed softly, and she knew that they hadn't known a thing about her night until she gave herself away.

"Jaime, just drive, will you, please?"

Dan was being wonderful.

True to his word.

He let Kaila sleep, waking with the kids, getting

them fed and dressed. He insisted that she make the most of his free time and go to lunch with her friends.

She played tennis, showered and joined some of her friends in the clubhouse. She didn't have to drive anybody anywhere, so she sipped wine throughout lunch. Toward the end of the meal, the waiter brought a silver tray with a small, beautifully wrapped box on it with a gift tag bearing nothing but her name.

"A secret admirer?" Candy Fox, a petite brunette married to another of the attorneys in Dan's office, inquired.

Kaila shook her head, smiling. "I think it's from Dan. He's been extra sweet lately."

"See what it is," suggested Tara Anderson, mother of two, part-time tennis coach at the club, and the third and final member of their lunch party.

She opened the box. Wrapped in delicate pink tissue was a pair of fragile "edible" panties. They were white chocolate with a red candy rose for the crotch. Kaila felt her face turn a million shades of pink.

"Whoa! How...how romantic!" Candy gasped. "How sexy. Boy, are you going to be getting some tonight, honey! I wish David would send me a gift like that now and then. The man is such a boob. On my birthday he goes out and buys me kitchen utensils!"

They were beginning to draw attention from nearby tables. Kaila quickly closed the box, flushing. "It's strange...."

"What's strange?" Tara asked her.

Kaila shrugged. "It's just...it's just not like Dan.

He did send me flowers recently, but most of the time, well, he's a kitchen-utensil kind of man, too.''

"Did you have a fight?" Candy asked. "You know how guys like to suck up after a fight!"

"No, not really. In a way, but it's already over. I mean, he's home watching the kids, being just great."

"A man home all day with his little kids—no wonder the edible lingerie. He's already planning to ease his frustrations!" Tara announced.

"Maybe," Kaila murmured.

"Honey, he's on a romantic binge! Enjoy it!" Tara advised her.

Kaila smiled suddenly. Dan was being good. So good. Twinges of guilt tore at her heart. She did act like a spoiled rich kid sometimes, thinking that the world was passing her by while she changed diapers. She prayed silently that God would forgive her; her children were so important to her! She loved them dearly, and they deserved a far more patient mother. Dan, too, was being great. Working so hard and still realizing that she needed a break. Lord, she even had Anna, for God's sake! So many moms with little kids had no help. She had so much.

She blinked furiously, realizing how close she had come to destroying her marriage. She had been so blind and selfish that she might actually have cheated on Dan.

She sipped her coffee and smiled at Tara. "I hope he's good and frustrated, because he's going to have one hell of a night!" She was going to be good to him. She was going to wear her gift and make up for being such a bitch lately.

Tonight…

* * *

Including airport time, it took less than an hour to get from Key West to Miami by plane. By noon, Kyle was back at Jimmy's office, reading and re-reading the forensic reports on all the victims, hoping that something else would jump out at him.

Jimmy came in, taking a chair and staring at Kyle. "Guess what?"

"What?"

"Remember Harry Nore, derelict, bad teeth, found with your father's Saint Christopher medal and the butcher knife that killed Lainie Adair?"

Kyle frowned. "What about him?"

"They let him go."

"What?" Kyle demanded incredulously.

Jimmy nodded gravely. "Believe it or not," he said in disgust, "the shrinks let him go. The doctors were supposed to let us know if they ever let him out, so they sent us a letter that we just got—but he's been out for about six months now."

"Six months?"

"And the murders started four months ago. All redheads, like Lainie, like you said."

"Redheads, yeah. Like Lainie." Kyle shook his head.

"So what do you think? Could he be doing the killings?"

"He's not the type. Can you imagine Nore romancing someone?" He shook his head. "But...do we know where he is now?" Kyle asked.

Jimmy shook his head. "He was supposed to be living in Stuart, and a social worker was supposed to have been looking in on him once every couple of weeks, but you know how things like that go. He disappeared after the social worker's first visit. I have guys looking for him now, but...he could be anywhere. Including Miami."

Kyle tapped a pencil against Jimmy's desk, then shook his head.

"It can't be Nore."

"Why not? He killed Lainie. He admitted it. Said she was the devil's spawn. Maybe he feels that way about redheads in general. Now that he's loose and out on his own, maybe he thinks God has told him to kill more redheads, more of the devil's spawn."

"I don't think so."

Jimmy groaned, aggravated. "Why can't anything ever be simple with you guys? Nore is a homicidal maniac! He butchered his wife, then Lainie, and it looks as if he's at it again."

Kyle shook his head, smiling slightly. "Nore never went to trial for Lainie's murder."

"Christ! He confessed to it!"

"Right. But he's a certifiable madman, and madmen confess to crimes."

"You had too many years of college, boy. Madmen don't confess to crimes, they *commit* them!"

"Jimmy, this killer is suave and sleek. He seduces his victims. Hell, remember what Nore looked like? His eyes were wild, his smile was a leer. He's about as seductive as a rabid dog. I don't think he's our man."

Jimmy was quiet. He sighed. "Damn it, I hate it when you almost make sense."

Kyle shrugged. "Nore shouldn't have been let out."

"No way in hell," Jimmy agreed.

"It would still be a good idea to find him, find out if he's been in Miami, question him."

"I've got an APB out on him now."

"Good. I think we're going to have an interesting afternoon."

"Oh, yeah? What's your suggestion."

"Let's hit the tattoo parlors ourselves."

"We've got beat cops on it already, you know."

"Yeah, but let's get involved ourselves. Unless you've got some other clue we could be following?"

"I always wanted to get inside a sleazy tattoo parlor," Jimmy said. "Let's go."

They spent the afternoon visiting tattoo parlors, showing pictures of the rose tattoos from the bodies of the two dead women to the various "body artists" at the different establishments. They found similar tattoos, but nothing exactly the same as either one. They also questioned everyone about Holly Tyler.

Toward the end of the day, near seven, they got lucky at a place in Florida City called Tammy's Tailored Tattoos and Tea Parlor. Tammy herself greeted them. She was a small woman wearing skimpy leather shorts and a skimpier vest that barely covered her ample bosom. Her hair was dyed a neon orange, teased and piled on her head. She flirted like crazy, until she made a sudden withdrawal, instinctively wary, when she realized they were the law. Kyle cut through her defensive stuttering, assuring her that they were interested in finding out about rose tattoos and Holly Tyler, nothing else.

Tammy studied the picture of Holly Tyler's buttocks for only a moment before staring wide-eyed at Kyle. "My God! She's dead? That pretty little thing is dead?"

"She was here?" Jimmy said quickly.

Tammy nodded, wide-eyed. "That's my work."

"When did you do it?" Jimmy demanded.

"Last Friday, late afternoon, early evening. She was in a big hurry, getting the tattoo to please some man."

Jimmy flashed Kyle a quick look.

"Who was the man?" Kyle asked.

"I don't know. He never came in here. She walked in by herself, real uncertain-like. She'd never had a tattoo before. She seemed to think we're the devil's den or something like that. The guy didn't come with her. I didn't make it as elaborate as I would have liked, 'cause she was in a hurry. She wanted the tattoo 'cause of this guy she had a real thing for. She was all excited and talkative, once she got comfortable. Said that good men were so hard to find these days, and this guy was a real prince. Nice guy, opened doors for her, paid for dates...and he was taking her for a romantic weekend on the water. They were just gonna lie around all weekend, drink wine, swim a little, fish a little, and make love like rabbits."

"Where were they going, do you know?"

Tammy shook her head. "South. I'm not sure where. Just somewhere south. Maybe Key Largo, maybe Marathon...hell, maybe they were going all the way down to Key West. All she talked about is how great a guy he was, how excited she was...and how he wanted her to have a rose tattoo where only he could see it."

"Did she say whether he was dark, light, blond, bald, Anglo, Latin, anything?"

Tammy shook her head.

"She didn't describe the guy at all?" Jimmy asked.

"I'm really sorry. I—'' She stopped suddenly, remembering something.

"What?'' Kyle asked.

"She was really proud of the guy. Said how good-looking he was, yet kind of shy. Refused to have his picture taken. She was telling me that she had sneaked a couple of Polaroids when he wasn't looking, but when she started digging around in her purse to find the pictures, she realized she must have forgotten them or lost them or something. She didn't have them, so she couldn't show me.''

"Damn,'' Jimmy breathed.

The understatement of the year, Kyle thought. "Call in, have Holly Tyler's house searched for photos and follow up every lead,'' he said to Jimmy.

Jimmy nodded. "We'll get guys right on it.''

Tammy looked at them sorrowfully, plainly realizing what a difference it would have made if she'd only been able to see the pictures. "God, I'm sorry. You know that I'd help you if I could.''

"Well, you've got us looking for photos now, so you might turn out to have been more of a help than you know.''

"If I think of anything else…''

"Sure,'' Kyle said. He took out a business card and wrote down the number to Jordan's house in Key West, along with his cell phone. "If you think of anything at all, no matter how minor you may think it is, please, *please,* call one of us,'' he said, watching as Jimmy also handed her a card.

They left the tattoo parlor, driving north, back to Miami. They went back to Jimmy's office, adding the new information to the time board they were constructing regarding Holly Tyler's last movements.

"You're really hung up on this tattoo thing," Jimmy told Kyle, driving him to the airport to catch a commuter flight back to Key West.

Kyle glanced at his watch, annoyed to see how late it had gotten. After ten. It would be nearly midnight when he got back to Jordan's house. He didn't like Madison being there alone.

He glanced at Jimmy, about to tell him that he was worried because Madison had a similar tattoo.

He refrained. Jimmy might wonder how he knew about the tattoo, and he felt certain that Madison wouldn't want anyone else knowing why he was so familiar with it.

It suddenly seemed important to him that no one know about Madison's tattoo.

No one.

Naturally Darryl Hart would know about his ex-wife's tattoo, but no one else had to know, and Kyle was determined to keep quiet about it.

He hesitated for a minute, then said, "Lainie had a similar tattoo."

"Lainie!" Jimmy eyed him, frowning. "How do you know?"

"She was married to my father."

"Oh," Jimmy said. He still sounded suspicious. He glanced sideways at Kyle.

"No, I did not have an adolescent affair with my stepmother," Kyle assured him dryly.

"I wasn't suggesting any such a thing, I was just..."

"Wondering?" Kyle said.

Jimmy shrugged sheepishly. "Yeah."

"I wouldn't have gone near Lainie with a ten-foot pole," Kyle murmured.

He realized that Jimmy was staring at him suspiciously again.

He glanced at Jimmy, smiling. "She was hell on wheels. Tortured my father and Jordan. And plenty of other men, I'm certain."

"How so?"

Kyle thought about it a minute. "She liked to hold things against people. If my father did something she didn't like, she always let him know that Jordan would be happy to be with her again. She did it subtly. And if she knew something that she could hold against you...she used it."

"Like what?"

"Like she caught me in the back seat of my old Chevy once, with the prom queen, when I was in high school. It hadn't gotten too serious, just a little heavy petting. My father would have hit the roof, though, because he was convinced that Patty Lawton—the prom queen—was out to get pregnant and trap me into marriage, and my father was determined that I was going to college. So anytime I wasn't doing exactly what Lainie wanted, she subtly threatened me with exposure. She always knew how to hit just the right buttons with people. It's hard to explain. Lainie manipulated people."

"Strange, isn't it, how differently we all see people? To me, Lainie Adair was a star, elegant, ageless, beautiful—on a pedestal. I wouldn't have thought she had a mean bone in her body."

"Ask Jassy how many bones are in the human body. Lainie had that many," Kyle said dryly.

"She couldn't have been all bad!" Jimmy protested.

"No one is all bad. The world isn't black-and-white. Everything has shades of gray," Kyle agreed. "Lainie did have her good points." He shrugged then, "You're right, it all depends on your point of view. The girls loved her. She was a good mother to Madison and Kaila, and she could be decent to her various stepchildren. Could be. She planned elaborate birthday parties for all of us. She loved to buy gifts. And she was proud and delighted when we did something well. Lainie was...unique. And no one deserves to die the way she did." Kyle fell silent, remembering how he had come from his room, alarmed when he heard his father's shouts of horror. Rushing to the bedroom, he had seen Lainie in his father's arms. Roger was crying out, choking, tears streaming down his face. Lainie was dead. In a huge pool of blood. Her killer's knife had struck through to a kidney, and she had died, in fear and agony.

He gave himself a shake as an old feeling of unease swept over him. At first, he had to admit, he'd thought that Lainie must finally have infuriated his father to such a point that Roger faced a moment of temporary insanity—and killed her. But he had become convinced that no one could feign grief the way Roger suffered it that night. And he believed in his father.

Then, and now.

"What is it?" Jimmy asked.

"Nothing. We're not supposed to speak ill of the dead, right? Lainie was many things. I pray she rests in peace," Kyle murmured. And yet, remembering

Lainie, he found himself thinking about Madison again.

Madison was nothing like Lainie.

And he cared more about her than he dared admit to himself, much less anyone else. But they'd both been hurt. They knew to keep their distance.

Well, he couldn't keep his distance right now. He had to stick to Madison. Like glue. Though how the hell he was going to manage it, he didn't know.

Jimmy left him at the airport, where he boarded the small plane. Despite the fact that the engines were noisy as hell, he dozed. At the airport, he hailed a taxi. The driver was slow, and as he sat in the back seat, Kyle began to feel twinges of unease.

It was nearly midnight as they drove through the quiet streets toward Jordan's house.

The closer they got, the greater Kyle's sense of unease grew. With Jordan in Miami, Madison was alone at the house, with only her father's maid, out in her room by the pool.

The uneasier Kyle felt, the slower the taxi driver seemed to roll along the street.

"Can you hurry it up a little?" he asked the man impatiently.

The cabdriver muttered beneath his breath, then hit the gas with such enthusiasm that Kyle was pressed against the seat by the force of it. Still, they sped along the last streets and around the last corner with a vengeance—wheels spinning and squealing.

"Thanks," Kyle said, handing the driver a more-than-ample sum. "Keep the change."

He stared at the house. The outside lights were all on; everything looked fine. But appearances could be deceiving.

Out of habit, he tapped his chest to make sure his shoulder holster and gun were where they should be. Then he approached the house, reaching into his pocket for his keys, moving quickly and quietly along the drive to the front door.

Just as he turned the key in the lock, he heard the first scream.

Short, high-pitched, seeming to quiver in the night air.

It was instantly followed by a second scream, this one long, terrified…bloodcurdling.

For a split second, he froze.

Then he burst into the house, drawing his gun and racing down the hallway.

Just as Madison screamed once again.

12

She was in the house again. Roger Montgomery's old house in Coconut Grove. The house where Lainie had died.

But there was more than one hallway.

Each hallway ran in a different direction. Silver mist lay in all the hallways, billowing thickly to a point about waist-high, thinning from there on up. She could hear her mother's voice, and she knew that she had to reach Lainie, but she wasn't sure which hallway she should be following.

She began to run.

She tried first one hallway, then the next. Lainie's cries were growing louder, more distressed, yet Madison couldn't tell from what direction her cries were coming. Each time she tried to turn, the fog became thicker and thicker, swirling around her as if a gust of wind had come along. Suddenly the fog began to settle back to the ground, and she heard her mother's voice—and there was only one hallway left.

She wanted to run, but she couldn't run anymore. She tried, she willed herself to run, but her legs felt like lead. She was moving in slow motion, trying to call out, but unable to utter a single sound.

As she moved through the mist in the hallway,

she saw the knife. It was high in the air, caught in the silver glimmer of the fog.

Suddenly it moved, slashing through the air.

She heard her mother's scream.

Felt her mother's pain.

Felt it as the knife slashed into Lainie's side. Cutting flesh, bone, sinew...

She tried and tried to scream. She knew that she was in a nightmare, where so often it was impossible to scream. But she needed to scream. She needed to awaken.

She saw the knife again, suspended in the silver mist, something dripping off its razor-sharp edge.

Blood.

Drip, drip, drip...

A pool of blood lay on the floor beneath the knife. Lainie's voice was forever silent.

Madison knew the nightmare; she had lived it. She struggled to awaken, but she was falling deeper and deeper into it. The knife couldn't be simply suspended in the air. Someone was holding the knife. Someone had wielded the knife. Still held the knife, would kill and kill again.

The knife was being held in a hand.

A gloved hand...

With a wrist, an arm...

Swallowed by darkness. Yet if she looked, waited for the fog to recede, she would see the killer. She had to see the killer, had to stop him from killing again, but the fog was so thick.

Then it began to fade away.

If she looked hard, really hard...

The knife was rising again. She couldn't see them,

but she felt the eyes of the killer on her. Watching her. Killer is watching! Killer is watching!

The knife was coming toward her. Any second now, it would fall, because the killer could see her, though she couldn't see him. The blade was so sharp, still dripping with her mother's blood....

Coming closer, closer, closer...

She turned to run, heard the blade swiping through the air. At last...

At long last...

She began to scream. Scream and scream and scream...

Arms came around her, holding her, shaking her.

"Madison!"

She awoke in terror, wildly fighting the man who held her.

"Madison!"

Her eyes were wide open, but it still took her several long seconds to realize that Kyle was the man trying to hold her, despite her violent struggles.

Martique was standing in the bedroom doorway in her flannel pajamas; she'd come running without grabbing her housecoat or slippers. "Dear Lord, Madison!" she murmured, concerned. She crossed herself.

Madison looked at Kyle, who was studying her with grave concern. He was still in his business suit, but he'd loosened his tie and opened the first few buttons of his shirt.

The air-conditioning was hitting her sweat-soaked body, and she started to tremble. He smoothed back her hair. "Are you all right? Madison, you were dreaming, right?"

She nodded.

"I'll bring you something," Martique said, staring sympathetically. "What would you like?"

"Something strong," Kyle said. He glanced at Martique. "A double shot of Jack Black."

"I can't drink bourbon," Madison said.

"That was for me!" Kyle teased. "You just scared me out of ten years of life."

She flushed, looking at him, realizing that she was wearing a short, sheer black nightgown that she had purposely chosen to be provocative—just in case he really came back—and that he was sitting casually next to her on her bed while Martique looked on. But Martique didn't seem to be concerned with the circumstances, only with Madison's state of mind. "I'll fix you both something good, and no arguments, young lady," she told Madison.

After Martique left them, Kyle ran his knuckles over her hot, flushed cheeks. "Tell me about it."

"There's really nothing to tell. I was dreaming about the night my mother was killed. It was so real, so frightening. As if I were living it all over again. I felt as if the killer were close to me again. As if he could see me when I was trying to reach Lainie."

Kyle was quiet for a minute. His fingers were interlaced with hers now, and he didn't meet her eyes, just looked down at their hands.

"You shouldn't have gotten involved in this."

She shrugged, not willing to admit that she was ready to agree with him at the moment. She shook her head. "I've worked with Jimmy before. Just nothing like this... I don't know. I mean, all murders are bad. Someone winds up dead, and dead is gone, and the mothers, wives, husbands, kids, lovers, are all left hurting, no matter how someone died. This is just so violent and so vicious.... I guess it's bringing back what happened to my mother."

"They're all redheads," Kyle murmured. He looked at her. "Like Lainie."

"Harry Nore—"

"Harry Nore is out," Kyle said bluntly.

"What?" Madison gasped, rising to her knees. "Kyle, if he's out, maybe he's the one committing these horrible crimes. Kyle—"

"Jimmy Gates has every cop in the state looking for him, so he'll be found."

"Oh, Kyle, maybe—"

"Madison, I'm going to tell you the same thing I told Jimmy. I don't believe that Harry Nore can possibly be guilty of these crimes. What woman in her right mind is going to get excited about a romantic weekend with a man like Harry Nore? He grins like a baboon, smells worse than a goat, and is so evidently off his rocker—"

"They let him out of an asylum for the criminally insane," Madison reminded him. "Maybe he's cured."

"Right. And that's going to make him as handsome and charming as Sean Connery, right? This guy picks up young, beautiful women. A broken, crazed old lunatic is not going to turn into Don Juan, trust me."

Madison swallowed uneasily, closed her eyes and sighed. "I know they found him with the murder weapon. He had the knife, and it had my mother's blood on it. But I never thought it was him. It just didn't feel right."

Kyle lifted his hands in an exasperated motion. "A point that I was far too young and inexperienced to pay attention to at the time. Think about it. There was Harry Nore, in a neighbor's kitchen, happily cutting bread. Yet when you 'saw' the killer, saw him holding the knife to kill your mother, he was wearing gloves. Flesh-toned gloves, the kind doctors use.''

Madison nodded. ''Well, if it wasn't him, and if the real killer was caught at the scene of the murder, all he needed to do was dispose of the knife—''

''And be clever enough to slip by me, you, Kaila, my father, and all the cops and everyone else flooding the property within minutes.''

Madison shivered again. She was soaking, and the air-conditioning was cold. And as the dream faded, her vanity was kicking in. She felt sticky and sweaty, her hair was plastered around her face, and she didn't feel the least bit enticing.

She eased away from Kyle, rising from the other side of the bed. ''I'm going to shower quickly.''

He nodded.

Once inside the bathroom, though, she was amazed to feel unnerved again.

She looked out the door.

''I'll be here,'' he promised her.

Madison slipped out of her gown and into the shower, turning the water on warm and letting it sluice over her face and body for long moments before she scrubbed her hair and sudsed lavishly. As she rinsed conditioner from her hair, she heard Kyle's voice.

''Madison?''

''What?'' she called.

He stepped into the shower behind her. Naked.

''I didn't want to scare you,'' he said.

His arms slipped around her, drawing her back against himself. He lifted her wet hair from her shoulders and neck, kissing her nape. His hands eased up her torso, caressing her breasts. She closed her eyes as electric flashes of pure sweet fire instantly began to sweep along her limbs.

His kisses moved lower down her spine. His tongue teased at the small of her back; then he turned her around, still kissing and caressing her flesh. Each stroke and touch grew more intimate and so incredibly erotic, blended with the heat of the water cascading down upon them both, that she began to fear that she would fall. She dug her fingers into his shoulders, desperately whispering his name. He showed no mercy. Her limbs felt like water, yet mercury seemed to tear throughout her, until she couldn't bear it anymore and she cried out his name. He was on his feet then, kissing her lips, and their tongues melded, with the taste of their lovemaking. Then he turned her, fingers laced with hers as he braced her against the tile. He entered her from behind, and the water poured down, hot and slick. He moved with an urgent passion, swiftly lifting her to a place she'd thought she couldn't possibly reach again so quickly. The thundering in her ears compounded with that in her heart, with the pulse in her body. Then he ground against her hard, fast, his body knotting with tension, and the volatile force of his climax precipitated her own. She felt as if the rush of the shower were around her and within her as the hot seed of his desire spilled into her.

She collapsed back into his arms without a murmur of protest. She heard him sigh after a long while, and she realized they'd been in there so long, the water was growing cold.

Kyle reached over and turned off the water. He stepped from the shower, reaching back for her with a towel, wrapping her in it when she came against him.

"Martique made hot brandied tea," he told her.

"Is it still hot?"

"I'm sure it is. She brought it in a coffee carafe, then left us to our privacy."

"She knows," Madison murmured, turning around and leaving the bathroom.

"So what?" Kyle asked, drying himself, then wrapping his towel around his waist and following her out to the bedroom. "She doesn't seem to be shocked. What difference does it make? You're over twenty-one. So am I." He poured two mugs of tea, then handed her one. "We're not biologically related, and as I pointed out before—although you assured me at the time that the situation wouldn't arise—we're not going to have children with pointed heads or anything."

She smiled, then looked at him gravely. "Kyle, I have a little girl," she reminded him.

"I know. I never forget that," he told her.

She held silent, turning away from him and wondering if he also never forgot that he had lost a wife he loved deeply.

Or that he had once called her a witch.

Or that they were usually at one another's throats within a matter of minutes during even the most casual conversation. So this...passion would surely burn itself out.

"I have a daughter, and I need to make sure she isn't hurt by anything I do," Madison said.

"She's with her father right now, isn't she?"

"Yes."

"So she's not being hurt by anything we're doing. She's being helped."

Madison arched a brow. "Oh? How's that?"

"I'm afraid for your safety. But anyone would have to come through me to get to you."

"Ah."

"And I'm damned hard to get through," he assured her. He finished his tea, set down his cup and took hers from her hands.

"Still obsessed?" she whispered as his mouth neared hers.

"Still obsessed."

"Are you sure you're not just in a protective mode, and sex is just a pleasant diversion?"

"Yep, I'm sure," he said flatly. "And you?"

"Still...curious" was the best she dared admit as his mouth molded over hers.

She gave up attempting to reason and gave into sensation.

Kaila snuggled against her husband, basking in a sea of contentment unlike anything she had experienced in years.

His arm pulled her closer, and he whispered against her forehead, "Wow."

"Incredible," she agreed.

And it had been. Absolutely. She would never have thought of herself as the kinky type, and she still didn't. She didn't judge others, but she was sure she never wanted to play some of the sex games she'd seen on the cable shows. She knew she didn't want to be handcuffed, hurt or whipped, or have Dan act like a child who needed to be punished. She had no desire whatsoever to call him "naughty boy" and make him grovel for her sexual favors. She didn't want to take part in an orgy, or get involved with couples who played switchies.

But tonight...

Wow.

And all because of his sexy little gift. He'd gone crazy, seeing her in the panties. And the things he'd done...and the responses she had given...

Just the two of them. So alone, so intimate. Having fun. As they hadn't in a very long time...

"What an idea. Thank you," she told him softly, kissing his lips, then snuggling back down beside him again.

"What do you mean? Thank *you*. Honey, you were awesome. So sexy. You have to buy more of those. What gave you the idea?"

She felt the strangest sensation of icy cold sweeping over her. It wasn't exactly fear, but it was awfully close.

She was silent too long.

"Kaila?"

"I..."

Dan was frowning, leaning over her and staring at her with angry eyes. "Kaila, where did you get those panties?"

"I—I didn't get them. They were a gift. They arrived at my table today at lunch, addressed to me. I assumed you had sent them."

"Naturally."

"Dan!"

He leaned back against the pillows, still staring at her, and the accusing glitter in his eyes was frightening.

"Dan—you didn't send them?"

"No."

"But—"

"No, I didn't send them."

"Then they must have been a mistake. Someone else was meant to have them."

"You just said they were addressed to you."

"Did I?"

"Yes, you did! Were they, or weren't they, addressed to you?" he yelled.

"Dan, stop it! This isn't a courtroom. You—"

"It might turn into a courtroom pretty damn quick. They were addressed to you, right?"

"Right! What are you getting so angry about? If you didn't send them, one of the girls must have been playing a trick—"

"Oh, Kaila, quit it."

"What the hell does that mean?"

"What does that mean?" he repeated. "It means that you've been flirting with someone. Flirting enough to give him the idea that you might be available. Christ! Here I am feeling guilty that you're so depressed, stuck home being a mother!"

"I'm not depressed being a mother!" she protested. "And I never said that. And I don't flirt!" She said the words boldly, then realized they were a lie.

She *had* given someone the idea she might be willing to have an affair.

She felt cold again. Really cold. *He* didn't know

that she had decided she was every kind of a fool and really truly loved her husband.

Oh, damn.

He might have sent the…gift.

"Look, Dan, honestly—"

"Save it, Kaila," he said softly, then rose. He slipped quickly into his robe and left the room, slamming the door in his wake.

Kaila stared after him, stunned. And cold, so cold.

The panties…

She shivered, feeling dirty. Had she really come so close to an affair? Worse, had she really already destroyed her marriage?

The next time she saw *him,* she was really going to give him a piece of her mind. She was going to explain that she had just been going through a bad period, that she really loved her husband.

Oh, God…

She still felt dirty. Squirmy. And afraid.

Dan had never looked at her like that before.

She got out of bed, wrapping up in her own robe, wondering how such wicked ecstasy could turn to something so horrible. She walked out to the living room. He was standing in the kitchen, staring out at the back, drinking a beer.

"Dan?"

"What?"

"I love you."

"Who sent you those panties, Kaila?"

She lied. She had to lie. "I have no idea, Dan. Honest to God. I swear on the kids' lives—I never cheated on you."

"Well, it's just interesting that another man would send my wife edible underwear," he said dryly.

"One of the girls must have done it as a joke."

"Sure, Kaila."

She walked to him, slipping her arms around his waist, really frightened that she might lose him.

"I love you, Dan!" she whispered.

She felt his muscles ease. His arm came around her. Tears slid down her cheeks, he brushed them away with his knuckles and kissed her lips.

"Every once in a while..." he murmured.

"What?"

"Well, you look like your mother. Maybe I get a little afraid you might want to try out several husbands."

"Dan, what an awful thing to say."

"You did receive edible underwear."

"I love you, Dan."

"Do you?"

"God, yes! I've just been afraid, I guess, because you're gone so much! Because you work with young, bright attorneys, so many women. And sometimes I feel that I can't compete with the excitement of your day because all I do is wear spit-up and baby drool, and all I can talk about is the most recent PTA meeting or the latest Disney movie."

He smiled and smoothed her hair. "That's my child's spit-up you're wearing, Kaila. And I love Disney movies, and believe it or not, the PTA matters to me. And you're intelligent and articulate and interesting. I love you, too, Kaila."

"Oh, Dan!" she murmured. "I'm so sorry. It's just that the kids are so little, I sometimes feel that I need three hands, and yet I adore them, and...and I adore you. You've been so good!" she whispered.

"You know what?" he told her, his voice growing harsh again.

"What?"

"I'm going to find out where the hell those panties came from."

His arms were around her, but despite that, she felt the devastating cold once again.

"I'm really not sure why you're so worried," Madison said. She was driving, and Kyle was at her side in the passenger seat, sipping coffee from a paper cup as he reached in the back seat for the *Miami Herald* she had just bought. "Kyle, this guy is a pattern killer, and if he goes by his past record, he isn't due to strike again for another several weeks. The middle of the month."

He was staring at the paper. "Damn it!" he swore.

She nearly jumped. "What?"

His knuckles were white as he clenched the paper.

"Kyle?"

He shook his head, staring at her. "Someone leaked the information that we were searching the last victim's house for snapshots of the killer."

"What?"

"Jimmy and I found the place where Holly Tyler, the last victim, got her tattoo. The woman who ran the place said Holly nearly showed her a picture of the man she was going away with, except that she couldn't find the picture. The cops are searching her home. And it's in the damned paper."

"Kyle, maybe it's not all that bad. I mean, the cops are already searching the house, right? So the killer can't come in now and ransack it to get his hands on the pictures himself, right?''

"Right," he said, staring out the front window, still furious. "And in a perfect world they'll have found the pictures by the time we reach Miami, he'll have a record, we'll find his identity by computer and arrest him by this afternoon."

"It could happen that way."

"It's not going to. What will happen is that we'll wind up tracking down Holly's third cousin twice removed who lives in rural Arkansas. And both crackpots and helpful friends will start sending in snapshots, and our needle will wind up in a giant haystack."

"Maybe not. The first scenario is still possible."

"Sure," Kyle said. He pulled his cell phone from his pocket and dialed headquarters, getting Jimmy on the line. Jimmy assured him that they were looking for the leak, and that there was going to be hell to pay for someone.

Kyle clicked off.

"Kyle?" she said quietly.

"Yeah?" he asked, looking at her.

"Remember what I said before? The killer strikes in the middle of the month. He isn't due for another three weeks."

"What are you saying?"

"I'm saying that you can't be so worried about me. I'm going home now."

"And?"

"And Carrie Anne is coming home tonight."

"And?"

"Kyle, I can't just...I can't just sleep with you at home. You've got to go back to your hotel tonight."

She felt him watching her as she drove. "Kyle, she's a little girl, and I don't know how to explain—"

"So you think Darryl never sees anyone when he has his daughter?"

"I'm the custodial parent," Madison said. "She's with me most of the time—"

"So you're going to spend your life having two-day affairs when your daughter is with her father?"

"You're being completely unreasonable—"

"I'm just curious. What are you going to do if you ever get serious about a man?"

"If I get really serious, I'll get married again, and that way I can explain to Carrie Anne that I'm married!" she explained, aggravated. "Kyle, she's a very little girl. And no matter how well Darryl and I get along, I don't ever want to give him any ammunition against me if he decides he suddenly wants custody."

"Darryl wouldn't do that."

"You never know."

She felt him watching her. "Well, you can always marry old Darryl again. That would solve that problem. Or sleep with him now and then—I guess that would be all right."

She stared at him, incredulous and furious. There was a gas station ahead. She pulled into it.

"What the hell are you doing?"

"Stopping. Get out of my car."

"What?"

"Out!"

"I don't think so."

"I'm telling you to get out."

His eyes narrowed. "And I'm refusing. I have to get to work in Miami."

"Call a cab."

"Out here? In the middle of the Keys? Call a cab to Miami?"

"Call a cab—call the damned FBI. I don't care. Get out of my car."

"Why?"

She stared at him, absolutely incredulous. "Because you're being hateful and vile and—"

"Scared!" he told her, his voice so deep and husky that she broke off, staring at him. He crushed his empty coffee cup in his hand, his knuckles white around it.

"Kyle..."

His coffee cup fell unnoticed to the floor, and he took her face between his hands, staring into her eyes. "Someone is murdering redheads in the middle of every month, and you're a psychic—whether you choose to be or not. You see the murder victims. Law enforcement is beginning to get a few leads. Just a few! But maybe enough to spook the killer. I don't want you to be alone. We don't have to sleep together, but I won't leave you alone at night. I can sleep on your couch, and we can explain to Carrie Anne that I'm a cop like Jimmy, and I'm just there to watch out for you both. Any objection?"

Madison tried to shake her head. "No, I guess not. And you can let go of my face now!"

He released her, easing back into his own seat. "May we go?" he asked politely.

They drove again. In dead silence. But fifteen minutes later they passed Theater of the Sea, one of the few facilities where people could swim with dolphins.

"I always wanted to do that," Madison mused aloud.

"Go to Theatre of the Sea?" he inquired, puzzled.

She laughed. "Swim with dolphins."

"You dive with sea creatures all the time."

She shook her head. "I've never run into a playful dolphin. Never."

"If it's something you want to do, the answer's easy. Do it."

"When you want to do something, do you usually just do it?"

"Yup."

"What was the last thing you wanted to do really badly?" she asked him.

He grinned slowly. "Sleep with you."

She couldn't help but smile in return. "Oh," she said lightly. Then she realized that he was looking at her gravely again.

"Madison."

"What?"

"What day was your mother murdered?"

She felt a strange, twisting tension inside. "June fifteenth."

"Right. The middle of the month."

"It has to be coincidence."

"Does it?"

Killer should have waited for the night.

But he didn't dare. And the challenge was actually getting quite intriguing.

The tattoo parlor didn't open until ten.

It was 9:03. He pulled on his gloves. Thin plastic gloves, taken right out of a dispenser designed for doctors' offices.

He parked in the grocery store lot down the street and walked the distance to the tattoo parlor. He was wearing a wig and dark glasses.

The front door was locked.

He went around the back and stepped in.

Good old Tammy, with her dyed hair and blowsy face, was at a desk in the back, going over her receipts. She looked up when she saw him.

"We're not open yet," she said.

He looked her over with disgust. Ugly old broad. He despised the fact that he had to waste his time and talents on her. But Holly had snapped a picture of him. The cops had searched her house. She probably didn't know she had it, but the old broad here had his likeness. Holly *must* have lost it here somewhere.

"Hi, Tammy."

"Do I know you?"

"I know you. And I know you're not open, but...well, I've seen you before. I had to figure out a way to talk to you...alone."

"Alone?"

He nodded. "Hey, you know, I just needed to ask a favor," he said, smiling charmingly as he closed and locked the back door behind himself.

Tammy rose from her chair. "Sure, sugar, talk to me. What can I do for you?"

He manuevered himself behind her, his breath at her ear as he whispered, "Die, lady, just die...."

He was behind her as he slit her throat. The killing was incredibly neat. He didn't spatter a drop of blood on himself.

She slumped to the floor, and he went to work, literally tearing the place apart.

And finally, wedged into the reclining chair where her customers lay as she worked, he found the Polaroids.

He looked at himself, as taken by Holly Tyler.

He slid the photos into his pocket and glanced at his watch. It had taken him less than fifteen minutes. He needed to get out.

But still...

He hesitated. He looked down at Tammy, and he couldn't resist. He had a few minutes left....

He looked over her equipment, and then he went to work.

13

By eleven that morning, Madison had made the drive back to her house. She'd wanted to leave Kyle at the police station or at his hotel, so he could pick his rental car, but he insisted on coming back to her house. He came in with her, searching the premises—despite the fact that her part-time housekeeper, Peggy O'Rourke, was in residence. And though he was polite to Peggy—it was hard not to be, because Peggy was round, rosy-cheeked, reassuringly matronly, with a touch of her old-country accent still remaining—he gave Madison the third degree, demanding to know exactly who had keys to the house.

"Peggy does. She comes three days a week."

"Which days?"

"It depends. We go on a week-to-week basis."

Kyle ran his fingers through his hair, looking exasperated. "All right, who else?"

"Jassy. My father."

"Anyone else?"

"Ummm...Kaila."

"And?"

"Trent...maybe Rafe, I don't remember if I gave him a key or not."

"Why the hell did you bother with keys? Why not just ask all of Miami in?" Kyle demanded.

"I don't always know ahead of time when I'm going to be traveling, and we have a cat, two hamsters and fish. Sometimes I call and have to hope I can catch someone just to feed the pets. And everyone I just told you is a member of my family, except—"

"Except..."

Madison hesitated. "Jimmy Gates might have a set of keys, too."

"Jimmy Gates?"

"Jimmy is a cop. You know, sometimes he'd meet me here so I could work with him, and I couldn't leave him just sitting outside if I was running late or—"

"Madison!" he snapped. He was losing his temper, he realized, running his fingers through his hair with such force that it was getting ragged. He shook his head, trying to gain control. "Interesting. I told Jimmy I was coming in here the other morning, and he didn't even tell me he had a key."

"Well, you shouldn't break and enter," she murmured.

"Madison, you've got to get your locks changed."

"The keys all belong to people I know and trust—"

"Who might accidentally leave them lying around somewhere."

"Kyle, you're getting paranoid."

"It can't hurt. Is Peggy with you all day?"

"All day."

"What time is Carrie Anne coming back today?"

"I get her at two o'clock."

"All right. Come right back here and—"

"Kyle, wait! I take her out on Friday afternoons. We go to the movies, to the ice-cream parlor for dinner, or something. It's her afternoon."

"Fine. Call me on the cellular. Let me know where you are."

"This is ridiculous," she assured him.

As she spoke, his phone started ringing. He patted his pockets until he found it, flipped it open and spoke his name tersely into the mouthpiece. His eyes were on hers as he listened. She saw disgusted dismay sharpen his green gaze and new tension tighten his features.

"Pick me up at Madison's," he said briefly, then clicked off.

"What happened?" Madison asked.

"The tattoo artist who gave us the information about Holly Tyler is dead."

Madison had to admit to a quickening of uneasy fear within her. "What happened?"

"Throat slashed."

"Where was she found?"

"In her tattoo parlor."

"Maybe it was a robbery attempt gone bad. The serial killer hasn't been leaving his victims where they can be found. Was she a redhead?"

"Umm, more like orange. Neon orange."

"And it's not the middle of the month—"

"The killer is a psychopath, but a clever one. He's able to don and doff his charm and respectability as easily as he might a coat. Usually—whenever we get lucky enough to make an arrest—this kind of killer eventually begins to lose control. He dons and doffs his coat too quickly, cracks somewhere, and becomes visible to his family or friends. But right now,

I don't think our killer is working from need or to satisfy the demands of his damaged psyche. Logic warned him that this woman had proven to be dangerous to him once and told him that she had to be silenced. Either that, or..."

"Or what?"

Kyle shrugged. "The snapshots Holly Tyler told Tammy about weren't in her house. They were lost somewhere between home and the tattoo parlor, so to find the photos, our killer might have thought he had to get rid of Tammy. So, Madison," he added, just as a horn began beeping outside, "you let me know where you are all day, you understand? And carry your cell phone with you at all times."

"People get mad at you when your cell phone rings in the movies!" Madison said.

"Skip the movies, then, or let them get mad."

"Kyle—"

"Jimmy's out there. I've got to go."

"But, Kyle, this might not even have been the same killer."

"It was."

"But how—"

"Because when the killer was done, he left his signature."

"His signature?"

"He used Tammy's own instruments to tattoo a rose on her back. Satisfied?"

Madison nodded, meeting his eyes.

"I'll be here tonight," he told her.

She nodded, following him to the door and watching as he met Jimmy on the front walk.

Jimmy began talking entreatingly. Kyle shook his head emphatically.

Jimmy wanted her to come with them, Madison realized.

Kyle wasn't going to let it happen.

She closed the door softly, leaning against it. She might be able to help at the tattoo parlor or she might not. She didn't want to go, that much she felt strongly.

Which meant that she should.

"Peggy!" she called to her housekeeper. "I've got to go back out."

Peggy came walking quickly from the kitchen, dusting her hands off on her apron. She was a bundle of energy. When Madison and Carrie Anne were both out of the house or she had a hard time finding anything else to clean, she started baking.

"Shall I get Carrie Anne?"

"That might be a good idea," Madison agreed. "The keys to my Cherokee are on the buffet there. I know, pick her up for me, then meet me in front of the movie theaters at the Falls. We can meet at three."

"Sounds like a fine idea, dear. I'll be there."

Madison cracked the door open again. The two men were still arguing.

"Will Mr. Montgomery be staying here? Do you need the guest room freshened?"

Madison looked around at Peggy. "I suppose. I should leave him out here on the couch.... No, fix the guest room, I guess. Thank you, Peggy. I guess I've got to hurry now—I think I have to break up a fight. I'll see you at three at the Falls!" she said, and hurried out.

"Madison only sees the victims!" Kyle was insisting angrily.

"But what she sees may be what we're looking for!" Jimmy pleaded.

"Kyle," Madison said from behind him.

She watched his shoulders tighten, then he turned around and stared at her.

"Kyle, it's all right. I'm coming with you."

"If you insist," he said coldly, and walked ahead to Jimmy's car, sliding into the front passenger seat.

Jimmy shrugged unhappily at Madison, then walked with her to his car, opening the rear door and ushering her in. As they drove, Kyle asked Jimmy curt questions, and Jimmy replied in kind.

Tamara Leigh Harding had been found at ten-thirty by one of her employees. The tattoo parlor had been ransacked. There were fingerprints everywhere, but the print people were already ninety-nine-and-nine-tenths-percent certain that the killer had been wearing gloves.

No murder weapon had been found at the scene or in a search of the nearby area. The coroner believed that the killer had been right-handed, seizing Tammy from behind, then slashing his knife from left to right across her throat. The killer wouldn't necessarily be covered in blood, because the blood would have spattered forward while the killer was protected from the spray by the body of his victim. Tables, chairs, desks and records were all in disarray, yet nothing appeared to have been taken. Tammy's purse had been dumped out on her desk, but her wallet, with approximately two hundred dollars in it, had been left undisturbed. There was almost five hundred dollars in cash in the register.

Yellow crime tape roped off the sidewalk and the front and back doors to the tattoo parlor. As they walked quickly to the scene, Jimmy flashing his badge to the street cops on duty, Kyle put a hand on the small of Madison's back to hurry her past the crowd of gawking onlookers.

She felt an uneasily little quiver as they neared the back door. She paused, looking around quickly, wondering if the killer was watching them. She didn't get a chance to test the feeling, because Kyle was anxious to keep her from being seen. He propelled her the last few feet toward the door.

The victim remained on the floor. Photographers were still taking shots of her from different angles.

She lay in a pool of congealed blood that resembled a big spill of cherry Jell-O. Madison braced herself, staring down at the woman. Her eyes remained open, as did her mouth, as if she had died in complete surprise. Her shirt had been ripped open at the back, and there was the rose.

It was sketched out as if a kid had done it. Stem, petals, flower—and thorns.

A fly buzzed, then settled on the dead woman's mouth.

Madison was afraid she was going to be sick. She breathed through her mouth.

Kyle stood slightly behind her, arms crossed over his chest. He was watching her, she knew. He didn't intend to lend any support. He was angry; she shouldn't be here.

Voices droned around her for a minute while she wavered, Jimmy and Kyle talking to the officers on the scene. Then Jimmy turned to her.

"Madison?"

She hesitated, stared at the victim again and closed her eyes.

She looked up then, toward the back door. It seemed to be covered in shadows. But there was someone there. She heard the dead woman, telling the man that she wasn't open yet. The man spoke again, his voice husky.

The dead woman smiled. Coquettishly. She was flirting; she was excited....

More excited as the killer came up behind her. Then, briefly, so briefly...she saw the flash of steel.

Tasted...tasted hot blood in her throat. Oh, God, she tasted it even before she knew what it was....

And that was that.

"Madison?"

She realized she'd almost blacked out, almost fallen. Kyle hadn't caught her, Jimmy had. He steadied her. One of the officers quickly brought her a cup of water. She thanked him.

Kyle wasn't even in the tattoo parlor anymore, she realized.

"What did you see?" Jimmy asked her.

"Nothing. A man in the shadows. She was flirting with him. She invited him in, even after she had said she was closed."

"What did he come for? Why did he do this?"

"I don't know. She didn't know. He just appeared at her door, she liked him, he came in...and killed her."

Jimmy nodded gravely, "All right, Madison. I know how rough this is on you. Thanks."

"It's all right, Jimmy."

"Come on."

He led her back out to the car. Kyle was already seated in the front passenger seat.

"She didn't actually see the killer," Jimmy said as he and Madison entered the car and he revved it into gear.

"Of course she didn't," Kyle said flatly.

"You never know—"

Kyle swung around, staring at Madison. "You watched the victim die."

"Yes. But—"

"And now images of that poor woman are going to haunt you, along with the dozens of others you've seen. Bit by bit, you're going to strip away your sanity."

"I'm all right, Kyle."

"It's madness, Madison. You can't be used this way."

"Kyle, if I can stop the killings—"

"Madison, you haven't stopped the killings! All you may have done is endanger yourself! What good is this doing?"

She inhaled deeply. "I know that Tammy didn't know her killer, or why he had come. And I know that…that she was attracted to him, and that he was able to kill her very quickly."

Kyle turned around again, staring out the front window.

"You're not going to see the killer, Madison," he said harshly.

"Why not?" Madison asked.

"Yeah, why not?" Jimmy demanded.

"Stay out of this, Jimmy!"

"Then tell me, Kyle!" Madison demanded angrily.

"The killer doesn't want you to see him."

"How can the killer stop Madison from seeing?" Jimmy asked. "How could he even know about Madison?"

"Oh, easily enough. Madison is a public figure. There have been articles in the paper about her gift. Maybe the killer is even someone close to her. There's a block in her mind for some reason."

"But could he really believe he could create a block?"

"Maybe. Maybe he thinks she can only see the victims of a violent crime. Maybe he believes that she just won't look at him. If you don't look, you can't see. Then again..."

"What?" Jimmy asked.

"Then again, maybe somewhere along the damned line, he's going to get nervous as all hell—and decide that Madison needs to be eliminated. Like that poor woman in there. She could end up with her throat slit!"

He was angry.

And maybe right.

The three of them drove in silence.

Kyle refused to just let her out of the car at the Falls, so he and Jimmy escorted her past the various shops until they reached the movie theaters. Peggy and Carrie Anne were already there. Carrie Anne let out a screech of delight and hurled herself into her mother's arms. They hugged and laughed, and Carrie Anne assured her mother that her daddy was fine, and they'd had a good time, and Daddy had even remembered to pay for her class pictures on time.

Carrie Anne greeted Jimmy with a hug, and Kyle

the same way—just a little more shyly. Carrie Anne wanted Jimmy and Kyle to join them for the movie and dinner, but though they both said they were really sorry, they had to go back to work.

Warning Madison to go straight home after dinner, Jimmy and Kyle left at last.

Madison watched them go, disturbed to realize that Kyle seemed to be growing more and more nervous where she was concerned.

"What a handsome man!" Peggy said approvingly before she left.

"Daddy said Kyle was a good guy," Carrie Anne told her gravely.

"He did, did he?"

Carrie Anne nodded solemnly. "He said that you always loved Kyle a whole lot."

"Well, you know, he was my stepbrother," Madison murmured.

Carrie Anne shrugged. "I think Daddy meant you were always in love with Kyle," she said, sounding incredibly mature for her age. "But he's okay with it," she assured her. "He's dating Lindy. She was real nice. It's funny. She kind of looks like you, Mommy. She's not as pretty, but she has green eyes—and real pretty dark red hair. Just like yours and Aunt Kaila's. He talked a whole lot to Lindy."

"Carrie Anne, you shouldn't have been listening, and I don't want to hear everything your daddy said to Lindy, okay?"

"Okay."

Madison shivered. Oh, God, she wasn't going to start suspecting Darryl of evil doings! she told herself. Damn Kyle! She couldn't run around being afraid of her own family and friends. There had to be somebody left to trust!

"Let's go see this movie. And it doesn't matter what Lindy looks like, as long as she's good to you and Daddy," Madison told Kaila.

Because it didn't matter what the woman looked like.

Did it?

While Kyle was at the morgue, drinking stale coffee in the lounge and awaiting a full report on Tammy, Jassy came to see him.

"Hey, big brother."

"Hey, sis."

"Lobster bisque, shrimp étouffée, fried potatoes, green salad with a vinaigrette dressing."

He arched a brow. "Jassy, I'm not hungry."

"Holly Tyler's last meal. Here's a copy of the lab report. We've already got guys from Dade and Monroe checking out restaurants from Miami to Key West."

"Tell Jimmy to get them to concentrate south of Florida City. We already know what time Holly got her tattoo. Dinner probably followed, and it looks like they were heading south."

"You sure?"

He hesitated, then shrugged. "Your sister 'saw' them driving south, past Lake Surprise. Yeah, I'm sure."

"I'll tell Jimmy."

There wasn't much else the coroner could tell them about Tammy's death that they didn't already know. She'd trusted her killer until she swallowed her own blood. She hadn't fought, hadn't protested, she had just died. There wasn't a smidgen of anything but ink beneath her fingernails. A number of the fingerprints they had been able to lift from her desk, the doorway and a few other places matched up to some guys with lengthy criminal records, and Kyle knew they would have to check them all out. He was certain, though, that the ex-cons had come for tattoos. The killer's fingerprints wouldn't be on record anywhere.

He spent part of the late afternoon and early evening interviewing Tammy's employees and friends and two ex-lovers. They all seemed to check out.

At six he called his office in Virginia, hoping that Ricky Haines would have something to tell him, either on Harry Nore's whereabouts, or on any similar crimes elsewhere across the country. Ricky sounded tired and defeated. "The only thing I found that might have some relation is a case that occurred in West Palm Beach about two years back."

"Tell me."

"There's not much there, because no one ever prosecuted. A young female cop tried to get some of the women involved to do something, but you know how rape cases go. It's hard to get the victims to testify against their attackers, because no matter how we try to bring things into the twentieth century, it's almost impossible to keep the victims from being victimized all over again."

"I know. Tell me about this case. Maybe I can go see this policewoman."

"Well, it's a tough one. The policewoman is a lady named Marge Krell. A friend of hers dragged her out to see another friend who had been roughed up. She'd been charmed into going out with a guy, then decided that it was going faster than she wanted. They wound up at a hotel, and she said no, and the next thing, he's wielding a knife at her. He doesn't cut her, but he threatens her, ties her up, and rapes her. The girl doesn't do anything, because she did go to the hotel with him. Plus she's married. She's been separated, but now she's got a chance to get back together with her husband, and she doesn't want the husband to know what happened. The guy supposedly works as a tennis pro at a Palm Beach club, but when the woman calls the club, he doesn't exist. Off the record, the policewoman finds out about a few other women he charmed and then raped, but the ladies were all afraid to testify, since they had gone with him.''

''No one was killed?''

''Not that we know about. Although, since then, two badly decomposed bodies of young women who had disappeared were found in some swampland in the general area. They were pretty much down to bone, though, and the coroner's office couldn't give an exact cause of death in either case.''

''There could be a relation here,'' Kyle commented.

''I'm sure of it, Kyle.''

''Why?''

''Get this—the women involved were all redheads.''

When Kyle hung up, he put a call through to Marge Krell. She wasn't sure what kind of help she could give him, but she was more than willing to try. ''Only two women ever talked to me. Claire Engle—and she's since gone back to her husband, had a child and moved to Iowa. She's denying what happened. You could subpoena her straight into a courtroom before God Almighty, and she wouldn't breathe a word. Then there's Josie Morgan. She'll talk with you, I'm certain. We've kept up with each other, become friends, so I happen to know she's out on a cruise ship, due back Wednesday morning. She's a good kid. I'm sure I can set up a meeting for Wednesday afternoon. I'll meet her ship when it comes in, and we'll come see you together. I'll have to ask my captain, of course—''

"The FBI can arrange the day for you," Kyle assured her. "How about lunch?"

"Great. Where are you taking us?"

"Where do you want to go?"

Marge opted for an Italian restaurant in Coconut Grove. He hung up, hoping he might have found his break at last.

Violence usually escalated. Their killer might very well have started off as a rapist.

Or...

What if their killer was the same man who had stabbed Lainie Adair? Had his hatred lain dormant all these years? Had the one killing sufficed for a very long time, until he had felt the need to take a woman and hurt her...

For not giving him something he wanted? Something he needed?

Thinking about Lainie, he read and reread the psychological reports on Harry Nore. Doing so, he became more and more certain that Harry Nore hadn't killed Lainie Adair. Yes, Nore had killed his wife with a butcher knife. But he'd been using the knife at the time, to cut meat in his kitchen.

His wife had pulled the plug on his radio in the middle of the NBA finals. A little drastic, but a man with severe psychological disorders might overreact. Domestic violence was often triggered by some small incident.

All right, so Harry had been found with the knife that killed Lainie. He was living like a bum on the street corners of Coconut Grove at the time. He could have found the knife.

Sitting at Jimmy's desk and going over and over the reports, Kyle rubbed the back of his neck.

"Hey."

He looked up. It was Jimmy.

"Are you going to get out of here? It's ten o'clock."

Kyle started, glancing at his watch. He packed up his papers. Ten o'clock.

Damn it. Why did he suddenly feel so panicked about Madison?

This dream was different.

She was in a car. It was her in the car, but it wasn't her, either. She was driving.

He was at her side. He was telling her where to go, but she already knew. She'd been there before. A long time ago, as a little girl.

They were headed for a place out in the swamps. Once, before the city got so big, before the environmentalists realized that the unique ecosystem of the Florida Everglades was being destroyed, guys had kept hunting shacks out in the swamps. They would go out there to hunt alligators, but mostly, they would shoot up beer cans. Both Jordan Adair and

Roger Montgomery had kept shacks out in the Everglades.

"I love you, and you love me, and tonight you're going to show me that you love me."

He was sitting next to her, in the passenger seat. She couldn't see him, but she was terrified. She was so frightened that she would have just stopped the car and run into the swamp and hoped to outrun him, except...

Someone was in the back seat. Whispering, "Mommy?"

Over and over again. In a frightened voice.

"You're going to love me...bitch. You're not going to hurt me, you're not going to cut my heart out, you're going to give it all back."

"Mommy?"

She opened her mouth, then gasped, feeling the point of something against her side. She looked down.

A knife.

Huge, with a six-inch blade. It was silver, glittering in the sunlight. The light reflected off it, blinding her when she tried to look up, into his face. The knife was touching her. Just touching her. Not cutting into her. Not yet. But as she stared at it...

Blood seemed to seep from it, and she knew it was the blood of those who had come before her....

She woke up soaked in a cold sweat.

And realized that someone was in her room. Someone watching her. Waiting...

She started to scream.

Kaila ran out to the store late.

She didn't usually go grocery shopping at ten at

night, but she hadn't realized that she was out of milk. Dan had run late, they'd just had dinner, and he would have gone to the store for her, she knew, but he looked really worn-out, and she needed to get out of the house for a few minutes, anyway.

She spent more time than she had intended, enjoying the solitude, though she didn't really buy much of anything. With her one brown bag, she walked out of the store at ten-thirty.

She was headed for her beige Lexus when, suddenly, she felt a tap on her shoulder. She turned around in surprise, then saw him.

And she shivered, dismayed, angry, oddly frightened.

"Kaila, let me help you."

"No...no, it's just one little bag."

"What are you doing out so late?"

"Just buying milk."

"Dan should have come out. The night is dangerous."

"No, lots of people shop on Friday night. The store stays open until eleven."

"It's still dangerous." He hesitated. "He doesn't love you enough. Like I do. When are you going to realize that? When are you going to come with me?" He leaned close to her, his voice husky. "Let me lick you all over. Let me eat those panties off you!"

She inhaled sharply. "How could you have done such a thing to me!" she demanded angrily.

"What? I sent you a present for us to share."

She shook her head. "I thought it came from Dan."

His face hardened. "Why would it have come

from Dan? You told me he was an ass who couldn't even come home on time.''

''I—I was wrong. Look, I know that I've kind of led you on, but…Dan is the father of my children. We're married, we've had problems, but we'll work them out. You've always made me feel good when I've been down, and I appreciate that, but…''

''But what, Kaila?''

''Please, no more presents. There can't be anything between us. Except the closeness we've always had.''

He shook his head. ''You're wrong,'' he said very softly, tenderly. ''You love me. Eventually you'll realize it. So screw Dan.''

''You don't understand,'' Kaila tried to explain.

''Yeah, I do. You're being a cunt, like most women. Like your mother.''

''My God, how could you— How dare you—''

''Sorry,'' he said briefly. ''All right, you're in love with your husband again. I'll put your bag in your car for you.'' He took the bag from her and walked to the car with it. She was suddenly afraid that he was going to force his way in with her.

He didn't. He put the bag on the back seat and closed the door. ''Look, Kaila, I'm sorry. What I said was awful. You have been leading me on, though. And you are going to have trouble with Dan again. You'll be looking for what I can give you again.''

''No… Please, I didn't mean to hurt you. I was just going through a bad time. And Dan is furious. I lied like crazy, but he's determined to find out where those panties came from. Please, you've got to be careful. We've got to stop talking, and—''

"Kissing?"

"Right. We have to stop kissing. Please, don't be angry with me. I care about you. Please, don't be mad."

"I'm not mad." He smiled at her. "Because you'll be back."

She shook her head. "I won't."

"Kiss goodbye?" he inquired.

"Sure."

It wasn't a chaste kiss. He wanted more, and because she was unnerved at first, she didn't fight him. Then she found the strength to pull away.

He drew away from her. "I still love you."

"The best of friends," she murmured.

"We'll see."

"Don't be mad."

"I'm not mad. Not at all."

He turned and walked away. She shivered fiercely. She wondered if she should come clean. Tell Dan what she'd almost done.

Oh, God, no, she couldn't. Too many other people were involved; she could ruin everything.

Kaila drove home quickly, called out to Dan that she was back and put her few groceries away. Dan was already in bed, watching television, when she went into their room. He patted her side of the bed, smiling hopefully.

"Just a sec—I'm going to shower."

She showered, then brushed her teeth and rinsed with mouthwash, assuring herself that the taste of another man's lips couldn't possibly remain on her own.

14

"Oh, right! Let's bring Madison along. Let's make her look at another damn murder victim!" Kyle swore.

The light was on, and he was pacing back and forth in front of her bed. He was wearing black-cotton boxers, looking as hard and sleek as a panther, and just as edgy and dangerous as any caged cat. She remained in bed—relieved, oh, God, yes, relieved!—sitting up against the headboard, feeling the beginning of a pounding headache. Kyle was in a dark, angry mood.

Not that he hadn't been reassuring at first, encircling her with his arms, holding her tighter and tighter until she knew it was him and her trembling stopped.

"You—you were in my room," she reminded him. "You scared me."

"You *knew* I was coming back. And you were shouting and crying out in your sleep. I figured you were dreaming again, but if you were, I had to wake you up. And if you weren't…well, hell, hopefully I was going to save your life."

"Then I'm sorry, but honestly, you scared me—"

"What was the dream?"

"I…don't remember."

"Bull. You remember all kinds of stuff you don't tell me. You had a vision off your father's boat that day, and you didn't say a word to me. You waited until we were with Jimmy, the next day."

"Well, Jimmy doesn't think I intrude on his life."

He paused, taking a deep breath, shaking his head. "Damn it, Madison, this isn't the time to make me pay for any of the stupid things I might have said to you when I was upset."

A violent shiver suddenly seized hold of her.

He stopped pacing, staring at her, coming back to her side. He sat on the bed beside her and drew her against him, and she felt the pounding of his heart, felt the different rhythm of her own.

"What is it?" he asked huskily.

"I'm all right. Just an aftershiver."

"What was the dream? Was it about Tammy?"

She pulled away from him, looking at him, and shook her head. "No, it was strange, I can't quite seem to remember exactly... It had the past mixed up with the present. I was driving west along the Tamiami Trail to the hunting shacks. It was me, but it wasn't me.... It was like when we were kids, except that I was grown up, and the killer was trying to take me away somewhere, but I couldn't run, because..."

"Because?"

"There was a child in the car."

"Carrie Anne?"

"I don't know. I don't think so. It was very, very strange. It was me, but it was someone else—"

"You always see through the victim's eyes."

"Yes, but, this was different from the dreams I've had before." She exhaled a long breath. "Some people have the gift of prophecy, but I never have. I've only seen what's already happened. This dream was different. It wasn't anything that's happened, and it was and wasn't me, in a different way. And the child…he kept saying, 'Mommy.' Weird, huh?''

"So you don't think that any of it actually happened?''

She shook her head. "No. I mean… Please, tell me there haven't been any children involved in any of these murders, right?''

He shook his head. "No. No kids.''

"Then maybe…I don't know, maybe I have seen one corpse too many.'' She hesitated. "How come Jassy never has nightmares?''

"She has a scientific mind.''

"I wish I did.'' She hesitated. "Kyle, I still feel I can help on this. I feel it more and more.''

"And more and more, I get the feeling that you're in danger. Besides that, you're suffering. You're suffering for every poor woman killed, and it's bound to take a toll on you.''

"I'm okay. Cops and doctors learn to live with pain and death. I can do the same. I *have* done the same. I have to stay on this case. I *have* to!''

"Damn it, Madison, only if you promise to listen to me.''

"Oh, really? Who made you the boss?''

"The FBI.''

"Well, they didn't make you the boss of my life.''

"If you want in on this one, I am.''

"Mommy?''

They both turned. Carrie Anne, her thumb in her mouth, was standing in the doorway to Madison's room.

Guilt swamped Madison. She wasn't even doing anything, but she couldn't help feeling guilty. She'd had the best possible divorce, but she still felt bad for Carrie Anne. Carrie Anne adored her father, and this just felt…uncomfortable.

"Hi, sweetie, come on in!" Madison said, pulling away from Kyle.

Kyle stood. "Hi, munchkin."

She glared at Kyle.

He hunkered down to her level. "Your mommy was having a nightmare."

"Were you sleeping in here?" she asked him.

"I'm in the guest room down the hall."

"No, you're not. You're right here."

"I *was* sleeping in the guest room down the hall. Then your mommy had a nightmare."

Carrie Anne glanced at Madison, then nodded gravely and looked back at Kyle. "She has a lot of awful dreams."

"Thanks, sweetie," Madison murmured.

Carrie Anne was still studying Kyle. "Are you going to marry Mommy?"

"Carrie Anne!" Madison gasped, stunned.

"There's nothing wrong with it, Mommy. He's not really your brother," Carrie Anne said. "That's what Lindy told Daddy. Daddy's worried because he said you were supposed to have your own little girl, Kyle, and he doesn't want you thinking that you're my daddy or anything like that. He told her that he liked you a lot, though, even if the only thing wrong with *him* was that he wasn't *you*."

Madison bounded out of bed, lifting her daughter up in her arms. "Carrie Anne, you know you're not supposed to listen to grown-up conversations, and you should *never* repeat things that Daddy says. Remember how I told you earlier that I didn't want to hear what Daddy and Lindy were talking about?''

Kyle rose, standing before her. He was trying to hide a very amused smile.

"I guess I should go back to the guest room.''

Carrie Anne nodded solemnly. ''You can't sleep in here unless you're married.''

"I know that,'' Kyle said. ''And you know what? I like your daddy, and I did lose a little baby girl a long time ago, so it's nice get to spend some time with you. I don't think he minds that. I'll ask him next time we talk.''

"Go ahead,'' Madison murmured. ''Because I'm going to kill him!''

"Who? Daddy?'' Carrie Anne asked, concerned.

"No. I mean... You know what? I'm going to make some hot chocolate. How's that?''

"I'll start the water,'' Kyle said. ''And I'm going to want Kahlua in mine!''

He left the room. Madison set Carrie Anne down. ''Now, you, young lady!''

Carrie Anne frowned, her little face puckering. ''I'm sorry, Mommy, what did I do?''

"Oh...'' Madison groaned softly. She hugged her daughter to her chest. ''So, you think maybe Daddy plans on marrying Lindy?''

"Maybe.''

"You know, Daddy comes down here a lot. I bet he's been getting to know her for a long time, making sure she'd be a good stepmother before he decided to introduce you to her.''

"Daddy would do that, wouldn't he? Make sure that a stepmother would like me? Stepmothers can be really bad, you know. Like in 'Snow White.' And 'Cinderella.'"

Madison laughed softly. "Daddy loves you more than anyone in the whole world. He would always think of you first. And so would I."

"Then it's okay."

"What's okay?"

"If Daddy marries Lindy. And if you marry Kyle."

"Honey, you know, Kyle really lives near Washington. He's here to work, but when he finishes, he—"

"Hey, water's boiling! Where's the powdered stuff?" Kyle called from the kitchen.

"I'll show you!" Carrie Anne cried out, running from the bedroom to help him. With a sigh, Madison followed.

Carrie Anne chattered as they drank. She began by telling Kyle about her friends in kindergarten. Then she told him about the great movie he had missed.

And he was good with her. He listened. He didn't pretend to listen, he *really* listened. When he asked her what she thought about the movie, he really wanted to hear answer.

Sipping her hot chocolate, listening, Madison was sorry again. His wife and child should have lived. He would have been a good father.

Finally she broke in. "Carrie Anne, you have to get some sleep."

"Okay, Mommy."

"Want to sleep with me?"

"No."

She kissed her mother. Then she kissed Kyle.

Madison walked her back to her bedroom. When Carrie Anne was tucked in, Madison went back to the kitchen, only to discover that. Kyle had returned to his own room. She did the same.

It was a very long night.

Saturday morning, Madison decided to get artistic with breakfast.

The coffee was already made when she woke up, and when she tapped on Kyle's door, she discovered that he was busy at his computer, which he'd plugged in on the desk near the window. "Sorry to interrupt. Thanks," she said, and lifted her cup of coffee to him.

He nodded briefly, looking at her.

"I didn't mean to disturb you."

"It's all right."

"I'm going to make Carrie Anne breakfast. Want some?"

"Sure."

"I'll send Carrie Anne to tell you when it's ready."

She told herself that she didn't need to impress him with her domestic skills—or lack of them. She wasn't really a great cook, but the things she could prepare, she did well. She decided to make French toast, strawberries with hand-whipped cream, omelettes with peppers, mushrooms and onions, fresh juice...and in the end, she broke down and fried bacon. She loved bacon, though she almost never indulged.

Carrie Anne helped her set the table in the breakfast nook. It was a pretty spot at the rear of the kitchen, overlooking the screened-in pool and patio.

She had invested in her house as her first big expenditure after her divorce, thinking a new home was the way for her to begin a new life. She still loved the house, even if it sometimes felt awfully big just for her, Carrie Anne and sometimes Peggy. A young couple with a baby had had the house custom-built before discovering the husband was being transferred to Toronto, and they had thought of all kinds of wonderful little details. The breakfast nook was one of them. It had a bay window that overlooked the bubbling spa end of the pool. It was pretty and peaceful.

"Wow!" Kyle said, arriving with Carrie Anne. He was in denim cutoffs, sandals and a black tank top decorated with the name of a popular rock band. A lock of his dark hair fell over his forehead, as if he'd been running his fingers through it while deep in thought. He absently repeated the gesture, looking at Carrie Anne, the breakfast table and Madison, behind the counter. "Carrie Anne, do you have breakfast like this every morning?" he asked seriously.

"Oh, no. I usually have Cheerios and Mommy eats stuff with raisins in it."

Kyle smiled. "Well, then, this is special."

"I'm feeling restless, I guess," Madison murmured. She looked reproachfully at her daughter. "And we do cook on weekends. Always."

"Always?" Kyle asked Carrie Anne.

She smiled happily and shrugged. They had become coconspirators.

"Sit down and eat and quit torturing me," Madison advised. As she was pouring juice, the phone began to ring.

Carrie Anne ran to the counter, then stood by the

phone. "Can I answer, Mommy, or should I let the machine get it?"

"Ah, so you usually do screen your calls," Kyle murmured, helping himself to food.

"And you don't?" Madison said, indicating that Carrie Anne should answer the phone.

"Hello?" Carrie Anne said into the receiver. She smiled right away and looked at Madison. "It's Auntie Kaila. She wants us to come over. She says she knows Kyle is here, and she thinks he should quit working so hard and come over this afternoon to swim and have a barbecue. Uncle Dan is home, and he wants to cook. Can we, Mom, can we?"

Madison hesitated. "Kyle may need to work."

"If I'm needed, they'll call me. I put in a dozen hours yesterday. I wouldn't mind an afternoon in the sun."

"Mommy?" Carrie Anne said hopefully.

"Sure. Tell her to give us time to eat, clean up and get some stuff together. What does she want us to bring?"

Carrie Anne turned studiously back to the phone. "Aunt Kaila, what do you want us to bring?"

She listened and turned back to Madison. "She said to bring ourselves."

Madison laughed. "Tell her we'll be along in a while."

Carrie Anne did so, then hung up. She was so excited that she didn't want to sit down and eat, but Madison warned her that they weren't going anywhere until they'd all had breakfast.

Kyle was an extremely polite guest, complimenting Madison and Carrie Anne on every dish. When they were finished eating, he offered to help pick up.

Madison thanked him, then said, "You two go get ready. I can manage quicker by myself. Maybe you could get your bathing-suit bag together, Carrie Anne, then run with Kyle to pick up some sodas or beer and cookies or something."

"Aunt Kaila said just to bring ourselves," Carrie Anne reminded her.

"Carrie Anne—" Madison began.

"We don't want to be empty-handed, now, do we?" Kyle inquired. "I don't know your uncle Dan that well yet. I've got to make a good impression, huh?"

"Sure. I'll show you the right kind of cookies."

"For Uncle Dan?" Kyle asked.

"For Justin, Shelley and baby Anthony," Carrie Anne said gravely.

"If we're going to impress Uncle Dan, get him some Guinness," Madison advised.

"Gotcha," Kyle said.

While they were gone, Madison quickly cleaned up and dressed in her bathing suit, throwing shorts and a T-shirt over it. She was slipping into her sandals when the phone rang, and she hurried to pick it up, thinking it might be Kaila, asking them to get ice or something else on the way.

"Hello?" she said, hopping into one shoe.

"Madison." It was Darryl.

"Hey! I've got a bone to pick with you," she warned him good-naturedly.

"Ouch. Don't talk about bones. I ran into your father and Jassy having dinner last night in the Grove. Naturally she gave me the lowdown on these corpses that keep turning up."

"Hmm. I guess she can't help it."

"So? What's the bone?"

"First, why did you call? What's on your mind?"

"A friend. Named Lindy. It's getting kind of serious, and I wanted to bring her tomorrow night, but it's Roger's show—your family's affair, in a way—and I wanted to make sure it would be okay."

She smiled, looking at the receiver, feeling a welling-up of affection for Darryl. She never should have married him, but still, she was glad she had. They both had Carrie Anne, and she had a good friend.

"Darryl, we've been divorced for nearly three years! Of course you can bring Lindy. I've heard all about her."

"You have?" He sounded surprised.

She sighed softly. "Darryl, that's my bone. You two weren't very discreet. Carrie Anne repeated all kinds of things you two were saying."

He was silent for a minute. "Oh?"

"Kyle likes you, too," she teased.

Darryl groaned softly. "So what's the story with him?" he asked. "I mean, you're right, we have been divorced a long time, but, well, we've both been so careful around Carrie Anne...."

"Darryl, don't worry. And actually...I don't know the story with Kyle. He's obsessed with the idea that I might be in danger, so he's staying here."

"That's all?"

"He's sleeping in the guest room," Madison assured him.

"Umm."

"What does that mean? Darryl, I wouldn't—"

"I'm not accusing you of lying, Madison. I'll just never forget the night you had that dream...or his wife's funeral, or the way you were after. You've always had some kind of a tie to him, Madison. I don't know exactly what. But it's not going to go away.''

"*He'll* go away again," she said dryly. "He works in D.C."

"So do I—supposedly. Though it looks like I'm being transferred down here. Permanently."

"Oh, Darryl! I'm so glad."

"Really?"

"Of course!"

"Anyway, you'll get to meet Lindy, and I hope you'll like her. She's cute as a button. A redhead."

"So I heard."

"Oh, yeah?"

Madison laughed softly. "I take it you've been seeing her longer than Carrie Anne knows?"

"Yeah. I met her almost a year ago, when I was down here for Carrie Anne's birthday party. I've been seeing her when I'm down...and she's come up to see me a few times, too."

"Good. I want your next marriage to be a success."

"Thanks. I'm grateful my first marriage left me with such a good friend."

"So am I. We'll see you at Roger's shindig, then. Can't wait to meet your girl."

"Good. Hey, Madison?"

"Hmm?"

"Are divorces supposed to be this good?"

"I try not to question my blessings in life," she told him.

"I'm a blessing?"

"You bet."

"Love you, kid. And, hey..."

"Yeah?"

"Don't let your pride get in the way of being happy, Madison. You married me because he hurt you. He didn't mean to. Take care."

He hung up. Madison slowly replaced the receiver. She was still staring at it when Kyle and Carrie Anne came back in.

"Anything important?" Kyle asked.

"Darryl is bringing Lindy to your dad's opening tomorrow. We'll get to meet her."

"She's nice, Mommy. Honest," Carrie Anne said.

"I'm sure she is," Madison agreed. "Go get your stuff, honey."

"I left the beer, Cokes and cookies in the car," Kyle said as Carrie Anne raced off.

"I'm all set," she told him, picking up her coffee cup, the last dish, to set it in the sink.

"You all right with that?"

"With what?" she asked, turning to him.

He was wearing his shades again. And he smelled like aftershave. A nice, subtle scent.

"With Darryl bringing Lindy."

"Why wouldn't I be?"

He shook his head. "I don't know. I mean, you were married. And it's hard to see what could have gone wrong between you."

"It didn't work."

"Was it me?" he asked.

"Kyle Montgomery, you do have an ego!" she protested. She wished he wasn't standing quite so close. "Let's get going, shall we?"

He nodded.

"Another man?"

"Let's go."

"Another woman?"

She slammed a palm against his chest, pushing him. "Let's go!"

Carrie Anne chatted all the way to Kaila's, making sure that Kyle had a good picture of all three of her cousins.

Madison just smiled.

An hour later she was really glad she had gone to her sister's. It seemed the farthest they had gotten from the dark shadow hovering over their lives for a long time. Dan was in a good mood, showing off for the kids, twirling his barbecue fork in the air and making wild slicing motions in the air as he turned the burgers. Later Madison helped Kaila wrap the leftover food and put it away, and she was glad to see that her sister seemed happy—and in love with her husband again.

"It's been a better week, huh?" Madison asked her.

Kaila smiled, shrugging, looking down at the dish she was rinsing. "A great week. Dan had a day off. He took over the chores.... We talked."

"Good. I know he loves you. He gets just as frustrated, you know. Being a lawyer is tough, time-consuming. It's hard for anyone to balance work and family these days."

"I just feel so guilty, and so scared...."

"Guilty, why?" Madison asked, frowning. "Kaila, you didn't—"

"No, no! I didn't go off and have an affair or anything."

"Then...?"

"I...I nothing!" she said quickly. "The thought, you know. You don't want to sin in thought, word or deed, right? My thoughts were pretty wicked, for a while.''

"Kaila! Did you actually have someone in mind?''

Her sister looked at her for what seemed like a long time.

"Kaila?''

"I—''

"Hey, sweetheart!'' Dan called, coming into the kitchen. He flashed Madison a smile as he slipped his arms around his wife. "Chicken fights!''

"Chicken fights?'' Kaila asked him.

Dan nodded. "You and me against Madison and Kyle. The kids are asking—no, demanding!—to be entertained!''

"They're like the old Romans, demanding Christian sacrifices in the arena. Send in the gladiators, bring on the lions!'' Kyle said, walking in behind Dan. They looked like best buddies, in similar boxer-style bathing suits and sunglasses, Guinnesses in hand. Dan was light, Kyle dark, but they were both fit and bronzed. Between them, Madison thought, they could make one great ad for men's swimwear.

"Madison?'' Kaila said.

"Uh…sure.''

"Come on, Kaila,'' Dan said. "We've got to be the lions. We must prevail. We can't humiliate ourselves in front of our children.''

"Well, now, I'm pretty good at chicken fights,'' Kyle advised Dan and Kaila solemnly.

"And I could always beat the shit out of Kaila,'' Madison warned Dan.

"Whoa, that's a challenge if I ever heard one!" Kaila cried.

Ten minutes later, she and Kaila were laughing hysterically, because no matter how hard they tried, they couldn't drag one another off the men's shoulders and into the pool. The kids were shrieking with laughter.

"Kaila, don't squirm so much!" Dan protested. "You're pulling out all the hair on my head. And I may be losing it already, you know?"

"Madison, let her go. You've got your sister's knee in my nose!" Kyle groaned.

"I'm going to beat her! I'm going to beat her!" Kaila cried, pulling with all her might on Madison's hands.

"Ha!" Madison declared, but then she and Kaila both went down.

They made tremendous splashes, and the kids demanded a rematch. Instead, Kyle set them up in the shallow end of the pool, Carrie Anne with baby Anthony on her shoulders, while Justin went into battle with Shelley on his own. Kyle helped both contestants balance and managed to let Shelley win, since she cared, and Anthony fall, since all he really wanted to do was create a big splash.

Before they left, Madison tried to take her sister aside again, but it was tough—Kaila didn't want to get taken aside. Madison finally managed to get a moment out by the car, as they were getting ready to leave. "Kaila, if something is going on, if you were almost involved with someone, please, tell me. Maybe I could help."

"Don't be silly," Kaila protested. "There...there wasn't anyone."

"Okay, I'm not going to call you a liar," Madison said quickly, seeing that Dan and Kyle were walking toward them. "But if you ever need to talk, if you ever need help, call me. Or Jassy. Or Dad!"

"Oh, yeah, Dad! He still treats Jassy as if she were sixteen."

"And she ignores him. So don't call Dad. Call me or Jassy."

"Of course, Madison."

"Honest?"

"Yeah. Sure."

Kyle was there then, along with Dan. Carrie Anne was already in the back seat, sound asleep. Madison and Kyle said good-night, Madison taking the driver's seat, since she wasn't sure just how many Guinnesses Kyle had consumed.

But when they waved goodbye and started backing out, she caught a glimpse of Kyle's eyes, and she realized he was stone-cold sober.

"What's the matter?" she asked him, smiling. "You were looking like a good old boy there for a while."

"Nothing's the matter."

"Something is."

He shrugged. "Your brother-in-law asked me to look into something for him."

"What?"

He glanced at her. "You don't know?"

She shook her head.

"She didn't say anything to you about...seeing someone?"

Madison felt as if a cold sweat were breaking out on her forehead. "Kaila's not having an affair."

"You're certain?"

"I— Yes," she lied. "Why?"

He glanced into the back seat to make sure that Carrie Anne was still sleeping, then turned back to Madison. "Because someone sent her edible panties."

"*What?*" Madison asked incredulously.

He nodded.

"But how did—how did Dan know?"

He shrugged. "Apparently Kaila thought he sent them. And she wore them for him."

"Well, then..." Madison trailed to a stop. "Obviously, if she wore them for Dan, then she isn't having an affair. Some prankster must have sent them—"

"Well, we'll find out," Kyle said casually.

Madison frowned. "Kyle, why would you want to do anything that might jeopardize Kaila's marriage?" she asked nervously.

Kyle shook his head. "You're forgetting something."

"What?"

"Your sister is a redhead. If some prankster is sending her things, I want to know just who the hell it is."

"But, Kyle, it could be—"

"Damn it, Madison, she can work on her marriage after we finish worrying about her life!" he said firmly.

Madison fell silent for a minute. "Give me a chance to talk to her, okay?"

"All right."

"All right."

"Tomorrow," Kyle said. "At my father's gallery opening. You know she'll be there."

"Right."

"Madison?"

"Yes?"

"If she doesn't talk to you, I will use every investigative avenue available to me to find out how your sister managed to get such a gift."

Madison pulled the car into her driveway. Kyle carefully lifted Carrie Anne from the back seat and carried her to the house while Madison opened the door and punched in the numbers on the alarm pad.

Kyle took Carrie Anne on into her room, where Madison thanked him. He left, as Madison got ready to change Carrie Anne into a nightgown.

Madison thought he might be waiting for her in the kitchen or the living room, but he wasn't. She hesitated, then went to the guest room door and tapped lightly.

"Yes?"

She opened the door. He was at the computer. "Sorry. Just wanted to say good-night."

"Good night, Madison."

She nodded and closed the door.

Well, so much for him dying of desire for her.

She went to bed herself, certain she would lie awake or, worse, that she would fall asleep—and dream.

She did. In her dream, she was driving. It was her, and this time she knew it was her, not some other woman. She was driving hard and fast, almost recklessly.

She was driving down the Tamiami Trail, far west, out of the city of Miami. There were old dirt roads out here. Some were roads that cut into the swamp, across canals and marshes, ending nowhere.

Some were roads that headed toward the old shacks that remained hidden deep in the pine hammocks.

She was driving in a panic, trying to get somewhere. Somewhere she knew. From a different life, she thought.

Or from a time when she had been very young.

She shouldn't be going, but she couldn't turn back.

She had to get...*somewhere.* It was like the time when she had come out of her bedroom. When she had known that she had to reach her mother. She had to move, move swiftly, because if she didn't...

Oh, God, if she didn't...

Someone else was going to die. Someone else she loved. Oh, God, she had to floor it, floor it, drive....

"Madison, shh, Madison, it's all right...."

Kyle was there. He'd gotten into the bed beside her, taken her into his arms. Now he was soothing her, running his fingers through her hair. "I'm here. It's all right."

She shivered fiercely. He held her close.

"What was it this time?"

"I was driving again. I was driving down the Tamiami Trail. I had to get somewhere really fast, and I was desperate, because if I didn't get where I was going, something awful was going to happen. I was trying to reach...one of the shacks. Remember the shacks, Kyle? When were young, Roger and my dad used to have them, until the government cracked down on the Everglades. Men used to go out there hunting, but they usually just got drunk and shot up beer cans. Your dad must have taken you out there."

"Yes, he did. They used to get so tanked up, it's

probably a miracle that the only things that ever got killed out there were beer cans.''

She smiled, then groaned, burying her face in her hands. "Am I ever going to stop dreaming?"

"Madison," he said, gently lifting her face to meet her eyes. "Those shacks were all torn down years ago. It's a new world. The environmentalists hate guys who shoot beer cans."

She half smiled, and he grazed her cheek with his knuckles. He was so close, but his arms drew her closer. She had been shivering; his strength warmed away the cold of fear. He was wearing only a robe. Temptation ruled. She slipped her fingers into the opening of the robe, running them along his chest. Lower. Her fingers brushed, then covered, the length of his erection, sending a fierce shudder throughout her. She stroked him beneath the robe, her lips coming closer to his. But he drew away suddenly, whispering softly, "The door."

Carrie Anne was in the doorway, rubbing sleep from her eyes.

"Mommy, you were screaming again."

Madison instinctively jerked away from Kyle. Loosely belting his robe, he rose, walking toward the doorway. He tousled Carrie Anne's hair. "Well, you're here now. You go snuggle Mommy, huh?"

"You can stay," Carrie Anne said politely.

He glanced over at Madison.

"I think I'll take a shower," he said pleasantly. "You girls get some sleep. Tomorrow's a big day. My dad's gallery opening."

Plagued with guilt, Madison welcomed Carrie Anne into her arms.

And tried to sleep.

15

"This just isn't working," she told Kyle over coffee in the morning.

"Oh?"

She flushed. "You haven't done anything. It's just...not working."

"This isn't about the delicacy of anybody's feelings—yours, mine, or even Carrie Anne's. You're in danger."

"We don't know that!"

"It's a damned good theory."

"But, Kyle—"

"You can't be alone."

"I'll go to Jassy's. She can shoot like a pro."

"She's never home."

"I can go to my father's."

"Maybe that's not such a good idea," he said, looking at his coffee.

Madison gasped. "You're accusing my father—"

"I know that your father and mother had a huge fight not long before she was killed. You didn't see it, because you were at school. I happened to be home, for some reason. She'd summoned Jordan to the house, crying over something my father had supposedly done, and trying to use Jordan to get my father riled. To his credit, Jordan wouldn't be used."

"Right! So he came back later to murder her! You're full of it! What about your father? He and my mother fought all the time, and I know that for a fact, because I had to listen to it just about every damned night!"

"Fine, my father is a suspect, too."

She threw up her hands. "Well, we can't keep doing this! It isn't working. What about Kaila's?"

"Do you really think Kaila needs someone else living in her house right now?"

"Darryl, then. I'm the mother of his child, for God's sake."

"Great. Then Darryl can soothe you from your dreams in the middle of the night."

"It would probably sit better with Carrie Anne," Madison murmured.

He rose, angrily walking to the sink. "Can we solve this later? I can sleep in the damned car or something, but right now I've got to get to the gallery. This event is important to my father. And you're coming with me."

She arched a brow, feeling her temper stirring. "I *am* coming with you, but *not* because you say so. I'm coming with you because Roger has always been good to me, and what's important to him is important to me!"

She spun around, leaving him in the kitchen and going off to get dressed. The opening was scheduled to run from two o'clock until ten; they arrived by twelve. Madison's job was to keep the local artists— the stars of the event—calm. For some of them that meant two tons of caffeine. For others, it meant breaking into the champagne early.

Roger was delighted that she had arrived early

with Kyle. After escaping the crowd around him, he took her hands, then stepped back, surveying her. "Gorgeous! They compare you to your mother. Rubbish. You're ten times more beautiful!" He kissed her cheek. "Thanks for coming and helping. Your dad's right over there." He looked at her assessingly again. "You are dynamite."

She hoped so. She'd dressed dramatically, in a short black silk cocktail dress that dipped in front and back, and contrasted with the vivid color of her hair. "Thanks," she told him.

"You're kind of pretty, too, son!" Roger teased Kyle. He wasn't pretty in the least. He was striking, in a black shirt with a casual pinstripe jacket and beige pants.

"Ah, Dad!" he murmured.

"Enough. To work!" Roger told them all.

By five o'clock, Madison was beat. She'd been taking care of the kids for the past hour. The gallery boasted a kids' corner, little tables with little chairs and buckets full of building blocks, crayons, stencils and so on. Kids could express their artistic vision while their parents, in Roger's words, spent "big bucks" on local talent.

She sank into one of the kiddie chairs, tired and bemused. By her side, Carrie Anne and Kaila's brood were busy doodling with a pair of five-year-old twins. Jimmy Gates was nearby, listening patiently as one of the artists explained the "surrealism" of her work. Dan and Kaila were inspecting a beautiful seascape. Madison frowned slightly. She was worried about Kaila again. Her sister seemed nervous. She kept looking over her shoulder as if she expected...what?

"Watch it! Watch it!" she heard suddenly.

She turned to see that Rafe, Trent and Kyle were carefully lifting a metal fountain sculpture of goddesses in a garden. The artist and purchaser were worriedly giving directions, along with Roger. The scene, Madison thought, was priceless.

"Hey, Jassy!"

"What?"

"Take over the kids, huh?"

"Sure."

Madison rose and wandered to the front of the gallery to observe the goings-on with the sculpture.

"Hey! Watch Athena's book there!" she warned.

"Thanks!" Trent told her, making a face.

"Got it!" Rafe assured her, grimacing.

Kyle arched a brow at her.

She smiled, following them to the doorway, then leaning against it as they struggled to get the sculpture onto the bed of its new owner's truck.

She closed her eyes for a minute. It was late spring, but the past few days had been hot as hell, and the breeze picking up this evening was beautiful. She opened her eyes and looked around. The gallery was situated just down the street from Cocowalk and Mayfair, two very unique malls. The area was also littered with charming specialty shops. The Coconut Grove area of Miami was popular with both the locals and tourists. Roger's gallery should do well.

"You!"

She didn't pay any attention to the voice at first; she was busy enjoying the breeze. And Coconut

Grove had its share of crazies, after all, most of them harmless.

"You!"

She turned then—and stared, stunned and incredulous.

There was Harry Nore. Bug-eyed, wild gray hair completely unkempt, unshaven face covered with a scraggly beard. He looked as mad as he had all those years ago, when he preened excitedly for the television cameras after Lainie's murder. Despite the heat, he was wearing a dirty old once-beige trenchcoat. And he was pointing at her—with the razor-sharp end of a switchblade.

"You! She-devil, she-bitch, spawn of Satan, seducer of innocents! You've come back. You've come back from the very bowels of hell! You've come back from the dead, like Satan's own, but Satan will have to take you back to hell, and you'll burn! You'll burn!"

The last was a screech, and with it, he catapulted toward Madison. She jumped back, slamming against the doorframe. He lunged again, and she was forced back again. She heard a crack. She had slammed against the gallery's big front window, and now she was losing her footing, sinking to the ground. She couldn't fall, couldn't let herself become vulnerable, but she couldn't regain her balance, either. She had to fight, or at least get away.

But even as she looked up into Nore's hideously contorted face and saw him so close that she could count every rotting tooth, she heard another hard slam.

Kyle had brought him down to the pavement.

Then pandemonium broke out. Trent landed on

top of Nore, as well, as people came spilling from the gallery.

Suddenly Rafe was at Madison's side. "Are you all right?"

She nodded, her mouth and throat dry. Jassy was there, ducking down beside her.

Madison grasped her sister's hands. "Get Dan. Have him take Kaila and the kids out the back. Please, I don't want Carrie Anne to see, to be afraid, please...."

"Stay with her," Rafe told Jassy. "I'll see to it that Dan and Kaila take Carrie Anne home with them for the night. The cops will be here soon. You'll have to talk to them, Madison."

"The cops are already here," a voice said. Jimmy. He, too, was kneeling beside Madison. "You okay, kid?"

She nodded.

"You've done something to your wrist, breaking your fall. Your hand is swollen."

"I'm all right."

"You need some X rays."

"The cops—"

"We can talk at the hospital," Jimmy said.

Sirens were screaming everywhere. The next thing Madison knew, her father was with her. She'd never seen him look so white, so tense.

So old.

"The ambulance is here."

"Dad, my wrist is swollen! I can walk, I don't need an ambulance."

"Right. But it's here, so get in it anyway."

Within the hour, her wrist and hand had been x-rayed. She was fine; she'd just sprained it, and an elastic bandage for a few days would make her right as rain.

As if everything that had already happened weren't enough, she wasn't even going to get to meet Darryl's new girlfriend. And she'd ruined Roger's opening. Talk about your basic day from hell...

When the nurse finished with her bandage, she returned to the waiting room. Her father, Roger, Jimmy, Jassy and Kyle were there, along with a young police officer. She gave him a brief statement, assuring him that she hadn't seen or heard from Harry Nore since her mother's death. He didn't need much from her; there had been witnesses to the attack.

"There are a bunch of reporters outside," Jassy warned her unhappily.

"I'll take the Cherokee around back and pick Madison up at a different door," Kyle said determinedly.

"That sounds good," Jordan Adair agreed. He kissed Madison on the cheek. "And stay with her," he cautioned, turning back to Kyle.

"I intend to," Kyle said, leaving.

Madison could see through the glass hospital doors that a group of reporters were milling outside. Did this mean that it was over? *Had* Harry Nore been killing women now, and had he really killed her mother all those years ago?

"Let's get you out of here," Jassy said.

She almost shoved Madison out the back. Kyle had the car running and the passenger door open. She slipped quickly inside.

He started driving in silence. He looked ashen, she realized, and his jacket was torn and dirtied from his tussle with Harry Nore.

"I really am all right," she told him. "And Carrie Anne—"

"Carrie Anne doesn't have the slightest idea that anything happened. She's with her aunt and uncle and cousins, and she's happy, because Dan is going to set up a tent in the living room so the kids can pretend they're camping out tonight."

Madison fell silent, looking down at her hands. "So, what's your plan?"

"We're getting out of here for twenty-four hours."

"How? Where?"

"You'll see. Trust me."

"I don't trust anybody anymore."

"Then consider this an abduction and do your best to enjoy it anyway."

"Where are we going right now?"

"The airport."

"The airport! I can't just—"

"Yes, you can."

"This *is* an abduction," she said angrily.

He shrugged.

"I could start screaming and pitch a real fit at the airport, and then you'd have some tough explaining to do."

"Would you please quit it! I'm taking you to do something you said you've always wanted to do."

"What?"

"Swim with dolphins."

"What?"

"You did say you wanted to swim with dolphins."

"Yes, but, we could just drive down to the Keys—"

"That's not far enough for this evening," he said determinedly. "We need to get away. I have a friend who runs a private facility on one of the islands off Martinique. We'll be there in two hours."

He was crazy. They both looked like refugees from *The Poseidon Adventure,* and he couldn't really be planning to just take off for an island with everything that was going on.

But he was.

She followed him through the airport terminal to a shop where they were able to buy T-shirts, baggy shorts, bathing suits and cheap sandals.

"You were the one who insisted I couldn't just take off without telling people!" she reminded him as they stood in line to pay.

"I've told your father and Jimmy what we're doing."

"You what? You told my dad that we were going off overnight to a Caribbean island?"

"Yes."

"How could you?"

"How could I not?"

"But—he didn't know anything about the two of us!"

"I think he did. Anyway, it doesn't matter. He wants you alive, Madison. There's the ladies' room. Change. Quickly. Our flight is already boarding."

He was in his new clothes when she came out. She almost smiled, seeing Kyle in a tourist shirt with brightly colored flowers all over it.

"Shut up," he warned her.

She didn't say a word.

"Let's go."

She raced after him to a gate that was so far out

she began to think they would be walking all the way to the island, then found herself on a tiny plane, facing the back of the pilot's head.

Kyle read a magazine.

"I can't believe you're doing this to me!" she protested.

"*We're* doing this. I didn't do anything to you."

"But this isn't my idea—"

"You forgot to scream in the airport."

"Damn you, Kyle."

"Hey!" he snapped. "Let's try to have one night without fear, without nightmares, huh? Harry Nore is locked up again."

"You don't believe Harry Nore committed any of the murders."

"This attack on you does make it appear more likely, doesn't it? He's back under lock and key, one step taken on the road. And you're safe—he could have killed you."

She fell silent, all too aware that she might have been killed. She couldn't forget Harry's eyes as he'd screamed at her, couldn't forget the flash of his switchblade as he'd pointed it at her.

"We can't stay away too long. Carrie Anne..." she murmured.

"We can't stay away too long or I'll get fired. Then again," he mused, "maybe I'd like to get fired."

"What do you mean? You love what you do."

"For a long time, I did. I'm tired now, burnedout. I'd like to open a dive shop. Maybe do some private investigating on the side."

"You want to follow roaming husbands, after the years you've spent on incredibly important cases?"

"Well, not exactly. I don't know, be a private consultant or something. 'Diving and Delving'—who knows. I don't feel definite about anything. Except a rum swizzler. Ever had one?"

"No."

"You will."

And she did.

The small plane brought them to Martinique, and from there they took another small plane to a private resort. She met Kyle's friend Gene Grant, proprietor of the place, a grizzled old fellow who looked like Hemingway. "Old CIA guy," Kyle whispered to Madison.

She didn't know whether to believe him or not, but Gene walked them around the reception area, showing them sweeping murals of dolphins at play and warning them about their excursions into the tank the next day. "Remember how strong they are. I don't let the guests swim with the males, because they can be very aggressive, and as gentle and wonderful as Flipper always looks, a knock from a dolphin's head can smash a person's ribs. They're wonderful creatures, though, intelligent, playful. They like to be stroked, but no poking. The trainer will tell you more in the morning. For now...I understand this rush trip had something to do with an eventful day. Have you eaten?"

"Not a bite in hours," Kyle told him.

"There's still a buffet out on the lanai. There's music, dancing. And your room is ready anytime after you've eaten."

Kyle thanked him and escorted Madison out to the lanai. The resort was beautiful, a huge white wooden structure with vast porches, wicker tables and chairs, and lanterns burning everywhere. A band played soft, laid-back island tunes, and waitresses in sarongs moved lazily among the scattered guests. Food was set up on a buffet table to one side.

Kyle caught the attention of their waitress and ordered two rum swizzlers. He spoke in French, which made Madison realize that French was the official language of the island. Then he led Madison to the buffet table. She suddenly realized she was starving. The atmosphere was so different, so far from home. She piled on ribs, pineapple casserole, something labeled Garden Delight and corn bread. When they returned to the table, their drinks were there, tall, icy strawberry-colored concoctions with oranges and cherries on top.

"Looks like a slushie," Madison said.

"Tastes like one, too," he assured her.

It did. It was sweet without being too sweet. She couldn't even taste the rum in it.

It went down like a slushie, too. Kyle ordered them both another.

"So is Gene really an ex-CIA man?"

"He is. He worked for the government for twenty-five years, then decided he'd had enough. He loved the water, so he opened this place. Now he bathes in tropical breezes and tries to enjoy the rest of his life."

"Tries?"

"In my business, you can never forget some of the things you've seen."

She nodded.

He reached out his hand, covering hers. "But you live with it. You learn that life is precious, worth fighting for as long as you're breathing."

"I know."

He sat back, sipping his drink. "I didn't. Not for a long time after Fallon died."

"It's hard," Madison said softly.

"And you never forget. You just go on."

She nodded, sipping the last of her second drink. A third magically appeared.

"You know I have no tolerance for alcohol," she reminded him.

"I know."

"I could pass out on you."

"I'll take my chances."

"You're not going to have to get me drunk to sleep with you, you know."

He smiled. "Yeah, I know that, too."

She tapped her cheek. The drinks were really deceptive. She couldn't feel her face anymore.

"Finish your drink, then we'll take a walk. There's a really pretty little church built by pirates about three hundred years ago down that path."

"I'm not sure I can walk."

"I'll help you."

The world was spinning. But it was spinning beautifully. Lanterns seemed to be ablaze everywhere. The island colors were vibrant. The breeze was like a balm. It seemed impossible that she had nearly been killed that afternoon. It seemed so far away.

She was totally tipsy, she realized. And tipsy was good. She didn't have a worry in the world. Tonight she was going to sleep without nightmares.

She wasn't tipsy, she realized. She was absolutely inebriated.

Sloshed.

She tried hard not to act it. "This is gorgeous," she told Kyle.

"Glad you like it. There's the church."

There were other people in the church. A priest, a couple of the waitresses in their sarongs. Candles were lit, and there were flowers on the altar. The floor was lined with memorials; stained-glass windows arched high over ancient tombs.

"It's great. This place is great."

"Glad you like it. We're going to get married here."

"No we're not!"

"It's the right thing to do."

"The right thing to do? I'm a little out of it, but people don't get married just because it's the right thing to do."

"Okay, I'll get down on one knee," he said, then did. "Marry me, Madison."

"Because I'm great in bed and you're trying to keep me alive? No!"

"There are worse reasons."

"Kyle, is this for real?"

"Yes."

"It can't be."

"It is."

"When did you arrange this?"

"When you were in X ray."

"I don't believe you."

"Look, I'm down on one knee, Madison. Just say yes."

"Yes to what?"

"To me."

"No."

"Think of Carrie Anne."

"I do think of her. Always."

"You *want* to marry me."

"I don't."

"You do. Say yes."

"I can say whatever the hell you want, Kyle. That doesn't—"

"Come here. Come with me."

He led her down the aisle. Everyone was staring at her, the priest smiling as he opened a book and started to speak.

She started to laugh. "Oh, God, Kyle! What kind of a setup is this?"

"Just answer the man."

She tapped her cheek again. She still couldn't feel her face. She was going to collapse any minute, she realized. Damn those rum swizzlers. Damn Kyle.

The priest was droning away in French. She had no idea what he was saying.

Kyle prodded her. "Say yes."

She stared at him. He put his arm around her, and he nodded her head for her.

"Say yes."

"Yes."

The priest smiled benignly. He had two faces. No, three. He started talking again, and Kyle murmured something in return. Kyle had her hand. She felt something cold.

"I'm going to pass out," she told him.

"Sure. Just another few minutes."

"I'm going to throw up all over you," she warned.

"Don't you dare!" he whispered.

She heard cheering all around her. The world was spinning, spinning insanely.

She started to fall.

Kyle swept her up, carrying her from the church and out into the night. The fresh air helped.

"You know better than to let me drink so much!" she told him.

"You'll survive."

They reached their room, a little bungalow on the grounds. It was air-conditioned, the temperature deliciously cool. He laid her down on the bed, where she stayed, watching the ceiling fan swirling above her. Suddenly she leaped up, racing to the bathroom.

Kyle was right behind her. "Breathe through your nose. I've made some coffee for you, but try the shower for a few minutes." He helped her shed her ridiculous tourist clothing, then helped her into the shower, heedless of the fact that his flowered shirt was getting soaked. The water felt good. She began to feel like living. She managed to get out of the shower and into one of the terry robes. Back in the bedroom area, she sank down to sit on the bed. He put a cup of coffee into her hands.

"What a wedding night," he said smiling.

"We aren't really married," she told him.

"We are."

"It's impossible. How could you have set up such a thing? You never asked me. This— Everything just happened today."

"I have friends in high places."

"I didn't marry you. Fear and good sex are not good reasons for marriage." She shoved the coffee cup back at him and threw herself down on the pillows. Her eyes closed. "Why do this? Why marry me? Just to keep me safe? You called me a witch.

You thought I was somehow responsible for Fallon's death.''

"I didn't."

"You did."

"Madison, I've seen you suffer. I know that you hurt for Fallon, nothing more. I'm sorry for what I said."

"You're sorry? Oh, Kyle, you can't marry someone just because..." Her voice trailed away.

Kyle sat down by her side, lifting her damp hair from her face, smiling.

She was out cold.

"I married you, you little fool, because I've loved you half my life, and I was too stupid to realize it most of the time. And I *am* going to keep you alive," he said.

She hadn't heard a word he'd said, of course, but that didn't matter. He lay down beside her and drew her close.

She sighed in her sleep.

Maybe it was him.

Most likely it was the rum.

But for once she slept soundly, without nightmares.

16

Madison awoke with a pounding headache, afraid to lift her eyelids. Her mouth was dry, her throat was aching, and she couldn't even croak to find out if anyone would listen if she begged for water.

She finally opened her eyes. The room was still spinning. As long as she lived, she didn't want to taste another rum swizzler. She tried to sit up. The spinning sensation was worse.

She crashed back down, groaning.

"You *are* going to live."

Kyle was there. If she'd had a prayer of actually managing the feat, she would have hit him. "No thanks to you," she groaned.

Then, despite her spinning head and the agony she suffered, she rose to a sitting position, staring first at her hand, then at Kyle.

There was a narrow, plain gold band on her finger.

Kyle was seated at a table in a little breakfast nook that overlooked the palm-covered lawn sloping down to the beach. He had a newspaper and coffee, was showered and shaved, and had even been shopping. He was wearing a surf-logo T-shirt and cutoffs and new Teva sandals. He looked comfortable and relaxed.

"What do you think you're doing?" she demanded in what felt like a shout. The sound of her own voice crashed mercilessly against her skull. She was going to have to whisper.

"Reading about yesterday's events," Kyle said. She realized then that he wasn't exactly happy. Something in the paper was disturbing him.

She wasn't worried about the paper at the moment, though. Her own situation was taking precedence. "You tricked me. You got me drunk on purpose. Tell me that everything that happened last night was some kind of sham."

"No. No, it wasn't."

"I'm an American citizen."

"And you think our marriage is illegal because it took place in a different country?"

"I don't know exactly what is and isn't legal, but I can find out. I have a brother-in-law who is an attorney."

"So?" he inquired politely.

"Kyle, what did you think you were doing? You can't protect me every minute, all of my life!"

He poured her a mug of black coffee and brought it to her—along with two aspirin.

She looked from the pills he had dropped in her hand to his eyes. "You even planned it down to the aspirin," she said resentfully.

"Madison," he said, sitting by her side, "you weren't unconscious—you did know what was going on. And the point here is that you're going to put yourself and Carrie Anne at risk if you don't let me protect you."

"But marriage? Kyle..."

"It *is* legal. But you can always change that," he told her quietly.

She sipped the coffee he had brought her, feeling strangely defeated. She stared into her cup. "I've been compared to Lainie all my life," she said softly. "I loved her, but I never wanted to be like her."

"Madison, you're not—"

"She was married four times. I think Dad's been married six times. Of course, he's been living longer."

"Madison, I'm sorry."

"About marrying me?"

"That you're so upset."

She drank the rest of the coffee and headed into the bathroom. "I'm going to take a shower."

"I'll order you some food."

"No!" she cried.

"It will help. Trust me."

"Trust you? Trust *you?* You must be insane."

"I'll order some toast. It will help."

She showered, then came back out in one of the hotel's big bathrobes. By the time she emerged, room service had come, and the toast did smell appetizing. There was also orange juice and more coffee. To her amazement, she discovered that she *could* eat, and afterward, she did feel better.

Kyle glanced at his watch. "Why don't you try to go back to sleep for a couple of hours? Then we can go on the afternoon dolphin swim before we head back home."

"We're really going swimming with dolphins?"

"Yeah, we're really going swimming with dolphins," he said, rising.

"Where are you going?" she asked him.

"Just for a walk. Try to get some more sleep. I'll see you in a couple of hours."

He left her, and she wondered where he was really going. But where the hell could he be going on a small private island where the traitorous natives spoke French?

She lifted her left hand—it only shook slightly. She stared incredulously at the ring on it. If someone had asked her when she was young what she wanted more than anything else in the world, she would have said—if she'd allowed herself to be honest— that she wanted to grow up to marry Kyle. And now it had happened. He had tricked her, but she had let him.

She closed her eyes. To her amazement, she began to drift. And she didn't dream.

She woke up to Kyle prodding her gently. "Hey, we have to be down at the pool in thirty minutes. You going to make it?"

She stared at him and nodded. She felt a lot better. "Yes, I'm going to make it." She bounded out of bed and into the bathroom, where she dressed quickly in her airport-purchase bathing suit.

Kyle was waiting for her on the bungalow porch, and as they walked down the lawn toward the shore, he pointed out the inlet where the pool was located. "Gene's lagoon is natural, but he's fenced off an area. He thinks that some of the people who get so nuts about releasing dolphins and killer whales are crazy—they can't make it in the wild any better than a French poodle. He's raised all his ladies, as he calls them, and they're affectionate, and accustomed to being fed. There's Judy, the trainer we'll be working with."

"Where are the rest of the people?"

"This is a private dive. Just us."

She arched a brow at him and realized that part of the reason he had left her that morning was probably to arrange for this private session. For a tough FBI guy not above pulling a few fast moves, he could be amazingly considerate.

"Mrs. Montgomery!" Judy called to her. The name was startling. She felt that she was playacting when she responded to it, but Judy just went on. "Welcome. I understand this is a long-time dream of yours. Come on over, meet the girls."

Judy was about thirty, an attractive, slender woman with a master's degree in marine biology from the University of Miami. She obviously adored the four dolphins in the pool—Heidi, Rachel, Debbi and Hannah. She introduced them one by one to Kyle and Madison, and warned them again that dolphins could be aggressive, even though the "girls" were naturally very affectionate. Madison and Kyle fed the dolphins fish, then led them in a few leaps and twirls under Judy's supervision before donning snorkels, masks and fins to jump in with them.

Madison had the time of her life.

The dolphins were wonderful. She quickly discovered that they were very strong and could shove roughly while playing, but they were also as affectionate as Judy had said. They loved to be rubbed and touched, brushing against her and Kyle. She glanced at Kyle as they surfaced together, laughing delightedly, and she saw in his eyes that he was every bit as fascinated as she was, and having just as good a time. For a moment, as she stared at him, she was able to forget the rest of the world. She had loved him almost all her life, and now they were together, sharing an experience she had dreamed of for what felt like forever. If only...

Heidi nudged her, trying to get her attention. Madison stroked the animal, marveling at her sleek feel, and ducked again to swim with her. It was incredible.

Madison was aware that they spent much more than their allotted time in the water, and she was grateful. Her skin was completely pruned when Judy swam over to Kyle and warned him, "I'm afraid you're going to miss your flight if you don't get moving. And you said it was important that you get back tonight," she added apologetically.

"Yeah, thanks," Kyle told her. He gestured to Madison, and she nodded. She patted each of the dolphins goodbye, then emerged from the lagoon, stripping off her fins.

Judy was at her side. "You know, Mrs. Montgomery, you can come back to the island when you have more time."

"That would be lovely," Madison assured her. She glanced at Kyle. "I'll have to brush up on my French first, though."

As she and Kyle walked back toward their bungalow, he asked, "Would that have changed anything?"

"What?"

"If you'd understood French? I mean, there was a church, a priest...."

"I thought maybe it was a game, a charade...."

"I made the whole thing easy for you, then."

"How?"

"Whatever happens, it's my fault."

"I...I don't want to think about that. But I do want to thank you for this afternoon," she told him.

"Oh. Then I shouldn't be jumping on you."

"It was thoughtful."

"So you forgive me?"

She shook her head. "You know I can't drink."

"I was counting on it. Anyway, we've got to hurry. We do have to get back. There's only one plane," he reminded her.

She walked ahead of him, straight into the shower.

She thought he might follow her.

He didn't, and she chided herself for her sense of disappointment. They did need to catch a plane, after all. Still, he was curt when she emerged, showering and changing very quickly himself, then pensive on the plane.

This time, she pretended to read a magazine while he stared restlessly out the window, but she couldn't keep herself from wondering what was going on, what had happened to change his mood.

It was late when they headed to the airport lot and got the Jeep. Kyle drove.

"I take it Carrie Anne is spending another night at my sister's?" Madison asked dryly.

He nodded. "I told Dan that one of us would get her after kindergarten tomorrow."

"Did you tell him we were married?"

Kyle nodded. "But I asked him not to say anything to Carrie Anne."

"What about Darryl?"

"He knows."

"How about my father? And yours?"

Kyle nodded, then glanced her way. "I made a lot of phone calls while you were sleeping."

"Did you happen to talk with anyone in the Storm Fronts? We're supposed to go into the studio Thursday and Friday."

She wondered why she wasn't surprised when he nodded. "Your dad told me, and he gave me some phone numbers. I got hold of Joey. There's no reason why you can't keep your date with them."

"Great," she murmured. "I'll just leave everything in your capable hands."

He didn't answer, choosing to ignore her sarcasm.

By the time they pulled into her drive, she was tired. She opened the door and keyed the alarm, choosing to ignore Kyle. It was nearly midnight. She should have been starving, but she wasn't. She could have fixed something for Kyle, but she wasn't in the mood. Let him fend for himself.

She went into her bedroom, showered quickly and donned a nightgown. She could hear him moving around in the kitchen. She went to bed, wondering if she should talk to him; but she didn't know what to say. She didn't turn on the television; instead, she pretended to sleep.

But he didn't come into her room, and in time, the pretense became real.

Killer watched her.

Enraged.

There she was, smiling at another man. Laughing. She had leaned on him, needed him, made him want her, love her, but she'd only been teasing.

Like the other one. The one who had claimed to care about him, yet meant to tell the truth about him. So that he would be an outcast. Thrown out. Taken away. The other one. Lainie. With her red hair and brilliant smile, all that beauty hiding a heart of ice. A rose, God, she had the beauty of a rose! But her thorns were vicious. Deadly. She could stab beneath the skin, cut to the heart, draw blood....

And now...

This one.

They could have made it. She could have eased all the pain and fury in his heart. He would have taken good care of her kids. Kids liked him. They always had. She could have loved him, but she was just a redheaded bitch in heat like the other one. She'd chosen not to love him. Maybe he would give her one more chance. Force her to see him, to be with him, to realize all that he had to give. Maybe...

He clenched his hands into fists at his sides and turned away.

He walked to his car and started to drive. Aimlessly.

He found himself on Seventy-ninth Street. Harlot Hangout, as he liked to call it. He saw one girl in particular. The bitch had dyed her hair a funky pinkish-red. It wasn't the red hair he liked, but it didn't matter. Not tonight.

He picked her up, paid her.

In a cheap downtown motel room, which he made her pay for so that he wouldn't be seen, he beat her up.

And slit her throat.

It turned out that the funky hair was a wig. He started to laugh. He'd made a mistake.

No. *She'd* made a mistake.

He decided just to leave her. He didn't allow himself to leave his signature on her body or anywhere near her. Let the cops think that this one had gotten it from a greedy pimp.

Killer drove away, laughing.

A wig. A damned wig. Her mistake.

The dream seemed to sneak up on Madison. First there was mist, then the mist began to settle, and she heard talking. Arguing.

She thought at first that she was a little girl again, back in Roger Montgomery's big house in the Grove, where her mother had died. It sounded like Lainie's voice, arguing. Then she realized that this voice was very different. Husky. She could also hear a male voice. Deep. Throaty. She knew it.

She didn't know it.

"Love me. Do it, just love me. You promised, you bitch. You smiled, you said that—"

"No, no, I didn't—"

"You will. Now stand still. You stand still, and you whisper that you love me, and you make love to me. Now. You don't want to upset the children, do you?"

There was silence. A long silence. Then a moan of anguish. "I'll do whatever you want. Just don't hurt the children. Please…"

"I just want you to love me!"

Madison awoke with a start. Once again, she was shaking. Once again, the dream meant nothing. She was drenched in sweat, and she was tired, so sick and tired of dreaming. She burst into tears.

"Madison?"

She opened her eyes. Kyle was coming into the room, in his robe.

"Yeah?"

He sat on the edge of her bed. "You're not crying because I didn't demand sex, are you?" he teased gently.

She couldn't help laughing. "No."

"Then..."

"Oh, Kyle!" she said, and slipped her arms around him. "I'm so tired of the dreams! I don't know what they mean, I don't know how to help. I feel like someone close to me is in serious danger, but I don't know who, and I don't know what to do, how to help anyone...."

"It will end, Madison. It will all end. We *will* get this guy," Kyle promised her. He held her, rocking with her. Then he eased her back to her pillows. "Want me to stay?" he asked huskily. Her arms were still around him; his eyes were locked with hers. "I *will* demand sex," he admitted.

"Well, you know, sometimes you've just got to pay the price," Madison murmured.

"Sometimes you do."

He took hold of her hand and kissed her palm, then drew it against his chest, where the robe gaped open. He drew her hand downward, closing her fingers over the growing length of his erection. "I think we were just about here the other night," he murmured, smiling. Then he rose, rising, sloughing off the robe and reaching for her and drawing her upright so he could strip away her cotton nightgown. His eyes on hers, he lifted her, caught her knees, parting them, as he settled her on the bed. Still watching her, he rubbed his engorged member intimately against her. She was amazed by the instant rise of mercurial excitement within her. Heat flooded her body, even before he forcefully pressed hard, all the way into her, deeper, deeper, deeper, his eyes on hers all the while.

When she thought she was about to die from the agonizing ecstasy of his hard, penetrating thrusts, he withdrew. He kissed her lips. He kissed her everywhere. Except where she burned.

Then he kissed her there, and she shrieked, called his name, and went wild, but he didn't come back to her until she was shaking with raw sensation. Then he reentered her, moving with hard, electric force, and when he ejaculated, she found herself crying out with the violent force of her own climax. She lay beside him for a very long time, overwhelmed by the way he could make her feel. Then she realized that he was leaning on one elbow, watching her in the shadows of the night.

"What went wrong with you and Darryl. What—what did he do wrong?" he asked quietly.

She bit her lip for a moment. "Nothing. He didn't do anything wrong. He just wasn't you," she told him.

He cradled her against him, and she fell asleep. And when he was with her, the nightmares stayed at bay.

When Madison awoke in the morning, he was gone. Peggy, however, was moving about the house, singing, "Danny Boy."

Madison stayed in bed, feeling the sheets where he had been sleeping, luxuriating in the subtle musky scent of lovemaking that remained.

She got up at last, showered and walked out in a terry robe.

Peggy smiled broadly at her. "God be praised!" she said, looking heavenward. Then she opened her arms and hugged Madison. "So, you've married the boy! A fine lad, I say. It's so wonderful. A real joining of the families, eh, love? All your assorted siblings will be in-laws now, eh?"

"Umm, I guess," Madison murmured.

"But what matters is you. And I've been given strict instructions not to leave this house today."

"Oh?"

"You're not to be left alone in it."

"Really? In my own house?"

"It never hurts for others to know there's an eagle eye about," Peggy said solemnly. "Your new husband says that he'll be back before dinnertime, so you and I can go pick up Carrie Anne together, and then you should do what you think is right about her—you go ahead and tell her that you're married if you want, or you can wait, and the two of you can tell her together. To tell you the truth, she likes him very much. I think she'll be very happy—like me. I'm delighted! Everything will be fine now!"

"Will it?" Madison murmured dryly.

"And your father is on his way, love."

"*What?* Dad is coming here?"

"He called just a few minutes ago. He's heading home to Key West, but he wanted to see you before he left. I said as how you were still sleeping, but he's on his way. I can keep breakfast warm for you both, if you want to get dressed."

"I'll do that. Tell Dad I'll be right out when he comes, will you?"

"That I will."

Madison nodded and returned to her room to

dress, wondering just what her father was going to say about her sudden marriage.

Kyle sat in an unmarked police car on the side of a road in Key Largo, going over the list of restaurants he'd just been given. Jake Ramone, the young rookie officer at his side, cleared his throat. "Sorry there are so many."

"Yeah, well…who would have thought this many restaurants would have had a shrimp étouffée special on the same weekend, hmm?" Kyle murmured.

"Must have had a good catch of shrimp that day."

"Yeah, and a bumper crop of brown sauce. It looks like this Rusty Rumhouse is next. Let's try her."

"Yes, sir. I'm right with you, sir."

The rookie revved the car into gear, and they moved forward.

God, it was a tedious morning! Despite the fact that a young desk sergeant had "let her fingers do the walking" to find out which restaurants in the Keys offered the menu Holly Tyler had last eaten, they'd come up with a longer list than anyone had imagined. He'd already been in ten restaurants, asking questions, showing Holly Tyler's picture.

He didn't have to do this. He could have sent out a half-dozen rookies to do the job. But he'd done everything else he could think of, and he was itching for action.

He'd even gone over to Kaila's tennis club and interviewed the waiter who had brought her the package with the edible undies. The man said he'd found the package on his tray and assumed his manager or the hostess had put it there. Questioning revealed that neither the manager nor the hostess had ever seen the box. Kyle left with a list of employees and club members.

His whole family—and Madison's—belonged to the club. He'd faxed the lists up to Ricky at the main office to see what the big computer could turn up.

Now he needed to move. Hands on. He needed to find this killer, and that meant getting out to look for him himself.

Even when he wanted to be...home.

Home had meant an apartment in Virginia for a long time now. It was odd to realize how quickly this place had become home again. How quickly Madison's place had become home, the place where he wanted to be. He didn't dare think about it too much right now. Not after last night. Not after she had looked at him and told him that Darryl had done nothing wrong, except that he wasn't *him.*

His blood quickened. Hell, he had just gotten married. He should be on a honeymoon. He'd been expected back to work, though; they'd sent him down here to help crack a case. And no matter how much he wanted to spend time with Madison, to guard her with his sheer presence, he knew that this case had to be solved if they were ever going to have a life.

And despite the fact that he was seriously considering resigning, he'd said he was reporting back to work. Well, hell, here he was—working.

Kyle thought about Jimmy Gates, back at his office that morning, awaiting forensic results. In spite of the condition of Holly's dismembered body, the coroner's office had been able to establish that she had engaged in sexual relations prior to her murder.

Whether they had been forced or not was impossible for the medical examiners to say, but they had been able to come up with a sperm sample for DNA comparison.

There had been other developments, too. Harry Nore had killed himself in his cell. An insane, pathetic ending to an insane, pathetic life. Kyle had known it on the island, because he'd read about it in the papers. But Harry's death didn't get him any closer to solving the recent rash of murders.

The dispatcher called in just as Jake Ramone stepped from the car to join Kyle. He paused to take the call, then turned to Kyle. "Sir, it's your Washington office, patched in on the radio."

Kyle took the radio. It was Ricky Haines.

"What's up, Ricky?"

"Nothing much. I heard you got married."

Kyle exhaled. Naturally. He'd reported in to his superiors, and word had filtered down.

"Yeah."

"You married your *sister?*" Ricky said.

"She was once my *step*sister," Kyle said patiently.

"Oh, yeah. Right. Sorry. Things just seem a little weird from this distance, you know?"

"Sure. Ricky, did you call to torment me, or is there a purpose to this?"

"Yep, there's a purpose. You remember how you told me to look for any connection between these murders and Lainie Adair's? I think you were on to something. I've been browsing through some old records. I wondered if you knew that one of Lainie Adair's last movies was called *A Rose among Thorns.*"

"I remember it vaguely. She plays a woman in the mountains of West Virginia, right?"

"Yep. It's a Cinderella story about a young woman who grows up with a pack of thieves. She's too ashamed of what she is to fall for the hero, until he discovers that she isn't who she thinks she is at all. She was kidnapped by the evil thieves from a rich New York family."

"I remember."

"Well, it gives credence to your theory that these murders are related to your stepmother's murder, what with the killer's 'signature' being a rose with thorns. You're talking classic-case here. A man with a grudge against Lainie Adair, killing her, controlling his urge to kill for a while, then killing again. Women who look just Lainie, this time."

"Thanks, Ricky. Call me with anything, no matter how small."

"Will do. Oh, and congratulations. On marrying your sister."

"Ricky, get a life," Kyle said, breaking the connection. "Okay, Jake, let's try the Rusty Rumhouse."

It was dark inside. Smoky, and dark. There was a central bar, with tables scattered into the four corners of the room. Kyle found the manager, a pleasant fellow by the name of Brad Maxwell, and when Kyle produced a picture of Holly Tyler, one of the waitresses let out a little squeal.

"Yes. Yes! I waited on her. It wasn't this weekend, but the, umm...Thursday or Friday before," the girl volunteered excitedly. She was young, petite, no more than five-foot-one, with a headful of bouncing blond curls.

"What's your name, miss?" Kyle asked her.

"Bitsy. Bitsy Larkin."

"Well, Bitsy, thanks for remembering, and for being so helpful. It's incredibly important. She must have eaten here on Friday," Kyle said.

"You're right! It had to be Friday, because she ordered the Friday special, the shrimp étouffée."

"Right," Kyle breathed, inhaling raggedly. He felt shaky inside. That was what police work was like. Weeks and weeks of work without a clue panning out, then some little step opened up the gates.

Please, God, he prayed in silence, let this be the step that gives us this lunatic!

"Can you remember who Holly was with?"

"Yeah, sure I can."

"Think you could identify him?"

"Absolutely!" Bitsy vowed solemnly. "Oh, absolutely."

17

Madison was just zipping her jeans when she heard her father's voice, and she quickly threw on a shirt, then hurried out to greet him.

Jordan looked a lot better than he had the last time she saw him, when he was so worried about her. His color was good, his long gray hair in a neat queue—he looked like the handsome, mature, sexy celebrity he was.

He smiled when he saw her, shaking his head. "Mrs. Montgomery."

"Dad!" she said, hurrying to him, accepting his warm hug.

"Breakfast is on the counter in the kitchen. I'll leave you to it," Peggy said, exiting to go about her work in some far corner of the house.

Madison looked anxiously at her father. "Do you mind?"

"Not at all. I'm delighted for you. You two did make a pretty quick decision there."

"I think he married me just to keep me safe."

Jordan caught her hands and leaned back, studying her. "I think he married you because you're a stunning woman with a wonderful mind and a warm heart."

"Dad, thanks! What a beautiful thing to say."

"I'm very proud of you, Madison. I'm proud of all my children. And I'm glad Kyle is my son-in-law."

"How about some breakfast?" she suggested, suddenly embarrassed. "I'm starving."

"Busy night, huh?" her father teased.

"Dad!" she protested.

They ate in silence at the kitchen table for a minute; then he cleared his throat. "Did you hear?"

"Hear what?"

"Harry Nore managed to hang himself in his jail cell. He had smuggled in some ultrathin wire and..."

Madison set her fork down. "God. I don't know whether to be sorry or not."

"He killed your mother, and he tried to kill you. I can't feel much remorse."

She shook her head. "I don't know why, I know the murder weapon was found on him and all, but...I just never thought he really did kill my mother."

"Madison! I'll never forget the terror in my heart when I heard him saying those things to you on Sunday! Then, seeing him lunge at you... The man was definitely homicidal."

Madison nodded, wondering why she was so upset. Then she realized that Kyle had probably read about Nore's death in the paper and decided not to tell her while they were on the island. Now he couldn't talk to Nore, couldn't learn from Nore. It was hard to clear a dead man. And it was hard to hunt for a killer if people believed the killer was already dead.

She shivered.

"Kyle didn't tell me."

"He *is* trying to protect you."

"Maybe he's trying too hard. Oh, Dad! I'm just not sure about this at all...."

Jordan Adair shook his head ruefully, staring out the window. "Honey, I'll be sure for you. I always liked Kyle. From the first time I met him. Even when he was really young, he had a way of looking at the world...wisdom, I guess. I don't know exactly what it was about him. But there was some chemistry between the two of you from beginning. At first you just adored him like a big brother. I'm not sure when that changed. Maybe he kept away from you purposely when you started getting older. He wanted to give you a chance to grow up, I think. And then, of course, he met Fallon...."

"He met Fallon, and I married Darryl. Well...I'm glad you're happy, Dad," Madison murmured.

He nodded again, as if there were more he wanted to say. Then he rose, slowly pacing the kitchen. "You know, he never accused me of murder, even though he was there when your mother and I had one of our worst fights ever."

"Dad..." she said uncomfortably.

"No, hear me out. I guess I've wanted to tell you this for a long time. The day Lainie was killed, she'd called me over. Roger had refused to cancel a personal appearance in Toronto to stay home to see her do a play in Miami Beach. She was furious—she really expected us all to jump every time she snapped her fingers. She wanted me to hang around so she could convince Roger it would be dangerous to leave the two of us in the city alone." Jordan shrugged thoughtfully. "I did still love her. I always loved her. I'll love her until the day I die myself.

But I knew she was using me, and I refused her, so she started throwing things. I grabbed her...and then I released her and walked out.

"She—she liked a physical fight. She'd been sure that if she could just get me to touch her, she could seduce me. But I managed to remember that Roger was a friend, and that Lainie had used me too often already. I left. Kyle was in his room, pretending not to hear us fight. But when it got violent, he came out—as if he could stop it if something really bad were about to happen. Lainie was furious—she hadn't known he was home. But he just turned away from her and walked me out. He was as smooth as a mature man that day, and the kid was just getting out of high school. Anyway..." He turned and stared at Madison, so much pain in his dark eyes that she found herself rushing to him.

"Oh, Dad! You can't keep punishing yourself over Lainie. We all loved her, and she hurt us all. But she loved us, too, in her way. I think she loved you very much. And I love you, Kaila loves you, Trent loves you, Jassy loves you—even Kyle and Rafe love you! You've been a great dad."

"In my way," he said softly, holding her. "In my weird way. I do love you, Madison. And you know, you're not like her. Not in the least. You and Kyle are going to stay married. Your vows mean something to you both. And I mean it—I couldn't be happier for you." He sighed then. "I guess I've got to go. I'm heading home. Roger's show is a success, and I've got to start on my new book."

"What's it about this time, Dad?"

"Pirates, sunken treasure. My macho hero is going to discover modern-day piracy, save the girl and discover hidden treasure. Thank God I'm old and have been at it a long time, so I don't have to be politically correct.''

''Sounds like a great adventure, Dad.''

He kissed her cheek, holding her close again. ''Life is the adventure, baby. I'm glad you're living it. I wish you and your new husband the very best. Tell him I said so. And somewhere along the line, we'll have to celebrate. I thought Jassy was about to run off and marry some guy, and instead it's you.''

''Oh, well...'' Madison teased.

''Who is he?''

''Who is who?''

''The guy Jassy is dating.''

Madison laughed. ''I don't know. In fact, if she doesn't tell me, I'm not inviting her to my wedding reception. When I get around to having one.'' She made a mental note to herself—it was time to tell Kyle they had to find out exactly who Jassy was seeing.

Her father grinned and kissed her cheek one more time. ''You be careful!''

She nodded. ''I will be,'' she promised him. She saw him to the door, kissed him again, waved and carefully locked the door behind him. She'd barely started picking up the breakfast dishes when the bell rang.

Being careful, she looked through the peephole before turning the first bolt. She thought maybe her father had returned, but it wasn't her dad, it was Kyle's.

''Roger!'' Madison said, opening the door. She began to wonder if she wasn't going to see every member of their extended family that day, one by one.

"Congratulations, Madison. I can't tell you how pleased I am." He enveloped her in a big bear hug.

She accepted the embrace, hugging him back. "Thanks, come on in."

He followed her into the living room. "What can I get you? The coffee is fresh."

"Coffee sounds great. Where's that son of mine?"

"Working."

"Humph! So much for a honeymoon, huh?"

Madison tried to keep her smile in place as she watched Roger. She decided that both their families were insane. She and Kyle had run off and gotten married less than two weeks after seeing one another again for the first time in years, and both their fathers seemed to think it was the greatest thing in the world.

"He was sent down here on an important case," Madison reminded him.

Roger frowned. "But Harry Nore came after you, Madison. Honey, he tried to kill you! He's dead, you know, and good riddance to him!"

Madison hesitated. "Maybe it's for the best. I think he was a tortured soul. And he probably did scare a few years off my life! But, Roger, honest to God, I don't think that he killed my mother. And Kyle doesn't think he can possibly be the same man who killed these other poor women."

Roger narrowed his eyes, frowning thoughtfully. He'd always been a handsome man, and age had done nothing to change that fact. Character was etched into the fine lines around his eyes and mouth, and his smile remained as charismatic as ever.

Kyle was going to look like Roger in another twenty-five years.

"It frightens me to think there's any way what's happening now could be related to your mother's death," Roger said.

"It does seem impossible," Madison murmured.

The phone rang, and she excused herself. It was Joey, reminding her that she was supposed to be working in the studio with the Storm Fronts later on in the week.

"I talked to Kyle. He said the two of you got married," Joey said. "Any truth to it?"

"Did you think he lied to you?"

"So you really did it, huh?"

"We really did it."

"That was fast."

"I know."

"Well, congratulations."

"Thanks."

"Sheila is going to be disappointed."

"Oh?"

"She really wanted to get to know him better."

"Well, tell her he's off-limits now."

"Yeah, she'll get over it. Frankly, I think she was just hoping for one night with him. Sheila and an FBI agent? Can't see it."

"What about me and an FBI agent?"

"You'll be fine."

"So what exactly are you saying about Sheila—and me?" she queried.

He laughed. "You're going to do fine, kid. See ya later." He hung up, and Madison guiltily remember Roger. She hurried back to the living room, apologizing.

Roger waved a hand in the air. "It's all right. I was just thinking."

"About what?"

He hesitated, looking at her. "Your mother."

"Oh?"

He shrugged. "You know I loved her."

"I know."

"But, Madison, she was hell on all of us. If she had lived, the marriage would never have lasted." He hesitated. "You know we had a huge fight the day she was killed."

Madison wondered if this was what it felt like to be a priest, with everyone coming to you with a confession to make. "Everyone fought with Lainie, Roger."

He lifted his hands. "That day, it was a bad one. She changed her schedule, and she thought I could do the same with a snap of my fingers. I told her no, and she completely lost her temper. She told me other men would go out of their way to be with her. She cried, told me I didn't care.... I told her she was a bitch, and she slapped me...and I walked out. And the next thing I knew, I was holding her after she'd bled to death in our bedroom."

Madison was quiet for a moment. "Roger, it's all right. I loved Lainie very much, she was my mother, but I'm an adult, and I know she hurt people. I don't hold you or my dad responsible for any of the pain in the past."

"I'm glad," he told her, rising. "Because I think you and Kyle are going to be something special together."

"Thanks. I hope so," Madison said, rising as well.

"It was good to have you as a stepdaughter. It's better to have you for a daughter-in-law."

"You're pretty great, too, Roger."

He gave her a kiss on the forehead. She walked him to the door, and was startled to see that Trent had just parked his Karmann Ghia at an odd angle on her lawn and was hurrying toward her.

"Hey, Roger."

"Hello, Trent. Coming with congratulations, as well?"

"What?" Trent said, frowning. "Oh...no, yes, yes, of course! Hey, sis, congratulations."

"Well, I've got to get going," Roger said. "You take care. Madison, since you and Kyle kind of ran away to get married, we'll have to plan some kind of family reception later, huh?"

"Sounds good, Roger, thanks," she said.

Roger walked to his car. Madison turned to Trent. "I know, you want to wish me well, then you're going to tell me that you had a big fight with my mother on the day she died."

Trent looked confused for a moment, then frowned. "I didn't fight with her. I stayed away from her."

"Oh," Madison murmured. "And you didn't come to congratulate me?"

A guilty flush spread over his cheeks. "Sorry. I *am* happy for you, I'm just not shocked. I mean, I thought you two would wind up together a long time ago, but then Kyle married Fallon, and you... Well, you know. But, honest, I am happy for you."

"Then...?"

"Madison!" he said, gripping her arms.

"What?" She gripped his arms in return.

"I sold my first novel. Without Dad's help. I didn't even use my own name when I sent in the manuscript. Madison, I got a six-figure offer for this book and its sequel! Oh, God, Madison, I can write. I can actually write!" He started hopping up and down with her on her front walk, and she started to laugh.

"Trent, I'm so glad! What's the name of it?"

"Right now, it's *The Color of Death*. It's a slasher book."

"A...a slasher book."

He flushed again. "It's not like Roger's books. Mine is...grittier. Hey, I hang around with a pathologist, and now there's an FBI agent in the family...."

"Yeah, there's an FBI agent in the family," Madison murmured.

He smiled. "Will you read it for me and tell me what you think? I've got the manuscript in the car."

"Of course. I'll be delighted. But you said it's already sold."

"I still want your opinion."

"Sure."

He grinned and went to the car. He returned with his manuscript, handing it her. "Now, I know it's not what you'd usually choose to read—I'm not such a rotten brother that I'm not attuned to the fact that you have enough bad things going through your own mind half the time. But I need your opinion. Madison, I've wanted to write so badly, but being Dad's son, actually getting a novel out was hard. I didn't want to use his influence with an agent or a publisher. You understand, right?''

She nodded. ''I understand.''

Trent took hold of her arms, pulling her close, smacking her on the forehead with a kiss. ''Like I said, I'm really happy for you, it's just not a shock. I mean, you've been sleeping together since he rode back into town, huh? God, I'm crude. Sorry. Well, we'll be having a party soon, I guess. Love you, and thanks a lot. I'll get out of here now!''

He turned and hurried back to his car. Madison followed after him. ''Hey! Don't go getting into an accident now!''

He shook his head. ''I'll calm down. I'm just on cloud nine.'' He saluted her. ''Honest. I can't wait to tell Dad.''

''He's headed back to Key West.''

''I know. I'm going to catch him. I know his favorite lunch spot, the Rusty Rumhouse in Key Largo. I'll catch him there.''

''Drive carefully!''

''Promise!''

He threw her a kiss. Madison started back into the house, reading the first few lines of the manuscript.

The giant teeth on the arm of the crane turned up dirt, garbage, and something starkly pink against the gritty black of the earth.

Pasty pink.

Crane operator John Laramore sat dead still, staring at the puddle of pink, gaping. He jumped down from the crane, moving closer.

Flesh. Human Flesh.

A woman. Now her naked body lay among the refuse, her murderer having discarded her as if she

were no more than a leftover meal. Her eyes, blue,
remained opened to heaven. Her mouth was locked
open, as well, contorted in a silent scream…

"Oh, jeez!" Madison groaned aloud, walking inside. She didn't want to, but she would have to read
the manuscript. It meant so much to Trent.

If he'd been trying so hard not to compete with
their father, why hadn't he opted for children's
books?

"Madison!" Peggy was calling brightly.

Madison dropped the manuscript on the kitchen
counter, staring from Peggy's face to her hand—she
was holding the telephone receiver.

"I know, it's a member of my family. Or Kyle's."

"Right on the first guess, dear. It's your sister,
Kaila."

"Thanks," Madison said, taking the phone.
"Hello, Kaila."

"Hey, cool! You went off and married our big
brother!"

"He's not our brother, Kaila."

Kaila giggled. "Of course he's not, silly. It's just
such a trip, isn't it?"

"It's that, all right."

"I called to say I'm thrilled. You're perfect for
each other."

"Thanks," Madison said. The phone made a dou-
ble-beeping noise—call waiting.

"Kaila, hang on one sec. Don't go away. You and
I need to talk big time. I meant to force you into
some nitty-gritty at the gallery, but… Hang on," she
said, and hit the button. "Hello?"

"Madison!"

"Hey, Rafe!" she said, shaking her head with amazement.

"Just called to say congratulations to you and my little bro. Where is the dude, by the way?"

"Working somewhere. I have no idea where."

"One-track mind! He marries the babe of the century and goes off to work. I'll have to speak with that boy."

She smiled. "It's all right, Rafe. We'll make up for it somewhere along the line."

"I'm sure you will. I just wanted to wish you both the absolute best."

"Thanks. I'll tell him you called. I know he'll be sorry he missed you."

"I'm sure he will. Bye, kid, take care."

"You, too." She clicked back to Kaila. "Kaila?"

"I'm here."

"It was Rafe."

"Wishing you luck."

"Yup."

"Well, that's all I was doing, too. God! I'm so happy for you both!"

"Thanks." Her line began to double-beep again. She groaned. "Kaila—"

"Go get it. I'm hanging up. I'll talk to you later."

"Wait, Kaila—"

"I really will talk to you later." Kaila hung up on her.

"Kaila!" Madison wailed, then clicked the phone again. "Who else can it be?" she murmured aloud. "Jassy?" she said into the phone.

"How did you know it was me?"

"I'm running out of family."

"No one else ever calls you?"

"Yeah, now and then. So what's going on?"

"What's going on with *me?* That's not the question. You *pretended* you weren't even happy to see Kyle," Jassy taunted.

"That's not exactly true. And is that your way of congratulating me?"

"No. I didn't call to congratulate you."

"Oh?"

"I need to talk to you."

"Okay. Talk."

"Not over the phone."

"Oh, Jassy, you don't want me to come to the morgue, do you?"

"No. I'm at Jimmy's place."

"Jimmy's place?" Madison said, surprised.

"Do you know where it is?"

"Vaguely. I've never been in his apartment, but I met him downstairs in the parking lot once. He's in one of the apartments on Brickell."

"Right." Jassy gave her the exact address. "Can you come right now?"

"I guess."

"Kyle isn't there, is he?"

"No."

"Good. I want you to come alone."

"Jassy, why this secrecy?"

"Please, just come over. I'll explain when you get here."

"All right. I'm on my way."

Madison hung up the receiver. "Peggy!" she called. "I'm off to meet my sister. I'll be back soon."

"No! Not alone!" Peggy called back to her.

But Madison pretended not to hear her, picked up

her shoulder bag and left the house to see Jassy alone. The midmorning traffic was light, and she made it to Jimmy's apartment complex in less than fifteen minutes. She parked, found the right apartment and rang the bell.

"Yes?" came her sister's voice.

"It's me, Jassy!"

"Come on in!"

She turned the doorknob, tentatively walking in.

Startled, gaping, she let the door close behind her as she turned slowly around, staring at the living room of Jimmy Gates's apartment.

It was a small, handsome room. Leather chairs and a matching sectional sofa filled the center of the room, arranged around an entertainment center with a stereo, laserdisc player and a television. The room was painted off-white.

Attractively framed posters were everywhere. Movie posters and playbills.

All of them featuring Lainie Adair.

18

"If I were to see him, I could identify him," Bitsy corrected. "I mean, how do I identify a guy if I can't see him?"

"Perhaps you could describe him. To a police artist. Face shape, eyes, hair," Kyle said. "Would you be willing to do that?"

"Sure. But I don't know how much help it will be."

"Why not?"

"Well, he kept dark glasses on the entire time he was here, so I don't know his eye color."

"That's okay. The artist can draw him with the glasses on."

"Then there was his hair."

"What about his hair?"

"I think he was wearing a rug."

"A toupé?"

"Yeah."

"So he was bald beneath?"

"Who knows? I had the feeling that he was trying to disguise himself. Like maybe he was cheating on his girl with this other one or something, you know?"

"Bitsy, you're all that we have. I'd really appreciate it if you'd come to Miami with us and work with one of the artists there.''

Bitsy looked at her boss.

"This man has brutally murdered a number of women," Kyle reminded her.

Her lip trembled slightly. "I know. I want to help. It's just that I have a kid, and…"

"We'll split tips just like you were here, Bitsy," one of the other girls offered.

"And you'll get your hourly wage," the manager assured her.

"That's good of you guys," Bitsy said, relieved. "Thanks!"

"Hey, honey," said a busty brunette waitress. "A killer's on the loose. You go get him, before he gets one of us!"

"Let's go," Bitsy said.

"What the hell…?" Madison exclaimed.

"What?" Jassy said, frowning. "Oh, the posters."

"Yeah, the posters! Of *Lainie!*" Madison said, staring at her sister.

Jassy curled into a corner of the leather sofa. "He kind of had an obsession with her, I guess."

"I guess!" Madison turned back and stared at Jassy, shaking her head. "Jassy, what are you doing here? What's going on? Where's Jimmy— Is he here, too?"

Jassy shook her head. "Jimmy is working. And I can't believe you haven't figured it out by now, but…Jimmy is the guy."

"What guy?"

"*The* guy. The guy I'm sleeping with."

"Oh, my God!"

"What do you mean, oh, my, God! What's the matter with Jimmy?"

"Nothing, nothing... I just didn't... I mean—I had no idea, and now...these posters! Jassy, these posters are...scary!"

Jassy shook her head impatiently. "He had a crush on Lainie when he was a kid. That's why it was so important for him when he worked her murder. And all those posters are collectibles now—worth a bundle."

Madison walked around to sit at her sister's side, still staring. "Life just gets weirder and weirder," she murmured.

"Hell, yes. You just married Kyle."

Madison exhaled, shaking her head again. "You and Jimmy Gates!" She stared at Jassy. "And I don't get it. Why aren't you at work? Why'd you have me come here?"

"You don't like the morgue."

"Jassy, this may surprise you, but most people don't like the morgue."

"Harry Nore didn't kill Holly Tyler."

"That's not a surprise to me. I never thought he did. I don't think he killed my mother, either."

"Well, he definitely didn't kill Holly."

"How do you know?"

"Holly Tyler had intercourse before she was killed. The DNA samples don't match up."

"So...they've got samples to match, if they can only find a few suspects."

"Yes."

"I still don't get it. Why am I here?"

Jassy shrugged. "Because I think someone we're

related to or at least close to killed Lainie—and these women, who are all redheads who resemble her.''

''Oh, Jassy, I can't believe that! I can't. I won't.''

''We need to start clearing people. Kyle needs to give us a sample.''

''Kyle!''

''He was there, Madison.''

''What about Jimmy-boy here, with his poster fetish?''

''Fine. I can see that Jimmy clears himself. Then we have to go to Dad—''

''To Dad?''

''And Roger Montgomery.''

''Jassy! Jassy, I'm not great at understanding the law, but I don't think we can just walk up them and ask for sperm samples!''

''We're not talking about the law, we're talking about clearing people. Our family.''

''You can't just ask—''

''Madison! People are dying here.''

Madison fell silent, looking around the room once again. She lifted her hands. ''Jassy—this doesn't bother you?''

Jassy shrugged. ''Well, I've suggested he might want to put a few of the posters away, but...they are art, and they are collectible.''

Madison was silent.

''She was your mother, and I'm really sorry, Madison, but Jimmy and I have actually only been seeing one another for about a month now. Everything about it feels right, but I can't dictate his life.''

''Oh! You don't want to dictate his life, but I should ask Kyle for a sperm sample.''

Jassy shrugged. "There are other ways to get it. You two can just fool around, and then—"

"Jassy, please."

"Well, if you don't want to say anything to him, it's one way to go."

"Great. And what about Dad and Roger and Trent and Rafe? You can just fool around with Jimmy, I assume, so—"

"Madison, this is serious. You just don't want to believe the truth."

Madison felt a chill steal over her, and she wondered if her sister hadn't hit the nail right on the head. She didn't want to believe the truth. Had that blinded her? In her dreams?

"It can't be Kyle. And I can't believe my father would have done something like that to my mother."

"Frankly, Lainie's murder isn't so hard to understand," Jassy said.

"Jassy!"

"Well, it looked like a crime of passion, and Lainie certainly made people feel passionately. The connection between then and now is what I can't quite understand, though the way Kyle explained it once, these serial killers need a fix. Killing Lainie might have been enough for a long time, and then the look of a certain redhead might have triggered the same emotions in the killer again."

"Jassy..." Madison began, then glanced at her watch. "Jassy, damn it, you're making me late. I have to get Carrie Anne."

Jassy stood, gazing at her own watch. "Just call Kaila, and she can get Carrie Anne when she picks up Justin. They're in the same school."

"It's too late. Kaila will have left already."

"It's not too late," Jassy said, going to the phone on a side table next to the sofa. "You're too much of a pessimist. Always saying 'can't' when you haven't even checked. See, Kaila answered. Kaila, it's Jassy, and I've got Madison with me. Can you get Carrie Anne when you get Justin, and Madison will just come to your house? Yeah, good." Jassy hung up, smiling complacently. "See, no problem."

"But I want to get my daughter, Jassy. I have to tell her I'm married."

"First you have to agree to help me."

"Jassy…"

"There's hypnotism, too."

"What?"

"You were never hypnotized."

"So?"

"You 'saw' Lainie's murder, right? Except you couldn't see a face. Maybe a hypnotist could lead you to see the face."

"Jassy, I didn't really see anything, except in my mind."

"You knew, Madison. You *knew*. Maybe a hypnotist could help you see."

"Jassy…"

"Why the hell not try before someone else is murdered?" Jassy demanded angrily.

Madison threw up her hands. "You want me to be hypnotized? Fine. Arrange it."

Jassy jumped up. "I happen to know the right person," she said, dialing the phone again. "I want you to talk to her for a few minutes, and if you like her, we'll go in tomorrow, all right?"

Madison sighed and took the phone from her sister.

* * *

Bill Decker, the police artist, was a good man, a talented man. But Bitsy was driving him crazy.

Police artists were accustomed to changing what they had drawn. It was the name of the game. Change, until the face came up right.

Now Bill was working over his sketchpad, with Kyle, Jake Ramone and Bitsy looking over his shoulder. Bill had been at it a long time.

"I'm sorry, ma'am, the nose was straight? Or bent? We've done both a few times now," the man said.

"I don't know, I don't know!" Bitsy cried. "It was there a minute ago...."

"Maybe I should just start over."

"You know what?" Kyle said, smiling at Bitsy. "Maybe I should have a go at this one. My father's an artist, and I picked up a little something from him. Okay, Bill?"

Bill lifted his hands gratefully.

"Hang around, give me a hand, huh?" Kyle suggested.

He started to draw, smiling at Bitsy. "From the beginning. The face shape, how am I doing? Oval here, broader forehead? And the mouth...?"

"Full, really sexy lips," Bitsy said. "I remember thinking that he was such a good-looking guy to be trying to wear some kind of a stupid disguise.... Yeah, that's it, the mouth is perfect! And the nose...it's straight."

Bitsy kept talking. Kyle kept drawing, shading, adjusting.

Somewhere in the process, he began to feel a sinking sensation. A heavy cold, like a glacier settled over him. The picture he was drawing was more than a face. It was an evolving personality. It made no sense.

"No," he murmured. "God, no."

"Yes, yes, you've got it right. Absolutely right."

Kyle stared up at Jake Ramone. "Where the hell is Jimmy Gates? I need to see him right now. Never mind." He pulled his cell phone out of his pocket and dialed Madison's house. Peggy answered.

"Peggy, let me have Madison."

"She's at her sister's house, Mr. Montgomery."

"Which sister's house?"

"Oh, now, I'm sure as I don't know. She just said she was going to her sister's."

"If she comes home, keep her there!"

He stood up, nearly knocking over the easel. "Jake, get on the phone and find Jimmy. I'm going to try to find my wife. You need to get an APB out now, this instant. I think he's going to start fraying soon, go out of control. Jesus."

"Who is?" Jake inquired, startled by Kyle's vehemence.

Kyle hesitated just briefly, feeling as if knives were piercing his heart.

Then he gave Jake the name.

Kaila left the house with Anthony in her arms and Shelley scampering along at her side. She had just put the two little ones into their car seats in her minivan when a car pulled in behind her, blocking her in.

Her heart pounding slightly, she saw Darryl get out of his Lincoln and walk up to her. "Hey, Kaila, have you seen the newlyweds yet?"

Kaila shook her head awkwardly. "Madison is

coming here in a while. I was just on my way to get Justin and Carrie Anne.''

"Then I'm glad I caught you. I'll get Carrie Anne.''

"But Madison will be coming here to pick her up.''

"I'll bring her over after we get an ice cream or something. Don't worry.''

"But—''

"Kaila, what's the matter with you? She's my daughter. I'll pick her up, and I'll bring her here.'' Aggravated, Darryl turned and got back into his car. Kaila got into her own car to pick up Justin. She wondered why she felt such a strange sense of unease.

She shivered.

"What's the matter, Mommy?'' Shelley asked.

"Nothing, baby, nothing.''

She started to drive.

At Justin's school, she left the two little ones in their car seats and stood about ten feet away, waiting to wave to Justin's teacher once she saw him coming out of the classroom.

Her son gave her a broad smile as he emerged. She smiled back. God, she loved her kids. She was so lucky, and she'd come so close to throwing it all away.

"Hey, kid!'' she said, greeting him and tousling his hair. "How was school?''

"Good!'' he said, and crawled into the back.

Kaila drove back to her house and got out of the car. "Justin, keep an eye on the other two one second while I open the door,'' she told her son, walking to the house. "Damn!'' she muttered then. She should have picked up some milk. And she had no snacks. If Madison was coming for Carrie Anne and ended up having to wait, maybe Kyle would come over, too, and she had nothing to offer anyone. She should just run back to the store.

She turned around and headed back to the car. Justin was giggling.

"What's going on?" she asked.

"Nothing!"

"Well, I thought we should go to the store." As she slid behind the wheel, the kids started giggling wildly.

"What is it?" Kaila asked, putting the minivan in gear.

She turned around and saw for herself.

At first she wasn't frightened. She was just puzzled.

Then the fear set in.

Somewhere along the way to Kaila's, a feeling of unease and urgency began to haunt Madison. She told herself not to panic, that Kaila had picked up the kids and would be back at the house by now.

Still, she looked at her purse, on the passenger seat, then reached into it for her phone. She couldn't get her fingers around it right away, so she dumped the contents of her purse on the seat. She picked up the phone and keyed in Kaila's number. She was dismayed to get the answering machine. She was even more dismayed when she heard a warning beep.

She glanced at the phone and swore. Her batteries were dying.

She threw the phone on the seat, angry, and growing more alarmed.

She was perhaps two blocks from her sister's house when she heard—or sensed—the taunting voice.

What could possibly be worse than fearing for your own life? Could it be fearing for your child's life?

The voice was so real, so clear, that she started, pulling to the side of the road, slamming on the brakes and looking around the car.

She was alone. Completely alone.

Her sense of panic escalating, she jerked her car back on the road. The irate driver of a diaper-delivery van blew his horn, but she ignored him, stepping on the gas as she spun around the corner to Kaila's house.

Kaila's minivan was ahead of her, about to turn onto a road that would bring them out to the expressway entrance.

"Kaila!" Madison shouted out her window. She knew it was useless.

The van didn't slow down. In fact, Kaila was driving like a madwoman. Madison sped after it. They left her sister's residential neighborhood behind and were soon on the expressway. She zigzagged around cars to keep up, driving more recklessly than she had in all her life. She couldn't believe that Kaila was taking so many chances with the kids in the minivan.

But then she knew. She heard the voice again.

What could be worse than fearing for your own life? Could it be fearing for the life of your child?

She'd seen it in her dream.

She knew long before they pulled off the westward extension that they would be driving along the Tamiami Trail, heading into the Everglades.

Dan Aubrey was standing in his driveway, scratching his chin, when Kyle pulled to a screeching halt. "Where are the girls?"

"I don't know. Was Madison supposed to be here? I don't even know where Kaila is. Jeez, just when I think we're starting to get it together again, she pulls a vanishing act. I came home early, thought we might see you two for a bit tonight. But who the hell knows what she's doing, huh?"

Staring at him, Kyle tried Jassy's number. He got her machine. Swearing, he sank against the car.

"Hey, Kyle, man, what's the matter? Want a beer? Can I do something."

"Yeah, get in the car with me."

"Why, what's going on?"

"I know who the killer is," Kyle said.

Kaila wondered how long he'd been hiding in the back of the minivan.

The kids thought it was a lark. Kaila was thankful that the kids were all in the back seats, Justin in the far rear, Shelley and Anthony in the middle, behind her.

Because *he* was next to her now.

His knife was in his lap. A switchblade. He'd opened it and closed it, opened it and closed it, over and over again.

"This isn't funny," she told him, trying for bravado.

"Not at all. Life is serious."

"Why are you doing this to me?"

"I'm not doing anything to you. You know you want to sleep with me, and you *are* going to love me. You just chickened out. You're not so much like her, you know."

"Like who?"

"Your mother."

A stab of pure panic ripped through Kaila's heart. She glanced over at him. He didn't look so handsome anymore. There was something in his eyes, in the angles of his face...

She moistened her lips. "I'm sorry. I didn't mean to lead you on. I made a mistake. I'm married."

"That can be undone."

"I have children."

"I can love them. Or—" he smiled, fingering his knife "—I can get rid of them. In fact, I'm going to give you a chance to love me the way you always insinuated you could...and, well, their lives will depend on it. Now drive. Faster. We've got another fifteen miles to go, then you can pull off."

She started shaking.

She was going to die, she told herself. She was going to die. She'd been a bad wife to a good man, and maybe God was getting even with her. She was so scared. She didn't want to die like her mother.

She couldn't die. The kids were in the car. She had to stay alive. No matter what happened to her, she had to stay alive until...

Until the kids were somehow safe.

The minivan turned off on an almost invisible road.

It would be insane to follow. She had to go back. Had to find a gas station, a phone.

But gas stations and phones were miles apart out here along the Trail. Miles and miles apart. If she didn't follow the minivan, she might lose it. Her sister, her daughter and all her sister's kids were in that van.

Oh, God.

She started shaking. It was just as it had been all those years ago. She had to go on. If she'd run down the hallway when she was afraid for her mother, she might have stopped the murderer. Now, if she left…she could lose her daughter. Her sister. Shelley, Justin, Anthony…

Oh, God…

She was so numb with fear that she nearly drove off the road. The minivan was barely visible ahead of her. Then it jerked to a stop. Quickly she slammed on her own brakes while swerving to the side. The Cherokee swung around in a complete half turn. But she didn't go sliding into the pool to her left, and she was pretty sure she'd inadvertently managed to hide the Cherokee.

They were fairly deep in the swamp, and she realized that they had come down an old deserted road leading to some abandoned hunting shacks. Now she hurried through the underbrush, getting close enough to see and hear everything going on.

The road ended just ahead, where the minivan was. Deep swamp stretched ahead, while some dilapidated old canoes lay beneath a tree on an embankment.

The occupants of the minivan were emerging. For a moment Madison didn't recognize the man with her sister. Then she gasped, disbelieving. And she knew why she hadn't been able to see. She knew why she hadn't *wanted* to see, to believe....

Anthony was crying, and the killer was telling Kaila to get the baby to shut up. Justin was trying to joke with him, but he was growing angry.

Desperately Madison searched the foliage for Carrie Anne. She didn't see her daughter. Terror gripped her heart. He had killed Carrie Anne.

No, no, no...that hadn't happened, she convinced herself. Carrie Anne just wasn't with them. Something must have happened, and Peggy had gone to get her. She would know if her daughter was...dead.

"Please..." Kaila was saying. "I'll handle the children. I'll do whatever you want, but please, just let me handle the children."

"They need discipline."

"I'll take care of it. Really."

"Get in the boat."

Madison nearly stepped forward, but then she saw that he was holding a switchblade.

And Anthony's hand.

"Wait, please—"

"Kaila, don't learn your lessons the hard way."

Madison kept quiet, biting her lip as she watched them step into one of the boats.

Madison stood behind a big pine, watching as the boat moved across the narrow expanse of water and its passengers alit on the hammock across the water. She inhaled deeply.

Go back, get help! an urgent sense of self-preservation warned her.

But she couldn't go back.

When the figures on the opposite side disappeared into the foliage, she scampered toward the boats. She felt ill. There were snakes in the water. Moccasins. God knew what else. Alligators. She wasn't exactly a nature girl. Oh, yeah, she loved the water, but...

Not moccasins or gators.

And spiders. Oh, God, there were spiders all over the boats. Which boat to take? One had a hole punched through it. Which of the other three was swampworthy?

She couldn't hesitate any longer. She chose one and pushed off. She moved slowly through the water. It was fairly shallow; saw grass was rising about its surface. In places, the grass was very thick, making it hard to maneuver. Don't think about the spiders, snakes and gators, she warned herself.

Right. Just remember that a man you loved as family all your life is a brutal killer. A killer who seduced your sister, just like his other victims, who has her here now...

She made it across the water and crawled from the boat, shaking. She hadn't chosen a great vessel. The water was two inches deep at the bottom. Don't think! she warned herself. Don't think!

She couldn't help but think. Kyle had been so afraid for her. She was the one with second sight, yet he was the one who had known she might be in danger. Kyle, oh, God, Kyle, if I'd listened, if I'd known...

Kyle...

If only she could will him to find her.

But he wasn't there, she was on her own, and she had to think!

She kept low in the foliage, managing not to scream when she walked into an enormous spiderweb.

She'd been here before, she realized. Years and years ago, when she was a child. This was Roger Montgomery's "swamp lodge," as he had called it. Abandoned so many years ago.

And yet apparently…it was still in use.

Oh, Kyle, where are you? I'm so scared. I'm so sorry. Kyle…Kyle…Kyle…

Please…

Madison's phone was apparently dead. Kyle swore in sheer frustration, slamming his fists against the wheel and throwing his own phone into the back.

Dan stared at him as if he'd lost his senses. Maybe he had.

"Kyle? Where are we going now?"

Kyle had cops moving all over the city, trying Jassy's place, the morgue, Jimmy's house, his father's house, Trent's, Rafe's, and checking the roads between Miami and Key West. People were obeying him without really understanding his sense of panic. His wife and sister-in-law had only been missing a couple of hours. No big deal. Women got together and went shopping. Nothing to worry about, according to most men.

But Madison wasn't shopping. She was somewhere…in danger—and looking just like her mother.

"Kyle?" Dan said worriedly.

He exhaled a long breath, looking at Dan.

"Where are we going?"

"I don't know."

God, it was almost as if he could hear her voice. Crying out to him. Was she hurt? Scared? Oh, God, was she dead? No, no, no…

She needed him. He sensed it, knew it. She was near, and she needed him. He had to reach her.

But where...?

All he knew was that he was searching for his wife. The woman he loved. Had loved, had shared something special with, all his life. That wasn't to take anything away from his marriage. He'd loved Fallon. But she hadn't been Madison.

He'd stayed away too long. Refused to admit how much he wanted her. He would never let her out of their marriage. Never. Not in a thousand years. Now that he'd held her, laughed with her, made love with her, listened to her nightmares...

"Jesus!" he breathed suddenly. It was as if he could hear her, as if she were really calling out to him. She needed help, *his* help. She needed him, and he wasn't there.

"What the hell is going on? What do you know?" Dan asked tensely. "The killer is the guy Kaila was having an affair with, right?" he asked thickly.

"Kaila never had an affair."

"She was seeing someone—"

"Not sleeping with him. If...if she had been, she would be dead now."

"They've got to be all right. I'm sure the girls are just off with the kids. They went shopping. For the love of God, they must have gone shopping."

Kyle looked at Dan. "They didn't go shopping."

"Then—"

"They're headed out to the swamp," Kyle said. Yes, that had to be it. He remembered holding Madison, feeling her shaking and trembling against him.

I was driving west along the Tamiami Trail. To the hunting shacks...it was me, it wasn't me...

Madison was with Kaila, or following her, not about to let her sister die as her mother had been killed.

19

Madison kept low, approaching the weathered old shack that sat on the pine hammock. Insects chirped. Things seemed to slither.

Yet as she neared the house, she was suddenly bombarded with mental images that left her gasping, doubling over for breath. Flashes of a knife wielded viciously in the flickering firelight danced before her eyes. Blood pooling on the floor.

And she knew. He hadn't necessarily killed his victims here.

But he had come here to see to their disposal.

Kyle was always telling her to breathe through her mouth. She did so now. She fought the impulse to be sick, staggering up to the wooden shack. She gained control, and looked through the window.

There was a loft inside the shack. Kaila managed to convince the kids that they were on an adventure with their uncle Rafe, and that it was really important for them to take a long nap so they could play games that night.

She was numb, trying desperately to think. Oh, God, if only she could talk to Jassy or Madison now! Just how did you try to placate a raving lunatic?

What did she have to do to stay alive? What about the children...

She wanted to laugh. All he had was the knife. She could run! But she couldn't, because she couldn't run with three little kids. This was absurd. She had to play along now and pray.

Pray for what?

That someone would find her in the middle of the swamp before he cut her and the children to pieces?

What about Darryl? What would happen when he came back with Carrie Anne, when Madison came looking for her daughter?

And Dan...Dan would think she had run off with the lover who had sent her the edible underwear. She almost laughed out loud, but she forced herself not to. Oh, God.

He was sitting in a chair in front of the fireplace. Rafe. Looking like himself now. Legs sprawled out, smile on his handsome face, blond hair only slightly ruffled. He had that beach-boy look about him again.

"Kids asleep?"

"Yes."

"Come here."

"Rafe, please..."

"Come here, Kaila. Now."

She inhaled, swallowed and walked over to him. He stared at her evenly. "Kaila, don't fuck with me. Don't turn out to be a bitch and a tease. I don't want to hurt you, and I don't want to hurt your kids. It's all up to you. We've got a chance here. You've just got to love me. Now, come here."

She was going to break down, Kaila thought. Break down and start crying and screaming. She couldn't believe she had ever thought him tender, sexy, attractive.

"You're almost exactly like her."

"Who?"

"Lainie. Your mother. She was the biggest cock-tease known to man. I look at you sometimes, and you *are* her. I almost call Madison by her name sometimes. What a bit of irony, huh?"

"I'm not my mother."

He smiled suddenly. "You're close enough. So, what would you do to stay alive?" he asked her huskily.

"Anything!" she whispered, feeling sick.

"Start doing it," he advised. "Convince me that I should let you live.

Through the broken window of the shack, Madison watched her sister strip off her T-shirt and kneel before Rafe, where he sat in the chair.

For the moment his switchblade sat on the rock ledge of the fireplace.

If she could just lure Rafe away for a few minutes, she could get the switchblade, grab the kids and Kaila and get them all out of there. Take the good boat back and sink the other one.

How could she get him out of the house?

Staring through the window, she saw tears streaming down her sister's face as Rafe stroked her naked torso. She wondered if Kaila was thinking about the amount of blood on those hands. Crouched on the ground, she curled her fingers into the earth. She looked down, realizing she'd picked up a large rock.

She rose swiftly, impulsively, and hurried around

to the front of the house. With all her force, she hurtled the rock against the front door of the shack.

She sped back to the window. Rafe had risen. Kaila was still kneeling on the floor, shaking. Madison waited until she saw that Rafe had walked to the front door, opened it and hurried outside, striding toward the edge of the water.

Then she crawled through the window.

Madison looked first for the switchblade. It was gone. Rafe had apparently taken it.

"Kaila!" Madison whispered.

Kaila didn't even look up. She was slumped with her arms crossed over her breasts.

"Kaila!"

At last her sister saw her. Her eyes widened in astonishment, and her lips began to tremble. "Madison, you have to hide. You have to get out of here, or he'll kill you, too. I think he's the killer. I think he killed Mom. Oh, God, Madison, it's not, I'm not..."

Madison grabbed her, dragging her to her feet, thrusting her T-shirt into her hands. "Put it back on!" she whispered. "Fast. Where are the kids? Where's Carrie Anne."

"In the loft. He'll kill them, Madison. But not Carrie Anne. She isn't here. Darryl has her. Oh, God, my babies... Maybe it's better if I just do...what he wants."

"He's sick, and he'll kill us all anyway," Madison assured her. "So get it together and help me! We've got to get them and get back out that window—fast! Come on!"

She dragged Kaila up the loft stairs with her. Justin wasn't sleeping. He was sitting up, his eyes huge and frightened. Madison motioned him to be quiet, and he nodded, instinctively understanding.

"Come on!" Madison told him, sweeping Shelley into her arms.

Kaila took Anthony. Just as they reached the bottom of the steps, they heard Rafe on the porch.

"Fast!" Madison advised. "To the window."

She balanced Shelley and Anthony while Kaila crawled out, reaching back first for Justin, then Shelley and Anthony. Just as Madison was handing Anthony out the window, the front door began to open. Rafe was there, standing in the doorway. He could undoubtedly see Madison, but in the shadows, he might not realize who she was. It was late afternoon now, and darkening.

"Get the kids out of here!" Madison whispered.

"Madison! I can't leave without you!"

"If I leave now, he'll catch us all. Listen to me, and listen to me good. Get in the boat you came over in and get the hell out of here. Get help!"

"Madison, no!" There were tears streaming down Kaila's face.

"Go!"

Kaila took the children and ran.

Madison backed away from the window.

Rafe was back.

20

She stared at him for a moment, then turned and headed for the loft, running up the steps.

Rafe stood below her, looking up.

"Kaila?"

"Just checking on the kids!" she called down.

"Hurry up!"

In the loft, she paused, breathing deeply. How long did she have? A matter of seconds. She needed to give Kaila a head start.

She closed her eyes tightly for a minute, praying. Were the keys still in Kaila's minivan? If not, had she left her own keys in the Cherokee?

"Kaila, hurry up!"

Time, time, she needed time. She couldn't let Rafe know that she had switched places with her sister, that Kaila and his littlest victims were desperately trying to escape....

Kyle, please, where are you? Do you know that we're missing? Can you remember where to come? Kyle, I love you....

"Kaila!" Rafe's voice was rising with fury.

She tousled her hair, letting it cover most of her face. She looked down the steps. Rafe had moved over to the dormant fireplace, leaning against it.

Rafe.

She felt dizzy, remembering how tenderly he had held her after Harry Nore attacked her. Rafe. Who had smiled, teased and joked with them all, year after year. They hadn't seen it. None of them had seen the other side of the man.

She had to get out of the house and heading in the opposite direction from Kaila, giving her sister and the children a fighting chance.

"Kaila!"

She took a deep breath. "Rafe!" she called back. "Let's play!" she said gaily, and went running down the stairs. He spun around, but she was already passing him. She burst through the front door and headed for the woods.

"Where, where, where?" Kyle muttered, swearing.

Dan, ashen, set the cell phone down. "Jimmy and the cops are on their way behind us. No sign of Madison or Kaila anywhere. Carrie Anne is with her father."

"Thank God for that," Kyle said. Dan was silent, and Kyle winced inwardly, remembering that Dan's wife and three children were in mortal danger.

"It can't be," Dan murmured. "It can't be your brother, Kyle."

"God knows, I wish it wasn't!" Kyle said vehemently.

"He must have been a kid when Lainie was killed."

"He was twenty-one. Older than lots of killers."

"But...why?"

"I don't know."

Kyle suddenly spun the car in a dangerous circle.

"What the hell?" Dan began.

"I nearly missed it."

He'd found the road. Overgrown, barely visible. He was amazed that he'd seen it at all. He'd been driving with blind desperation.

But now...

He sped down the road, the wheels sending rocks, grass and gravel flying up around the car.

He nearly slammed into Madison's Cherokee. As his car jerked to a halt and the dust settled around them, he saw Kaila. Running to them, Anthony clutched to her breast, Justin and Shelley running behind.

"Oh, God!" she threw herself into her husband's arms, sobbing hysterically.

"Kaila, Kaila..." Dan whispered.

She gathered herself together enough to pull away. "Kyle, he's got Madison. He thinks she's me. Maybe he thinks we're both Lainie. Oh, God, Kyle, she's alone out there with him!"

Kyle needed no more. He tore down the path.

At first it was easy enough to stay ahead of him. But she was trying to make sure he didn't realize that the boat was gone, so she had to keep to one side of the shack, which didn't leave her much area to run in.

"Kaila!"

Gasping for breath, she forced herself to giggle. "Catch me!"

"Kaila, no more games. I'm tired, and the kids will be waking up soon. I want you, and then we've got to get some dinner going. We've got to make plans. Get back here."

"Catch me!" Madison insisted, trying to make sure she kept the trees between them. One good look and he would know he wasn't chasing Kaila.

The area around the shack was heavily overgrown. She ran around vine-laden pines and wild orchids. Trees were down, branches were everywhere. It was growing darker and darker.

She suddenly realized that she didn't hear him crashing after her.

She held still, looking anxiously through the trees. She barely breathed. She started to turn and realized that he was coming around behind her.

Playing her game.

He was about to catch her.

She let out a shriek and started running again.

She was ahead of him, too—until her foot caught on a root and she went sprawling, cracking her head on a fallen limb.

Suddenly he was straddling her, laughing. She was stunned at first, unable to struggle when he wrenched off her T-shirt, muttering. "Why's this damned thing different from the one you were wearing before?"

He smoothed the hair from her face, and suddenly she was looking into his silver eyes. The eyes of a killer.

"You!" He grated out the single word.

She blinked furiously, trying to force herself to reason, to find strength. "Rafe."

"Where's Kaila?"

"Don't you really want *me?*"

"Where's Kaila?"

"I'm more like my mother."

He sat back on his haunches, staring at her. "Yeah, you're more like her."

He slapped her suddenly. A cruel blow that made her head spin.

"Bitch! Where's Kaila?"

"Gone. You'll never touch her."

He was silent for a minute, then he started to laugh. "Fine. I'll touch you. You are right. You're more like your mother. And you know what? I was always afraid you were going to see me. But you didn't want to see me. I'm your stepbrother. No... that's not it. I'm Kyle's brother. Now there's an irony for you."

"Why?" she whispered.

He smiled, leaning toward her, stroking her hair. "Because it isn't true. That's what Lainie was holding over me."

"What? I don't understand."

"Lainie could never let anything be. You never knew where my mother was, did you? Roger divorced her because she was kind of off-the-wall. She was a beauty, too. He always went for beauties. But she ran around. She was wild. She liked to play around herself, but she couldn't tolerate it in old Roger. She tried to poison him once, when she thought he was seeing another woman, and then they got divorced. Anyway, my good old mom wound up in the loony bin. And leave it to Lainie, she went to see her. And lo and behold, Mom lets her know I'm not Roger's kid. And Lainie...well, you know Lainie! She'd tease me like the cocksucking little bitch she was, threatening me all the time. That one night...I guess I just freaked out. She was the first. She was easy. And now... You know, I'm a bright guy. I don't really think all redheads need to pay. It's just that sometimes it's like an itch I just have to scratch...and it's so much better when I see a woman crying, pleading for her life..." He paused, grimacing. "And then bleeding," he said with a shrug.

"Rafe, I never did anything to you."

"Well, you know, you married Kyle. The good son. The real son. That should be enough."

"He's probably on to you, Rafe."

"You think? I'm not so sure. You were all such a blithering pack of blind idiots!"

He sat back again and reached into his pocket. He produced his switchblade and snapped it open.

"You know, I did Lainie with a butcher knife. Then there was Harry Nore, standing in the middle of the street, begging. I tossed the knife into his hat. Turned out to be a good idea, huh?"

He laid the flat side of the blade against her cheek, then moved it across her face, down to her collarbone, around the swell of her breast above the lacy cup of her bra, without drawing blood. She kept her eyes on his, swallowing tightly.

"You really are beautiful."

"Rafe, please don't kill me," she whispered.

"You sound like your damned bitch of a mother, too!"

"Rafe..."

He stood up suddenly, reaching his free hand down to jerk her to her feet.

"All right. I'll give you the same chance for a few more minutes of life that I gave Kaila. Come on. Convince me that you deserve to live."

She stared at him, then turned in a panic. He

dragged her back, whispering against her ear. "Oh, come on, Madison! Cheat on the great Kyle. Make love to me. Isn't it worth it to breathe? Feel this? Feel the blade against your throat...?"

All he had to do was twitch his fingers and the razor-honed blade would slip into her. She closed her eyes.

She thought of Kyle, crying out his name silently in anguish. She thought she heard his voice and opened her eyes.

Kyle hadn't called out to her, not with words. But, to her astonishment, she saw him. He was dead still, hunkered down in the bushes. He put a finger to his lips as her eyes fell on his.

"Rafe!" she whispered.

The knife eased slightly.

"Whatever you want," she whispered huskily.

"So you'll buy time. You're pathetic."

"I want to live. Let me...let me get my jeans off. Let me show you how I can make love to you."

"You run again and I'll put this blade right through your heart when I catch you."

"I'm not going to run."

His hold on her eased. She backed away from him, keeping her eyes locked with his as she gained a greater distance, unzipping her jeans.

"That's it, freeze!" Kyle commanded, stepping from the bushes, aiming his .38 special at Rafe.

For a moment Rafe froze. It was long enough for Madison to cry out and race to Kyle. He slipped his free arm around her while she shook, but he kept his gun leveled at his brother.

"Madison?" he murmured.

For a split second he looked at her, and in that

split second Rafe sent the switchblade whistling through the air. It caught Kyle in his right biceps, and the gun fell from his hand on impact.

Rafe hurled himself across the few feet between them, wrenching Madison from Kyle's arms. But Kyle let out something like a roar, catapulting himself after his brother, and they all went down. The weight of both men slammed Madison to the ground. Then they went rolling off her, down toward the marshy water. Madison staggered up, looking for Kyle's gun. She could see the two figures wrestling desperately at the water's edge, and she couldn't find the gun. Groans, thuds and shouts rose from the two men struggling so desperately. Then, even as Madison continued her frantic search, she heard a cracking sound.

She looked toward the two men. One of them rose. In the semidarkness, she didn't know who. She got slowly to her own feet, watching, barely breathing, waiting.

Then she heard sirens. The cops had arrived.

The man kept walking toward her. It was Kyle, she realized, weak with relief. Kyle, covered in mud, his arm bleeding fiercely, though he didn't seem to notice.

"Oh, Kyle!" She threw herself against him. "Oh, Kyle, Kyle, come on, let's go. The cops are here, but I can't find the gun. If Rafe gets back up..."

"You don't need the gun," Kyle told her wearily.

"But—"

"And he won't be getting back up. I broke his neck. But yes, let's go get out of here!" He took off his jacket and wrapped it around her.

There was so much pain in his eyes. She wanted to say something. "Oh, Kyle..."

"Let's get out of this darkness," he told her, and kissed her forehead.

"How did you find us?" she whispered.

"Hocus-pocus. I followed your dreams. My wife is a witch," he told her.

"Oh, Kyle..."

"I wouldn't have it any other way."

_____ Epilogue _____

The sign read Diving and Delving. Parking her car after her trip to the doctor, Madison still couldn't quite believe that they were using the name, but Kyle had been adamant about it.

She still shook her head every time she looked at the sign.

Now, however, she walked beneath it, heading out not to one of their dive boats but to their private vessel, a forty-five-foot sailboat—one with a strong motor and all the amenities known to man. If Kyle was naming the business, she was naming the boat. It was called _Tomorrow's Promise,_ named for all the tomorrows she'd once thought she would never get to have.

The aftermath of the day in the Everglades had been traumatic. Kyle speculated to Jassy that Rafe had confessed to Madison only when he'd been certain he would soon kill her as well. Something in his mind had come unhinged when he'd been very young, leading to his obsession with Lainie, as well as her death and the deaths of the women who resembled her—and almost to the deaths of Madison and Kaila. Roger Montgomery had grieved for the man he'd always thought of as his son and taken on the guilt for every woman who had lost her life, including Lainie.

Kyle had spent an equal amount of time wondering what he could have done to change the path of his brother's insanity.

It didn't matter that they'd discovered that Rafe wasn't biologically related to either one of them. Roger had raised him, Kyle had always lived his life as if he were his brother, and he was probably never going to forgive himself for the things he hadn't seen.

Madison tried to tell him that they'd all been blinded.

Naturally the papers all across the country carried every conceivable piece of news regarding Rafe and his family. It was painful for all of them, but Madison could worry only about Kyle.

She was upset when he immediately offered her an annulment, saying there was no reason why she should stay married to the brother of a murderer. She'd told him that Rafe had been more her brother than his over the past few years, and that he wasn't getting out of his marriage quite so easily.

He didn't leave her, but he didn't touch her, staying up nights and staring into the darkness. When he told her that he was leaving the FBI, she was upset, though it wasn't totally unexpected. She told him that she refused to allow him to leave until they talked. Really talked.

She managed to get him back down to the Caribbean. She rented the same bungalow they'd had the night of their marriage.

And she managed to get him back to the church. Once inside, she'd spun him around and shaken him. *Hard.* When he looked at her, anger blazing in his eyes, she smiled.

"Good. Glad to see that you're alive!" she told him. And then she knelt down before him. "I love you, Kyle. I've loved you forever and ever. Please don't let our marriage die. There's been enough tragedy. I need you."

He looked at her, still without touching her.

"You needed me, but it took me so long to get there. I failed Lainie, and I nearly failed you."

"My mother failed herself!" Madison assured him. "Please, Kyle, I love you...."

And it was then, in the church, that she finally got through to him. He cradled her in his arms, holding her. "You do know why I married you, right?"

"To protect me," she said, her words muffled against his throat.

He shook his head. "Because I've loved you forever. And I was afraid. I had to have you. God, I do love you...."

That night, for the first time since the events in the swamp, they made love. Again and again. They talked without stopping. They worried about everyone around them. And he told her that he really did want to change his whole life. He loved the Keys, and he wanted to own a diving business.

"Although..." he said, his voice trailing off.

"What?"

"I'd like to consult now and then as an investigator. Maybe privately, maybe for the cops. Then there's that mysterious mind of yours...."

"*My* mind? I heard you calling to me when my eyes were closed," she told him solemnly.

He smiled. "I heard you calling to me. In my heart."

And so they began to heal.

Roger and Jordan remained good friends, supporting each other through the barrage of media attention.

Jassy married Jimmy so they could converse happily about police work and body parts whenever they wanted.

Kaila and Dan renewed their marriage vows, and Kaila started modeling on a part-time basis.

Darryl married Lindy.

The movie rights to Trent's book sold for a million dollars, and everyone expected the book itself to become a bestseller.

Madison still modeled and sang. Kyle took out some of the dive trips himself, but he hired people so he could be dive master when he wanted to be and lie in the sun when he didn't.

Six months after the incident, they were all beginning to find their lives again.

Now as Madison walked toward the boat, she saw Kyle standing on the deck, reading the newspaper. He was in dark sunglasses and cutoff denims. His bronzed chest was bare, as were his feet. His dark hair was lifted by the breeze, and Madison decided, stopping to stare at him, that he wasn't just the man she loved, he was gorgeous.

She was smiling as she approached the boat.

He sensed her coming, looked up and hopped out to help her in.

She wasn't quite six months pregnant, but she was as round as a tub.

"Well?" he asked her.

"Carrie Anne is going to be with Darryl and Lindy for three days. They're going to Disney World."

"That's great. She'll have a really good time. And…?"

She smiled.

"Come on, this is torture! I should have made you reschedule your appointment when I couldn't get out of my meeting with the Board of Tourism."

"Is it?"

"Madison, boy or girl?"

"Boy."

"Wow!"

"*And* girl."

"Madison!" His voice held a warning growl.

She ignored it, kissing his lips. "Both, my love. One of each. Twins."

He sat down hard by the helm.

Then he drew her onto his lap and kissed her, very tenderly.

"Can you read my mind right now?" he whispered.

She shook her head.

"Good. You'd get all bigheaded and uppity."

She laughed. "Why?"

"Because I was thinking how much I love you. And that you're the most stunning pregnant woman in the entire world."

"Can you read *my* mind?" she asked him.

He shook his head. "No. Why, are you thinking that you love me and I'm a stunning pregnant father, as well?"

She shook her head solemnly. "No, I was thinking it's a good thing you married me, because I must have gotten pregnant the first time we fooled around.''

He started to laugh, lifting her up—and heading for their cabin.

''Actually…''

''Yes?''

''You are pretty stunning,'' she told him.

He smiled and carried her down the narrow steps.

Take 3 of
"The Best of the Best™"
Novels FREE
Plus get a FREE surprise gift!

Special Limited-time Offer

Mail to The Best of the Best™

3010 Walden Avenue
P.O. Box 1867
Buffalo, N.Y. 14240-1867

YES! Please send me 3 free novels and my free surprise gift. Then send me 3 of "The Best of the Best™" novels each month. I'll receive the best books by the world's hottest romance authors. Bill me at the low price of $3.99 each plus 25¢ delivery per book and applicable sales tax, if any.* That's the complete price and a savings of over 20% off the cover prices—quite a bargain! I understand that accepting the books and gift places me under no obligation ever to buy any books. I can always return a shipment and cancel at any time. Even if I never buy another book, the 3 free books and the surprise gift are mine to keep forever.

183 BPA A4V9

Name	(PLEASE PRINT)
Address	Apt. No.
City	State	Zip

This offer is limited to one order per household and not valid to current subscribers.
*Terms and prices are subject to change without notice. Sales tax applicable in N.Y.
All orders subject to approval.

UBOB-197   ©1996 MIRA BOOKS

Available in October from
New York Times
Bestselling Author

HEATHER GRAHAM POZZESSERE

A luxury cruise liner, warm caressing
breezes and long, sultry nights. It was the
perfect setting for a passionate affair—and a
terrorist kidnapping. The only way out for
Amber Larkpur is to entrust her life to
Michael Adams, the man she's falling in love
with—a man she doesn't *really* know....

A PERILOUS EDEN

Temptation awaits...October 1997
at your favorite retail outlet.

MIRA The Brightest Stars in Women's Fiction.™

Look us up on-line at: http://www.romance.net

MHGP9

CATHERINE LANIGAN

the bestselling author of
ROMANCING THE STONE and *DANGEROUS LOVE*

Searching—but (almost) never finding...

Susannah Parker and Michael West were meant for each
other. They just didn't know it—or each other—yet.

They knew that someday "the one" would come along and
their paths would finally cross. While they waited, they
pursued their careers, marriages and experienced passion
and heartbreak—always hoping to one day meet that
stranger they could recognize as a lover....

ELUSIVE Love

The search is over...August 1997
at your favorite retail outlet.

"Catherine Lanigan will make you cheer and cry."
—*Romantic Times*

MIRA The brightest star in women's fiction

Look us up on-line at: http://www.romance.net   MCLEL

National Bestselling Author

MARY LYNN BAXTER

"Ms. Baxter's writing...strikes every chord within the female spirit."
—Sandra Brown

LONE STAR *Heat*

SHE is Juliana Reed, a prominent broadcast journalist whose television show is about to be syndicated. Until the murder...

HE is Gates O'Brien, a high-ranking member of the Texas Rangers, determined to forget about his ex-wife. He's onto something bad....

Juliana and Gates are ex-spouses, unwillingly involved in an explosive circle of political corruption, blackmail and murder.

In order to survive, they must overcome the pain of the past...and the very demons that drove them apart.

Available in September 1997 at your favorite retail outlet.

MIRA The brightest star in women's fiction   MMLBLSH

Look us up on-line at:http://www.romance.net

Also available by
New York Times bestselling author

HEATHER GRAHAM POZZESSERE

#66000	SLOW BURN	$5.99 U.S. $6.50 CAN.	☐
#66005	A MATTER OF CIRCUMSTANCE	$4.99 U.S. $5.50 CAN.	☐
#66038	STRANGERS IN PARADISE	$4.99 U.S. $5.50 CAN.	☐
#66019	KING OF THE CASTLE	$4.99 U.S. $5.50 CAN.	☐
#66089	EYES OF FIRE	$5.99 U.S. $6.50 CAN.	☐
#66069	ANGEL OF MERCY	$4.99 U.S. $5.50 CAN.	☐
#66079	DARK STRANGER	$4.99 U.S. $5.50 CAN.	☐
#66146	BRIDE OF THE TIGER	$5.50 U.S. $5.99 CAN.	☐
#66160	NIGHT MOVES	$5.50 U.S. $6.50 CAN.	☐
#66171	FOREVER MY LOVE	$5.50 U.S. $6.50 CAN.	☐

(limited quantities available on certain titles)

TOTAL AMOUNT	$	
POSTAGE & HANDLING	$	
($1.00 for one book, 50¢ for each additional)		
APPLICABLE TAXES*	$ _____	
TOTAL PAYABLE	$ _____	
(check or money order—please do not send cash)		

To order, send the completed order form, along with a check or money order for the total above, payable to MIRA Books, to: **In the U.S.:** 3010 Walden Avenue, P.O. Box 9077, Buffalo, NY 14269-9077; **In Canada:** P.O. Box 636, Fort Erie, Ontario, L2A 5X3.

Name: _____

Address: _____ City: _____

State/Prov.: _____ Zip/Postal Code: _____

*New York residents remit applicable sales taxes.
Canadian residents remit applicable GST and provincial taxes.

MIRA The Brightest Stars in Women's Fiction.™

Look us up on-line at: http://www.romance.net

MHGPBL11